PRAISE FOR MELODY GROVES

"Melody Groves was not born in the Old West, but it's fair to say it lives inside her."

— *ALBUQUERQUE JOURNAL*

"Groves' breezing writing style puts the reader in the story...plenty of action."

— ANNE HILLERMAN, *NEW YORK TIMES* BESTSELLING AUTHOR

"Readers should make sure their saddles are properly cinched."

— *ALBUQUERQUE JOURNAL*

THE MAKING OF THE TEXAS KID

ALSO BY MELODY GROVES

Lady of the Law

The Colton Brothers Saga

Trail to Tin Town

Showdown at Pinos Altos

THE MAKING OF THE TEXAS KID

NOLAN GANG UNLEASHED
BOOK ONE

MELODY GROVES

WOLFPACK
PUBLISHING
— EST 2015 —

The Making of the Texas Kid
Paperback Edition
Copyright © 2024 Melody Groves

Wolfpack Publishing
1707 E. Diana Street
Tampa, FL 33610

wolfpackpublishing.com

Paperback ISBN 978-1-63977-457-9
eBook ISBN 978-1-63977-703-7
LCCN 2024937385

THE MAKING OF THE TEXAS KID

CHAPTER ONE

APRIL 1872—BLANCO HILL, TEXAS

RUBBING MY LOWER BACK DIDN'T HELP. I groaned and rubbed harder. Stretching my arms way up overhead and twisting my torso didn't help. Cursing, even, didn't help. But what would? I brightened. A beer down at Sam's Emporium. Definitely. And a rubdown by one of his fallen angels wouldn't hurt either. That kind of rubbing for certain would take my mind off aches and pains for a bit. If I had enough money, she could rub half the night.

But I didn't have money. All I had was a sore back and odors of horse *shite* and sweat—mine and the horses'. At least working at Alphonso's Livery Stable provided me with something to do with my day instead of making a real wage. I rubbed again, then bent over and picked up the horse's rear hoof. It needed a new shoe and a bit of filing.

I worked hard knowing Alphonso had taken a risk hiring me, especially with me so fresh out of prison. I'm sure it was Sheriff Becker's idea to have me work off my three months' parole at a livery stable. No doubt his and the judge's. Kind of his perverted way to extend punishment for stealing the sheriff's horse. *Borrowing* was more accurate. In choosing that roan, I hadn't thought about who it belonged to. It was simply there in the stable, already saddled, just like the one my best friend, Wink Tannen, had picked. We'd intended to get them back before anyone noticed. And it for sure wasn't my fault that stupid horse came up lame.

Somehow, maybe my punishment wasn't so much about the horse as it was the sheriff's daughter. The daughter who turned out to think I was a scourge of the earth? Someone to be used and then put out to pasture. Well, she wasn't perfect, either. True, she was a great kisser, and allowed me a bit of fondling, although she'd done her share of fondling me, but she certainly wasn't a keeper.

Good thing that fella from Louisiana rode into town one day, married her and took her off into the sunset. Maybe that was why Becker hated me so much. Thinking on it, maybe it wasn't so much the horse at all.

But was one little misstep worth nine months of my life in prison? Not hardly. And what about Wink, my partner-in-crime? True, he hadn't taken the sheriff's horse, just one that wasn't as fast as mine. And he hadn't been quite as drunk as me. Guess he'd made the better decision when it came to horseflesh.

Still.

I finished filing hooves and currying the four horses in my charge. Tomorrow I'd take that one over to the farrier for new shoes. For now, they'd be there overnight, standing in the stalls munching on hay or sleeping. Once the saddles came off, all four had a chance to roll out behind the stable when they arrived, so I figured they were ready to be left alone for the evening.

Sun in the west turned the world a light pink and gold. Definitely time to head for home. I shucked off my thick chaps, plucked my hat from the peg and peeked in at my boss. There he sat behind his desk, his droopy brown eyes scanning papers clutched in gnarled, callused hands. Not my idea of a good time.

"Horses're tucked in for the night, sir." In the six days I'd been working for him, those words had become my go-to phrase for *I'm done for the day*.

Alphonso Romero looked up at me, stubbed out a cigarette, and put down the paper. "Tomorrow's payday, Tate." He nodded up and down like watching a fly. "You've done good so far. Guess you deserve your six dollars."

Once a week. I got paid once a week, and the notion of accomplishment, job well done, straightened my shoulders, brought a smile to my face. I'd worked hard for the money and was looking forward to either spending it mostly on those dime novels about Jesse James or saving my coin. I hadn't decided which. "Thank you, sir." I headed for the door. "See you tomorrow."

He picked up the paper instead of waving or saying good night or any of the common things people say when leaving. That was all right with me. Maybe in Mexico, where I figured he was from originally, based on a light accent that wasn't typical for Blanco Hill, they didn't say good night.

Pondering on various customs, more used to the German around town and the Irish of my parents, I strolled down Main about to take a shortcut home. I rounded the corner of Second and Dawson and froze. Four men, all War of Northern Aggression veterans, rolled around in the street like a bunch of feral dogs. Growling, they yanked at something. Another grabbed the treasure, started to run, but the three tackled him.

The men tumbled in a knot of humanity. I moved closer just as they somersaulted toward me. Even though the light was dimming, I spotted a knife blade come up, then plunge downward. Somebody yelled, groaned.

Bang!

A gunshot from the other end of the street jolted me back into reality. Eyes narrowed, I made out Sheriff Becker, the worthless piece of trash who'd put me behind bars. The Yanks scattered like terrified mice while I kneeled to see about the man.

Blood oozed down one arm, over his chest. Whoever had done this, was strong. I looked right hoping to see who it was. A hand clamped around my arm and hoisted me to my feet.

"Not enough to steal a man's horse and sully my daughter's good name? Now you gotta kill too?" Sheriff Becker spit those words in my face. "Nine months didn't teach you nothing, except how to kill? Should've expected that from a piece of *scheisse* like you."

"Sully?" I wanted to sully him, but the strength of his grip numbed my arm. I changed subjects. "Me? I didn't kill him." Handcuffs around my wrists clicked. "Just walked up on four of 'em fighting." I chinned down at the victim. "Got stabbed. They were fighting over something. Looked like a round of bread."

"You expect me to believe that? All you do is lie to save your worthless skin."

I pointed. "Look at his hand. Something's in it."

We both kneeled. Becker pried a torn piece of bread from the man. He examined the evidence like he'd found gold instead of bread.

"Told you, Sheriff." A light breeze kicked up and with it brought smells of home cooking. Supper time. I cocked my head back toward the stable. "Go ask Alphonso. He'll tell you we were talking a few minutes ago. There wasn't time for me to buy bread and have those fellas try to get it."

Becker stood, bringing me with him. He studied the body, me, the body, town in the distance, then back toward the livery. Mumbling, he cursed words I'd heard in prison. He grabbed my wrists and unlocked the handcuffs. "Gotta get my deputy to take care of this body. I'll talk to Alphonso." He poked me in the chest, hard. "You. Go right home. I may change my mind tonight. If you ride outta town, I'll arrest Joe."

"Joe? You can't do that!" How dare he try to arrest one of my brothers. That was against the law.

"Can and will." He pointed toward my folks' house. "Or maybe I arrest Eagan, your poor baby brother, all crippled up." His meaty hand pushed my shoulder. "Now git."

* * *

I'D ALREADY CAUSED enough heartache around the house what with my mediocre decision-making, so I didn't mention my run-in with Becker or the man who was stabbed. Ma didn't need to hear such things. I sat at the supper table, quiet.

Joe spoke over a mouthful of crispy fried potatoes, my favorite. "A group of them misplaced Yanks been causing trouble again."

My head cantered toward the front door. "Where?"

"Down by the telegraph office. Ed Whalen took 'em on."

"Your boss?" I figured the German had enough muscles to hold his own.

Pa held his fork mid-high, a speared slice of ham halfway to his mouth. He narrowed his eyes at me. "What'd they be doon?" His Irish accent thick this evening.

Avoiding Pa's stare, Joe turned a beady eye instead on my youngest brother sitting across the table. Eagan pointed a fork. "Hell, Pa. Ask Joe. He was there."

"I'll be havin' no such language in this house." Ma glared first at me, then at Joe and then at my youngest brother, Eagan. "I know you're all grown men now, but I'll not be havin' it, lads, I won't."

We all spoke in unison. "Sorry, Ma."

"If ya want to be cussin' 'n carryin' on"—she pointed toward the door—"ya can just take your plates down to that swillin' place, that saloon, and there ya can talk like yer a sailor, ya can."

I regarded my family. Certainly, I loved them without question and would give my own life for them. But to be treated like a schoolboy? Told how to speak? At twenty-two, I was a grown man. The nine months I'd recently spent in jail had opened my eyes to more colorful language. I'd learned how to swear plaster off cell walls. But I'd learned to be careful around Ma. Eagan had learned too, tonight.

Joe eyed Ma, then Pa, and set his fork and knife on the plate's rim. He shrugged and wiped his mouth on a cloth napkin. "Those ex-soldiers did nothing special, Da. They're searching for food, a handout. Poor lads are hungry, is all." He held out one hand, palm up. "I saw 'em on the way back to the telegraph office. Got kinda insistent they did, hollering about wanting food, they deserved to eat, and looked like they were gonna push Mr. Whalen around. But they didn't."

"They simply walk away after that?" Eagan's gaze turned to Joe who nodded. I thought back to an hour ago when probably those same men were fighting over bread.

"Wish we could help them out." Ma sipped from her water glass. "We're fortunate, we are, to have food on our table and,"—she looked upward—"a roof over our heads. Many are not like we."

Ma's rich Irish accent brought me a half smile. While I'd been gone less than a year, had I already forgotten what Ma sounded like? Impossible, but there it was.

Awkward silence filled the small dining room, chewing and swallowing the only noises.

Ma's cooking, the mouth-watering aromas of baked ham and bacon-grease fried potatoes, filled my stomach, soothing taut nerves. I held up a water glass and considered. I'd been home, what, eight days now and here I was already irked, questioning what I was doing living under their roof. Wasn't I old enough to be out on my own? No doubt. At this age, my folks, with a babe in arms, had already spent months on a ship sailing the seas from Ireland to England to New Orleans. Within two years, Ma would give birth to Joe somewhere on the Texas trail, no less.

And what did I have to show for my years? Menial jobs, prison time, and now working at Alphonso's Livery Stable mucking out stalls, piling manure, and feeding cantankerous old nags. There had to be more to life than this. I mean, look at the James brothers, Frank and Jesse. They were doing something thrilling. And getting rich. A familiar clot of nerves embedded in my chest. I fought to control building anger. Time to be grateful for what I had, as Ma had just said. But why'd Pa—

"Heard talk about the James boys down at the telegraph office this afternoon. Those brothers are robbing again."

I perked up. My idols. I listened carefully.

Joe waited until most pairs of eyes were on him. "Took out a bank up in Minnesota, they said."

"Who said?" Eagan leaned forward, his copper-colored eyes wide. "Imagine."

"Yeah, imagine." Ma wagged her head and crossed herself. "A family of brothers takin' the wrong side of the law. 'Tis a shame. Lord help them mend their evil ways."

Pa crossed himself, then glared at us boys until we did too.

Evil ways? I would've laughed out loud except Da would cuff me right off this chair. Then, I'd end up going ass over teacups onto the floor, and then we'd go to blows, just like—

"All I know is, when they get caught, and they will, it'll be long years in jail." Joe finished the last swallow of milk, emptying his glass. He held it up. "Can't imagine being behind bars the rest of my life. Must be—" He sucked in air and stared at me. "Sorry, brother. Forgot."

I nodded, food no longer inviting. I pushed away the plate, mostly empty. Eyes avoided me like I was a leper. All right. Maybe I'd let my family down, soiled the good name of Nolan all because, well...it hadn't been my fault. Not really. But I'd spent the good part of a year behind bars and Joe was right. That wasn't anywhere I wanted to be again. Ever again. Where I wanted to be wasn't in jail or under Da's roof anymore. Working at the livery stable wasn't going to bring me enough money to strike out on my own. Maybe I should go to California. Or Mexico. And do what? Buy a ranch? Get a wife? Kids? I played with tines on the fork.

Joe's firm pat on my shoulder brought me back to the table, to the dining room, to Da's house. Everyone else had gotten up from the table, plates in hand and were heading for the kitchen. Eagan banged the back screen door as he limped off to get the nightly firewood supply. Ma hated him banging the screen, but despite the endless ways she'd asked him to quit, she couldn't make him stop. He probably never heard it slam.

Joe picked up the last of the dishes, met my frown. "Wonder if the James boys' mom hollers at 'em for slamming the door."

My mouth turned up. Only Joe would think of something like that.

Joe stepped toward the kitchen. I held his arm and lowered my voice. "How much longer you gonna stay here? With Da and Ma telling you what to do? Huh?"

Joe's shoulders rose and fell. "Hadn't much thought about it."

"Brother. You're twenty. Time you made your own way in this world. Out of this dumpy, dusty town. Blanco Hill ain't no place to be, except away from."

"What're you saying, Tate?" Joe set down the plate. "You fixin' to leave for good?"

I pursed my lips and nodded. "Soon's I can."

"What you gonna use for money?" Joe raised both eyebrows, thick like Da's. He lowered his voice and glanced side to side. "You ain't gonna be like those James boys? Rob a bank, are you?"

Snickers punctured the room's silence.

"That's exactly what I'm planning." I leaned in close. "Wanna come?"

CHAPTER TWO

"DON'T WORRY, I KNOW HOW TO STAY OUTTA jail." My gaze roamed over my brother who seemed to have grown half a foot since I went behind bars. He stood next to me on the back porch watching me smoke. It was a habit I'd picked up in prison and couldn't seem to stop. We both were enjoying the cool evening breeze. Days had already warmed too much for my liking. At least it wasn't as hot and humid tonight as the past few days. For that I was grateful. I puffed out a stream of smoke. "If I learned anything this past year, it's that. How to keep away from prison."

Joe pulled in air and ran his hand along the thin wooden railing which suddenly held his interest. Chirruping night crickets broke the silence. Somewhere down the road a dog barked.

I elbowed my brother. "Let's walk down to the stream. Mosquitos aren't too bad tonight." I glanced back over my shoulder and took a long drag on the cigarette. "We can talk down there."

Our path was a familiar one. Over a short hill, around

a stand of oaks, and through tall grass. We stopped at the water's edge, a half-moon reflecting off the slow-running stream. The water glistened, coming alive, as if the stream had a life, a purpose, its own existence. And if this water trickle had a name, I didn't care. It was simply water. And there was plenty of that everywhere. One creek looked like all the others.

Blowing out the last of the smoke, I tossed the cigarette butt into the water. Another long look over my shoulder, then right and left. Nobody around. This was a place we could talk quietly, but freely.

"Done a ton of thinking, I have." I picked up a pebble and tossed it into the water. "Need money. Piling up horse shite isn't the ticket outta here."

"You've only been home—"

"I know. But I need money, and a lot of it, now. I gotta get out on my own." I turned to Joe whose moon-lit silhouette revealed a man, not the *gossoon* I remembered. His shoulders had broadened. "We could go in together. Partner up. Rob banks and trains." I spoke faster. "We could go clear up into this Minnesota and rob what the James boys do."

"But—"

"Joe." I lowered my voice and thumped his chest. "We could be the feared Nolan Brothers. Get our names on the front pages, just like those James fellas. And when Eagan gets older, he can join us. People'd stand up when we walked into a room." My smile pulled at my cheeks. "Just think. We'd be rich *and* famous."

"How you plan on not getting caught? Not going to jail?" Joe broke off a stick from the closest tree and began peeling the bark. "I ain't going to jail. I'm not."

Thoughts of the rolled cigarette waiting for me on the porch rail paraded through my head. Why hadn't I remembered to bring it? Another smoke would be good right now. How could I convince Joe, or at least make him seriously consider this proposition? It would be great having him by my side. I mentally snapped my fingers.

"Understand you're sweet on that banker's daughter. What's her name?"

Joe's wide eyes met mine. Had him where I wanted him. "How d'you know about Frieda?"

"Well, brother." I patted his shoulder. "Everybody knows."

A smile climbed onto Joe's face. "She's lovely, she is. Can read Shakespeare, write, and easy to look at. She makes me happy. And even though she's seventeen, she helps keep the books at the bank, you know."

My shoulders straightened as I sucked in air. Oh yeah, Frieda would be quite useful. In more ways than one. "You serious about her?"

Even in the soft moonlight, Joe's red cheeks glowed. One shoulder rose. "About as serious as can be." He pointed the stick at the water. "Might elope someday. Her parents aren't keen on me being Irish."

Germans. Hated them. Seemed like all the *Teutons* had more money than us Irish and certainly didn't hesitate to mention that fact every time they met. They held jobs where they didn't get their hands dirty or callused. No, the Irish got to do that. Who did the *Kofs* think they were? Some high and mighty founders of the feast? No. They'd come over on the same boats like Ma and Da— and me. True, they hadn't been starving from rotten potatoes like so many of the countrymen, but they were forced out by civil strife. They weren't so proud then. But look at them now.

Joe waved the stick in the air, then towed it through

the water. "Maybe next year when I have money saved, we'll get married and head west. Clean over to California."

"I'd like to meet this princess."

"What're you *jungs* doing down here this late at night?" A rich baritone voice, thick German accent, boomed behind us. "Causing trouble again?"

Like a poked rabbit, I jumped. Joe spun, letting out a soft squeak as he turned. He gripped the half-peeled stick like a weapon.

A man stepped out from under a tree and into a splash of moonlight. Sheriff Fritz Becker. Again tonight? Did the man ever sleep?

Becker drew a revolver and aimed the Colt at Joe. "Put down that weapon, Joe. I'd hate to shoot you."

"Then don't, Sheriff." I inched closer to my brother. "It's just a stick, and we're not causing trouble. We're here talking. Catching up. That's all." *That's all I'm gonna tell you, at any rate.* Rising bile burned in my throat. Stupid sheriff. Stupid *schweinehund.* Has to throw his weight around, trying to be tough. Just because he wears a badge doesn't make him God.

Both hands up, Joe glanced at me then back at the sheriff. "I'm putting the stick on the ground. Please, don't shoot." He squatted, placed it carefully on the stream bank and stood, one arm still upraised.

I flapped a hand at my brother. "Put your hands down, Joe. Sheriff Becker won't shoot." I cocked my head to one side. "Will you?"

"Hope I don't have to." Becker turned his revolver on me. "Might shoot *you*, though. You armed?"

I wished I was. How satisfying would it be to pull out a .45 and shove it in this lawman's ugly face? I spread my arms out wide. "No, I'm not. Neither of us are."

"Keep those arms up. Don't move." Becker spent time patting my chest, pockets, rear. Twice. Any place a potential weapon could be hiding. Satisfied, he moved back. "Time for you *unruhestifter* to go home. No need to be here."

Knowing enough German that we had been called troublemakers, and by this worthless piece of human, anger ran up and down my body. "It's a free country. I can be anywhere I want, any time I want." I knew to control my voice, keep the words low and from shaking, but with the unfairness of it all, anger sat on my chest.

Sheriff Becker moved within inches of my face. "You're dying to go back to jail, aren't you? I just may oblige."

"You got no right—"

Becker clutched his .45 and, using it like brass knuckles, walloped me upside the head. Fire raged across my cheek, lightning bolts racing up and down my legs and arms. I spun, crumpling to the ground. Holding my burning face, blood coated my fingers.

Joe jumped between me and the lawman. "I'm sorry, Sheriff. I'll take him home. Won't be causing you any trouble tonight."

I rolled onto my back, face throbbing, head pulsating in rhythm with my heart. If I could, I'd stand and pound that man into mush. Instead, I lay still letting Joe do the negotiating.

Words and gestures sailed over me, but nothing was clear. Minutes, or possibly hours passed until Sheriff Becker leaned down and pointed a finger in my face. "Count yourself lucky this time." He turned to Joe. "You, too."

"Thank you, Sheriff." Joe's voice sounded strong

enough, but I knew otherwise. He was scared. And right-fully so.

Becker disappeared into the dark, his voice trailing behind. "If it ain't the *wortlos* Yankees causing trouble, it's the Micks."

Joe kneeled and pressed a wet bandanna against my left cheek. "Here. This'll get the swelling down." Joe pulled me upright, looked over his shoulder. "Best be getting home. Do what the sheriff says."

Although I thought I was strong, I let him help me up. Standing yet wobbling, I considered. *Yeah, I'll go home.* But within a fortnight, I vowed I'd leave this shite-filled dump for someplace better.

I'd hoped Joe would come along.

CHAPTER THREE

THERE WASN'T MUCH TO BLANCO HILL. Businesses of all stripes lined the one wide, main street, wide enough to run a small herd of cattle through, four abreast. The one mercantile carried a variety of goods. There, a customer could get a bag of Bull Durham, a sack of potatoes, new boots, a plow, and a fancy dancing dress, all under one roof.

Starting at the first building, which happened to house Sam's Emporium, a rowdy and favorite saloon and dancehall, I ambled east along the boardwalk, enjoying my one day of the week off. No stinky horses to clean up after, no raking until the calluses on both hands had calluses. No putting up with horses that would kick when I walked behind them. No, today was a day to myself and despite a swollen, aching cheek, I reveled in being alone.

But the cheek still throbbed and was tender to touch. I thought back to that next morning, having to explain to Ma and Da how I'd received the crimson welt on my face. Both me and Joe claimed we'd been roughhousing down by the stream, and I'd ended up smacking into a fallen limb. Ma had seemed to believe the lie, lecturing us boys we were both too big to play rough like that. Da simply studied our faces and then went back to eating breakfast. Now, two days later, I looked into the mirror to shave. All I saw was a ghastly purple mark about the size of a dollar, tinged with green. Fortunately, the healing bruise wasn't bad enough to make people on the street stop and ask questions.

Today, Ma had sent me into town for a few items, but I considered it surely had been a ploy to get me out of the house. Afterall, how important was it for me to buy a new thimble for her and a new razor for Da? Maybe she simply wanted me gone for a couple of hours. Had I been that hard to live with? By now, I'd been home ten days, and in that time, I'd had one shouting fight with Da and a shoving match with Joe. Typical family events.

Even without Ma's urging, I'd planned to go to town anyway and begin cementing my robbery ideas. Would I choose a place in town or ride elsewhere? Probably elsewhere since Blanco Hill claimed less than a thousand people as residents. Everyone knew everyone and their business.

Plus, how much money could there be in town?

But I could start small here and then move up to some town like San Antonio or even Austin, the capital of the great Republic of Texas. I allowed a grin to push up my mustache. Ideas were coming together now and maybe by the end of the day, I'd have a real plan in place. Then me and Joe could finalize details.

We'd be on our way to becoming the most feared western outlaws, the Nolan Brothers Gang. I walked, dodging women who failed to step aside as I passed, and glaring back at the men I ran into. No matter. I was busy envisioning the gang's first wanted poster. Like pictures I'd seen on those posters, big as brass right in the middle would be me and Joe's smiling faces, a gleam in our eyes showing true cleverness, skill, and cunning. Our remarkable outlawry. People would gasp. Lawmen would hitch up their gun belts and vow to capture these outlaws who, like ghosts, evaded capture.

Life would be everything I wanted.

This being Tuesday meant the stores were open. A normal day of operation. Perfect to figure out how to rob them. First, who had the most money? Probably the bank. Maybe I should start there. Or try something smaller, something less guarded?

I stood on the boardwalk and glanced across the street. Ed Whalen's telegraph office sat smack in the middle of the long block. My brother Joe would be there now taking down coded messages or sending one. And while surely Whalen didn't carry a ton of cash in the office, clearly, he'd have *some*. People had to pay to send messages.

An irritating little bell over the door tinkled as I stepped inside. Why they had a bell like the one at the mercantile was beyond logic. It was a small room and not many people came in. Maybe Whalen simply liked the dinging.

Locating Joe was easy. The only person in the room, he perched at a high desk, a bit stooped over scribbling something on paper. Joe looked up at the bell, located the source, and flashed a smile. He climbed down from the tall stool.

"Tate?" Joe walked over to me. "What brings you here? Supper time already?"

I'd never been in the telegraph office before. Another new business which had come into town while I was away, rotting in jail. I pushed down bitterness. Did stealing a couple of horses and then bringing them back deserve nine months of my life? True, one had been Sheriff Becker's horse, lame, but still, he got the nag back.

I took a closer survey of the office. Progress was about and seemed to be taking over, like the wild dandelions in the spring.

"Wanna go have a beer?" I scanned the room. Yep. No one else. Where'd they keep the money?

Joe pulled a watch from his vest pocket and frowned. "Isn't quite ten, big brother." He looked up at me. "Kinda early to be drinking, don't ya think?"

I shrugged. What did time of day matter? Shoot, it was only a beer. But I'd placate Joe. "Never too early for a beer. But"—I nodded—"how about I meet you down at Sam's at noon? You're off for an hour then, aren't you?"

Straightening to his six-foot-one frame, Joe's muscles stretched his sleeves, the buttons on his shirt straining. "I am. Boss'll be back by then."

Where'd he get those muscles? I considered. Probably from helping Da plow the little field down by their house. With me gone, Joe would have had to fill in. Another victim of my ridiculous incarceration.

Still, I had research to do. Without spilling the beans as to my plans, I wandered the small room, taking special notice of the papers tacked to the wall.

"Special notices we get in." Joe pointed to one in particular. "From the government. Says the Kiowa have been pushed back in this area and aren't a problem anymore."

"So, why's it up there? Haven't been Indian attacks in at least five years that I know of."

Joe shrugged. "Guess the boss likes to show off official notices."

I pointed to the high desk with some contraption, probably a telegraphic machine, in the middle. "And this your desk?"

"Where I spend most my day. Yep."

Nodding, I headed for the door and that nerve-jarring bell. I stopped and turned. "So, if I want to send a message to say, the president, what'd it cost?"

"Let's see." Joe let his gaze roam the ceiling. "From here clear up to Washington?" He glanced at a piece of paper on his desk. "Ten words. Looks like two dollars, seventy cents. But seeing as you're special, I'd give it to you for two dollars, sixty-five cents." A smile lit up his dark blue eyes. He thumped me on the back. "Meet you at Sam's."

* * *

THERE WEREN'T many places to go in town. Afraid I'd be waylaid from a beer, I planned to stay away from the butcher's where Da and Eagan worked. Sauntering up and down Main, I finally ducked inside the mercantile in search of a thimble and a razor. Why Da couldn't stop in on his way home or at lunch and get his own razor was beyond sense. And Ma? As a seamstress who did piece-work, wouldn't she prefer to select her own? But when Ma had asked as kindly as she had, I'd do anything for her. I couldn't say that about anybody else, not even Joe, but for Ma, I'd walk over hot coals in the middle of summer if she requested. Plus, she'd given me fifty cents. I'd be sure to get what she wanted.

Locating the items was easy and took a couple of minutes. After all, how many razors and thimbles did this mercantile carry? I spent time locating a cash box underneath the register. From my standpoint, that was like finding the pot of gold at the end of the rainbow. In days, I'd be rich. Well, maybe not rich exactly, but certainly wealthier than I was now.

Should I rob the mercantile first or the telegraph office?

I paid for the items, standing within inches of that pot. I carefully watched the clerk tally up the thimble and razor, deposit the money in the register drawer and hand me change. Nothing seemed to be locked. Good news. And I'd glimpsed a small stack of bills and plenty of coins.

Even better news.

On the way out, package in one hand, I gripped the door handle and pulled. Before I could step out, in came a young woman followed by an older man. New to town; had to be. I scanned her, shoes to bonnet. Definitely new. I would have remembered this woman.

I tipped my hat. "Welcome to Blanco Hill, ma'am." Then realizing a man was also standing there, I turned to him. "Sir."

A perfect smile blossomed on her face, the cheeks pinking. "Thank you, sir." An accent, light but certainly there. Italian? Spanish? Not the usual German or Irish.

"Grazie." The man bobbed his head at me.

Italian. I returned the enchanting lady's smile. While she wasn't what I'd call pretty, she wasn't homely either. And no way would I kick her out of bed for eating crackers. I chuckled at that. Something one of my friends used to say.

I stepped back into the store and hoped I produced my most enchanting smile. Girls had told me I was good looking, handsome even, but then again, they were paid to say that. Besides Sheriff Becker's daughter, only one other "non-professional" woman had been a sweetheart of sorts, but by now she was long gone. Out to California I'd heard.

A longer look at this woman and I knew I had, absolutely *had*, to get to know her better. "Ma'am? You new in town?" What a stupid question. I mentally kicked myself.

The man closed the door and scanned the display of goods. I spread one arm out wide to present the store's contents like they were mine. "We have a wide assortment of household and personal goods here."

Something about the woman was beyond words. A scent? Her smell was like early mornings at home when I'd work in Ma's garden. Gardenia? Honeysuckle? I explored her coffee-colored eyes. There was intelligence behind the kind face. No doubt, I'd like to get to know her. And soon.

I lowered my voice into what I hoped was honey smooth. "Looking for anything in particular?"

She spoke to her da in the most beautiful language I'd ever heard. It rolled off her pretty tongue, past her charming lips, and out into the world connecting with her father's ears. Words sailed back and forth. Finished, she looked up at me. "We're moving here and need supplies to eat. We have furniture in our wagon already."

My heart beat a bit harder. Excellent. Since they would become Blanco Hill residents, I'd see her often. Maybe take her to dinner one night. And who knew where that might lead?

Before more questions could spring from my mouth, a clerk stepped up, a smile blooming on his wide face. "Ah, *signore!* Good to see you again." He stepped back. "*Benvenuto.* Welcome."

They'd been here before? And I'd missed seeing this woman? Obviously. She probably didn't venture inside livery stables. A woman like her certainly would not be interested in a man who shoveled shite for a living. My shoulders slumped. Not many women would. Loser. I was a *bosthoon,* a dolt. What chance would I have with this woman? None. So why stick around this stupid town? I gazed at the woman now being led off by the store clerk, heading toward canned goods and food items.

The back end of her skirt swished as she walked. Pure poetry. Someday, some *day* when I had excess coin jangling in my pockets, I'd escort her to supper at the finest dining establishment in town. In a burg this size, there were only two places to go, but I'd choose the more expensive. Maybe even order champagne, that bubbly fizzy drink I'd heard about. No doubt I'd even raise my pinky when I drank out of a crystal glass. Exactly like I'd seen pictures of in magazines. I'd raise that pinky and toast her beauty.

"Excuse me, Tate." A deep voice boomed in my ear. I jumped. "Need to ask you to stand somewhere else. You're blocking the door."

That same clerk now stood in front of me pointing toward the door. He nodded, an obligatory smile plastered to his face. "Good seeing you again. Thanks for stopping by."

A bell tinkled as the door shut behind me. Finding myself standing on the boardwalk in front of the store, I chomped down on humiliation. Bitterness threatened to rise to my throat. I needed a plan and needed one now. Why not amble up to Sam's this minute, down a beer or two before Joe arrived? Give me time to start formulating a way out of this miserable town, this miserable life.

I traveled past two stores, glancing in the window of the first, a hat maker, and then slowed and finally stopped at the newspaper office. A copy of last week's edition, stapled page by page to the wooden bulletin board, caught my attention. Six pages held plenty of news. Here, from this position outside, the smell of ink assaulted my nose and jangles of *tink-tink-tinking* roiled out the open door into the street. Could that be a mechanical typesetter? What else would sound like a miniature hammer and anvil making miniature horseshoes? I chuckled at the image of elves busy at work.

If I perused the weather-worn newspaper, would I find mention of me in there? Probably not. I'd kept my nose clean so far. But I'd only been home less than two weeks.

Running my pointed finger under a sentence on page two as I read, it was clear more and more businesses were coming to town. Right there a story mentioned a bakery about to open. *A bakery? Wouldn't Ma love that?* But at home, nobody had mentioned such an enterprise.

Imagine. A bakery in shite-infested Blanco Hill.

Visions of soft pastries filled with fresh strawberries, apple pies wafting a hint of cinnamon, cookies bursting with sugary smells rumbled my stomach, and made me lick my lips. When would this store open? I read on. Next week. The first pie would be sold next week. That meant *this* week since the paper was a week old.

I stepped back, nodding. I knew right away what I'd do. Surprise Ma with something from the bakery. Wouldn't she be thrilled not to have to bake? Firing up that stove in the middle of summer crowded the house with godawful heat. We opened doors and windows, fanning ourselves with wet towels.

This time, the oven would stay cold while Ma and the

family dug into a sweet treat. Maybe the bakery would be open today. I might have just enough money to buy a beer *and* a pie.

I took another step back and bumped into someone bigger than me. I spun ready to apologize. Sheriff Becker stood at my shoulder.

"Causing trouble again, I see." He glanced down the street, left to right. "Come in to steal more horses? Or bother our women?"

Hands immediately fisting, I moved aside, imagining what it would feel like to hear the crack when I broke this man's jaw. So satisfying. If I did, however, I'd be tossed in jail for years. Heart in my throat, beating like I'd finished running a marathon, I stood up straight, threw my shoulders back and unclenched my hands.

"You following me, Sheriff?"

"What you got there, Tate?" Becker poked the wrapped package under my left arm. "Wouldn't be a gun, now, would it?"

I stepped back to the edge of the boardwalk. "No business of yours."

"If that's a gun, it is."

"Just running an errand for Ma. No law against that." This *Jackeen* didn't deserve a better answer. Did this obnoxious, self-asserted man have nothing better to do than harass me?

"Let's see what's in that package you're holding." Becker grabbed the paper, ripping a corner.

I clutched it to my chest. "Ain't your business. Told you. I'm buying something Ma asked me to."

Becker whipped out his gun, poked the end against my chest. "Tired of your mouth, *stalljunge*, you stable boy. You broke my daughter's heart. Or don't you remember her?" He snorted. "Oughta shoot you right now and save me walking you down to jail."

"Daughter? Heart? Jail?" I stepped off the wooden boardwalk and into the street. "Jail? I ain't done nothing. Just standing here reading." My voice swelled. A familiar icy fist spun in my stomach. "Your daughter left me for another man. There was no broken heart about it."

He grabbed, holding me tight against his shoulder. He snarled into my ear. "Why d'you think she left so suddenly? Huh? Why?"

I had no idea why. She liked the gravelly voiced gambler better than me? He promised her things I couldn't give her? I shrugged.

"I'll tell you why." Becker moved in front of me close enough I could see where he missed shaving this morning. "Because you weren't man enough for her. You broke her heart going out with those fallen angels. She...lef--... because of you."

Why didn't I have a gun? Even if I spent years in jail the time would be worth seeing this *bopach*, this useless piece of trash, die. However, a tiny part of me felt sorry for the man. A real tiny bit.

Becker pointed up Main. "Talk respectful to me, boy. Put your hands up. And I'll take that package." He ripped the bundle from under my arm then prodded me with the gun barrel. "You know where to go."

All the curse words I knew melded together into one long Irish rant. I had no choice but to comply, for now. Arms over my head, I marched the three blocks to the sheriff's office. I refused to look either way, refused to be the loser everyone knew I was. I'd show them.

And soon.

* * *

BY THE TIME Joe found me, I was lathered into full fury. I paced bars to window back to bars. Stopping long enough to clutch the iron bars, I shook them.

Joe, with Sheriff Becker right behind, stepped into the room housing both cells. "Here you are. Couldn't find you." Joe tilted his head. "Looked all over."

"I didn't do anything!" I shook the bars hard. "Get me out."

Joe nodded. "Already did. Cost me five whole dollars." He moved aside for Becker to insert the key into the lock.

The click echoed against the stone walls. The door swung open, and I pushed out, past Joe, past Becker, stopping at the sheriff's desk hidden under stacks of papers.

I spoke to the sheriff's back, trying to keep my rage civil. "Need my package." I waited for what called himself a lawman to close the cell door and turn around.

Pulling out a pocket watch, Joe looked at the hands. "Couple more minutes before I gotta be back, Tate. Still have time for a beer." He thumbed toward the door. "Maybe a sandwich, too."

Becker fished around in a desk drawer, then handed me the thimble and razor, shreds of paper and string hanging limp around them. "Had to make sure it wasn't a gun." Strong, unapologetic words bounced off the walls. "That razor's weapon enough."

Holding my breath kept me from hollering at this man. Joe's light touch on my arm helped me focus. I clutched the two items and leaned close to Becker. "Tell Da he's shaving with a deadly weapon next time you see him." Two steps toward the door, then I turned back to the sheriff. "*Póg mo thóin.*"

Red flamed on Becker's cheeks. He used his long arm

to point toward the door. "Out! You and your filthy mouth. Your smart attitude. Out before I shoot you."

Joe tugged me outside before I could tell the sheriff what I really thought. We walked down the street past one store, then Joe stopped, waiting for me to stop, too.

Joe shook his head and glanced over his shoulder. "Good thing Becker doesn't know you told him to kiss your ass." A hint of a smile created a dimple. He locked narrowed eyes on me. "Listen, brother. You've got to make amends with Becker. Otherwise, one of you is gonna kill the other. At the very least, he's gonna lock you up for good."

He was right. I knew my little brother was right. Couldn't I simply stand and read something without being harassed? Apparently not. Well, I'd forget all this. Inside a week, I'd be gone.

CHAPTER FOUR

WIPING PIE CRUMBS FROM MY MOUTH, I LOOKED over at Ma. Her eyes were closed, a satisfied, silly-looking grin engulfing her entire rounded face. Yep. Buying a dewberry pie with the last of my money was a great idea. This evening after supper, quiet had taken over the room as the rest of the family chased dark berries and crumbs around their plates.

Buttons on my shirt strained a bit. Yep, finally I'd done good, as they say. Finally, something went right. I folded the napkin and leaned back. Supper had been meat and potatoes, Ma's forte. Not much on sweets, she made cookies during the winter and, for special occasions, a cake, but nightly dessert? This pie was a rare treat. Especially of this caliber. Maybe I should've worked at the bakery. Surely, they needed someone to taste the products. Make sure the cookies, pies, cakes were edible. That would have been easy. And fun.

Ma folded her napkin, emitting a light sigh. "'Twas delicious, it 'twas." She turned her green eyes on me.

"And thankee for getting me thimble and your da's razor."

"You're welcome." Would I tell her how much trouble it'd been? Would Joe? I studied my brother who was still busy chasing pie crust flakes. No, neither of us would tell Ma what going to town truly cost. She didn't need to know, and Da would again lecture me, loudly, on how to speak to the sheriff. Probably end up in a fight. A fist fight. But hitting your folks wasn't done. The church forbade such disrespect and somehow, I had managed to sit through enough endless sermons about that very thing. Looked like the rule had sunk in.

I'd never intentionally put a fist in Da's face, or stomach for that matter. No, not intentionally.

* * *

DISHES DONE, Ma and Da sat quietly in the front room, him enjoying the last few puffs on a pipe, Ma peering at a piece of cloth, her needle rising and then sinking into the calico. *When was the last time she had made something for herself?* I struggled to remember. She'd made all her men's work shirts and even shirts and trousers for special occasions. But for herself? I stood in the open doorway feeling the warm outside air pushing its way inside and counted the months. Years?

When I had enough money, I'd buy Ma a new apron. Or maybe a skirt. Maybe a whole dress. *Wouldn't tha' be grand?* Without her saying a thing, her Irish accent echoed clearly in my head.

Time to plan my new life. I pushed open the screen door and ambled outside, pausing at a century-old Texas oak standing halfway between the front porch and the stream. Would Becker bother me here? I gazed upstream and then down. Nobody out and about. Nothing but big, hungry mosquitos.

I'd spent all afternoon deciding which to rob first—the mercantile or the telegraph. While the store would undoubtedly have more money, they'd also have more people around. I made a few decisions. First, no breaking in at night. I'd need a lantern, and surely somebody would notice a light in the room. Besides, the owner, or a trusted clerk, would have taken the cash to the bank, where it got locked up nice and secure. Probably did this every day at closing time which, for most days, was six.

Second, I'd have to start small, which meant the telegraph office or the bakery. Alphonso's livery, where I worked—thanks to Sheriff Becker who insisted Alphonso take me on in order to work off my prison parole—didn't have enough revenue to count. And what coin and cash Alphonso made, he stuffed into his vest pockets. Out of sight. Probably a good idea what with the poor Yankee ex-soldiers continually looking for handouts. To them, a dollar would be a fortune.

Pulling an already-rolled cigarette from my shirt pocket, I struck a parlor match, waited for the tip to flare orange-gold, then held it to my cigarette. I drew a lungful of smoke, then exhaled against the slight breeze as the tip burned into ashes. Another draw. Nerves now calm, I made the decision. Telegraph office. And Joe would help.

Finishing my cigarette, a habit I needed to kick, I went in search of Joe, idly wondering if my brother would prefer to be called by his front name, Michael. He'd been Mike until starting school, then Joe it was from then on. I thought about my own front name, Seamus. Ma called me that only when she was angry and knew I'd done something wrong. I hadn't been Seamus in a while now.

A single lantern glowed, lighting half of the barn in a golden hue. I spotted both of my brothers currying the only horse Da owned. They took good care of that animal, probably hoping to borrow her on Saturdays. Joe to go courting that Frieda Aertker, but Eagan? Did he have a girl, too? Hardly. Like me, he didn't go out much. Soon as I had coin jingling in my pockets, I'd change that.

I leaned against the barn wall watching and enjoying the camaraderie between my younger brothers. They'd grown much closer since I'd been gone. Guessed they'd had to. Hell, all three of us had been close as kids. Roughhousing, chasing, fighting. No matter what we had done, or trouble we'd gotten into, we did it together.

But not anymore. Now I'd become the outsider. A ball like thick clay stuck in my chest. Breathing over the blockage was hard. I pushed it aside and joined them at the horse.

I ran my hand down her muzzle. "Well, boys. She's pretty enough to show off at the county fair."

"That she is." Eagan brushed the muscled brown shoulder. "Da says I can ride her if I take care of her." His wavy blonde hair swept his shoulders as he straightened.

"Got a sweetheart I don't know about?" I regarded my brother. In 1857 and on the trail to this hellhole called Blanco Hill, three-year-old Eagan had fallen out of the back of our wagon. Fourteen years later, the incident was etched on my memory. I'd been sitting next to baby brother and before I could grab him, Eagan had tumbled out, breaking a leg, and twisting an ankle. Ma's tears were hard to bear, but always the stalwart, she helped Da set the leg and then made a nest for Eagan in the wagon bed. I had to walk since my brother now took up the space I had been assigned. But that was all right. Eight was plenty old to walk with the wagon from west of New Orleans clear over to Blanco Hill in Texas. Most times, six-year-old Joe would walk with me.

I didn't mind walking. In fact, hoofing along was better than riding in the swaying wagon. It was crowded, and when Da hit a hole, all the things inside tumbled into me. Walking, Joe and I found bugs, rocks, rabbits and all sorts of discarded items from wagons before us. The best I ever spotted was a four-poster bed with a wide straw mattress. Joe and I took turns lying on it until Ma made us catch up.

Although excited about my robbing ideas, I hesitated to talk about them in front of Eagan. That seventeen-year-old seemed happy enough, making a bit of money working alongside Da. Besides, the fewer people who knew my plans, the better. I'd wait to be alone with Joe where we could talk without prying eyes or ears.

The chance came when Ma called Eagan into the house to help with a chore. The moment he limped away, I began, my voice low enough only Joe could hear.

I spoke for a good three minutes while Joe's eyes grew wider and wider.

"Awful risky, Tate." Joe stared toward the barn door, standing wide open. "You sure you wanna try this? What happens when Da finds out?" He moved in shoulder to shoulder with me. "Hell, when Becker finds out. You'll be lucky just to get life in prison."

"Only one who'll know is you." I rocked his shoulder. "And if it goes like I think it will, you won't know much. It'll be the first of the Nolan Brothers Escapades."

"But—"

"It'll be good practice." I turned my most charming smile on Joe. "Trust me."

CHAPTER FIVE

In the stable, I bent over, hoof gripped between my knees, and picked out clods of manure and pebbles while I thought. Joe had said that his boss, Ed Whalen, took the cash to the bank only a couple times a week. Sometimes Tuesdays, but always on Friday around three. The bank closed at four, giving Whalen time to wander over, deposit the money, chat with the good-looking cashier, and then amble over to Sam's Emporium for a habitual Friday afternoon drink. Like clockwork, Joe reported.

Exactly what I needed to know. My plan seemed simple enough. I'd need a small pouch or at least a big pocket, enough to hold the cash, a mask—my old gray bandanna would do—and something solid to use as a weapon. And...I knew I should wear a different hat and shirt. Something people couldn't immediately identify as mine.

For a shirt, I'd see if Ma had one I could borrow without her knowing. But a hat? Eagan's maybe? No. Stealing a hat or messing with one was almost as bad as stealing a horse. You simply didn't mess with a cowboy's hat. I'd seen men beaten near half to death for lesser crimes.

I brightened. Those derelict former soldiers might give me one of their kepis or sell it to me. That would be the ticket. I'd check with them on my walk home.

Now, for a weapon. A gun? No. I wasn't a killer, never intended to be. Plus, I didn't own one and certainly didn't have the money to buy even a cheap one. I lowered the hoof, satisfied all dirt wads were gone. Straightening up, I spied my new weapon of choice. Leaning against a post was an old branding iron my boss had used back in his cowboying days. He didn't use it much anymore. Alphonso would never miss the iron rod.

I whistled as I picked up the horse's next hoof. Yep, plans were coming together. Friday couldn't come soon enough. Two more days.

* * *

I TUCKED the war-torn kepi under my shirt before walking away. Two of the men had fought over the quarter I offered. In the end, I chose the one that came closest to fitting and even then, the fit was snug.

When I got home I'd look for a shirt, one Ma had put aside to mend. I was sure there were shirts at the bottom of her mending pile that would fit me. I wasn't big enough in the shoulders, chest, or belly to warrant an extra-sized shirt. And if she didn't have one, maybe I'd go back to those crazed soldiers. No doubt they'd sell me one. Also, I'd need a sack for all the money. I spied just the thing—a tobacco pouch. It would be big enough.

Things were certainly coming together.

* * *

FRIDAY DAWN PROMISED rain and close to unbearable warmth. This early in the morning with the sun hesitantly spreading its glory across the horizon, the horses were especially ornery despite my soft words and gentle touch. I gave them an extra scoop of oats and rubbed down two of them. But they were antsy, keeping their ears back or flicking them side to side as if listening to important discussions.

Despite the oppressive humidity, I was as on edge as the horses. At half past two I'd make my way over to the telegraph office, take the money and skedaddle. Shouldn't take more than ten minutes; my boss wouldn't miss me.

I curried the latest horse to be stabled, a broad-shouldered feisty dun, and in my head went over my plans. A shirt I'd rescued from the bottom of Ma's mending pile now lay hidden under a mound of straw along with the kepi. The branding iron still leaned against the wooden wall where it'd been for weeks. I decided against telling Alphonso I'd be gone a few minutes running an errand. While that would explain my disappearance from the stable, it was too complicated. I'd have to find an alibi and, well...too complicated. In answer to my absence, if questioned, I'd cite an off-tasting mid-day ham sandwich upsetting my stomach. A quarter hour in the privy had helped. That sounded reasonable enough. No one in their right mind, not even old man Becker, would search the privy for confirmation. No one.

Then again, Sheriff Becker might check out of spite.

Minutes stretched into what felt like hours until I thought the world had stood still. Off-and-on rain hid the sun; a gray gloom shrouded the town, shrouded my thoughts. I about wore out my pocket watch checking before two o'clock.

Another look. Thirty more minutes and I'd execute my plan. If all went well, and there was no reason it wouldn't, I'd become richer than I was at the moment. Plus, I'd learn how to rob and steal and, most importantly, how to get away with criminal activity. Especially pulling the wool over the eyes of Becker and any other *gombeen* law officers who happened to wander by. No, this plan wouldn't fail.

Now…if Joe did his part, we would be on our way to fame and fortune.

At precisely two twenty-five, I retrieved the kepi and changed shirts, carefully pushing my regular shirt under a pile of straw in one stall. The tobacco pouch I shoved up under my shirt. On the way out of the stable, I picked up the branding iron, and stepped out into a rainy world. I'd have to be careful to leave obvious boot prints. I stomped to the privy making sure my prints were there, then tiptoed down the alley toward the telegraph office.

Joe's detailed description of the inside of the office paraded in my brain. I could navigate the room in my sleep. An added bonus was the supply room which I hadn't taken special notice of when visiting earlier in the week.

Standing in the alley, I put an ear against the back door. No voices, simply *clack-*

clack-clacking of the telegraph machine. Was that Joe humming? I listened harder. Yes. The tune was "Camptown Races," the all-clear signal we'd agreed upon.

Glancing right then left and seeing not a soul in the alley, I eased open the door, branding iron clutched in one hand. Joe wasn't to notice the squeaky door close behind him and the fact I was sneaking in. True to his word, Joe stayed slightly bent over his desk, busily writing whatever words were coming in.

I edged toward Joe, pulled in a lungful of air, and brought the iron down over the back of his head. Hopefully, I'd swung gently enough not to cause too much damage. Joe needed to be knocked out so he could honestly say he never saw who or what beaned him. My brother hit the floor and lay still.

"Sorry." I kneeled, touched the egg-sized knot on the back of Joe's head, and put a hand on his chest to be sure he was still breathing. Knowing time was important, I then dragged my unconscious brother, who was heavier than he looked, across the room to the supply closet, tied his hands behind him, loosely wrapped the gray bandanna around his mouth, stuffed him in the closet, then closed the door. Was conking your brother the best way to make money? Doubts rattled around in my mind. This wasn't right. But then again, Joe had agreed to being hit, knew the blow was coming. I threw back my slumping shoulders, nodded, and pulled in a deep breath.

Within seconds, the pouch was full of cash and coin. I took a moment to stop at the closet door, touched it, then headed out the way I'd come in, now all the richer.

Again, no one stood in the alley. No one would be outside today if they didn't have to. I glanced upward. *Thank you for the rain.* I shut the door, then slogged through mud, cursing the prints left behind. Hopefully enough rain would erase some or muddle them enough that I couldn't be followed.

On the way, I whipped off the hat, offering no explanations, and returned the kepi to the beggar now taking refuge in a side alley. The man twisted the hat onto his head, muttering what could be thanks or oaths. I wasn't sure what he'd said and certainly didn't want to stick around for clarification.

Privy in sight, I veered toward the wooden structure hoping to make visible boot prints back to the stable. Luck was with me. I opened the privy door, stepped in, back out, and slammed the door in case anyone was within earshot. Trudging up to the stable, I couldn't hide a smile. No matter how much money I'd stolen, this was proof positive I was an outlaw. A successful one at that.

I changed shirts and, then careful to replace the branding iron, checked the rod for blood. How hard had I hit Joe? Enough to draw blood? A close inspection revealed no red splatters. Good. By now Joe should've been awake and complaining to Ed Whalen.

What felt like years dragged by as I fed the horses, curried the newest arrival, and rubbed a plaster poultice over a swollen fetlock. My stomach rumbled. Must've been close to suppertime. Butterflies stomped in my chest.

I paced stall to stall, cleaning one, adding fresh hay to another. Rubbing the back of my neck as if it was dirt-encrusted, didn't help with the growing headache. I needed to get home, return the shirt to Ma's mending pile, be sure Joe was all right, listen to his tales of being robbed, and then...count the money. Of course, I'd share with my brother, but we'd agreed I would keep eighty percent since I was taking all the risks, and Joe was the innocent victim.

A shadow crossed my face. I squinted toward the open door, now beams of waning sunlight pouring into the stable. I shaded my eyes and my heart stopped. Or at least thudded like a rock. Sheriff Becker. The Devil incarnate. I made a mental rundown of what I had hidden or replaced. Branding iron back? Check. Shirt off and stashed under straw? Check. Money in a small pouch I'd carried in a different stall? Check. Even if Becker patted my pockets, he'd find nothing. The usual.

Sheriff Becker strolled in like he was there for a friendly visit. I knew better. Becker ran his hand down the dun's rump, his hooded park eyes scanning me.

"Where've you been, boy?"

Not now, not now, I repeated. *Keep a civil tongue in your head*. I swallowed irritation. "Right here. All day, sir." *That's it. Show respect*.

"Not over visiting your brother?"

How the hell does he know? Fear strangled me, but I forced out words. "No sir. Like I said, been right here all day."

Becker *humphed* air from his nose and moved in close. He took his time inspecting the horses, the straw, the harnesses and then turned eyes on me. "Got some bad news for you."

This is when it counts. Play along. Keep your words civil. I furrowed my forehead. "What kinda bad news?"

"Seems someone robbed the telegraph office today and your brother took the brunt of it." A smile raised one side of his grayed mustache. "Got clobbered darn good, then stuffed into a closet."

This sounded worse than what I'd intended. "Joe's dead?"

"*Nein*." Becker wagged his head. "Got a skull thicker'n yours. He's over at Doc's. Your pa's with him. Eagan ran." He stopped and chuckled at his own joke. "Well, he *hobbled* home to fetch your ma."

I reached to run my hand over my face but put it back on the fence. Doing that might have given me away. I hadn't counted on this. The plan was Joe would come home with a knot on the back of his head and tell the family he'd been robbed. Maybe I'd hit Joe too hard.

"Thanks for telling me." I turned to my boss who'd walked in. "My brother—"

"Sheriff already told me." Alphonso thumbed outside. "Go to your brother. I can finish up here."

Well, damn. Would my boss find the shirt and money if he 'finished up'? What would that entail? Would I have time to move it? No. I prayed Alphonso wouldn't discover the loot, or the shirt.

I nodded to the stable owner. "Thank you, sir. I'll get my hat and go see Joe." Knowing I shouldn't but couldn't resist, I turned to Becker. "You say they robbed the office?"

Becker nodded.

"They get much?"

The sheriff grunted. "*Nein*. Not much more than fifteen dollars the owner said." He started for the door then turned back. "Fifteen more'n you'll make in a year, kid."

I balled a hand then relaxed the fist.

Becker stepped in closer. "Don't think of leaving town, *junge*." He jabbed a thick finger at my face. "My eyes are on you."

* * *

MOANING SOFTLY, Joe lay on the examination table holding his bandaged head. Da stood across the room, his back to the door, staring at a framed document on the wall. He muttered like he was reading the fine print.

Doc Patton met me at the door. "Glad you're here." He looked over his shoulder at Joe. "He's been calling your name."

Well bollocks. How hard *did* I hit him? And would that make people, especially Becker, think I had something to do with the robbery? My long legs took me to Joe, and I patted his shoulder.

"Hey, brother. Heard you've been sleeping on the job." I smiled when Joe's blue eyes opened and seemed to focus on me. Faint beginnings of a smile claimed Joe's face, but within moments turned more into a grimace.

Joe stretched out a hand, which I took. "Hurts." Joe whispered. "Head really hurts."

I started to apologize, wanting to take back the idea to hit my brother, wanting to rewind the clock. But none of that would happen. I'd apologize, grovel, if necessary, later. I'd give Joe all the money.

I clutched Joe's hand harder than I should have. Releasing the pressure, I turned attention to Da, now standing on the other side of Joe. Da's glare stabbed right through me. How did he know what I'd done? Would Da tell Becker? No way Da knew unless Joe had told him. And that didn't seem likely.

Da ran a meaty hand over his mouth, down his beard. "Durn Yankee *buggars*. Look what they've done." He looked from Joe to me to the doc and back. "Gone to robbin', they have. Gone to attacking innocent boys, they have." He straightened, pulled in air, ran a hand across his balding head.

I allowed a slight breath to escape. Da thought it was the ex-soldiers. Should I push my luck? "What makes you think it was those men?"

Da shook a finger toward the window. "Somebody reported seeing a *duine* wearing a kepi near the telegraph office. That's proof enough for me."

Good God. Somebody saw me? Well, that was the chance I'd taken. So far, so good, though.

A nurse, glass in hand, appeared at the door, followed by Ma, then Eagan on her heels. They pushed into the small room. With nowhere left to stand, I stepped into the waiting room at the front of the office. From there I listened to Ma's soft voice cooing at Joe, and then hardening toward the doc, asking questions and searching for answers.

Left alone, I sat thinking about what damage I'd caused. Joe would have a lump for a long time, probably a nauseating hangover type headache for a week. Of course, Ed Whalen was out fifteen dollars, and those ex-Yankees would be hounded and harassed by Becker and maybe by the good citizens of Blanco Hill.

Would the soldiers confess they'd sold a hat to me? And if they did would their word hold up? After all, they were bums, drunken, half-crazed, half-starved men. Who'd believe them? No one, except Becker. If anything, just out of spite.

I kicked myself for not planning this entire endeavor carefully enough. The little things were what mattered. Next time, I'd know better.

Eagan rushed past me toward the door. He pulled it open. "Gonna get the horse so's Joe can ride home." His copper-brown eyes glowed in the lantern's light. "Da said I could."

"He's good enough to come home?" I stood, a weight off my chest.

My brother nodded. "What with the laudanum making him groggy, he can't walk too good. Walks even worse than me." Eagan moved outside and held the door. "Gotta go. Be right back."

Good news indeed. I closed the door and made my way back to Joe's room where I found my brother sitting on the edge of the examination table, eyes glassy. Ma fussed and Da stood resolutely next to her.

Doc patted Joe's shoulder. "Be fine in a day or two, son. Gonna have a splitting headache for a bit, but no real damage done." He turned his gaze on Ma. "Don't let him sleep more'n a few hours at a time tonight. Make sure he drinks plenty of water."

The nurse handed her a small bottle. "This laudanum should do the trick. It'll keep the headache from getting too bad."

"Thank you both." Da shook hands with Doc Patton. "What'd I owe you?"

I shook my head. Another detail I hadn't figured on. I'd have to plan better next time.

While Da and the doctor tallied up expenses in the outer office, I stood outside on the boardwalk, watching for Eagan. Usually, it was a ten-minute walk from town, but for Eagan, probably fifteen. A pound of guilt about my little brother's accident sat on my chest. I hadn't pushed him, hadn't made him fall, but I couldn't save him. Remorse and sad memories flooded in at bad times.

At long last, Eagan rode up, dismounted like he was born a cowboy and produced a star-lit smile. "Took longer to saddle her but got 'er done."

Before I could comment, the door opened and Joe stepped out, arms draped around Ma and Da's shoulders. Doc and his nurse followed behind.

Joe wobbled like a cowboy at the end of a four-day whoop-em-up, a sappy smile pushing up his reddened cheeks making the dimples extra deep.

It took four of us to get Joe on the horse without him sliding off the other side. Once settled, I swung up behind and wrapped arms around my brother. Reins in hand, I headed for home, the rest of the family walking right behind.

THE MAKING OF THE TEXAS KID   55

hand. I headed for home, the rest of the family walking
right behind

CHAPTER SIX

I BROUGHT A CUP OF TEA TO MY MOUTH AND held it there without sipping. Chitchatting, forks *tinging* against plates, tea slurping, and everyday breakfast noises filled the dining room. Aroma of scrambled eggs and ham wafted throughout the dining room. This morning at the table, the main topic of discussion was Joe and his head and how lucky he'd been. Thoughts of my younger brother, now lying on the living room sofa with white gauze wrapped around his head, kicked me in the stomach. Joe, still trying to make sense of the world. Softly answered questions, none of the answers clear.

Ma hustled to finish her eggs and ham while Da pushed the last of his breakfast into his mouth. But Eagan was most excited about the horse, going on and on about his heroics of getting the horse...and so quickly. Yes, he was sorry about Joe, but getting the horse and retrieving his brother was the single thought on his mind. I smiled at his passion. Indeed, he'd been the best man for the job and clearly, Eagan thought so too.

Da pushed back his chair, rose as a knock at the front door turned heads. He opened it and ushered in Doc Patton.

"Wanted to make sure my patient was mending properly." Patton nodded as Ma waved her hand toward Joe. Da and I followed.

Joe pushed himself upright, a blanket bunching around his legs. Doc peered into Joe's eyes, felt his forehead, listened to his heart. "How're you feeling, son?"

Clearing his throat, Joe sipped water and fought for words. "All right, I guess." He patted the bandage. "Head hurts, but it's more like a fuzzy toothache. Upsets my stomach though."

Doc patted Joe's knee. "All part of the laudanum and that whack you took." He turned to Ma. "He'll be right as rain in a day or two. Just keep an eye on him and if you see anything that worries you, send for me."

I turned at another knock on the door, this one harder than the Doc's. Now what? Criminy. It wasn't even six yet and already we'd had company. With Da and Ma and now Eagan talking to Doc, pointing to Joe, that left me to open the door.

Ed Whalen stood there, concern etched on his face. "How is he?"

"Come see." I stood back while Joe's boss stepped into the living room. The room wasn't too big, enough for the five of them, but not much more. Now with seven, the air felt clogged, thick.

Whalen sat on the couch next to Joe. "Afraid we'd lost you there." He looked up at Ma, then Da. "When I found him in the closet, hands tied like that, thought for sure he was dead. Can't imagine anyone doing that to Joe just for a few dollars." He shook his head and patted Joe's hand. "Doesn't make sense."

Joe turned glazed eyes on me.

Icy fingers wrapped around my throat threatening to strangle me. What *was* I thinking? I wagged my head. "Sure doesn't."

Rap-rap-rap. I blew out an exasperated sigh. Now what? Had to be Becker. Sure enough, when I opened the door, there stood Sheriff Becker, staring at me with a smug combination of power and superiority on his face. What did he want? *Behave yourself. I've come too far to screw it up now.*

I stood back allowing Becker entry. Conversation stopped and eyes turned to the lawman. Da shook hands with the man.

"Glad you're here, Sheriff." Da nodded to Doc and Whalen. "We've been real worried about Joe but looks like he'll be fine."

Becker stood between Doc and Ma and looked down at Joe. "You're heavier than you look, son." Becker turned to Ma. "Tried to carry him down to Doc's. But *heilige kuh*, Mrs. Nolan, you must feed this boy well. He's full of muscle. Ed, here, and me were lucky a wagon came by and offered to help."

Whalen nodded confirmation. "That Italian man and his daughter came by at the right time. Took him down to Doc's then offered to stay with Joe until Mr. Nolan arrived." He tilted his head at Joe. "She's a pretty young lady too. About your age, I'd say."

A grin wrinkled Joe's cheek. "Guess I'll have to thank her." His words, soft, slurred.

"That you will, my boy." Whalen chuckled and patted Joe's knee. "That you will."

Great. I pressed my lips together, hoping frustration wouldn't explode. Had to be the same woman. I'd seen her first. On second thought, why couldn't *I* thank the woman and her father on behalf of my brother? That would be the gentlemanly thing to do. Would give me a great excuse to come calling.

All at once, everyone spoke at the same time. I fought the urge to put my hands over my ears. Whalen and Doc and Becker couldn't leave soon enough. In fact, if someone didn't leave right now, with all the racket and words flying around, echoing off the walls, I would scream for everybody to shut up. No, I couldn't do that. It would be a dead giveaway and as it was, daggers of guilt were busy gnawing at my soul. I had to get away. Going to work should do the trick. Shoveling *shite* would make me feel better.

Pushing through the crowded living room, I plucked my hat from the pegs on the wall, fitted the narrow-brimmed hat down tight and opened the door. Becker's firm grip on my arm stopped me.

"Where you going?"

"To work."

"Need to ask you some questions first." An oily tone seeped into Becker's words. "Stay here."

I thumbed toward town. "Gotta go. Alphonso's expecting me."

"I'll write you an excuse." Becker waved a hand like he was swatting flies. "Just like you're a kiddie in school."

I remained uncomfortably still. Even though I didn't move, I knew I was walking the knife edge of danger. What I did now determined the rest of my life. Panic wadded itself into a ball and slid down my throat. With the panic, I swallowed pride. "Thank you, sir."

Doc pushed his way to the door. "I'll stop by tomorrow," he said to no one in particular, and disappeared into the early morning light.

Ed Whalen shook hands with Da and addressed Ma. "Got a fine son there, Mrs. Nolan. I'm lucky to have him work for me."

"*Thankee*, sir." Ma's Irish lilt was in full force this morning.

"Tell him, for me if you will, I don't want to see him back until at least Wednesday. Today's Saturday, so that should give him enough time to heal up." Whalen opened the door. "And I won't dock his pay. I think he's earned a couple days off." With that, and just like the Doc, he retreated into the morning.

"Would you like tea, Sheriff?" Ma pointed toward the dining room, a real luxury in the Blanco Hill residences. Most families ate in the kitchen.

"You have coffee?" Becker clutched his hat in his hand. "Not much on tea."

Ma pointed toward the dining room. "Afraid we don't. But I do have water."

Becker nodded and crooked a finger at me. "Let's talk in there."

As much as I wanted to be walking toward that stinky livery stable right now, I sat at the table, dirty dishes disappearing as Ma whisked them off to the kitchen. Becker sat on the end, near me.

Eagan, clutching his hat, shook hands with the sheriff. "Sorry I've got to go, sir. I hope you find whoever did this to my brother."

"You can count on that, Eagan." Becker turned razor-sharp eyes on me. "He'll be sorry when I do."

Da and Eagan closed the door. Ma helped Joe to bed, which left me alone with Becker. As much as I had wished for quiet, now I wished they were all back. I'd appreciate a roomful of bodies. Would this be my final moments as a free man?

Becker drank half the glass of water then said, "One of the ex-soldiers said they'd sold you one of their hats." He cocked his head. "That true?"

I couldn't breathe. "Why would I want one of their lice-infected hats...sir?" I said, adding "sir" as an afterthought.

"Why would they give me your name? Why, Tate?"

Scrambling for an answer that made sense, I leaned forward as if telling a secret. I lowered my voice. "Don't tell Da or he'll wring my neck. And Ma doesn't know either." I wished I had a glass of water, too. Suddenly, my throat was desert dry.

Becker lowered his voice also. "Know what?"

"Sometimes I give them a coin or two. Occasionally, I get tips from the horses' owners, and I give it to those poor men." I made a show of peering down the hall. "Ma feels sorry for them, but says they need jobs not hand-outs. Says the Texas government should be helping them. Da thinks so too. Don't tell them I told you, please."

Would Becker believe me?

The sheriff leaned back in his chair, studied me and then the inside of the room. A slight squint of the eye, a sideways movement of the jaw. "Guess jail did you some good after all." He let out air. "All right. I'll keep your secret...for now."

"Thank you, sir." How had I managed to sound civil with my teeth gnashed? Would this jackass ever leave?

Becker rose as Ma hurried into the room. She nodded to both me and the sheriff. "Finally got Joe all settled. Slept on the couch last night, he did." She addressed Becker directly. "We all took turns staying up with the boy."

The sheriff nodded, then looked at me. "I'll stop by

the livery stable and tell Alphonso you'll be a few minutes late today."

"Thank you." Seems like that's all I'd been telling the sheriff for hours. I certainly didn't mean it. What I wanted to say was graphic things. But I'd resist. Especially since Ma was in the room.

"I'll let myself out." And Becker was gone.

Ma plopped down into his vacated chair. "What'd he want with ye?" She twirled the empty water glass. "Nothing bad I hope."

I stood, bent down, and kissed the top of her head. "Just talking, Ma. Asked if I'd heard from his daughter. I told him no." I ambled toward the door. "I'll try to stop by at noon."

* * *

I CHECKED IN WITH ALPHONSO, then rushed to the stall which held the money pouch. Luck was shining that morning. There it was, way back under a pile of straw left undisturbed. I tucked it under my shirt. Would the other shirt still be hidden this morning as well? Straw undisturbed. I let out a long sigh. Again, lucky. Apparently, my boss had seen no need to rake more straw into the stalls.

Whistling, I scooped manure from the farthest stall while mentally listing the things

I'd learned: small details matter. Have an excuse for everything you do. Don't hit your brother.

The hardest part of the past twenty-four hours was having to wait until I was in the privacy of my own bedroom, well mine, Joe's, and Eagan's, to count the money. Then I'd divvy it up with my brother and no one would be any the wiser. As soon as I got home, I'd count.

But I'd also make plans for my next robbery soon. Maybe I'd stick around Blanco Hill a bit longer, just until Joe was back on his feet and the sheriff wasn't looking. Might be as much as a month. Could I stand being here that long?

Thoughts turned to the Italian girl. Maybe I *could* last a bit longer.

Tomorrow being Sunday, perhaps she'd be going to church. Although I worked Sundays, I could sneak off for a few minutes when mass was over and "run into" that angel. I'd listen for the bell announcing the end and then dash over. Ma and Da, definitely Eagan, who liked going to church, would be there. Joe would probably stay home, enjoying the place to himself for a change.

What was her name and who would know? I couldn't be too obvious. Couldn't simply walk up and ask. Maybe the ladies at the mercantile. I stopped raking. They would know if anybody would. And if I stopped in at noon today saying I needed another thimble for Ma, I could ask one of the female clerks. Then I'd walk home to check on Joe. Guilt refused to dissolve. I'd nearly killed my younger brother.

Noon came at last and with the newest horse curried, combed and full of oats and water,

I waved at Alphonso and wove my way downtown. The mercantile was busy most Saturdays and today was no exception. I kept an eye out for the Italian woman, but all I saw were ladies with children in tow, picking out material, the kids sneaking candy from the jars on the counter. I chuckled. It hadn't been that long ago since I'd done the same thing.

I waited for a clerk to finish helping an older woman select buttons for green fabric. Foot tapping, this was taking way too long. I had only so many minutes and those were being eaten up with waiting. I headed for the door when a woman's voice in my ear stopped him.

"Can I help you with something, sir?"

I jerked back and took in this woman who wasn't tall but held herself like a queen. A dusting of freckles danced across her cheeks. I stared.

"Can I help you?" Her voice, deeper than most, broke my reverie.

"Uh." Was that all I could utter? Please. I was a man of the world. I could do better than that. "Looking for a thimble." Would I tell her why I was really here?

She pointed to the far side of the store. "Over there. Follow me."

I selected the same one from the other day, then decided to go ahead and ask the Italian lady's name. And hers while I was at it. I asked.

She smiled broadly. Not one saved for everyday customers. "Of course. She's new to town. Angelique Rossi." She leaned into me, a hint of lilac wafting under my nose. "Isn't that a beautiful name? Wish it was mine."

How perfect could that be? I stuck out a hand. "I'm Tate Nolan. What's your name, if you don't mind my asking?"

"Nothing as pretty as Angelique." She took my hand, shaking it gently. "Miss Anderson. MaryBeth Anderson."

I produced the type of smile that made one grin back. I'd perfected the look, I was sure. "I think MaryBeth Anderson is a beautiful name." I tipped my hat and held up the thimble. "I best be going now." I put it back into her hand. "Not sure which one Ma wants."

"For your ma? Not your wife?"

"Yes ma'am. Ma. Maybe I can stop back in some time." I'd make sure I did.

She dipped her head. "I'd like that."

I whistled partway home and then changed to humming. Two women. Two. Neither one a raving beauty, but both pretty in her own way. I turned the corner on my street and stopped cold. On my front porch stood Becker. What the hell? Didn't he have anything better to do than harass me?

Serious thoughts of turning around and running back to work took over. Maybe that German *bopach* hadn't seen me.

Becker pointed a finger. "There you are, Tate." He stepped off the porch and waited.

Could I drag my feet any harder? I stopped a good yard away from that lawman. "Just came home for food, Sheriff." Surprised civil words came out, I moved toward the door. Maybe Ma would save me.

"Your meal can wait." Becker pulled out my faded gray bandanna, the one I'd used on Joe.

Icy needles pricked my skin. I swallowed. Hard. "What's that?"

"I'll speak slowly so even you can understand." Becker held up the cloth. "This is a bandanna, like the one you're wearing now. Only the one around your neck is blue."

Without thinking, I fingered the material. I wore one every day. Most men, working men, did. Entire chest on fire, I envisioned wrapping the cloth tight around Becker's neck until his face turned purple and the man stopped breathing. I struggled to keep my voice normal. "Yes, sir, I know what it is." I shifted my weight to my right hip. "Just wondering why you have it and why you're showing it to me."

"Because it's yours."

Nerves on fire, I fought to keep my breathing even. I

wrinkled my forehead. "Why do you think so?" I peered at it closer. "Certainly isn't mine."

Becker used the hand with the bandanna to point toward the house. "Your ma says it is."

"You asked her?"

The lawman *humphed* with disdain. "*Ja*. Why not?" Another *humph*. "You afraid?"

I plucked the material out of his hand, studied it, then shook my head. "Used to have one kinda like that a long time ago. Sheriff, plenty of men have gray neckerchiefs. Where'd you get it at?" I handed back the material.

"Used to gag your brother yesterday. Tied on kinda loose, Whalen said. Almost like whoever did this didn't want to hurt him."

That much was true. I stepped past Becker and onto the porch. "Well, sir. Like I said, it's not mine and I don't know anything about the robbery." I opened the door just as Ma stepped out.

"Sheriff Becker? Ye're still here." Ma pointed inside. "Would ye care to stay for a ham sandwich and buttermilk?"

Becker squinted at me, then softened toward Ma. "Thank you, ma'am, sounds delicious, but I'm needed back at the office." He turned to me. "I'll stop by the livery later; see if you've remembered." He tipped his hat and ambled away.

* * *

I KEPT one eye on the horse and the other on the stable door. All afternoon I'd jump when a shadow passed and especially when a man led in a horse. I barely listened to

the instructions—how much feed, horse brushed or not
—the usual. Could Becker actually figure out the robber
simply based on an old neckerchief? And would that be
enough evidence to send me back to prison? I kicked
myself again. Small details really *did* matter.

The afternoon dragged while I waited, watched. No
Becker. Maybe that poor excuse for a lawman realized a
gray bandanna was just that—a common gray bandanna.
One anybody could own.

Stomach grumbling was a sign quitting time was
around the corner. How about the bakery? German
women ran the place. Would they have strudel? I licked
my lips at the vision of flakey crusts filled with cinna-
mon-laced apples, all baked to a crispy brown. I checked
my pockets. All my money was at home in the tobacco
pouch.

"Hey there, brother."

Eagan's voice spun me around. Thank the Lord it
wasn't Becker.

"Thought I'd walk home with you today." Eagan
hobbled in and ran his hand down a horse's rump. He
patted the chestnut mare. "Good looking animal." And
then as if remembering why he was there, he explained.
"Da went home early to see Joe, so figured I'd walk with
you."

I glanced at the stalls, all full today. They usually were
on the weekends. "I'm about done here." I plucked my
hat from a post. "You got any money?"

Digging around in his vest pockets, Eagan produced
four coins and a grin. "Sure do. Why?"

"Let's make a stop on the way home."

* * *

THE STRUDEL WAS EVERYTHING the bakery ladies had promised. Apple parts melted in my mouth. Forking the last bite, I looked at the family all seated around the table. Was that a sigh I let out? I'd certainly taken this for granted—sitting around a table sharing food. But after being gone for so long and then almost losing Joe, a sense of family engulfed me. I pushed back my empty plate, all crumbs gone. This good feeling still didn't change my mind about leaving. Now maybe I'd move on later than I'd planned.

Table cleared, dishes done, I leaned against the front porch rail taking in the slightest cooling breeze. I lit a cigarette and blew smoke into the wind and thought about the money now in a sock in my drawer. Before supper, while everyone fussed over the strudel, me and Joe had counted the booty. Fourteen dollars and seventy-five cents. Not as much as I'd wanted, but certainly more than I'd had.

Guilt roaring, I'd offered all of it to Joe. After much bargaining, we settled on fifty-fifty. All right. My remorse was still running in spades, but I was content. And I'd never again hit Joe. Or Eagan for that matter.

Slam! Screen door. I spun around. Eagan walked toward me, that leg making his gait lopsided. Eagan patted his stomach. "Good idea about the strudel. Best I ever ate."

"Yeah? How many have you had?"

He cocked his head and took time answering. "Maybe none. But this one was sure tasty."

Nodding, I stared into the dark expanse of Texas. Out there, somewhere, was the answer to my problems. Somewhere was a trunkful of money just waiting to be stolen. But, instead of stealing and having to look over my shoulder the rest of my life, did I want a regular job like Da and my brothers? Making enough to keep a roof over my head and my belly full? Seemed to be a tradeoff for a clear conscience. Being tied down to a job wasn't what I wanted. But then again, the law—

"Saw the paper today." Eagan stared where I was looking. "That James Gang sure has been busy. Robbing stages, even trains." He turned to me. "Imagine robbing a train. I ain't ever even rid one and here they are robbing them."

"A train you say?"

Eagan nodded, his youthful enthusiasm beaming. "Think I'll get to ride one, Tate? Wouldn't tha' be grand?"

Ma's lovely Irish accent brought a smile to my face. Even though I was the only brother to be born in Ireland, I spoke like the others who had picked up Ma's and Da's accents. Occasionally, a German phrase or two would slip in. Couldn't be helped since most of Blanco Hill was German immigrants.

"You ever ride a train, Tate? What was it like?"

It would take more money than I had to buy a ticket. A ticket out of here. Maybe that's what I'd do after I robbed something else. Take my little brother on our first train ride.

"Tate? You listening?"

I stubbed out the cigarette and tossed the remainder into the darkness. "Haven't been on a train, but I think I hear them at night. Wonder where they're going."

Fervor bubbling over, Eagan pointed north. "Probably clear up to Austin, don't you think? That's a ways off." He changed directions. "Or maybe down to San Antone. They got trains down there?"

"You're asking a lot of questions. You look at a map or something?"

Bobbing his head, Eagan turned his back to the porch rail and leaned against it. "Been reading. You know I like to read, and this lady loaned me a book about trains. Said her husband had been a...a...engine man back east and the story reminded her of him. Guess he died or something."

I hadn't seriously thought about robbing a train until right then. How hard could it be? You jump on, find where they keep the money, take everything you can carry, then jump off. How hard *could* it be?

Eagan rambled on about trains and the *clackety-clack* they made. How he'd give almost anything to ride one and how do you know where they're going and how do you know when you get there and who all rides the train and...

I tuned him out. If the James boys could rob a train, why couldn't I? Sure, they'd had more practice at robbing, but that didn't mean much. To get ready, I'd rob another business, move up to a bank or two, and then the train. I paused. How much money did a train carry? Was it worthwhile to rob one? Maybe I'd rob the station where they sell the tickets. Surely, they had more money than a train.

I'd definitely have to do a lot of planning and research.

"Tate, you listening?" Eagan's tug on my shirtsleeve brought me to the present. "You been staring at that old tree like it's about to walk away." He leaned over the railing, peered into the darkness, and pointed. "Yep. There it goes."

I couldn't help but smile. Eagan always found humor

and a sense of adventure in everyday life. A trait that apparently had bypassed me.

My thoughts moved from trains to women. Maybe Eagan could help. "You get a lot of customers a day. Ever meet the new Italians, the Rossis? A man and his daughter?"

"You mean the ones what helped cart Joe over to Doc's?"

I nodded. Maybe this wasn't a good idea. Eagan didn't always watch what he said and to whom. He'd probably tell her that his older brother was interested.

Eagan tapped my upper arm. "Sure do. She's kinda pretty, don't you think? I mean for an old lady."

Smiling, I nodded. "Old? Guess she would be to you."

"Comes in all the time. Most times her da comes too."

Now the conversation was truly interesting. "Any particular day of the week, like regularly?" That question was way too obvious. "I mean, being as they're new to town, just curious."

Eagan's grin lit up the porch, his smile like a full moon. "Sure you are." He stepped back and pointed a finger at me. "You're in love. I can tell. You're in love."

"Just—"

"Tate's in love!" Eagan turned and shouted through the screen door. "Tate loves the new Italian old lady!"

I grabbed Eagan around the shoulders, put him in a headlock, and knuckled his head. "Am not. Am not." I knuckled harder. "Don't go spreading rumors about your big brother."

Thrashing and laughing, Eagan pulled out of the brotherly embrace and limped toward the safety of the door. "Are too."

Before I could grab him again, Eagan jumped inside, slamming the screen door.

Ma and Da's admonishments about slamming the door and waking Joe made me laugh. I felt good. For the first time in a year, I felt good.

CHAPTER SEVEN

I LEANED ON A SHOVEL HANDLE, BREATHING IN nothing but hay and horses. From the stable, I listened hard. Only a few more minutes until the church bell declared the service over, the sound always a relief. Attending church was a chore, nothing I ever looked forward to. Eagan, on the other hand, loved the singing, the fellowship, even the message the priest would drone on and on about. How many times had my snoring resulted in a sharp elbow in the ribs? Today, brother Joe had the right idea. His headache still made him sick to his stomach, he'd reported, so he didn't dare go.

I smiled at the smirk on Joe's face when he'd come up with the excuse early this morning. Maybe that knot on the back of his head would get him out of church for a month.

Over my growling stomach, church bells sounded the end of another saintly service. How many attendees were secretly glad to leave the confines, ready to go home to fried chicken and potatoes? I remembered those days—that string tie drawn so tight I'd about strangled; rear end numb from sitting and squirming on that hard pew, head spinning from the "these" and "thous" the priest interjected at the beginning of each sentence. No, the only good part of this stupid job mucking stalls was I had to work Sundays. I chanced a look skyward. Maybe there were miracles, after all.

Horses fed and watered, standing in their stalls, there was no reason I couldn't take ten minutes. Angelique the Angel might be coming down the church steps now, her long dark tresses billowing in the breeze.

Alphonso nodded when I asked to go talk to Ma and Da since they were nearby. I jogged up Main and then over a block. Sure enough, paroled parishioners stood in small groups on the landscaped lawn in front of the steepled building. I caught snippets of "Lovely sermon," and "How's your rheumatiz?" and "Did you hear about...?" I ignored them while navigating through the crowd. One, maybe two, seemed to notice I was there, the rest irritated when I pushed past. Ma and Da stood with another couple, all deep in conversation. Eagan and two other teenaged boys huddled together peeking over each other's shoulders at a cluster of girls nearby. Soon, my brother would be courting one of those. Which one?

And then...descending the church steps like an angel of mercy was Angelique Rossi. And her da. Of course. Any da worth their salt would escort such a fine young woman out in the world. No telling what might happen. Or who she'd meet.

I rethought. Was I one to be warned against? Would her da let me come courting? Probably not. Here I was working in a stable and recently out of prison. My shoulders slumped. Definitely not someone worthy.

But still, I had to try. I was on a mission. I squared my shoulders, marched over to the Rossis now at the bottom of the steps. I stuck out a hand and tipped my hat with the other one. "Mr. Rossi? Miss Rossi? I'm Tate Nolan."

Rossi's face lit up. "Ah! *Sí. Sí.*" He shook with me.

Encouraged, I continued. "Wanted to thank you, thank you both, for helping my younger brother the other day. Joe? At the telegraph office?"

"Ah! *Sí. Sí.*" Mr. Rossi's head bobbed like it was on springs, his face lighting up like the sun. He mimed a chop block to the back of his head. "*Colpito alla testa.*"

"Yes. Head. That's the one." I cringed at the memory. "Wanted again to thank you for carting him to Doc's and then staying until my da came."

Breeze picking up, Angelique scraped a wind-swept strand of hair from the corner of her mouth. "How is your brother?"

Her words. That accent. Heaven. Pure heaven.

"Mr. Nolan?" Her words brought me back to earth. "How is he?"

"Got one big headache, but he's already on the mend. Up and about. Going back to work Wednesday."

Angelique nodded to her father and said something in Italian. He beamed, "*Bene, Bene,*" and nodded again while she smiled, a beautiful, perfect smile. Her lips curled on the ends. "Good news, indeed. Please tell him we wish him well."

Taking her elbow, Rossi led Angelique toward the road. I walked alongside. "Can I pay you for your trouble, Mr. Rossi?"

"Pay?" Rossi seemed to understand some English. "Money?"

I nodded but studied the woman. Definitely pretty.

"No. No pay." Rossi waved his hand and started walking again.

"If you won't take money, then for my gratitude, may I escort your daughter to supper one evening?" Had I just asked her out? I blinked, hard.

Angelique blushed, then interpreted the question. Italian flew back and forth, gestures accompanying them. After what seemed fifteen minutes, the furor stopped.

"He says yes, but he watches you." She smiled the kind of smile that set my toes tingling.

Mr. Rossi pointed at me and then back at himself. "I watch. My only girl."

I bowed slightly. "She's safe with me, sir."

Me and the lovely lady decided to go to dinner Wednesday evening. Since that was my only day off, I'd have time to bathe and shave. Would fourteen dollars be enough? Wait. Half of that was Joe's. Could I borrow his half?

If not, could I stretch seven dollars to cover supper? If I took her to the cheaper place, we could eat for two dollars each, but with desserts and drinks...I needed more money.

I waved as the beauty and her keeper walked away. I strolled the other way toward the livery paying no attention to people around me. Where would I take her? And then it hit me. What was I thinking? I couldn't have her ride Da's horse, and Da didn't own a buggy. And renting one from Alphonso would cost almost as much as supper.

We'd have to walk.

* * *

I STEWED ALL AFTERNOON. Here finally I was allowed to court this lovely young woman and again, I had no money and no way to get any. Maybe Alphonso would give me an advance. Not a chance. I could ask my folks for a few dollars, but that would be embarrassment beyond endurance. Eagan? He'd never let me hear the end of it. Joe would loan it to me, but I already owed that brother too much.

Three days until Wednesday evening. Could I rob someplace else in that time? Could I come up with a plan soon enough? Raking manure, tossing straw, currying horses kept my body busy, but my mind stayed on this lack of funds. Surely, something would come up. Some way I'd get my hands on a few more dollars. Just a couple more.

Stomach rumbling, I sighed. End of another day. Home for supper, a couple hours on the front porch planning, then bed.

"Time to head home." A man's baritone voice startled me.

I turned toward the barn door and spotted Mr. Carmichael, wealthiest rancher in the area. And I'd heard, head of the town council. I liked the man. He treated his stock well, and men had told me he was equally good to his hands. Paid decently and at least once a year threw a party for his crew, their friends and family.

We shook hands. "That time again, sir?" I opened a stall door, backed out a fifteen hands-high chestnut. I patted the animal's neck and tossed the reins over the fence rail. That horse was a beautiful bit of Texas. Strong, shiny sorrel coat, a reddish hint among the tan.

Carmichael patted his stomach. "My wife'll skin me alive if I don't get home in time for Sunday supper. Right now she's busy frying chicken and making dumplings." He lifted his nose. "Can almost smell it, can't you?"

He had a kind of face, the kind of sincerity I admired.

Saddling the horse, I mentioned the new bakery. "Bet

the missus would appreciate their dewberry pie, or the apple strudel." I chuckled. "I can tell you from firsthand experience they're both real tongue pleasers."

The rancher smoothed his mustache. "Appears I'll just have to go try it myself. Thanks for the suggestion."

I led the sorrel into fading sunshine, handed Carmichael the reins. "See you soon, sir."

Carmichael offered a hand and when I stretched out mine, the man dropped a dime into it, followed by two quarters. "This's for more strudel for you and thanks for caring for my horse so well. Like usual."

I wanted to give back the surprise, but the idea of that kind of money in my hand made me stutter. I hated myself for that. "My family will be extra happy tonight, sir. Thank you."

I followed the rancher to the street. "Excuse me, Mr. Carmichael. I've been thinking. I have Wednesdays off and if you've got extra chores need doing, I'd be obliged if you'd think of me."

"Money's that tight, Tate?"

Pursing lips, I fought embarrassment. "I've got a girl—"

"Say no more." Carmichael swung up into his saddle. "Come see me Wednesday." He nodded, flashed a wide grin, then clucked to his horse.

I let out a held-in breath. Maybe things were finally looking up. And, if I liked working out at the ranch well enough, maybe Becker would let me work there instead of this stable. Three more months of parole and I'd be a free man. Free to work where I wanted.

I counted the coins in hand. Sixty cents sat there, shiny, like they were smiling back. Pocketing the money, I returned to the stable, found my hat, waved goodbye to Alphonso, and headed home.

No pie or strudel tonight. I'd save my money for Wednesday's supper. Besides, dessert like that twice in one week was enough. I'd want to surprise Ma, but again so soon would be no surprise.

On the way home, I spied two of the ex-Yankees sitting on the boardwalk, slumped against a wooden wall. Neither looked well nor with full stomachs. If I gave them the ten cents Carmichael had given me for a tip, they'd at least get something to eat tonight. Yep, that's what I would do. And it would prove to Becker that what I'd said was the truth.

I kneeled in front of the men, their body odor competing with the horse smells clinging to my own clothes. "Had anything to eat today?"

The two perked up when I spoke. Both shook their heads. "Yesterday, I think," one of them mumbled. I leaned back. If I could see the man's eye-watering bad breath, it would spew out green.

I pointed toward the nearest café. "If you go around back, bet they'll give you enough supper for both." I produced the dime. "Here. This's for you two. Don't fight over it, all right?" I chose the least dirty hand to put the coin in.

A strong hand clamped around my upper arm. "Tate Nolan. You're under arrest." The hand yanked me to my feet. Sheriff Becker grabbed one arm, then the other and jerked them behind my back. Before I could protest, the familiar *click* of handcuffs battered my ears, my wrists again weighed down with rough iron.

I twisted around to face that son-of-a-gun. "What, Becker? What?"

The sheriff's smug expression revealed an air of conquest. A hammy forefinger drilled into my chest. "Got you this time for sure."

"What? For what?" Panic wouldn't help right now. Confusion pushed in. "Under arrest?"

"*Ja.*" The man on the short side of six feet, slim but powerfully built, leaned back, enjoying the spectacle. He turned to people still on the boardwalk. "Under arrest for robbing the church and attempted murder." Both eyebrows slid up. "By now, might be outright murder. The Padre may not make it."

"The priest?" I trembled. "Who'd murder a priest?"

Becker tugged me into the street, pointed toward the jail. "Got your room ready."

Legs refusing to cooperate, I planted my feet on the ground. "I'm not going anywhere with you. I didn't do anything. I was at work all day. Ask Alphonso. What makes you think I did anything?"

Becker balled a thick hand and plowed it into my stomach. Wind knocked out, I doubled over, then crumpled to my knees. I groaned. Within seconds, uncontrolled anger brought me back to my feet. Still bent over, I ran at Becker, ramming him square in the chest. We hit the ground.

I rolled off and onto my bound hands, the iron digging into my back. Huffing, my chest heaving, Becker stood over me and kicked. I took the force in my ribs. Stars. Circling stars. Another blow and a rib broke.

I rolled into a fetal position, hoping, praying Becker would stop. A savage kick to my head, and then the attack ended. German words, curse words, assaulted me. With undeniable strength, Becker pulled me up and planted me onto my feet.

"Robbery, murder, *and* assault." Becker snarled, spitting words in my face. "I'll watch you hang then dance on your grave."

By the time I'd wobbled all the way up the street,

then stumbled into the cell thanks to Becker's shove, I realized life was over. Twenty-two years. Way too soon to be hanged for something I didn't do. Twenty-two years. Ma would be devastated.

Shoulders aching, I managed to stand and peer between the iron bars. The door from the cells to the office was open. No sounds came from there. No paper shuffling, no coffeepot scraping against the potbelly stove, no conversation between Becker and his deputy.

Silence. Was I alone?

I stretched as best I could, moving right then left, tugging on my hands, hoping the cuffs would snap off. My head, ribs and shoulders shouted at me that I'd been assaulted. Their throbbing, pounding, aching was relentless. Somehow, I had to get these handcuffs off or my shoulders would pop loose. "Becker?" I shouted over an aching jaw. "Sheriff! Can you get these cuffs off me?"

Hearing no response and figuring Becker had left the office, I called again hoping a deputy was around. Becker sauntered in, daubing a corner of his mouth with a white handkerchief, red streaks marring the material. He stood back against the inner wooden door and smirked. "You. Think you're so smart. And good with the robbing." His gaze trailed up and down me. "You're not so smart. I catch you this time."

"These cuffs?" My wrists burned. I inwardly smirked at causing that piece of shite to bleed.

Becker raised an index finger and waggled the digit in a circle. I turned, back to the bars

and listened for the distinctive *click* of freedom. Finally free. Rubbing my wrists, gently, I turned back around. "What is it exactly you say I did?"

"You know." Becker, an intense, humorless individual,

pulled a chair from the outer office, arranged it in front of me, and sat.

We stared at each other. I held burning ribs which matched my pounding head. If I could have a swig of Joe's laudanum, I would feel much better. Becker rubbed his chest and glared at me.

Unable to continue the silent staring contest, I calmed my nerves and hoped I spoke civilly. "You think I tried to kill Father Connor? Why would I do that?"

Becker snorted. "To take all the monies from the collection plate. They found it empty when they found Connor."

"I haven't been inside that church for a year."

"Until today."

I pulled in air and with that movement my ribs screamed. I winced. "Look, Sheriff. I was at work all day. Ask Alphonso."

"I did. Said you took time off at noon to go to the church."

I'd forgotten. My shoulders slumped. "He's right. I went to see Ma and Da before they walked home."

"About what?"

None of your business is what I wanted to shout. Instead, I chose to level with this man. "Wanted to ask Da if I could borrow the horse Wednesday. I'm going out to supper."

"With who?"

"A friend." Should I continue answering this ridiculous line of questioning? Maybe.

"A girl?"

"Miss Rossi. Angelique Rossi." Maybe they could vouch for me.

I looked up as a deputy I didn't recognize appeared in the doorway. Becker turned. The deputy thumbed over his shoulder. "Thought you'd want to know. Priest just died."

Plunging into icy cold water couldn't be as terrifying. I struggled for a breath. My life was over. For certain now. No way out of this.

Becker nodded at the deputy then turned back to me. "How does hanging Friday at sunrise sound?"

I gripped the bars, shaking them. "It wasn't me. It wasn't." I calmed. "How did he die?"

Head tilting to one side, Becker frowned. "You don't remember? You hit him with a brass candlestick on the back of the head. Just like you did your brother." He whacked at the air.

"Then you emptied the collection plate. You robbed, just like at the telegraph office."

"It wasn't me."

Becker jabbed a long finger at me. "I saw you give money to those men." He pointed to his face. "With my own eyes."

"You saw wrong. I got a tip at the stable and gave it to them so they could eat. Just like before when I said I did. Gave 'em ten cents." I brightened. "Ask Mr. Carmichael. He's the one who gave it to me." Would that rancher be my ticket out? Not likely, but at this point, anything would help.

Becker groaned up to his feet. "Oh. And found your kepi hat under the priest. The one you bought from the soldiers." He walked off leaving a trail of sniggers behind.

I slumped to the cot, head in my hands. Not even a miracle could save me now.

CHAPTER EIGHT

"YOUR MA'S HEARTBROKEN." DA STOOD IN front of me, iron bars separating us.

"How many times I gotta tell you?" My voice rose over the conversation in the outer office. "I didn't kill the priest. I didn't rob the collection plate." I took a breath. "Believe me, Da, I didn't rob the telegraph office. Didn't hit Joe." No doubt I'd go to hell for lying, especially to my father, but being accused of something I didn't do brought a kind of anger, rage I'd never felt before. Not even when I was sentenced to prison—for *borrowing* a horse, no less.

I rethought. Borrowing the *sheriff's* horse. But I'd brought back the animal. Safe and sound. Me and Wink Tannen had decided to take two horses and ride up to Austin, simply out for a joyride, a lark, on a beautiful spring morning after a couple of beers. I remember we'd planned to be gone only a full day, coming right back, returning the mounts safe and sound. Unfortunately, mine stepped into a gopher hole and came up lame.

We rode two up on his sturdy horse all the way back

to town, lame horse limping behind. When we came in, it was full dark, with Becker in a pure lather. I couldn't get the animals to the barn before the sheriff's rifle pointed at my chest.

Da gripped one bar. "I don't have the money to bail you out." His shoulders slumped. "In truth, Becker says no amount of money could bail you out now."

"Da, we gotta fight this." I stepped back, sighed, glanced over my shoulder at the window to watch light clouds dance across an awakening blue sky. "A judge won't hang me without evidence, would he?"

"I talked with Becker a few minutes ago. He's saying it's too much of a coincidence between the telegraph office and the church to be two different people. Says he saw you negotiating with the Yankees to buy another kepi." Da sighed the sigh of a man defeated. He hung his head. "Don't know if I can help you, son."

Bollocks. "Da, you *gotta* believe me." I reached through the bars and held his arm. My gaze searched the face I knew so well. The face which looked much like mine, only older. "Besides the drunken one here in town, there another lawyer maybe?"

"I've sent Joe over to San Antone to get one."

Good news then. But the cost would be too much for the family. We'd have to mortgage our house, maybe sell the horse. Ma would have to take in more sewing, Da and Eagan take second jobs. Joe works extra hours. All because of me.

Was that pressure building up behind my eyes? Something wet trickled down my cheek. "I'm sorry, Da. Can't seem to do anything right."

Da patted my hand still clutching the shirtsleeve. "Seems like you were born under a dark star, son." He gave a heartier pat and then stepped back. "Maybe Eagan and Joe and me...and your ma, can find a way out of this." Da turned when the sheriff appeared in the doorway and spoke softly to me. "Keep the faith, Tate."

With that, he disappeared into the office. An outside door slammed, harder than necessary. I slumped to the cot. From in here, I couldn't explain to Alphonso, explain to Angelique Rossi, explain to the world.

Damn Becker. Damn whoever killed the priest. Who *would* kill a priest? Obviously, a man with no morals and who needed quick money. Part of me chided myself for not thinking of the collection plate. Fairly easy pickings. But I'd certainly never hit a man of the cloth. God would never ever forgive me for a sin of that caliber. Had to have been one of those beggars on the street. Maybe two of them. Was Becker out there right now chasing down the real killer?

"Becker? Sheriff Becker?" I yelled through the partially open door that led into the office. "Becker? You out there?"

"Shut the hell up, Tate." A wheezy voice. Not Becker.

I stared at the man lumbering through the doorway. Walter...Walter something. I struggled for a last name. We'd gone to school together many years ago. Walter had been the school bully, always teasing girls, throwing rocks at boys, spilling ink on papers, especially mine, generally making life a living hooligan for Miss...Miss Simmons. Her last name came more easily than Walter's. But now, a badge replaced the last name.

"What d'you want? I'm busy."

"Where's Becker? Need to talk to him."

"About what?"

"None of your business, Wagner." That was it. Walter Wagner.

Wagner launched himself to the cell, reached in,

grabbed my shirtfront before I could move away from the ferocious grip. The deputy yanked me forward, my head slamming against the bars. A push back and then another yank forward, this one harder. Stars danced around my head. Blood poured from a broken nose.

"Always wanted to do that, Nolan." Wagner's smirk took up most of his surly face. "Looks like now I get the chance every time you come in here." He released my blood-spackled shirt.

Agony attacked my face. I held both hands under my nose, the blood gushing. I untied my blue neckerchief and held the fabric against my throbbing face. Tilting my head back only sent the blood down my throat. I leaned over, coughing, spitting red goo.

"That'll teach you." Wagner stood back admiring his work. He pointed a wagging finger at me. "Remember me from school? You and the others, always laughing at me, calling me names. Well, now it's my turn."

"We were just—"

"You'll show me respect. I'm a deputy now. Deputy Wagner to you." He walked away, then returned and lowered his voice. "I can make your life, what you have left of it, a living nightmare."

The door shut soundly. I sat on the cot, neckerchief soaking up blood. Could life get worse than this? If I'd just kept the money from the telegraph office, taken a horse from Alphonso and galloped out of town, I wouldn't be behind bars right now. I'd be down in Mexico, a shot of tequila in one hand and a pretty *señorita* on my lap. Maybe two *señoritas*.

If I ever got out of this, *ever*, the first thing I'd do would be steal a horse and ride away as fast and as far as I could. Leave behind this miserable life. I'd turn to full-time robbing and become better known than Jesse James.

I'd hold up not only stages but trains, and plenty of both. My name would be splashed all over the newspapers back east. Headlines would read: *Feared Outlaw Leader, Tate Nolan, Strikes Again.*

I pinched the bridge of my nose, held my head back a bit and waited for the blood to stop dripping. My stomach rumbled. I'd almost forgotten about breakfast. Would I get fed?

* * *

NO TRAY OF FOOD, aromatic or otherwise, appeared in my cell as the day dragged by. Occasional wafts of something cooking sailed in through the window, but certainly nothing within reach. Despite calling for Becker and food, no one came to the rescue.

Mid-morning, the door opened and in stepped Alphonso, Becker on his heels. The sheriff's sneer accentuated his graying mustache. Alphonso's brown eyes roved up and down me. I squirmed under such scrutiny. Neither man spoke.

I had had enough. I gripped the bars and spoke, words full of determination and honesty. "I didn't do it. Whatever Becker told you, wasn't me." Would he believe me? Somebody had to.

Wagging his head, Alphonso faced him, but didn't look directly at me. "You've been a good hand. I'm shocked you would do such a thing."

"But I didn't!" Frustration burst from my chest. I ran trembling hands down the bars, desperate to control my temper. If I could, I'd kill Becker right now. "I had nothing to do with the Padre's murder. It wasn't me."

An uncomfortable silence enveloped the room. My steam engine breathing, chest rising and falling with the air, Alphonso's throat clearing, Becker's subtle snickers pierced the quiet.

Alphonso stepped back. "I'm sorry, Tate. I've found someone to replace you."

"What? I'm fired?" Could life get any worse?

Becker's snickers grew into full-blown chortles. "Why should you care? You be swinging in three days."

Before the sheriff and Alphonso reached the outer office, I called to him. "Alphonso?" I waited for the man to turn around. "Would you give my wages to Joe? Please?"

Alphonso nodded then closed the wooden door.

What else could go wrong? Another thought hit me. If I really, truly was at the end of my life, I should get things in order. Not much to arrange, but things needed to be said. I'd give Joe all my money. All seven dollars tucked in my sock. And the two quarters Carmichael gave me were now the sheriff's, taken when Becker patted me down. What else did I have? Nothing. I had nothing. Both hands balled, my sore jaw ground. What kind of man was I? A loser.

I lay on the cot, hands folded over my chest. Is this the way they'll bury me? A shudder ran over me. No, I couldn't give up yet, but...still, I needed to make final plans.

Unless Becker had changed the schedule, supper wouldn't come until around four. And judging by the sun, it was barely noon. My stomach grumbled and complained. My eyes closed despite the hour. I hadn't slept, and a nap would work wonders, make me feel better at least.

"On your feet, Nolan."

I jumped at the command. Eyes fluttered awake while I fought to make sense of my world.

"Stand when I talk to you." Becker stood near the bars.

Behind Becker waited Mr. Rossi. My shoulders slumped. I knew what he would say. I dragged myself upright and moved closer to the bars. "Hello, Mr. Rossi."

Rossi shook a finger. "No, no, no, no, no." The Italian accent thick. "No see my girl." The finger shook through the bars and into my face. "Never. No see." The man's cheek muscles pushed out when he clenched his jaw.

"I didn't do it, Mr. Rossi. I didn't kill the priest." How many times had I already said this? "Remember yesterday? I spoke to you, then went back to work." I pointed toward downtown. "I didn't go inside the church. Remember? I went back to Alphonso's."

Becker touched Rossi's arm. "Let's go to my office. We can talk there. This prisoner's too irrational. No telling what he'll say next."

"Wait! Mr. Rossi! You gotta believe me. I didn't do it."

I continued yelling even after the wooden door clicked shut. I sank into the cot. What else? Would at least one thing go right? Just one? I gazed upward. God, one thing. Please.

I lay back, one hand under my head, the other massaging sore ribs. To square things, I had to talk to Joe, Eagan, and Ma. Those three needed to hear what I had to say. But first, a trip to the privy was becoming increasingly necessary.

Standing, I hollered, "Becker? Deputy?" Before I could shout again, the door opened and a deputy I didn't know walked in, a tray of food in hand. Aromas of baked ham, potatoes, green beans, and a biscuit sailed into the room. I grinned and rolled my eyes skyward. Thank you, God.

"Ladies at the café must like you." He nodded to the tray. "Even *I* don't eat this good."

"Smells great, but—"

"Stand back against the wall and I'll put this on the floor." The deputy eyed me. "No trouble now."

"Deputy, I gotta get to the privy first." I nodded at the tray. "Haven't eaten since yesterday noon, but other matters appear more important at the moment."

"Understand." Balancing the tray in one hand, he searched his pocket for keys. He unlocked the door, one eye on the tray, the other on me. "One wrong move, Mr. Nolan and I'll have to shoot you."

"No trouble, I promise." Getting to the privy now was becoming truly urgent.

We went through the back door, out to the privy. I wanted to run, but if I did, there would be a good chance of catching a bullet in my back. If I had to choose between a bullet or wet pants, I'd choose wet over dead.

Three, four minutes later I stepped out and froze. Deputy Wagner stood waiting, the other deputy walking away. Wagner crooked a finger then pointed. "Let's go, scum."

Inside the room which housed the two cells, Wagner grabbed my arm, jerking me to a stop. He nodded to the full tray on the floor in my cell. "I see you've finished your supper." He opened the door and shoved me against the far wall.

Wagner scooped up the tray, stepped back and slammed the cell door. The lock clicked. Chortling, Wagner walked away. "Um. I love ham." He closed the wooden door separating the office and the cells.

What was happening? "Becker? Sheriff Becker?"

No answer, of course. Maybe if I stood on tiptoe, I could flag the attention of someone on the street. I tried.

Nope. The window faced the side of a building with no windows or doors.

* * *

TUESDAY DAWNED CLOUDY, but warm. I stretched, ribs reminding me of the assault, my jaw swelling overnight. I worked the muscles around until I could speak. Although my headache wasn't as intense as the day before, when I touched my face, I discovered the bridge of my nose now sported an extra bump. My stomach cursed him. I had to get something to eat.

And then like a savior, Eagan pushed open the wooden door and stepped in, the second deputy right behind. Aromas of fried chicken and potatoes wafted into the room. I'm sure my grin filled the rest.

Eagan held up a cloth sack. "Ma sent some food. Didn't know how much they give you in here." He glanced to his side until the deputy nodded, then passed the sack between the iron bars. I snatched the bag before Eagan could let go.

Chicken leg in mouth, I rolled my eyes skyward and then let them rest on my youngest brother. I spoke over a mouthful of heaven. "Thank you." Guess God was paying attention, after all.

"Ma says she put lots of love in there." Eagan pointed to the sack. "Plenty more back home, if you want." He turned to the deputy, thumbed over his shoulder toward the house. "Ma made the best fried chicken. Ever. It was crispy and moist. Made it every Sunday. Sometimes we had stewed tomatoes to go with it, tomatoes she grew last summer. After church, we'd go home, and she'd get busy dunking those chickens into flour—"

"He probably knows, Eagan." I grinned, more chicken in my mouth.

"I do." The deputy ran a slim hand across his mouth. "My ma used to do the same."

"Maybe they all do. I appreciate you letting me come in to see my brother, deputy." Eagan held out a hand. "But I didn't get your name."

He held up both hands. "Sorry, don't shake. You never know."

I agreed. From what I'd seen, lawmen couldn't afford to shake hands with strangers. A strong grip could bring the sheriff in close, pull a gun and shoot pointblank. Or bring in a fist and deck them. Or...the list went on.

"I'm Deputy Tommy O'Sullivan. Born in Ireland, as it sounds like you were."

Eagan shook his head. "Not me, sir. Born on the trail, somewhere in east Texas. But Tate here was. Came over from Queenstown, County Cork when he was but a wee one."

I nodded at Ma and Da's Irish accents again, picked up by all three boys. My stomach, so appreciative of being fed, settled down. It didn't grumble as loudly as before. Maybe I wouldn't starve to death before being hanged.

Eagan thumbed over his shoulder. "Those hammers're louder in here. Been hearing them all day yesterday. *Bang, bang, bang.*" He frowned at me. "What're they building?"

Glaring at my brother, the knot in my throat refused to move. Didn't he know what was going on? How could he be that naive? Before I could tell this dimwitted brother it was the gallows, Eagan blanched.

"Holy smokes, Tate." He stepped back. "The gallows? For you?"

Finally, he figured it out. I nodded, no words coming forth.

Eagan's gaze trailed the room, the empty cell, me still eating, the door, the ceiling. He drew in a breath. "Sorry, Tate. Guess I'm dumber 'n a fence post."

I understood. I'd prefer to ignore the sounds too.

"Well, sorry, gotta get to work." Eagan thumbed over his shoulder, then stopped. "Oh...and bad news, I'm afraid. Joe rode in at sunrise this morning and said he couldn't find one lawyer, not one, who'd come help. Said they were too expensive or not interested."

"Well, dammit, Eagan. What'm I supposed to do now?" I gripped the bars, the sack of chicken forgotten. "I didn't do it. Didn't kill the father. I didn't."

"I believe you. We all do. Well, not Becker or the other deputy. But a lot of the town does." Eagan narrowed his eyes. "Well, not Mr. Rossi. He thinks you're Satan. Mrs. Schmidt, down at the café, thinks so too. But I don't. Da doesn't either."

"Is Ma coming to see me? Why hasn't she been by?" My heart ached. Too much guilt, too much angst...too much everything.

Eagan shrugged. "Been real busy. But I think she'll be by today." He stepped through the wooden door, stopped then turned back to me. "I'll see you before...well, before Friday morning."

I finished the last bite of potatoes, fished around in the bottom of the sack for crumbs, then sat wishing for a glass of cold water. Or a beer. Or whiskey. All of that. Before I could holler for the nice deputy, the wooden door opened, Becker stood in the doorway, O'Sullivan behind him.

"Thought you should know—"

"You found whoever killed Father Connor?" My hopes soared.

Becker *hmphed*, shoulders rising then falling. "*Ja.*" He nodded, finger pointing at me. "Found you!"

I exploded. "How many times I gotta tell you? I didn't do it." I paced the cell. "While you're busy gloating over locking me up, you're letting the real killer get away!"

Becker lumbered in closer.

Like a crazy man on fire, I kept pacing, pointing at Becker and toward the office. "You and your so-called deputy. You're busy eating my supper *and* breakfast while pretending to be on the side of law and order. Becker, you should be in here, not me! Besides, it was probably you who killed the priest."

Becker's beefy face melted into rage and fury. He lurched forward. Instinctively, I backed against the stone wall. Yet, I couldn't control my mouth.

"*You* killed him, took the money." I wedged my entire body into a corner. "Everybody knows sheriffs make nothin', so you decided to rob the church." I sneered. "That's real classy, Becker."

Like lightning, the sheriff unlocked the door and dove at me taking the full brunt of a man four inches taller and forty pounds heavier. Fists in my face, punches in stomach, German curses encased my graying world.

"Stop it, Sheriff. You can't do that! Stop it!"

Becker growled. "Get your hands off me."

"You're gonna kill him! Stop!"

And suddenly, the assault stopped. Heavy breathing in my ear. Still on my feet, crammed against the wall, I opened one eye, the other too swollen to comply. Swallowing blood, I slumped to the floor. Which hurt worse? Head, jaw, stomach, or ribs? Each vied for dominance.

Eyes narrowed, I blinked through blood. There stood

Becker, arms held back by Deputy O'Sullivan, both men struggling.

"Let go of me, you imbecile!" Becker wiggled out of the hold. He bent down nose to nose with me. "Next time, Nolan. Next time. Another smart word out of your mouth and you'll be dead before you hang."

I rubbed the dirty sleeve under my dripping nose. For the first time, I relaxed at the distinctive *click* of the cell lock. I was safe in there, for the moment anyway. The wooden door closed. I dragged myself up onto the cot and held throbbing ribs. Closing the one good eye, I considered my life. Something had to change. If I didn't hang, I'd have to change my life. I'd need more money and get out of town. Those were givens.

I wiped as much blood as my crusty shirt allowed, laid back on the cot, careful not to aggravate my ribs too badly. Despite the constant hammering, from inside the cell, I could plan.

* * *

THE WOOD DOOR CREAKED OPEN. I rubbed my eyes. Must've fallen asleep. Ma, mouth set in a tight line, stood in front of the cell. She held her shoulders back, chin up. I limped to the bars, my hand over hers. Darn it. She'd already seen enough hardship in one lifetime, and now here I was, bringing her more.

"I'm sorry—"

"I'm sorry—"

I patted her hand. "You go first."

Ma breathed in. "I hear yer trial is Thursday. Morning."

"It is?"

"Becker didn't tell ye?" Ma glared toward the outer

office. "Of course not." She held up a blue shirt. "Made this for ye. Thought ye could use something new."

I hadn't considered what I wore, but certainly a clean shirt would help. Immediately, I felt better.

Ma passed the present through the bars and looked me up and down. "I'd say I come in time. Look at the shirt what yer wearin'. Looks worse than yer Da and Eagan comin' home from a day at the butcher's." She wrinkled her nose. "Smells like it too."

I lifted my mouth into what I hoped resembled a smile. "Thank you, Ma." I held up the shirt. "I like it."

"Wish I could do more."

"How's Joe?"

"Wanted to come himself just now, but still, he's dizzy. Took a long ride for nothin', he did, and his head is still spinning."

I felt the exact same way. The room spun. I stumbled back to the cot and sat. Not where I wanted to be. Ma's concerned face, worry wrinkles lining her forehead, mouth drawn down into a frown, anger in my heart. I'd get out of this mess one way or another.

Maybe I'd break out. Would Deputy O'Sullivan help? Maybe. Possibly.

Ma threaded an arm between the bars. "Yer face. Becker do that?"

I nodded. Part of the skirmish was my fault, shouldn't have egged him on like I had, but I wasn't the one with a badge, a gun, and a fist the size of an anvil. But, I realized, I'd held my own. Sort of.

Room no longer tilting, I eased off the cot and patted her hand. "I'm sorry to put you through this. Again. I'm just a sorry person." I searched her blue eyes. "Never meant for any of this to happen. But know I didn't do it."

One hand planted on a cocked hip, Ma shook her

finger at me. "Seamus Tate Nolan. I know ye didn't. Ye're a good person. Got a kind heart, ye do. Ye're just a little...*unsettled* yet." She patted my hand and pulled away. "Someday ye'll be a great man."

Ma daubed at the single tear under her right eye, smiled at me, then walked through the wooden door out into the sheriff's office.

* * *

ALTHOUGH HIGH CLOUDS blocked the sun's attempt to brighten the world, Wednesday looked much like the day before. Da and Eagan stopped by on their way to work; Becker continued harassing me, calling me all sorts of names—in German and English; Wagner pulled a knife and threatened to slice me like a pig; O'Sullivan brought breakfast *and* supper.

Sunlight faded along with my hopes. The next day was Thursday. The trial would be over in ten minutes and then first thing Friday morning, I'd swing from the gallows being built at the end of the street. The incessant hammer blows tortured me, my nerves recoiling with each bang. Even with my hands covering my ears, I couldn't escape the inevitable.

The inner door to the cells squeaked open and in walked Mr. Carmichael. Becker stood at the doorjamb leaning against the wood, arms folded across his belly, smirking like a hunter who'd taken down a prized grizzly. Carmichael stretched out his hand and shook with me through the bars.

"Mr. Carmichael." I tried not to stutter at the surprise. "Good to see you again, sir."

The rancher cocked his head to one side and allowed his eyebrows to raise. "When you didn't show up today, figured you had a good excuse." He glanced around. "Didn't think it was this drastic though."

Was that a hint of a grin on his face? I hoped so.

I chin-pointed to the man standing there, smirking. "Sheriff Becker says I killed Father Connor. But I didn't. Didn't have anything to do with it. I was at work. Just went over to the church for a minute. But he says I'm gonna hang Friday morning at sunrise. I'm innocent." I couldn't stop the words. Couldn't fight the panic rising. Couldn't keep the tears from clouding my vision.

Carmichael half turned to Becker. "What kinda evidence you got, Sheriff?"

Becker puffed out his chest and thumbed over his shoulder. "Found a kepi Tate bought offa one of those soldier boys. Just like the one he wore when he robbed the telegraph office. Hit his brother."

Carmichael's eyes widened then narrowed as he fully turned to Becker. "You mean to tell me, you've locked him in here, denied bail, beaten this young man, simply because of a hat?"

"Don't need anything else. That's enough."

"A hat?" Carmichael's furious voice rose, lifted to a shout. "A damn hat? You think that's enough?" He moved in nose to nose with Becker and spoke over a clenched jaw. "You get him out of here right now. I'll pay the bail. Take responsibility for him."

"You can't—"

"I *can*." Carmichael motioned to me. "Get your things. I'll take you home and then get you tomorrow in time for your trial."

"Who do you think you are?" Becker's face clouded into a mottled red. "Telling me what to do. You can't—"

"Open that door." He pointed and waited for Becker to fumble with the key.

I stepped into freedom, the night air sweeter than I'd imagined. Me and Carmichael

stopped on the boardwalk. "Can't thank you enough, sir." Would I push my luck with the next question? I had to know. "Wondering why you've gone to all this trouble. I mean…" I searched the sky, the town, the man's face. "Why bother with me? I'm nobody."

Light chuckles jiggled Carmichael's shoulders. "Why?" He untied his horse's reins. "I'll walk you home."

CHAPTER NINE

THE JUDGE, BLACK ROBE FLOWING BEHIND HIM, strode in like he was the King of England. He made his regal way to the desk while everyone rose. Surveying his kingdom, the judge stopped behind his chair and gazed over the audience. Without a word, he sat, picked up the gavel and waited for the spectators to sit. He whacked the desktop.

"Court is now in session."

Wearing what I hoped would be a *good luck* shirt, the blue one Ma had just made, I sat up straight, the wooden chair under me hard and spiteful, just like Becker sitting to my left. On the other side this warm morning, sat Mr. Carmichael. I still wasn't quite sure why this man, this savior, had taken interest in me, but still, I was grateful. I vaguely remembered something about a son Carmichael had tried to keep on the right path. Guess it didn't end too well for the son.

The courtroom, tucked into a back room of the mercantile, allowed about fifteen, no more than twenty people inside. This morning, air was at a premium. I glanced around and behind me. Full. People stood in the doorway while others peered through the single window. Me, Becker, and Carmichael were up front, chairs set aside for us. The judge's desk, big enough to hold a gavel, and a glass of what I assumed was water, sat no more than ten feet in front of me.

Whispers, idle chitchat, and a roaring in my ears made me turn halfway. Behind me sat Da, Ma, Joe, and Eagan. Da nodded encouragement. I couldn't stomach the sets of family eyes looking at me, some sorrowful, some doubtful, all hoping for the best but assuming the worst.

I turned back around. Breathing wouldn't come. Not quite a year ago the same thing had happened. Same judge. Same words. Would this time be different?

Half leaning over the desk, the judge stared at me. He waved a hand. "Stand up, Tate Nolan."

Swallowing dread and pulling in air, I managed to stand, although shaky legs and knees threatened to abandon me.

The judge leaned back allowing his gaze to start at my well-worn boots and work its way to my head. He looked at the water glass then me. "I see you're here before me again." He pointed the gavel at my face. "Judging by those bruises and split lip, you're still a rabble rouser. Didn't learn anything in prison?"

I squirmed. I wanted to explain, tell my side of the truth, but would I even get a chance? No one had asked for my side of the story. And here I was, in the middle of this nightmare, about to hang, and I couldn't help myself? If I ever got out of this—

"Sheriff Becker explained how he found the kepi and how it related to the telegraph office robbery. And how you are at the center of killing Father Connor."

I opened my mouth but thought better of saying anything. Surely, I'd get a chance to explain.

The judge continued. "While I agree with Sheriff Becker that you must have had a hand in these two crimes, Nolan, I've done a lot of thinking and weighing the evidence."

Carmichael pushed to his feet. "Sir?"

"Sit down, Mr. Carmichael." The judge held up one hand. "I'm not finished."

I turned to my new friend who was easing back down. A nod wasn't enough to say thanks, so I faced the judge, forcing my knees to keep me upright.

"Now," the judge cleared his throat. "Tate Nolan, I have no doubt you were involved in at least one, if not both, of these incidents. Your past records point in that direction." He pulled in a deep breath. "However, I agree with Mr. Carmichael that an old army hat is not enough evidence to convict you. It's circumstantial at best."

Breath held, fire raged throughout my body.

"Approach the bench, Nolan."

Would my rubbery legs take me that far? I prayed they would. I stopped on the other side of the desk.

"Hear me and hear me well." The judge pointed the gavel at me. "This will be the last time you'll stand before me. Do you understand? There will be no more reasons for you to take up this court's time. Understand? From here on out, you'll earn a living like the rest of us— by working. You'll get up every morning, go to your job, work hard, go home, sleep, then go to work the next day. No more stealing horses, no more robbing." He paused. "You understand me? And understand me good?"

"Yes, sir."

"I hope so." The judge stared at me, switched his gaze to the spectators. "So, it's the ruling of this court that Seamus Tate Nolan is found not guilty of the murder of Father Connor."

The courtroom exploded into one intense gasp. Murmurs, a few loud enough for me to make out "Killer's free?" and a few sighs. Probably from my family.

The judge looked at me again. "You are hereby released into the custody of Anthony Carmichael, owner of the Lazy Six Ranch and head of the town councilors. You will work for him until he, and only he, deems you ready to be on your own." The judge whacked the gavel.

What had just happened? Was I free? I shivered. I wasn't going to hang after all? A tenuous smile blossomed on my face. I turned to Becker now barreling toward me.

The sheriff grabbed the front of my new shirt, and planted a finger in my face. "One wrong move, Nolan. One. You breathe wrong, I toss you in jail. You say the wrong word, I toss you in jail. Next time, won't be no judge." He pushed me back. "My eyes are always on you."

From the back of the room, Deputy Wagner pointed to me and then his own eyes. He made a slicing move across his neck. I knew the warning. I'd try almost anything to stay out of Becker and Wagner's reach.

I shook hands with Da, Joe, and Eagan, and accepted a hug from Ma. Words of congratulations sailed into my ears, but there were enough glares in the room to make me shudder.

On the boardwalk, the fresh air brightened my spirits. While I was basically a free man, still, I couldn't simply ride out of town and start a new life. A better life than Jesse James. No, I had to do what Mr. Carmichael said. And maybe that wouldn't be so bad.

Mr. Carmichael spoke with my family and then turned

to me. "I'm gonna let you spend the rest of the day with your family, then first thing tomorrow I expect you at the ranch. You'll move into the bunkhouse with the other hands and the foreman will assign you a job." He straightened to his full six-foot height. His words had a bite. "I'm taking a chance with you, Tate. We talked yesterday, so you know how I feel. But one step out of line—one—I'll have you back in jail within an hour. I'm fair to work for, pay fair wages, fair to my men. But I don't allow shrifters to work for me. You do your job and work hard. As we all do."

Maybe this wouldn't be such a great deal. I peeked at Ma and her sparkling blue eyes. I'd make it work. "Yes, sir."

A smile grew on Mr. Carmichael's face. He stuck out a hand to Da. "I'll treat him right, Mr. Nolan. He'll be fine." He tipped his hat at Ma, shook with Joe and Eagan, then untied his

horse's reins.

"Mr. Carmichael?" I looked up at the man now in the saddle. "I'll have to borrow Da's horse tomorrow. Can I stable him at your ranch?"

"Of course." Carmichael patted my shoulder. "The foreman can get you a horse, so next time one of us comes into town, we'll bring your pa's horse back." He turned to Da. "How's that sound?"

Da nodded.

I shook hands with my new boss. "Thank you, sir. See you first thing tomorrow."

"Yes. You will."

CHAPTER TEN

ONE THING I LEARNED EARLY ON BEING AT THE Lazy Six Ranch—never miss chow. In the three weeks I'd worked there, I hadn't been late once. And this morning was no exception.

I picked up a fork and spoon and straddled the wooden bench in the dining area of the bunkhouse where me and the other hungry hands waited. This morning, before the sun had fully claimed the ranch, the men had already fed the horses while the cook prepared food. Aromas of sourdough biscuits browning, bacon frying, beef steaks sizzling, and beans warming in a pot hanging over the fire whetted my already-ferocious appetite. Following two long days branding, dehorning, and castrating calves, and despite my substantial supper the night before, I was starved. Had I ever eaten? My stomach thought not.

Smitty, the old, grizzled cook, hollered, "Come and get it, 'fore I throw it out!" He didn't need to. All hands hovered close by.

I jumped up, leaving utensils and coffee cup at my

place, grabbed a tin plate from the stack at the end of the counter, and waited my turn to get breakfast. Another day branding and maybe roping horses was ahead and I'd need good grub—a lot of it—to keep going.

Pushing beans into my mouth, then a chunk of steak, I chewed and thought. So far, with three weeks under my belt, I'd stayed out of trouble. The other hands were good to work with. No one tempted me with whiskey or sneaking out of the ranch. Even the poker games were tame compared to the ones at Sam's Emporium. The men stayed sober and worked hard. I did too.

Biscuit in hand, I swallowed the last of the meal, finished off the coffee, and stood. I bit off the biscuit, my third, I think. Maybe I could stuff one more in my shirt for later in the morning.

"Kid?" The foreman stood in the doorway. From the first day on, everyone had called me Kid. I took exception to the new moniker, even coming close to hitting one of the men, then was told everybody who was young, especially one around more grizzled, seasoned men, was called Kid. By now, I'd gotten used to it.

"Yeah?"

José pointed toward the main house. "Big boss wants to see you, pronto."

Although I couldn't think of a single thing I'd done wrong, still, that cold knot of dread squeezed its way into my chest. I handed my empty plate to Smitty and spoke over my shoulder to José, "You know why?"

"*No se, exactamente.*" The foreman shrugged, then turned to the others now heading for the door. "*Vamanos, muchachos.* Let's get those calves branded today. Finish up if we can."

Maybe it was news about my family. My rushed stride across the ranch yard brought me to the house within a minute. Were they all right? Somebody get hurt? Was I in trouble? For as long as I'd been here on the Lazy Six and as far as I knew, I'd done what was asked.

I stepped onto the veranda and came face to face with Mr. Carmichael who extended a hand.

"Haven't seen you for a week." Carmichael shook with me, then stood holding a ceramic cup. Aromas of coffee floated from it. He peered into the rising sun. "Understand you've taken to ranching life like you were born to it. José tells me you've learned to rope horses, brand calves, and mend fences."

"Yes, sir." Where was he going with this? "My family all right?"

"Far as I know." He sipped the black brew. "You're staying out of trouble, I hear."

"Yes, sir." Relieved but still confused, I chanced a look at my boss's face. No hard lines, no anger there. "Haven't had a chance to get into trouble. Just doing lots of hard work."

Carmichael's lips rose to a slight smile. "Good." He finished his coffee and tossed the grounds onto the dirt. "Foreman suggested I send you and Tex out on the far range to bring in a couple of stray steers. Job's gonna take sunup to sundown." He regarded me. "You up for it?"

I was, especially if that meant I didn't have to brand more calves. The stench of burned hide and hair, all the blood from castrating, had turned my stomach more than once. Especially when I first started out, two days before. I'd had to run behind a mesquite bush to throw up an embarrassing three times. The men teased me mercilessly the rest of the day. However, I suspected they'd done their fair share of retching a few years ago.

I nodded at Mr. Carmichael. "Up for it? Yes, sir. I

haven't been that far yet. Looking forward to seeing the rest of your spread." We shook hands before I bolted down the steps and headed for the stable.

I swung up into the saddle, my wide-brimmed hat shielding my eyes from the first rays of sun. Today would be another hot, humid, stifling, Texas June day. I slapped a mosquito gnawing on my neck. The foreman stood looking up at me.

"Reports say five, maybe six steers are trying to break down the fence over by Clearwater Creek." He pointed south. "Kid, you and Tex round 'em up if you can, and bring 'em back to the west pasture. If the fence's broken, I'll send somebody to fix it tomorrow."

"No problem, boss." I nodded. "See you at supper."

Me and Tex, a man with no other name, wheeled our horses around and trotted out of the yard, leaving behind the rambling main house, Mr. Carmichael still standing on its wide veranda. The bunkhouse, blacksmith shop, barn, icehouse, chicken coop, and various other outbuildings took up a good city block all within shouting distance of Carmichael's house.

As we rode, I thought about the past month. Neither of my shirts fit now, the material stretched tight enough the seams showed. I'd need new britches soon. The seat of this pair was wearing thin and if I moved the wrong way, the fabric would split, my drawers showing. Not that I much cared. In the bunkhouse, the hands walked around in their drawers or nothing on at all.

Nobody was shy.

Of course, I hadn't been to town to buy new pants or anything else. The fact I still had no money, and was bone tired by sundown, kept the temptation to rob at arm's length. However, more and more often, I'd wake up thinking about my hands digging into a barrel of coins, savoring the feel of hard currency sliding down my body.

And if it wasn't thoughts of money, it was of women. Angelique Rossi filled my nights. More than once I'd awaken with the pillow in my arms, lusty images of the Italian beauty dancing throughout my body. So far, Mary Beth Anderson from the mercantile had kept her distance, but it was only a matter of time. Most of my thoughts had been at night, but more often I saw women in the horses I tended. Even one time I saw a face in the stew.

I had to get to town.

With money. As we rode, I thought about who to rob next. Immediately, I ruled out the butcher shop since Da and Eagan worked there. They might get accused of robbing and that would never do. The mercantile would have to be at night and the manager always took the day's money to the bank.

Sam's Emporium. Biggest and noisiest saloon in all the hill country. I considered how best to do it. A gun in the owner's face? No, too brazen. And then the scene popped into my head like I was already there. Joe and I would start a fight. We'd get to throwing punches at each other and then whoever else stood nearby. At some point, Joe would toss me over the bar, and I'd grab as much money behind there I could. I'd need to know where exactly ol' Sam kept the money, but it was behind the bar somewhere. He didn't have one of those fancy register contraptions I'd seen down at the bakery.

Holding up Sam's would be perfect. We'd have our fight Friday or Saturday night. Soon. Soon as I could get off the ranch. Then I'd come back and be richer than when I left. I'd start planning a bank robbery then.

I ducked under a low Texas oak branch, glad of

noticing the wooden beam before I got knocked off my horse. Although Tex was quiet, he'd undoubtedly share my humiliation with the entire ranch.

I glanced right at the quiet man. Tex, at least fifteen years older than me and a hundred years more experienced in the world, never said much. Especially about his past life. All he admitted was he'd been with Carmichael three years now and had never caused trouble. Those were pretty much the only words I had coaxed out of him. Tex wasn't rude or standoffish, simply one of those cowboys who kept thoughts to himself.

Stands of more oak dotted the pastures while mesquite and sage grew along the stream. I'd never been this far south and was amazed I was still in Texas. How much land did Carmichael own? More so, would someday I own that much? Did I want to? Instead of land, what would I buy with all my money? Beautiful women and lots of them sprung to mind. I'd get different sizes, ages, and hair colors. But after that? A new horse? An expensive saddle? A house? Mentally, I looked back over my shoulder. Would I want a ranch and house like Carmichael's? No. That was too much like being tied down. I would be free...and rich. Richer than Jesse James. And Frank James. Combined. I'd be richer than President Grant.

I reined up next to Tex who had stopped, sitting in his saddle, one leg hitched over the saddle horn. Tobacco pouch in hand, Tex liberally sprinkled flakes onto a thin paper, rolled it, and offered the cigarette to me. Tex started a second.

"Thanks." I twisted the end, found a match in my vest pocket, lit both cigarettes. We sat enjoying the relative freedom until most of the cigarette was ash. In front stood a line of thin trees and underbrush. Had to be the creek. To my left, a rolling hill promised good grazing.

Tex stubbed out the end of his smoke, swung his leg back into the stirrup, glanced sideways at me and cocked his head. A light *cluck* to his horse and Tex trotted off.

I set spurs to the horse, Honey, a sturdy chestnut mare with one white sock. She loped smoothly, enough to make my eyes close. The ride took me down onto the stream bank. Tex, who had wandered upstream, whistled, and pointed.

"Fence's cut."

That was never a good thing. I followed the fence across the creek and met Tex, now leaning, one end of the cut wire in hand. Tufts of hair fluttered in the breeze.

"Recent, you think?" I examined a bit of black hair I'd yanked off the wire.

Tex nodded.

Waiting for more words from my partner, I lifted a leg to swing off my horse but then thought better. Within a week at the ranch, I'd learned the most important rule of being a cowboy—never get off your horse unless you're bucked off or it's time for chow. Most everything else was done from the saddle. And heaven help anyone bucked off. The men would ridicule endlessly, never letting the cowboy live down the embarrassment. Apparently, there was absolutely no honor in being thrown, especially from a tame horse.

I retook my seat. The other side of the fence was Stinson's Ranch and old man Stinson was as opposite of Mr. Carmichael as possible. I had heard stories about Stinson hiring men and then right before payday, firing them, claiming they'd stolen from him, paying them no wages. I'd also heard Stinson hired known gun hands to do his bidding, especially to patrol the fences. I'd keep a keen eye on the horizon.

Tex pulled back the wire allowing enough room for his horse to walk through without being scratched. I followed, figuring Tex knew what he was doing, but technically, we *were* trespassing. I surveyed the area. Trees and bushes dotted low rolling hills. On the ground, distinctive cattle and horse prints. Those steers had been encouraged to go through.

I caught up to Tex. "Shouldn't we go back and tell Mr. Carmichael? I mean, this is Stinson's land."

"Just looking for our stock." He pointed to a stand of cedars to the left. "Probably there." He gigged his horse into a lope.

Determined to keep up, I rode beside the man. Maybe we'd find the strays, herd them home without any of Stinson's men finding out. The ranch covered hundreds of acres, so the chances of being discovered were low. Or so I hoped.

Sure enough. Five steers sporting our Lazy 6 brands milled around in between the trees. I rode to the other side, gripped the lariat, and waved the coiled rope at the animals. "How come you're so far from home? Let's go, boys." The black yearlings picked up their heads, turned.

"What d'ya think you're doing?"

I jumped at a deep voice. I turned and stared into a .45's muzzle. Within mere feet sat four men, all with weapons pointed at me and Tex.

My first inclination was to turn and gallop away. My pounding heart told me retreat was a good idea. A look at Tex, sitting stock still, glaring at the men, I decided I'd have to stay and see this through. Odds were not in our favor. Well, go to Jericho, I didn't even have a gun. Tex's was still holstered. Could Tex draw a weapon without being shot? No. If we couldn't talk our way back onto Carmichael land, we'd be in one Herculean fix.

When Tex didn't say anything, I spoke up. "Came to get our cattle. Don't want any trouble. Just what's ours."

A man, well over six feet and thick in the chest, raised the gun higher. "These're ours now. Best you two scat, unless you enjoy feeling a bullet in your chest."

Tex pointed. "Lazy Six brands're on their rumps." He moved in closer. "You gonna deny that?"

That was chest bumping at its finest. My shoulders drew back, and I sat taller. Obviously, Tex rode for the brand, and I would too.

"Maybe they can't read, Tex." With those words, I'd just dropped the gauntlet, so to speak.

The leader chuckled, glanced at the three men, and then swung off his horse. He grabbed Honey's bridle, and glared at me. "Off. Now, *cabron.*"

As if a silent signal blew, the three other men dismounted, as did Tex. My boots touched ground and before I could step out of the man's reach, the leader grabbed my leather vest and pulled me in close. "Don't know when to cut your losses, kid." Odors of stale onion and bacon spurted out with each word.

"We gonna shoot 'em both, Larkin?" A man hitched up his pants and stood next to the leader. "Or kill one of 'em so's the other can spread the message."

"Message?" Tex narrowed his eyes.

Larkin leaned forward with an air of ownership. "Don't see brands on these animals." He turned to his men. "Do we boys?"

Three heads shook.

"If you want to keep breathin'," Larkin continued, me still in his grip, "you'll get back on those nags of yours and ride off. Tell your boss not to mess with Stinson's property."

"Let go of me, you dry shite." I swiped at Larkin's powerful hold.

Larkin let out a deadly chortle. "Kinda feisty for a stinkin', wet-nosed pup."

My fists plowed into Larkin's chin. The uppercut took the man and his .45 to the ground. Within seconds, my arms were pinioned behind me, men taking turns pounding my face, my stomach. Tex's grunts told me the same thing was happening to him.

Unable to breathe, I slipped to the ground, gasping for air. I looked up at Larkin whose Colt was aimed at my heaving chest. Fear, like the quick, hot touch of the Devil, bolted through me.

I flinched.

Larkin pulled the trigger.

A red-hot poker plunged into my shoulder. Ears ringing, arm on fire, I tasted acrid gunpowder.

My shoulder. How could something hurt that much? I blinked. My world twisted into black.

CHAPTER ELEVEN

RINGING, POUNDING, THROBBING. AGONY. FIRE in my shoulder, down the arm to the fingers. I pried open one eye, the other coming with it. The world, a dark world, piece by piece pulled itself into focus. I lay on the ground, that much I was certain. Hands tied behind me, I struggled to roll over, only to discover my ankles tied too. Could I speak over the pain? Tex? Was he close by?

Thousands of questions flashed through my mind. I closed my eyes, pulled in a long drink of air despite complaining ribs, and listened. Crickets called out to other crickets not too far off. Fallen leaves rattled as something small dove for cover. No breathing except my own. Was I alone? And where?

Although swollen, my eyes opened completely and stared up into an endless canopy of stars. Some twinkled, some sat shining above. Some winked at me like the girls at Sam's Emporium. But judging by the darkness surrounding me, the time was well past midnight, sunup yet hours away. I squirmed against the bindings, and succeeded only in aggravating my throbbing, burning, hurting shoulder.

When I opened my eyes next, wet drops splatted in my face. I looked up into a sky no longer filled with stars but with sun trying to peek around sky-shrouding clouds. Heavy, rain-laden clouds. The kind of clouds that produce gully washes. Not a good time to be outside.

"Tex?" I yanked against ropes holding my wrists and ankles. "Tex? You all right?"

I didn't expect much of a reply, knowing the man, but at least a grunt or a groan would be welcome. "Tex?" I used my elbow to roll over. There lay Tex by a tree, dried blood spread across his chest, a bullet hole in the middle.

I couldn't help the man now. Based on the dried blood, looked like he'd been shot right after I had passed out.

Cursing the men who'd done this wouldn't do any good right now. Getting out alive should be the single thought on my mind, but I had to grin. Right now, I envisioned Ma's breakfast of ham, eggs, and potatoes. Wouldn't they be grand? My stomach rumbled in agreement.

I squirmed, fidgeted, twisted my arms until the pain in my shoulder made me vomit. There wasn't much to bring up, but I shook just as hard as that time I drank all of Da's whiskey hidden in the shed. Recovered, I scooted across the grass to a tree and rubbed the rope against the trunk. I'd throw up, rub, throw up, rub, eyes peeled for the return of Larkin and those men. Sun stood minutes shy of overhead when the rope snapped. I untied my ankles, sat rubbing my wrists. Pulling in more air, I closed my eyes for a moment, then crawled to Tex.

Definitely dead. And why? Senseless killing. Tex sure didn't deserve to die, and especially not like that. I pushed up to my knees, then feet. Wobbling like I'd been on a three-day binge, I gripped a tree branch to keep myself steady. But I was upright and alive. That much I was grateful for, despite the rain soaking my head and shirt.

Locating the horses wasn't hard. They hadn't gone far, finding a buffet of branches and grass to munch on. Tex's horse didn't want death on her back, but I tied her tight to a sturdy branch, hobbled her, then somehow—I have no idea where my strength came from—slung Tex over my shoulder then over the horse's back. She whinnied and shied but didn't go far. I tied him down with two rawhide ropes.

By now, my shoulder was bleeding and throbbing again, but I wouldn't let Tex down. I knew he'd do the same for me. Part of me was sorry *I* was the one bringing him home. The other part was sorry this had happened. I replayed the scene over and over trying to figure out how to have prevented this. Nothing came to mind.

* * *

HEAD DOWN HOPING to fend off even a few drops of this incessant rain, I cursed the men, again, for taking my hat as I rode into the ranch yard. Tex slung over his horse, trailed behind. The scene, I was sure, looked like bedraggled soldiers returning from war. It felt that way. The return ride had been long, wet, and painful.

I aimed for the main house, reining the horse past the bunkhouse left of Carmichael's. I pulled up short. There. Tied to the hitch rail was a big bay I recognized. Becker's horse, the one I'd stolen, but still I preferred the word "borrowed." What did that scum-sucking, son-of-a-gun want now?

Before I could back the horses and head for the barn to hide out, Mr. Carmichael and the sheriff stepped out onto the covered veranda. Caught. I couldn't run. With the last of my energy, I lifted my head and blinked through the drenching rain.

This had to be the worst day of my life. Worse even than the day before. Could I simply curl up and die right now? Cold, wet, that embedded bullet burning like the Devil's fires in my shoulder, head thumping, dead man in tow, and now...the sheriff. Good Lord. What had I ever done to deserve this?

Carmichael stepped into the yard, then trotted over to me. "What in thunder, boy? Supposed to be back last night. What happened? Come inside." He turned and shouted over his shoulder. "Ellie! Get bandages and dry clothes."

Unable to take much more, I allowed my boss to help me off the horse. Usually, a sign of pure weakness, but I had to admit, I was weak. By now, three of the other hands, including the foreman, ran toward me. Of course, Becker remained dry under the porch roof.

Knees refusing to hold my weight, I sagged against the rancher. Muttering apologies and explanations, I hoped I was telling everyone what happened.

"Tate, you're not making sense. Can't understand a word you're saying." Carmichael wrapped an arm around my shoulders and nudged me toward the house.

I stopped, then turned back to Tex, and the men now sliding him off the horse. Another hand had both reins and would take care of the horses. I relaxed. After drying off, a cup of coffee, and maybe something to eat, things would make sense.

And they did. Wearing dry clothes, I sat in the living room on the good sofa, cup of hot coffee in hand. From here, kitchen sounds wafted to my ears. Was that for me? I hoped so although I wasn't sure anything would stay down. Right arm useless with the shoulder bandaged so heavily and arm in a sling, I used my left to hold the shaking cup.

When I had arrived at the ranch house, Mrs. Carmichael and another woman, I vaguely remembered, had given me laudanum, a big dose to last long enough for them to dig the bullet out of the shoulder. Flashes of intense pain, squirming, someone holding me down, and then…nothing. But now I was awake, and the aching not too bad. Must be thanks to the heavenly pain killer Joe had enjoyed. Now I understood the attraction of that elixir. Could I get more?

World now in focus and back to the living room, I looked at Carmichael sitting in a wingback chair, Becker at the end of the sofa.

"What happened?" Carmichael leaned in closer.

Before I could explain, Becker pointed his cup at me. "I'll tell you what happened. Like I told Carmichael before you came dragging in, you and Tex were at Sam's last night causing quite the scene. Eyewitnesses say you two started a fight over a girl. Busted up the place to shambles. Sam had to close today for repairs." He glared. "Course you'll pay for damages."

"What?" The cup slipped out of my grip, coffee splashing on the rug. I glanced up at the rancher. "Sorry. I'll get a rag—"

"Stay. It's only a few drops."

I stared open mouth at the sheriff. "Tex and I weren't anywhere close to town. We followed the cut fence down by Clearwater Creek, found our strays, and were waylaid by a pack of Stinson's hired guns. Leader was a fella named Larkin. They killed Tex and shot me. Tied me up. Took all night, most of the day to get loose."

Becker stood. "No." He shook his head. "No. You broke up the bar, killed your partner there, then someone shot you." He nodded at Carmichael. "That's what really happened."

Pulling up my sleeve, I held out a chaffed wrist. "What d'you think did this?" I pointed to the red-skinned places. "A rope is what did. What those men tied me with."

"*Hmpf.*" Becker snorted disdain. "My eyewitnesses say you tried to lasso one of the upstairs women. They used the rope on you instead."

Good God.

"Eyewitnesses?" Mr. Carmichael stood also, chest puffed a bit. "Sheriff. I want to know exactly who they are." He pointed at me. "If my hand says he was way out in the south pasture, then that's where he was. I'll send a couple boys out tomorrow, but I'm sure we'll find a cut fence like Tate here says."

Becker planted his hat on his head and leaned down to me, still sitting. "I'll be back tomorrow and arrest you for destruction of property. Oh, and murder." He smirked. "*Ja.* Murder."

I retreated into the sofa's softness, closed my eyes. If I could just get out of Blanco Hill, out of Texas, maybe I'd lead a normal life, not one hounded by an idiotic sheriff. And if I didn't go to jail, how long would I need to work at the ranch until I could afford to ride off? I counted. Thirty-five a month from Carmichael, plus the seven in the drawer at home. Carmichael hadn't paid me yet, but payday was the end of the month, and that was coming soon. Forty-two wasn't much to start a new life on. Definitely time to rob again. This time, it'd be some-where with more than fifteen dollars.

A touch on my shoulder jerked me upright. Mr. Carmichael stood in front of me looking down. "Can't imagine Tex and you riding off to town instead of where José sent you. Don't worry about Becker. I'll take care of him."

I nodded, wishing "I'll take care of him" meant putting the man six feet under. Heck, I'd dance on his grave, like he threatened to do on mine.

Mr. Carmichael pointed south. "I'd heard Stinson hired professionals but didn't realize they'd stoop to this." He offered a hand. "You've had a long, hard two days." Mr. Carmichael pulled me to my feet and cocked his head toward the front door. "Go get some sleep. Take that laudanum with you. We'll work this out tomorrow."

Not sure I could walk alone to the bunkhouse, I stood as straight as I could, bottle in hand. "Thank you, sir. Good night."

Mr. Carmichael followed me to the door, held open the screen. "Oh, I sent word to your family about your getting shot. Told them you were sore but would be all right. I suggested they come by tomorrow to see how you're doing."

Did I want my family to come out worrying and fret-ting about me? On the other hand, I hadn't seen them for weeks, and I wondered how Joe was doing. I dragged into the bunkhouse greeted by the other hands who offered condolences about Tex and inquiries as to my health and what the hell happened. I gave short answers and headed for bed.

CHAPTER TWELVE

A FIRM HAND SHOOK MY BANDAGED SHOULDER. Groggy, coming out of a fog, I pried open one eye, the other, then focused on the person standing there. José Montoya, ranch foreman, cocked his head and shoulder toward the main house. "Your father and mother are here. Talking to Mr. Carmichael. Thought you'd want to say hello."

Lips dry and cracked, I ran my tongue around my mouth and tried muttering what I hoped was a response. "Be there soon's I get my feet under me."

Apparently, he understood. José offered a hand. "Well, kid. Look like you met the wrong end of a stampede. So you know, this morning I sent four men out to Clearwater Creek to repair the fence. Two to work, two with guns and rifles."

Now sitting, I ran a hand across my sandpapery face. "Hope they come back in one piece."

"Sí. Tambien." The foreman held my arm as I stood. His gaze fixed on my face while he waited for me to steady myself. "When your shoulder heals enough, in a day or two, you'll do lighter work here." He turned, then turned back. "You've been a good hand, hard worker, kid. I'd like you to stay."

Before I could make sense of the words, José walked away. A compliment? Surely I'd heard wrong, especially coming from a rough-and-tumble man such as him. Besides, nobody gave me compliments.

Mulling over the words, and like a man all used up, I peered into the shaving mirror, and decided another day or two without a razor would be fine. One eye was turning black, but it paled in comparison to the purple bruises on my chin and cheeks. Two long pulls of the laudanum dulled the headache, the body ache, and most importantly, the throbbing shoulder. The life-saving elixir bottle snuggled in my vest pocket, I wobbled and staggered across the muddy yard to the ranch house. Tied at the rail was a buggy I recognized from Alphonso's.

One step onto the porch and Ma and Da burst out the door, Ma hugging me despite my groans which slipped out. Da fumbled to shake hands with my left.

Ma stood holding me at arm's length. "Lookin' a wee bit off yer feet there, son. Yer face's sportin' lots of pretty colors, it is." She moved in closer and touched my cheek. "Not broken, is it?"

I winced and held her hand away from the sore places. A hardier pat would send tears down my cheeks, and I couldn't have that in front of her. "Probably not broken." Were those words clear? I looked at Ma to confirm. She narrowed her eyes and lowered the eyebrows.

Standing at the door, holding it wide open, Mr. Carmichael pointed to the living room. "Let's go in there where we can be more comfortable."

We three Nolans sat on the down-filled sofa while Carmichael took his leather wingback chair. Ellie Carmichael, tray in hand, appeared from the kitchen. Balancing water glasses and a plate of cookies, she set the tray on the coffee table. "Please, help yourself to water and cookies. Afraid we're out of lemonade right now, but the cookies're fresh out of the oven."

Oh yeah. That's what I'd smelled as I walked in. Reminded me of the German bakery with the strudels and pies. My stomach nudged me.

Settling for cookies, although I'd rather have breakfast, I nodded at Mrs. Carmichael and selected a morsel. When I brought the cookie up to my mouth, my jaw had other ideas. I tried opening but couldn't get it wide enough to slip in one cookie. I held my jaw, hoping that would help. No, jaw still achy and swollen. So much for breakfast.

Returning the cookie to the tray, I eased back against the cushions. Their softness, like arms embracing me, brought a sense of warmth and security I needed. That and home-cooking aromas added to my sense of well-being. Would life make a turn-around soon? I had to believe. On the plus side, at least this morning Becker wasn't shoving his authority into my life. I'd fully expected Satan Incarnate to be here already, handcuffs and noose in hand.

We passed an hour catching up on town and ranch news but mostly listening to my garbled account of the shooting. Ma gasped on occasion while Da gripped the water glass, knuckles glowing white.

"When the men get back from mending the fence," Carmichael glanced at his wife sitting in another wingback chair, "I'll see what they say, then go over to Stinson and figure this out. Way I look at it, he's guilty not only of rustling, but murder and attempted murder." He nodded toward me. "I'll take Becker with me."

Like a wild boar coming to life, rage filled my chest. "Becker?" I sat up straight while my voice rose. As much as I tried to reel them in, the words grew louder, garbled, but louder. "Becker? Don't, Mr. Carmichael. Get somebody else. Anybody else."

"Tate." Da tried to bring me down from the ceiling. I didn't feel well, hurt everywhere and was hungry. Words spewed.

"Mr. Carmichael." I let loose with both barrels. "Stinson killed one of your men, almost killed me. Took your livestock." I jerked my good arm south. "You need to find somebody with big b..." I changed course. "*Strong enough* to arrest that sonofabitch." Oops. I had said a curse word in front of Ma. If I lived at home, she'd probably kill me.

"Sorry, Ma." I looked at her with what I hoped was pity. "Don't feel well—"

She patted my hand. "It's all right, Tate. I'd of used those words meself."

Although she'd been quiet, Ellie Carmichael turned to her husband. "Suppose that new deputy, O'Sullivan, could go with you, Anthony?"

"Deputy won't do. Gotta be somebody with more authority." Carmichael sipped, thought, sipped again, draining the glass.

My ranting had shoved needles and knives, maybe a hatchet, into my shoulder. I unplugged the laudanum bottle and took a good, long slurp.

Thoughtfully, Carmichael set his cup on the coffee table. "Closest law besides Becker is down in San Antone." He regarded us. "Besides, half of Stinson's property is in another county out of Becker's jurisdiction. Might be worth a ride down there after all."

"Might be." Da scooted forward on the sofa. "Law around here's darn one-sided if you ask me." He looked from Ma to Ellie. "Excuse my poor language. But we need outside help."

At last. Maybe something good would come of this. Felt like my tirade had used up all my energy. It ran out through my toes. Were there rocks on my eyes? I struggled to keep them open. I'd have to lie down within a minute if I didn't want to pass out right here in the main room. That would be too embarrassing.

A strong hand helped me to my feet and walked me to the porch. I stared at Da, his shamrock-green eyes moist. "Glad you're still alive, son."

"Me, too, Da." I found myself wrapped in his strong embrace and whispered, "Me, too."

CHAPTER THIRTEEN

FEELING STRONG ENOUGH TO JOIN THE MEN AT supper the evening two days after the shooting, I sat at the bunkhouse's long table and rubbed my shoulder. I never knew something could hurt so much as when that laudanum, that heaven-sent nectar of the gods, wore off. When it did, my head pounded like a blacksmith's hammer on tough iron. My shoulder throbbed, itched, pulled, screamed, and burned when I moved wrong. Even when I was still. Every time that bullet wound hurt, I cursed those men again. Sometimes aloud, sometimes to myself. I was sure those *bodaches* knew I'd come for them. Some day. Somehow. What gave them the right to kill Tex and shoot me?

Relaxing my clenched jaw and left hand, I pulled into the present. This long table served not only as a place to eat, but to read, to clean weapons and to share jokes. A gathering spot. More than a few hands of poker had been played on that wooden plank, too. Right now, me and my stomach looked forward to a helping of chicken stew with a tortilla. Yesterday, my achy jaw cooperating a bit more, and I'd managed a few spoonsful of broth Mrs. Carmichael had sent over. Tonight, instead of broth, I needed more—stew, steaks, fried chicken, venison stew, coleslaw, apple pie. The vision brought moisture to my mouth. I wiped the drool, hoping no one had noticed.

And then like a miracle, courtesy of the cook, a bowl appeared in front of me, the aroma wafting under my nose and around my head like a benevolent angel. Massaging the jaw, inch by inch, I pried it open, managing to get the spoon in. One bite. Heaven. I closed my eyes enjoying the taste of chicken and then realized how silly I looked around the other men. Would they understand or just think me an idiot?

Bowl in hand, José scooted along the opposite bench until he was across from me, and a fella named Charlie sat to his right. Without words, they spooned food into bellies like mine—gnawing and complaining.

A soft pat on my unbandaged shoulder made me look up. I grinned at my brother.

"Figured you'd be feeding your face about now." Joe plunked down next to me and nodded to José and Charlie. He leaned almost face first into my bowl, then reared back and smiled. "Chicken stew?"

My mouth lifted on one end. "Darn right. Smitty's a right fine cookie." So good to see Joe again. I'd had many dreams about hitting him. Not dreams, more like nightmares, and I was relieved to see him in one piece. Remembering how hard I'd hit him before, I tapped his arm—lightly. "'Bout time you came visiting your big brother. Thought I'd been abandoned."

I introduced Joe to the hands. Smells of stew swirling around my head I asked him, "You hungry?"

"Like a bear coming out of hibernation." He patted his stomach. "Didn't get much at noon and this sure smells good." He turned to me. "Hey, brother. If I'd known you ate this well, I'd come hire on here. How come you didn't tell me sooner?" He nodded at Smitty who handed him a filled bowl and a tortilla.

We passed the next half hour in conversation with the rest of the hands who came in for chow. A few of the men tried to wow Joe with tales of ranch derring-do, touting their cowboy prowess. Some stories were true, I figured. At least they were entertaining, and Joe seemed to eat them up, along with a second helping of stew.

Stomach at long last full, I eased up to my feet. A sideways glance around the bunkhouse, I was surprised to realize I liked it here. The men were good to work with and apparently José appreciated my efforts. Maybe my luck really was turning around.

I put my bowl, along with Joe's, into a big tub at the end of the table. Cookie's helper, known as a hoodlum, would have the honor of washing. I turned to Joe. "How about poker? We can play for matches."

Joe tugged off his hat and gripped the brim tighter than I thought necessary. His mustache, which was growing into adulthood, looked good on him. I guessed that at twenty, he truly was becoming a man.

He eyed me, probably taking in my black eye and exquisite bruises, which I'd examined this morning in the shaving mirror, and shook his head. "Nah, no poker tonight. I need to be getting back. Got work tomorrow." He started to poke my bandaged shoulder but then withdrew his hand. "Ma's been worried about you. Promised I'd report back."

"Fair enough." I flashed a crooked smile. "Be sure to say good things." A twinge of pain shot through my shoulder. Time for another big swallow of that potent pain killer. I stepped toward the sleeping room.

His hesitation made me stop and frown. "What's wrong? Something else?" He was keeping me from my medication. This needed to be quick.

"Hoping I could talk to you." Joe glanced at the men finishing their chow. "Somewhere private. It's important."

I pointed toward the room with the bunks, and Joe followed on my heels.

Although I wasn't in bad pain yet, I soon would be the moment the laudanum's effects wore off. Even more, the draw of that elixir was undeniable. I slipped the bottle out from under my pillow and brought the glass to my mouth. Nothing. Empty. Had I used it all? No. I frowned at Joe. Had he finished it off when I wasn't looking?

I gripped the bottle like it held answers to all problems. Eyes narrowed, my gaze trailed up to Joe. "You finish it off?"

Joe stepped back. "Course not." He shrugged. "Didn't even know you had some."

"Well, I sure as hell did. A full one. Where is it?" Hands shaking, I tossed the pillow then sheet off the bunk. I searched under the mattress and on the floor. "Where is it?"

Shaking, stomach lurching, I slumped on the floor and leaned against the bedpost. Joe kneeled next to me. His words were strong, definitive. "Brother. You're relying on that medicine too much." He pried the empty bottle out of my hand. "This stuff's good for the pain, but it'll take over your life if you let it."

Even in my frantic haze I realized he was right. But one more swallow. Just one. A long, deep satisfying swallow. Then I'd never have another. I'd quit. But still, just one more. "You have som,e don't you? I've seen it.

Listen, I'm not allowed to leave the ranch, so bring me yours. One more pull and I'll quit. Promise."

Joe scrambled to his feet. "Sorry. Don't have any and even if I did—"

"You're no brother of mine!" My words, which I immediately regretted, echoed off the wooden walls. I climbed to my feet, stood glaring at Joe.

Joe spread his arms out wide, bottle held far away from my grasp. "Can't help you."

My face burned, words uncontrolled. I yelled. "Yes, you can! Get me more. Joe, I need more!"

José, along with two other hands, rushed into the room. "Problem?"

Joe moved between me and the men. "Family drama, that's all. He'll calm down."

Eyeing me and then Joe, José nodded at the bottle clutched in my brother's hand. "Powerful medicine. But makes men crazy." He lowered his voice to Joe. "I'll make sure he gets through this. He won't like it, my grandmother's medicine, but it'll cure him."

"Thanks." Joe looked at me now sitting on my bunk. "I don't like seeing you this way."

My burning eyes trailed up to my brother. "Just get me more."

CHAPTER FOURTEEN

THE NEXT TWO DAYS WERE PURE TORTURE. THE first night, when I thought I was sleeping, José yanked me out of bed, shoved me outside, across the yard and into the barn. "What the—?" I stumbled, barefoot, yelling at him. At the world. "What?"

"You keep the men awake with your fits. Shaking, crying, yelling." José pushed me into an empty stall. Before I realized what was happening, he tied my good arm to a post. "*Siéntense!* Sit."

When I didn't obey, he pushed me to the ground, the rope slid along the post too. I cursed him soundly, yanked at the restraint, cursed him again, and tried untying my wrist. No way was that right arm going to cooperate. "What the hell, José? What's going on?"

He kneeled close enough I could see how dark brown his eyes were. Like camp coffee. How lines jutted out from the sides of his mouth. "Tomorrow, *mañana*, I'll brew up tea like my *abuela* did when her husband turned loco. It will help you get through this."

"Through what?" Had everyone gone crazy? "Just

need more laudanum. José, get me some, please. *Por favor.*"

He stood and looked down. His head moved back and forth. *"Buenos noches*, kid." With that, he marched out of the barn and closed the door. A wooden beam scraped along the outside holding the doors in place.

Tears rolled down my cheeks. I cried, cursed, hollered, and yanked at the rope until I couldn't anymore. Odors of horse, manure, hay, harnesses and whatever else lived in the barn attacked my nose. I sneezed. Coughed. Sneezed. Threw up.

* * *

I SPENT the next day shaking, crying, and drinking bucketsful of an ungodly concoction José brewed. So far, that mud-colored, foul-smelling excuse for medicine was working. By day three, I no longer craved the pain killer, instead preferring coffee. But I was weak and didn't trust myself yet. My shoulder, head, and jaw still ached, but I pushed through the pain without anything to dull the agony.

As part of the recovery and because my right arm was still useless, I was assigned to help Smitty, be his hoodlum. Besides stirring pots of stew and beans, I also brought in water—managing one bucket at a time. Bringing in firewood someone else had chopped took more time. But I enjoyed the aromas of simmering beans, biscuits, and mesquite, somehow, all melding together. My stomach rumbled often, but not from lack of food. This morning, I was looking forward to helping cook and then eat cubed potatoes, eggs, and ham.

José stepped into the kitchen and crooked his finger

at me. "Big boss wants you up at the house." He cocked his head. "Think you can ride?"

With one hand, I untied the apron snugged around my chest. "Ride? Yeah, I can ride. I'm going somewhere?"

Shoulders rising, José walked away. "Maybe. Boss didn't tell me. But he asked."

Unsure what to expect, although I figured Mr. Carmichael knew about my brush with addiction, I knocked on the ranch house door and waited to be let in. So different from a week ago when I had ridden into the yard, beaten, and shot, barely hanging on to consciousness. Then I was carried in by Mr. Carmichael. Or was it a hand who had picked me up and brought me through the door? Fuzzy faces. That was all I remembered. Pain and fuzzy faces.

I nodded to a woman I thought I recognized who opened the door and stood back. I scraped my boots on the thick mat, hoping to dislodge whatever had attached itself. I took off my hat and stepped inside. Mouth-watering cooking smells floated around my head. Seemed like most of what happened on a ranch was cooking or preparing to cook. Cutting firewood, cleaning out the stove, stirring food, chopping meat, salting, tasting, enjoying. Maybe I should be a cook full time. Someday open my own restaurant.

Deep in thought, hat in hand, I stood by the sofa.

"There a hole in the rug I don't see?"

I recoiled like I'd been caught with my hand in the cookie jar, and almost dropped my hat when I turned. Mr. Carmichael stood in the doorway, a grin taking up most of his face.

"No sir, just thinking." I returned his grin. "Enjoying the smells of a house is all."

Carmichael pulled in air and stepped into the room. "Sit. We need to talk."

Here it comes. I'm fired. Going back to jail. I eased to the cushion's edge, gripped my hat. "Sir?"

"José tells me you're helping the cook. Been busy, in fact, and Smitty reports he appreciates the assistance." The boss sat in his favorite chair and eyed me. "Looks to me you're healing up well. The eye isn't quite so black."

"Yes sir." Where was this going? If I was going to be fired, do it immediately. None of this chitchat to prolong the agony.

Carmichael sat upright. "Rode down to San Antone yesterday, spoke with the sheriff there. Man by the name of Samuels. Alton Samuels. Told him about Tex and you and the cattle. Says he's had complaints about Stinson in the past, and he'd like to meet us out at Stinson's ranch today. Talk to the man. Get his side of things." He leaned forward and studied my face. "Those bruises and black eye make a mighty convincing argument. Even your swollen lips. I'd like you to go, if you're up to it."

"I am, sir. Still got enough aches and pains to remind me all the time what those fellas did. Can't get Tex, lying there, all covered with blood, out of my head either." I nodded. Maybe there would be justice in the world after all. "Yeah, I'd like to go." I hesitated. "But can I get breakfast first?"

I'd never seen Mr. Carmichael actually laugh, but he did right then. Not sure what struck him as funny, me, I guessed, but he nodded all the while waving in the bunkhouse's direction. I took that as a yes, told him I'd be back in a few minutes, and headed out the door.

Fifteen minutes and two helpings later, my stomach complaining of too much food, I polished off the final bit of coffee and stepped out into the yard. Like being hit by a fist in my gut, I skidded to a stop. Becker's horse stood at the hitch rail.

Before I could turn tail and run back to the safety of the bunkhouse, Becker and Mr. Carmichael stepped off the porch.

"Just coming to get you, Tate." Mr. Carmichael's mouth and eyes had narrowed.

I waited for them to come to me. I wasn't making Becker's life one ounce easier by walking to him. They stood looking at me, Becker's gaze traveling from my boots to my hat.

Mr. Carmichael sighed, studied the sky, lowered his eyes to stare at me. "Where were you last night around eight?"

"Sir?"

"Answer me truthfully, son. Last night. Around eight."

I leaned back, a cold knot pressing against my chest. "In the bunkhouse. Went to bed early. Still don't have much energy."

Mr. Carmichael tilted his head. "You sure? Can anybody vouch for you?"

How should I answer? "Just the men, sir." And then rethought. "Wait." I held up a hand, knowing honesty was everything. "I needed some thinking time, by myself, and I was enjoying that the durn wind had finally died down." I looked from a glowering Becker to a concerned Mr. Carmichael. "I walked down to that little creek maybe a quarter mile from the bunkhouse. Stayed about half hour. Then went back and to sleep."

"Anybody see you?"

I shook my head. "Don't think so. What's going on?"

"I'll tell you what's going on." Becker moved in so close I had to back up. "You robbed Delilah's Café last night." He made a chopping motion behind his head. "Knocked out the owner with a frying pan, took all the monies. That's what you did."

"What?" What a coincidence. Here I was working as a cook's helper, go off on my own for less than an hour, and someone in town robs a restaurant.

"I didn't do it, Mr. Carmichael. I haven't been off the ranch since the day I rode in, most of a month now. Unless you count the night I was tied up on Stinson's property."

Becker planted a thick finger in my chest. "That's what *he* said. But I don't believe either of you."

I didn't take kindly to having a finger planted in my chest and knocked his hand away. "Don't touch me." I glared at him. "Didn't do it."

Both of Becker's open hands slammed against my chest. "You lie!"

Wind knocked out, I gulped air and stumbled back. My shoulder caught fire. Becker came at me again, this time whacking my bandaged shoulder.

I fisted my left hand but a firm grip on my upper arm stopped me from pounding that sonuvagun. I glanced at Mr. Carmichael and then realized José and a couple of the hands were standing with me.

Becker glared at each of them.

José stepped forward. "Sheriff Becker, sir." He pointed at me. "We overheard you questioning the kid about last night."

"*Ja*. What's it to you?"

"Well, sir. Kid didn't want to tell you, probably *un poquito* embarrassed, but we all played poker last night 'til way past ten. He lost. Lost everything. Then got mad, stormed off to bed." José feigned a smile and lowered his voice. "Truth is, he's not a very good poker player. Took losing hard."

Mr. Carmichael looked from man to man. "You were all there? Eyewitnesses?"

Nods all around.

Becker shook a finger in my face then turned to Mr. Carmichael. "I'll be back. Soon." He leaned into me. "You'll hang."

We all let out sighs of relief when Becker swung up onto his horse and galloped away. What an ass. Could I hate anyone more? I turned to the men now walking away. They didn't have to do that. I *had* walked down to the creek by myself. I really hadn't played poker. But they had backed me. Lied for me. My smile reached ear to ear; I was sure.

Mr. Carmichael patted my back. "You didn't rob that café, did you?"

"No sir." I rubbed my shoulder and touched something sticky. As much as it hurt right now, visions of that laudanum teased me. But I knew better.

"Let's get that bandage changed. Clean shirt." Mr. Carmichael studied my bloody hand.

"No bother. I'm fine, sir," I lied. I'd push through this, although I could feel the stitches had pulled loose. "Doesn't hurt at all." Would I go to hell for lying? "I'm fine to ride."

Shrugging and giving me an "I don't believe you" look, Mr. Carmichael cocked his head toward the house. He walked. I followed.

CHAPTER FIFTEEN

AS WE RODE TOWARD STINSON'S RANCH, I massaged my shoulder and thought about what happened this morning. Mrs. Carmichael and the house-keeper Miranda, as she had introduced herself, had peeled off my blood-soaked shirt and tsked about its condition. Then they peeled off the bandage and tsked about my shoulder. So much tsking made me wince. But just as I had suspected, those stitches had been pulled loose. I looked away and fought down rising breakfast.

When I saw the needle and thread in Mrs. Carmichael's hands, I knew those eggs would come back up. I squeezed my eyes shut and thought of Angelique Rossi. Lovely Angelique. Would I ever see her again? Get to take her to supper? And before I knew it, the two women had re-sutured me and helped me slip my arms into a new shirt. This one was light blue with tiny yellow stars on it. I liked the way it fit and had to ask.

"Is this one of Mr. Carmichael's shirts?" I wouldn't feel right wearing my boss's clothes. But then again, what about the one I just had on?

Mrs. Carmichael, rolled bandage in hand, stopped and turned to me. She looked down. "No."

Before I could ask further, she helped me with one button. She spoke matter-of-factly. "This was Jefferson's. My son. After he died, I saved his clothes thinking they may come in handy one day."

What should I say? Nothing came to mind except, to say, "I'm sorry."

She swiped at a tear and stepped back. "Glad you're the same size. And it looks good on you."

Miranda finished helping me button and nodded slightly.

I thanked both women, slipped my arm back into the sling and met Mr. Carmichael outside at the hitch rail.

Attention back to the present, I noticed what a smooth ride my horse gave. Loping felt like a ride on butter. My shoulder much appreciated it. We rode along a wide trail that led to San Antonio. Many times I started to ask the questions bombarding my mind, but I stayed silent for most of an hour. He did, too, although he looked over at me on occasion. What was he thinking?

And finally, like a petulant two-year-old demanding attention, my question slipped out. "Do I remind you of him?" Immediately, I tried to reel more questions back in, but they weren't having any of me. In fact, more came. "When did he die? What happened?"

Without a word, he pulled back on the reins and sat looking at me. His gaze traveled across my face, my new shirt, down across the grassy plains, the valley, and up to the sky. I squirmed in the saddle and mentally kicked myself for asking. José would have known. Should've asked him.

Mr. Carmichael rubbed his freshly shaven chin. "Yes and no." He turned to me, his eyes now so sad. "Two years ago, Jefferson decided ranch life wasn't for him. Wanted something 'better,' more exciting." He stared at the saddle horn. "Took up with a gang of outlaws who managed to get themselves all killed in a stage holdup."

"I'm sorry." That wasn't enough, but it was all I had.

He nodded. "Jeff was your age, twenty-two, and had a full life ahead of him. I tried talking to him, long father-son conversations, but he wouldn't listen. Instead, he threw away his whole life. Just threw it away." His eyes met mine. "Like I told you when I bailed you out of jail, I hope you have better sense. Don't do what he did."

After a long swig from the canteen, he set spurs to his horse. I spent the next half hour riding across flat plains, up and down swales, still following the road, all the time pondering on what he'd said. Was this a second chance for me? And then my brain went its own separate way and changed course. Robbing a restaurant like Becker accused me of this morning. Why hadn't I thought of that? Sounded easy. And surely, they had money. If I robbed at the right time, nobody would be around except whoever was counting the day's income. And I'd try not to hit anyone. Why hadn't I tried an eatery first?

Mr. Carmichael and I pulled rein at the entry to Stinson's ranch. The road stretched south over a hill with no house in sight. At the intersection, a long wooden plank suspended over the ranch road had SSS carved into it. Had to stand for Stinson. And maybe his sons?

As if he had read my thoughts, Mr. Carmichael pointed to the sign. "Three S Ranch. Used to belong to Schumacher and his boys, but they got run out."

"Run out?"

He sipped from the canteen and let his gaze roam the vast countryside. "Yeah. Comanches, Texicans, slave hunters from New Orleans, and finally the government forced them out. Something about back taxes." He hung the canteen around the saddle horn. "Stinson's been here about ten years now, since right after the war. He's been a nuisance ever since, but never killed one of my hands before."

Before I could ask more questions, a lone rider loped into view. Samuels? Hopefully the sheriff from San Antonio. He was. That badge he wore seemed to shine extra bright. Would he arrest Stinson, make him pay for Tex's death? And my bad shoulder?

Sheriff Samuels pulled rein, greeted Mr. Carmichael who introduced me. We exchanged quick pleasantries and shook hands awkwardly since I had to use my left.

"After speaking with you yesterday, Sheriff," Mr. Carmichael pointed at my bruised face and arm still in a sling. "Thought it'd be a good idea to bring Tate along. You can see yourself

what Stinson's men did. But I'll let him tell you."

My stomach knotted thinking about that late afternoon. Poor Tex. We sat our horses, facing each other and I explained every detail, leaving out nothing. "It's a fact we were on Stinson's land. I won't deny that. But, Sheriff, truly we were simply looking for our cattle. Found them, too, on Stinson land. But Larkin and his men... well, said those steers were now theirs." Was I shaking? My voice sounded like it was. "Then they beat and shot us."

Samuels nodded at the right places, huffed at others. Was he going to do something? Or be like Becker and blame me? I searched a face even older than Mr. Carmichael's, both having been shaved this morning.

When I was finished talking, I took a long pull of

sweet water from the canteen and ran the back of my hand over my mouth. Did he believe me?

The sheriff let out the longest breath I'd ever heard. His steel-gray eyes, lines jutting out from either side, narrowed as he looked down the ranch road. "Don't know which is worse—stealing cattle or murder."

Mr. Carmichael reined his horse toward the ranch. "Murder, when it's a good man like Tex."

We trotted along the dusty ranch road avoiding wagon ruts. Horses had been known to break legs navigating the rough ground and I certainly didn't intend for that to happen to mine.

The closer we rode to the ranch house, the tighter my chest squeezed. Could I even breathe? Met at the door by a tiny Mexican woman, we followed her pointing hand.

Behind a wooden desk covered with papers sat a man, much older than I expected. He rose when Sheriff Samuels strode in. Stinson's thin, pointed nose accentuated thin lips, a pencil mustache etched over them. His iron-brown eyebrows and powder-white hair fought each other for dominance. His face looked like it had been put together with leftover parts. If I hadn't been so nervous, I would have laughed. Smiled, at least.

Within seconds, I distrusted this man. Something about Stinson set me on edge, especially since he'd allowed his men to roam the range as killers.

Stinson took a seat at his oak desk, fingers steepled as he surveyed us standing in front of him. At long last, he pointed. "Sit, gentlemen. What brings you out this way?"

Samuels explained and allowed Mr. Carmichael to fill in the gaps. Hat twirling in hand, I gave my eyewitness account, hating to relive—again—seeing Tex like that.

A stinging silence permeated the room. Heavy breathing, throats clearing, boots shuffling. Not a word spoken. Seconds dragged into a long minute.

Stinson leaned forward, elbows on desk. He pointed at me. "You should become one of those fantasy writers someday, son. You tell a whale of a cockeyed story." Stinson's dark eyes bore a hole clear through me. "Now, Sheriff, Carmichael." He glared harder at me. "Boy. Let me tell you what actually happened."

Boy? How condescending was that? I really disliked him now. Plus, that was not what I had expected the man to say. He was supposed to say he was sorry; he'd bring in the men who'd done such horrific deeds. But he didn't.

Stinson leaned back in his squeaky chair. "Lazy Six Ranch hands cut the fence wire, trespassed onto my property—which Tate here admitted to—for the express purpose of stealing my cattle." He took a beat and stared at me. "Isn't that true?"

Most of it was. "I didn't—"

"My men, my hands, discovered you and...Tex, you said? In the process of rustling *my* steers. You and Tex shot at them, they shot back. You got wounded." Stinson dropped his voice into an icy timbre. "More 'n likely, *you* shot Tex. Then to make it look good, you go running back to your boss, telling him it was my men who did all that."

Mr. Carmichael sat straighter, leaned forward. "Now wait—"

"Seems to me, Tate here is the one who needs arresting. *He* trespassed, *he* rustled, *he* shot." Like a cougar ready to pounce, Stinson oozed to his feet. "Sheriff Samuels, he even admitted he was on my property. I want Tate Nolan arrested for cattle rustling and murder."

He turned to me. "Those are hanging offenses." He pointed to Samuels. "Sheriff?"

"What?" Anger burbling to the surface, I jumped to my feet, looked from Mr. Carmichael to the sheriff. "What? He's got it all wrong. The way I told is the truth." I fought to breathe. "I got shot. Beat up. Look at my face. *They* killed Tex."

Stinson strode from behind the desk. "You see them kill this partner of yours?"

My world crashed around my ears. Rage shook my head. My good hand fisted and unfisted.

"Then you don't know for certain it was one of my men." Stinson puffed out his narrow chest, moved in closer to me. "If you don't swing for murder, you'll swing for attempted rustling."

A hand on my arm kept me from decking the old man.

Sheriff Samuels's voice rose to a deep bass. "I'll need to talk to your men, Stinson. The ones Tate encountered."

The man shrugged. "Just missed them. Sent them down to Mexico to pick up a bull. Mexican bull with tremendous breeding history. Cost a good penny, but I need to strengthen my herd." Part of a smile rose on one end. "Should be back in a month or so."

Wasn't that simply a bit too convenient? Anger somewhat under control, I wanted to shout but kept my voice lower. "Didn't take your steers. Ours were being herded toward a group of cattle with your brand."

Stinson chuckled, his cheeks pushing wrinkles around his eyes. "Then Sheriff, Carmichael. I welcome you to check my herds. Find yours if you can." He chinned toward the outside. "I run five thousand head. Please, help yourself, if you think yours are there."

Mr. Carmichael, Sheriff Samuels, and I stood, hats now on heads. Shoulder throbbing, head pounding, I looked at my boss. Would he let me be arrested? What would happen if he did?

Stinson followed us to the door. "I'll come into town the next day or two, Sheriff. I expect to see this rustler behind bars." He paused. "Oh, and when my men return, I'll have them come see you."

Anger surfaced before I could reel it in. I spun to Stinson and stood within spitting distance. "*Your* men killed Tex and shot me. That's the way it was." I shook a finger in his face, almost brushing his nose. "I'll find those men. That Larkin and his bunch. And when—"

"Let's go, son." Mr. Carmichael stepped between me and Stinson. "Nothing we can do right now."

Mr. Carmichael probably saved me from considerable jail time right then. Another three seconds and I would have pounded that sonuvagun into his plank flooring. Only thing left would be a pile of quivering shite.

The tug on my arm from Samuels twisted me around. He pulled until I found myself standing at my horse. Could my heart pound any harder?

I pulled in two, maybe three long gallons of air, determined to calm down. Envisioning that old man with a bullet hole in his chest would have to do for the moment. Unless I wanted to swing at the end of a rope, I'd need to get on my horse and ride away.

Mounting aggravated my re-stitched shoulder. Yet, that didn't hurt as much as the cold knot in my chest. Going back to jail. That wasn't the plan.

We reached the end of the ranch road and reined up. Samuels let out a long stream of exasperated air. "Don't seem right arresting you Tate. I know there's two sides to every story, but something about Stinson's isn't quite right."

"It doesn't, for a fact." Mr. Carmichael studied me, turned to Samuels. "Are you really arresting him? Can I bail him out right here?"

The sheriff pursed his lips, huffed through his mustache. "It's his word against yours, Tate, the way I see it." He leaned close to me. "You stay on Carmichael's ranch, out of trouble. Heal up. When those fellas get back with the bull, if that's what they're really up to, I'll talk to them. Get their side. I'm thinking they won't be back though."

I extended a hand. "Thank you, Sheriff. This sure didn't go the way I figured."

Samuels leaned in close. "Tate, you seem like a nice enough fella. You've been hurt," he nodded toward my shoulder, "and you've been wronged. Stay away from Stinson and those men of his. I'd hate to have to arrest you. Or bury you." He patted my bandaged shoulder. "Understand?"

I'd been warned thoroughly. I nodded. "Yes, sir." Was he more like Becker who turned a blind eye to everything except what he wanted to see? I sure hoped not, but after all, Samuels *was* wearing a badge.

CHAPTER SIXTEEN

SILENTLY CURSING THE UNENDING PILE OF dirty dishes here in the kitchen, I wondered how a cook could use so many pots and pans. Sudsy water dripped down the side of the heavy pot gripped in my left hand. Using a soggy dishtowel, I swiped the dented side and considered. How could a week have passed already? *Wasn't it just yesterday I was over at Stinson's place expecting that old man to go to jail?* Hell, as it turned out, I almost got arrested. Certainly not what I had anticipated. Nevertheless, the days had flown by, and now with my shoulder healing, stitches out a day ago, I was expected to do more. José and I agreed that chores like bronc busting, throwing hay, mending fences even, would be too much right now. So, besides washing and drying dishes, I got assigned to muck out stalls.

Great. The bouquet of day-old manure, urine-soaked hay, mite-infested dust, combined with non-stop buzzing flies, created a nose-assaulting, stomach-turning dislike for a necessary job. My time spent with Alphonso had taught me how to manage dirty stalls. I thought I'd left that behind when I came here. But no. There was no escape from manure.

I picked up another pot and dried. But there was escape. Yesterday had been payday and Mr. Carmichael hadn't insulted me by suggesting he keep my money for "safekeeping." Like everyone else, he gave me thirty-five dollars cash which felt like heaven in my hands. After pawing my well-earned pay for a good half minute, I tucked the bills and a shiny Liberty head five-dollar coin into my vest pocket. No way would I put them under my pillow like others did. No, I'd keep my money on my person.

This morning, as I dried endless pots and pans, I thought about my pay. That was the most I'd ever received. It was double what Alphonso gave me. Now, what to do with my fortune?

Thirty-five certainly wasn't enough to start a business, buy a ranch, marry a gal, or even buy a good horse, much less a decent saddle. But...I froze, dish towel in hand. It *was* enough to buy a gun. Last time I'd been in town to shop, more like window shop, I'd seen a .38 Colt Navy Revolver over at Elroy's Hardware store. He'd said I could have it for fifteen dollars. Back then, he could have said fifteen cents. Didn't matter. Couldn't afford one. But now I could.

A hearty shove on my good shoulder unfroze me. Smitty, the cook, tossed me his best glare and I continued drying and planning. Would a gun be good use of my money? Maybe. What else could I spend it on besides Angelique?

I gave up, realizing I had no answers, and turned to Cookie busy chopping meat for tonight's stew. Hemming and hawing, I finally got down to the question. "What do you do with your pay? Got a gal to spend it on or what?"

He whacked gristle off a chunk, stopped and looked at me. "What the hell kinda question is that? Do I look like I got a gal?"

Can't say he did, but one never knew. I tried again. "Don't mean insulting you. It's just that—"

"Save it for my old age. Every penny." He glanced around the kitchen. "Got everything I need right here. Place to lay this tired head, three squares a pay—even though I do hafta cook 'em myself—good men to work with, boss who's fair." He shrugged. "Don't need nothing else."

I had no response other than, "Huh." In all honesty, I'd never considered being old and what all that meant. Would there come a time when I couldn't work, earn money? Of course, I'd never heard of elderly outlaws since they didn't seem to live all that long. Should I rethink being a train robber? How long would Jesse and Frank James live? Would they end up in rocking chairs on their front porches, stroking their long gray beards? From that perch, would they entertain grandchildren with wild tales of robbing stages and trains? I couldn't see it.

But I'd be different from the James boys. I'd be better. Faster. Richer. More famous. First, I'd need a gun.

Pots and pans now dried, I nodded to Smitty and headed outside to muck out stalls. Between drying or mucking, I'd take kitchen duty any day. But Mr. Carmichael and José had been good to me, and the least I could do was what I was told. Didn't make the chores any more enjoyable though.

On my way to the barn, Mr. Carmichael strode up. I stopped, wondering what I'd done now. Did he want his money back? Maybe there was word from Sheriff Samuels about that scum Stinson.

"Hear your wound's about healed, Tate." Mr. Carmichael chinned at my shoulder, arm no longer in a sling.

"Yes, sir. It's feeling fine, thanks to your wife and Miranda. They took good care of me."

Half a smile rose on his face. "Unfortunately, they're both practiced at it. As you know, cowboying takes a toll on the body."

"Yes, sir." I studied his face waiting for bad news.

His face revealed nothing. The fact we were about the same height made looking into his eyes easy. And when I did, I saw kindness and sincerity.

"Tomorrow's Saturday, Tate." Mr. Carmichael hooked a thumb in his waistband. "The missus wants to go into town, do some shopping and have tea with her friends." He paused as if considering whether to continue, and then did. "If you're feeling strong enough, I'd like you to drive her into town. You'd have to carry packages and then wait while she gossips with the girls." He chuckled. "Don't tell her I said that."

I nodded, giving him my fullest smile.

"I'm trusting you, son."

"Yes, sir, I understand. I'd be happy to go." Finally. Off the ranch. Change of scenery.

"I'm not sure you completely understand." Mr. Carmichael gripped my good shoulder, hard. "I'm entrusting the well-being of my wife to you. She's the most valuable thing I've got. Also, I insist you stay away from anything that smells or hints of trouble. No drinking, no card games. Avoid Becker if you can. If you see anything, anything at all that might lead to trouble, find Ellie, and leave town."

I nodded again.

He shook my shoulder. "Good. Tomorrow after breakfast you'll take the buckboard—in case she finds lots to buy." He took two steps toward the house then spun back around. "Listen, as you know, Sundays we have church service here. Why not invite your family to join us? Miranda and Smitty always set out a hearty chicken dinner afterward. There's plenty room for four more. It'd be good to see your folks again."

"Yes, sir. I'll ask tomorrow when I'm in town."

Not sure my boots touched ground as I headed for the barn. Me? The boss was trusting *me* with his wife? Allowing me to go into town? And inviting my family to Sunday dinner?

Rake in hand, I pushed around straw and manure. Thoughts returned to the night José had tossed me into one of these stalls and tied my wrist so I couldn't escape and then left me in the dark with the critters. I'd hated him for a week, especially when he made me drink that godawful cure. But, when I came to my senses and realized what he'd done not only for me, but for the rest of the hands, I'd apologized to him as well and told him how grateful I was.

But still, the memory was painful every time I stepped foot inside the barn. And then, as my brain tended to do, it shifted course and thought about Joe. He'd come here that night, having supper with us and then I'd had my meltdown. Something he'd said sprang to the front of my mind. I hadn't thought about it until now. Said he needed to talk. It was important.

My brush with laudanum, fuzzy brain, bad shoulder, had blocked out that until now. How could I be a good big brother if I'd ignored him? My heart grew too large for my chest. I hated myself. How could I treat him that way?

Tomorrow when I went into town, after being sure Mrs. Carmichael was busy shopping, I'd find my brother and see what was so important. That made me feel a little better. But not much.

* * *

BUCKBOARD HITCHED, I waited in front of the ranch house and brushed any remaining dust from my shirt, vest, and hat. I needed to be presentable for such an auspicious occasion. Checking again for the millionth time this morning, all my pay was nestled in my pocket, waiting to be exchanged for something wonderful. Would I get a chance to buy that gun? I'd also need ammunition. What did that cost?

Mr. Carmichael escorted his wife onto the porch. She wore the prettiest dress I'd ever seen, and her hat matched the sky-blue color. She was stunning with her blonde hair braided, pinned up in the back and her blue eyes, reminding me of a lake, matched her dress. If she hadn't been married, I would've courted her. Instantly, I was in love.

Loping over to the porch landing, I held out an arm for lovely Mrs. Ellie Carmichael, old enough to be my ma. She took my extended crooked elbow, looked side to side at her "men." Mr. Carmichael stood on her right.

"Why, thank you, kind sir." She smiled a full-bodied smile at me, then turned to Mr. Carmichael who helped her into the buckboard and arranged her skirt around her shoes. Her radiant cheeks flushed a tinge of pink when she kissed Mr. Carmichael on the cheek. In return, he turned a deeper pink and looked down to investigate the tip of his boot. The love and respect between them were undeniable, and suddenly I longed for a relationship like that. But one thing I knew for sure—I wouldn't find it cloistered here at the ranch.

Mr. Carmichael waved as I flicked the reins over the two horses' backs and started off with a jerk. Not the smoothest way to get going, but no harm done. His wife turned on the hard seat and returned the wave. My stomach clenched, flip-flopped, gurgled, and churned. Not too fitting for a man of my capabilities.

If I'd been alone on a horse, I could've made the trip to town in half an hour. As it was in this buckboard, we could lope, but even so, the trip would take forty-five minutes, maybe longer. We spent the time in small talk, she asking about my shoulder, I wondering how she had come to live on a ranch. Her response was she enjoyed it very much and had been raised on a ranch in Colorado. She and Mr. Carmichael had met at a dance in Denver. I avoided asking about her son, although certainly it was on my mind.

Instead, I asked her about the evening I came riding in after being shot. So many details were fuzzy at best. She filled me in and then surprised me with, "Mr. Carmichael is the one who pulled out that bullet. Neither Miranda nor I could get a grip on it. You'd lost a lot of blood."

He'd never mentioned it. Another thing I had to thank him for.

Her sparkling blue eyes turned to me. "Why does Sheriff Becker seem to dislike you so much?"

How to answer? I chose the quickest one. "A year ago, a friend and me decided to ride up to Austin. We borrowed two horses—just for the day. I happened to pick Becker's. It went lame. Brought it back though, but he still pressed charges. Judge gave me nine months in prison, three months parole saying I was lucky he didn't hang me."

She wagged her head with appropriate tsking. Would she think less of me now? Probably. I considered explaining the rest of his hatred for me which involved my courting his daughter, who was something of a party girl. She was wilder than most, and I found her exciting. But she didn't like me enough to stick around. Guess I wasn't bold enough for her. No, she took up with a New Orleans gambler and off they went. No wonder Becker blamed me. But still.

We rode in silence for a long minute until, like mirages rising from the mist, buildings appeared when we topped a hill. We both grinned.

"Once a month my friends and I have tea at the Imperial Hotel." Mrs. Carmichael opened her purse and studied a pocket watch. "Always at two. Usually, we spend an hour, maybe hour and a half catching up."

I wanted to snicker at what my boss had said about "gossiping with the girls," but I bit my tongue. "Take your time, ma'am."

Since it was now around ten, we decided to go to the mercantile first. But I needed to be honest with her as to why I didn't plan to hang out on the sidewalk until she wanted me to carry packages.

"While you're in there shopping, ma'am, I'm hoping to go find my younger brother over at the telegraph office. Then stop by the house and invite my family to Sunday service and dinner tomorrow." I froze. Had Mr. Carmichael mentioned it to her?

"Of course. Anthony told me he'd invited them. It'll be so good to see your ma again."

Her face lit as she spoke. Was she an angel, or a real person?

I shook my head to rattle the marbles back into place. She regarded me with questions written on her face. I rushed to explain. "I didn't mean no I wouldn't ask. Sometimes I just shake my head."

Boy, did that sound stupid. Why had I become tongue-tied around this woman? She's the one who not only had peeled off my wet, muddy clothes, but sewed up my shoulder. Twice. I should be able to say anything to her.

We pulled up in front of the mercantile. I jumped down, tied the reins to the hitch rail, then helped her down. While her skin was definitely wind-worn, she was beautiful. I was surprised none of the men on the board-walk rushed to her aid.

Keep your eyes straight ahead, I kept telling myself. This lovely dove is taken and has been married longer than you've been alive. I walked her into the store hoping to catch a glimpse of Mary Beth Anderson. Did she still work here? Mrs. Carmichael headed directly to the fabric area, and I followed. Sure enough, I spotted Mary Beth helping another customer.

I stood back, looking at bolts of calico, and without warning, Mary Beth turned her big, brown eyes on me, and her face lit up. "Mr. Nolan. What a pleasant surprise. It's been what? A month since you were in here last?"

She remembered! "Yes, ma'am. Little over a month now."

"Wondered if you'd moved away." She turned to look at Mrs. Carmichael now running her hand down an emerald-green fabric bolt. Before I could answer, she said, "Sorry, I need to help Mrs. Carmichael, one of our best customers."

No doubt she was. Maybe I could get Mary Beth to come to Sunday dinner, too. Before I had the chance, she left me in favor of my boss's wife. All right, there would be time later. I touched Mrs. Carmichael on the elbow. "I'm gonna go find Joe. Be back in thirty minutes, if that's all right with you."

She held up the green bolt. "Wouldn't Mr. Carmichael look good in this color?"

I nodded. What did I know about stuff like that?

"Oh, I'm sorry, Tate." Mrs. Carmichael flashed me a soft grin. "Make it an hour. I've got quite a list."

"Yes ma'am. One hour." I started off then turned back and spoke quietly in her ear. "Please don't go anywhere. Stay right here. All right?"

"Don't worry." She waved me off. "Go find your folks."

As much as I hated to leave, I truly needed to find Joe. This time of day he'd be at the telegraph office. Would he hate me? Never speak to me again?

I navigated through men trucking down the board-walk, women with children in tow. Seemed like everyone was out enjoying the hot, humid day. Across the main road, down three blocks, I found myself at the front of the office. Inside, tap-tap-tapping clacked. How could he stand that racket all day?

Deep breath drawn in, I pushed open the door and cringed at the bell's tinkle. On his high seat perch, Joe looked at me, held up one finger and finished pushing little buttons. Done, he climbed down, jogged over to me, and wrapped me in a bear hug.

All was forgiven, apparently.

He stood back, keeping me at arm's length. "How the heck are you, big brother?"

My grin probably matched his. "Fine, just fine, Joe.

Shoulder's about healed," I leaned in close since I spotted his boss at the other desk, lowered my voice. "Off the medicine too. It was rough, but I'm in control now."

"Good to hear." Joe's brotherly grip on my upper arm was comforting. I hadn't realized how much I'd missed him. Missed the long talks at night after "lights out." How, as kids, we'd plotted and planned to be pirates and plunder ships on the high seas. I struggled to remember my pirate name.

Before I could, he introduced me to his boss, even though we'd met before. He nodded. Joe thumbed over his shoulder. "Mr. Whalen? Mind if Tate and me take a couple minutes outside? I'll be right out here if you need me."

"Go ahead, Joe." His boss waved a hand toward the door.

We stood around the corner, away from the main street. Tension gnawed on my chest. What was so important? Waiting was killing me. "And?" I couldn't help myself. "First of all, I apologize for not listening to what you had to say when you came out to the ranch. Second—"

"She's leaving, Tate. Going with her family to California. Her da's opening a bank up in Sacramento." Joe's mouth tightened. "I'll never see her again."

I'd not seen his grief like that since our old dog died. "Frieda Aertker? That who you're talking about?"

Joe nodded. "They're leaving in ten days."

I scrubbed my freshly shaven chin. What to say? What did he want? "And you want to go with them?" Ma and Da would be sad to see him go. Then again, so would I.

He looked into the sky. "Don't want to. But if it's

staying here and losing her, then I'd go." Sad eyes turned to me. "I intend to marry her. But..." He shrugged. "Don't have enough money, no house. Tate, I can't offer her anything but love."

Feelings from the depths of my soul burbled up. I finally understood my kind-hearted brother. "That's pretty much what Da and Ma had when they came over from Ireland. Besides love, they had me too." I hoped my attempt at levity helped.

Studying something down the side street, Joe sighed. "What do I do, Tate? How can I keep her here?"

"What does she think?"

"Says it's her duty to go with her family." Joe rubbed an eye. "But maybe if we married, her folks wouldn't mind going without her." He seemed to brighten a bit.

"So, go ask her. Right now." Was I giving the best advice? "If she says yes, the rest will fall into place." I rocked his shoulder. "I don't have a place for you two to live, but Ma and Da do. She can move into your bedroom. It won't be ideal, just temporary."

He looked down. "Don't have much money. Fifty, maybe."

Now I knew where to spend my pay. I could buy a gun next month. I dug around in my vest pocket and pulled out thirty dollars. I'd keep five, which I thought was fair. I gripped his hand and plunked the bills into his open palm. "This is for you and Frieda to help start your new life with."

A tear rolled down his cheek while pressure behind my eyes caused me to blink more than usual. A hearty hug took the wind out of me. I hugged back.

Released, Joe started for the office. "I'll ask Mr. Whalen for half an hour off. This can't wait for lunch."

"By the way." In all the excitement, I'd almost

forgotten about tomorrow's doings. "Mr. Carmichael's invited our whole family to come out to the ranch for Sunday service and then a picnic. Miranda's fried chicken is delicious."

Stopping, he turned back to me. "Can I bring Frieda? We could announce our engagement then." His face blossomed into pure sunshine.

I nodded as he trotted off.

CHAPTER SEVENTEEN

TEN MINUTES LATE. TEN MINUTES. I TORE UP Main Street leaping over mounds of fresh road apples and kicking at excited dogs nipping my boot heels. I'd spent way too much time visiting with Ma. Her freshly baked sugar cookies and hot tea had caused the tardiness. She'd shared town gossip and I'd asked too many questions. Fortunately, I'd remembered to invite her for tomorrow, and she assured me they'd all come.

But ten minutes felt more like ten years. Was Mrs. Carmichael all right? Was she waiting for me at the mercantile's door, foot tapping, glancing at her watch every two minutes? She'd scold me and make sure I'd never drive her anywhere again. My fault. Should've watched Ma's Regulator more closely.

Half a block from the store, I spotted two old men sitting in chairs on the porch next to the door. No Ellie Carmichael waiting impatiently. At least not that I could see. I added speed and slid slightly past the door, all the time the men watching. I grabbed a sign on the side of the door which helped me slow. I stopped. A big breath in, shoulders thrown back, I stepped into the store as if I didn't know I was late. Now to find Mrs. Boss.

I checked the fabric area. No Ellie. Pick and shovel aisles? Empty. No woman stood behind barrels brimming with shiny nails. Where was she? A twinge of panic climbed to my throat and stuck there. A clerk I didn't recognize approached.

"Can I help you find something, sir?"

Nodding, I hoped to hide my panic. "Looking for Mrs. Carmichael. Supposed to meet her here." Another survey of the store revealed no Ellie.

The clerk turned side to side. "Huh. She was here a moment ago." She shrugged. "Must've left."

"Left? As in gone? Are you saying she's gone? Where'd she go to? Did she leave with someone?" My concern escalated into pure panic.

"I'm sorry, I—"

"Thank you, Ms. Anderson. You've been a great help." Mrs. Carmichael's voice.

I spun halfway around. And there she was, coming out from a curtained area behind the counter, Mary Beth following on her heels. Mrs. Carmichael clutched a small box in her hand. Both women were smiling, so I figured nothing out of the ordinary had happened. No attempted robbery of the store. No armed men coming in looking for unescorted women to harass. Nothing untoward.

However, still panicked, in my mind I bolted over the counter, past the clerk, knocking over a jar of gumdrops to rescue them. But hopefully, what they actually saw was me, no cares in the world, sauntering their way.

We met at the register counter where I spotted boxes of various sizes stacked sky high. One guess who they belonged to. I waited while she paid for the goods, then choose a few of the bigger ones to cart off first.

Now, buckboard close to full, Mrs. Carmichael, Mary Beth and I stood at the hitch rail, Mary Beth shielding her eyes from the sun while she had a last-minute chat with Ellie. I'd wanted to speak with the lovely clerk alone, but I guessed it wouldn't happen this trip. Instead, I tipped my hat at her. "See you soon, I hope."

"I'd like that." Mary Beth flashed a disarming smile and disappeared into the store. My heart did a baby bird flutter.

I helped Mrs. Carmichael onto the buckboard seat. "Where to now ma'am?"

She pointed toward the end of town. "How about lunch at Delilah's Café? My treat."

My stomach growled an answer. "That's kind of you, but I couldn't let you pay." I picked up the reins but her hand on my arm stopped me.

"Nonsense." Her words were smooth like a lake in summer. "It's the least I can do for having you drive all the way out here and back. I'm sure there's other things you'd rather be doing."

"No ma'am, not really." Did I stutter? "But thank you, kindly. I'll take you up on an offer of food."

Sitting at a cloth-covered table topped with a small vase of yellow flowers, we spent a pleasant hour chatting. Eating something besides Smitty's stew was a true pleasure although a piece of ham stuck in my back tooth, and I tried to mind my manners not to pick or suck at it. The sugary sweet potatoes had come from heaven, obviously. And I could've eaten the entire white cake with buttercream frosting. It was almost as good as the pastries at the bakery. I made a mental note to buy some today if I could. The boys at the bunkhouse would be mighty surprised and grateful.

She took out her pocket watch, glanced at the time

and shut the case. "This has been a delightful hour and a half, Tate." She hesitated. "You don't mind me calling you by your first name, do you?"

"No ma'am." Heat rose to my face. "I'm pleased."

"Good. Then Tate it is." She stood, pushing her chair back while it screeched across the wooden floor. "It's about time to have tea. I've been so looking forward to it."

I jumped to my feet hoping to run around the table fast enough to hold the chair for her, but she had already pushed it in by the time I got to her. She set coins on the table, took my arm, and out we went.

I'd never been inside the Imperial Hotel. Never knew anyone who'd stayed there, and I definitely couldn't have afforded to eat there, even just for tea. So, when I opened the door which had to be ten, twelve feet tall, my mouth opened too. The ceiling, painted sky blue with little cherubs dancing across it, must have been fifteen, twenty feet high. Silver and red striped tufted wallpaper adorned the walls in an unimaginable opulence. Brocade wing-back chairs graced the room and a round mahogany table held an extravagant spray of flowers. All at once, I felt rich and poor. How could two such feelings flow over me at one time? The desk clerk across the lobby greeted us like old friends.

"Ah, Mrs. Carmichael and sir. Delightful to see you again." He beamed rushing toward us, his gloved hand outstretched.

Mrs. Carmichael took it and shook ever so daintily. She smiled. "Good to see you again, too, Mr. Bertram." Turning toward me, she nodded. "And this is Mr. Nolan. He works for us at the ranch. He's been good enough to drive me into town today."

"Nolan." Was my name uttered between clenched

teeth? Part of his lip pulled up into a sneer, then his eyes cocked toward Mrs. Carmichael, his mouth turned into a straight line. Mr. Bertram took my hand, squeezing, crushing until I pried myself loose. He let go and used that hand to point to our right. "A few of your friends are already here, Mrs. Carmichael. Let me take you to them."

Wondering what I'd done to aggravate this perfect stranger, I followed Mrs. Carmichael and him to a separate dining room where four, maybe five tables took up most of the space. Three women at one table waved, two stood while we wound our way past a table filled with well-dressed men. Obviously bankers or some such.

Mrs. Carmichael smiled and returned the wave. She hugged the women, introduced me and sat when I pulled out a chair for her. I bent near her, hoping to speak quietly enough. With the other women all talking, I figured they wouldn't listen anyway.

"I'll be right outside, Mrs. Carmichael. I don't plan to go anywhere." Straightening up, I tipped my hat to the four women. "Enjoy your tea, ladies."

Tittering and whispered words came my way as I walked off. I took in snatches of "good looking," and "where did you find him?" Were they talking about me? I hoped so. I stood straighter.

Determined to stay out of trouble, I parked myself on a bench outside, next to the door. From this point at the far end of the street, I could see most everyone coming my way. Relaxing in the portico's shade, I wondered what the women inside were talking about. Lulled by the warmth and full stomach, I stretched out my legs, tilted my hat down over my eyes, and closed them.

"Is that you, Tate Nolan? Say it isn't so." A woman's voice opened my eyes. I looked up into a face I recognized but couldn't believe.

Easing to my feet, I took off my hat, ran a hand through my hair. I must've blinked a million times. There stood a woman and a girl, about seven or eight, I figured.

"It's you, isn't it Tate?"

I nodded, words refusing to come.

She flashed a wide smile showing her teeth. "You don't recognize me, I bet. Imogene? Imogene Daley."

Boy howdy, now I did. She was the first girl I'd ever bedded, proud of the fact I was fourteen at the time. She was fifteen. I swallowed hard.

Unsure whether to hug her, stick out my hand to shake, or simply melt into the boardwalk, I stood still, studying her and then the little girl holding her hand. Her daughter? Had to be.

Somehow, I found my voice, although I was sure it was several octaves above normal. "Imogene? My God. Good to see you. Thought the world had swallowed you up. You just disappeared, if I remember right."

Her brown eyes were every bit as brown as I remembered. We'd known each other in school, and I'd made it my mission she'd be my first conquest. I'd walked her home daily for a few months and stayed an hour or so before her da came home from work. We were alone, her ma having passed on years before. Well, nature took its course. We'd had many passionate after-school sessions.

Since her da didn't allow visitors in the house unless he was home, the stream bank near the house had made a soft alternative to a bed. And then right as school term was done, so were we. She vanished from town. Her house sat empty, and eventually another family moved in. I thought about her often, then not so often, and up until a few minutes ago, rarely.

"You're back." I warbled the obvious.

She put one hand behind her back, something she'd

done when I'd known her. "Not back to stay. We are passing through, and I was hoping I'd see you." She glanced down at the girl. "I wanted you to meet my daughter. Louisa Margaret. She's almost eight."

Even I could do the math. My heart about exploded right out of my chest which was impossible since ice water attacked my body. I shook off total shock, stuck out a hand to the girl. "Louisa. Pretty name for a pretty girl."

She smiled a shy smile and ducked behind Imogene's skirt.

I raised my eyes up to meet Imogene's. As quietly as I knew how, I asked, "You sure?"

She nodded. "For sure. No one else."

I wasn't surprised no one else had tried to get under her petticoats. In school, she was fairly homely, not popular, and an average student. But looking at her now, she'd grown into her own kind of pretty.

"We're on our way to California, probably. At least somewhere west." She glanced at the empty bench and settled Louisa there while she continued to explain. "Pa died last spring and it's just the two of us now. Thought we'd head west and here we are."

"Sorry about your da."

From the bench, Louisa scraped her feet against the boardwalk. "My papa's gone. I cried."

Imogene touched my arm. "Was hoping to see you. Introduce you two." She rushed her words. "I'm not asking for support, or help. Don't want to interfere in your life. Just thought you should know."

A different female voice came up behind me. "Is Mrs. Carmichael still at tea?" I whirled around and almost plowed into Mary Beth Anderson. She halted. "Oh, my apologies. I interrupted."

Imogene saved the awkward situation. She flashed a smile, held out a hand. "No worry. We're old friends, just catching up. I'm Imogene Daley."

"Pleased to meet you." Mary Beth nodded, smiled at Louisa, then pointed to the hotel. "I told Mrs. Carmichael I'd let her know if I could come tomorrow."

"And?" I'd finally found my mouth but was surprised a word came out.

"I'd be delighted to."

I turned to Imogene and invited her too. She immediately said yes.

"Great!" Mary Beth's smile produced one lone dimple on her left cheek and turned to Imogene. "How about I drive since I know the way?"

"Thank you. We don't have a buggy here."

Oh boy. This would be quite the party. I vaguely wondered how Smitty and Miranda would feel when they're told how many more mouths they'd be feeding.

Imogene opened her mouth to say more but her gaze riveted behind me. Before I could turn to see what had caught her attention, something round and hard pressed into my back. I grunted.

"Hands up. High." Becker's voice. Now what the hell? I did as commanded and then pivoted around to face him. The women stepped back.

"Now what, Sheriff? There's no law against standing on the boardwalk talking to ladies. Is there?" My arms drooped.

A distinctive click of a gun being cocked brought up my arms until I was sure I could touch the sun. Becker patted my vest pockets and pulled out my five-dollar Liberty head coin. He held it up, turning my money front to back allowing the sun to glint off the shine.

"That's mine, Becker. Part of my pay." Why did I feel

the need to explain? I looked down at my chest and at the gun pointed within inches. A twitch of his finger and I'd be dead. I chose to be polite, especially in front of the women. But if I'd had a gun…

Becker used the coin to thump my nose. "This is part of what was stolen just now from the café. Ten dollars is missing and now I've found half." His hand dug into my other pocket again. "Where's the rest?"

"Café? Missing? The rest?" Heat pounded my head. Anger built and I fought to push it down. I spoke through gritted teeth. "Mrs. Carmichael paid. We left. I didn't take any money." My arms sagged a bit and I felt silly standing like that with more and more bystanders stopping to stare.

"Nah. You did. This is proof."

As if that wasn't bad enough, I spotted that no-good deputy of his, Walter Wagner, gun pulled, come loping across the street, making a beeline for us. A shiver, then I turned to Mary Beth and Imogene. "I can explain. It's what's left of my pay from Mr. Carmichael. I gave the rest to my brother."

"Cuff him, Deputy." Becker eased down the hammer on his Colt. I relaxed my arms and Wagner yanked them behind my back. My shoulder wound caught fire and I wondered if it had broken open again. Sure felt that way.

"Sheriff Becker." Mary Beth moved in closer, her eyes wide and sad at the same time. "I'm sure he didn't steal that money. He's a good man."

While I appreciated her standing up for me, it was wasted breath. I was on my way to jail, a trial, and a noose, in that order. I'd never see my brother get married or my daughter grow up, which was a foreign thought.

Wagner locked too-tight iron handcuffs around my wrists. Within seconds, my fingers turned numb. All sorts of curse words circled my head and while I was choosing which ones would be best, Mrs. Carmichael and her girlfriends opened the hotel door and stepped out. All froze. And gasped.

"Mrs. Carmichael!" I prayed she could pound sense into Becker's addled brain. "He says I stole money from the café. But I didn't. You were there."

"Sheriff Becker." Mrs. Carmichael drew in a deep breath, narrowed her eyes, and lowered her eyebrows. That bull was about to charge. "I was with him the entire time. We walked out together." She looked at her friends, then Mary Beth, Imogene, me and before glaring at Becker. "Release him right now. I insist."

"No ma'am." Becker gripped my upper right arm, now turning numb, too. "He's a scalawag, a thief, a liar, and...a murderer. I'll see to it this time he hangs."

If it hadn't been so dire, I would have laughed at his theatrics and the huffing I heard from the congregated women. A knot in my chest threatened to rise.

"Fact is, he's going to jail right now." Becker planted a meaty hand on my back, roughly shoving me forward.

Before we could get too many steps in the jail's direction, a man I didn't recognize rushed toward the crowd. Great. One more person to complain about me. Half a block away, he waved his arm like flagging down a buggy. "Sheriff Becker! Becker. Wait!"

We halted, all of us in this Pied Piper-like throng. Would he now say I'd robbed the mercantile, bakery, saddle shop and also the bank? I vowed right then and there that if I got out of this mess, I'd start robbing. I'd been accused, might as well do it for real.

Out of breath, the man stood in front of Becker. "Sheriff," he wheezed. "Glad I caught you in time."

"Oh? He steal more money?"

The man shook his head. "No. I made a mistake. I'm not missing any money. Nobody robbed me." He looked at me. "Found the ten dollars under a napkin."

"Huh." Obviously unhappy, Becker's frown moved into a scowl. "You sure?"

Nodding, the man turned to me. "I apologize, Mr. Nolan. I pointed my finger at you because of...well, because of your reputation. I assumed it was you." He stuck out a hand. "I'm sorry."

I couldn't shake with my hands cuffed behind me and even if I could, wasn't sure I would.

Mrs. Carmichael took his outstretched hand. "Thank you, Mr. Hennessey, for coming forward. I knew Mr. Nolan hadn't taken your money."

A collective sigh ran through the group when those handcuffs came off. I rubbed my wrists then my shoulder while Becker and his minion marched off, defeated for the moment. They'd be back, I was sure.

CHAPTER EIGHTEEN

THE ROAD BACK HAD STRETCHED FROM A FEW miles into thousands, Mrs. Carmichael and I passing most of the time in silence. My head, full of questions, doubts, panic, wishing I was somewhere else far away, didn't make for good conversation. She'd apologized for the café owner's behavior which I'd nodded and grunted at.

I fumed over the fact Becker had kept my five dollars. In all the commotion, I'd forgotten to demand its return. But losing the money only added to my other concerns.

What was I going to do about Imogene, Louisa, and Mary Beth? What about Joe and Frieda? Those two were the least of my worries. More than once I turned to ask Mrs. Carmichael her opinion, tell her what I'd gotten myself into, but words wouldn't form. If they had, no doubt she'd think less of me than she already did.

About the time I figured we'd missed the turnoff and we'd be seeing the outskirts of San Antone any minute, the ranch road appeared. I reined the horses right and we trotted down the dusty path. My rear was about as flat as a flapjack and needed a good rub. Anticipating a get down, unloading the wagon, and then supper, I let out quite the sigh when the ranch house popped into view.

Before arriving at the main house, Mrs. Carmichael touched my arm. "Tate. I've been thinking." She gave me a full-out stare, those blue eyes concerned. "I apologize for asking you to drive me today. Looks like the town wasn't ready for you to return. Maybe it's too soon after...well, after Becker accused you of murder. I'd hoped otherwise."

I shrugged and pulled rein in front of the house. "Other than that, it was a most interesting day." *Interesting* being an understatement. "No major harm done."

Before I could say more, Mr. Carmichael appeared on the porch and then bounded down the steps. He helped her out before I could and held her at arm's length. "Looks like you had a marvelous day, my dear."

She glanced at me, gave her husband a wide smile and a peck on the cheek. "I did. But missed you."

He slid an arm around her waist and guided her toward the door. "I'll bet you're exhausted." He looked back at me and smiled. "All that shopping and tea drinking. Exhausting."

They disappeared into the house, and I looked at the mound of packages to be unloaded. I untied the ropes holding them down and, like a miracle, another ranch hand appeared. We had the wagon bed empty in no time.

My stomach rumbled and grumbled. Surprisingly, Smitty's stew was calling.

Supper finished, the pots, pans and dishes demanded to be washed. Smitty and I dug into the chore with less gusto than when cooking. I held up a pan, swiped it once with an old dish towel.

"Tate." José's voice stopped me. I looked behind me

and he had his thumb pointed toward the main house. "Boss wants you."

Now what? "I'll see him when I finish drying."

"He says now."

Bollocks. I shrugged to Smitty whose frown showed he was definitely not happy at me or maybe at life in general. I nodded to the ranch foreman. "Be right there."

Before I could gather all my thoughts, trying to put them in some sort of order, I found myself in Mr. Carmichael's office. A wide mahogany desk, papers piled on top, took up half the room. A brown and blue-striped rug under foot relaxed my back. Before I could take a longer look, Mr. Carmichael walked in, coffee cup in each hand. He closed the door with a boot heel, handed me a cup and pointed his toward a leather chair near the desk.

We both sat, sipped, before he started. "Looks like tomorrow's going to be quite the party." He raised eyebrows. "Not sure Smitty or Miranda are too happy. But it'll work out just fine."

I nodded, sipped, nodded again, not sure where this was leading.

Fingers steepled, he leaned forward, elbows resting on the desk. "Heard there was trouble with Becker. Again. Also heard it clearly wasn't your fault."

"Yes, sir." Deciding to explain as much as my heart could handle, I let it all out. I told him about Imogene, Louisa, my money, the accusation, and Joe's dilemma. I opened up and no doubt my voice trembled. And then everything crashed in on me. I rubbed my eyes, my shoulder, my temples.

My boss sighed, leaned back, studied his coffee cup. Something outside the window caught his attention, although it was now dark. He sighed again and finally looked at me. "First off, thank you for letting me know. For confiding in me. I'm sure it wasn't easy."

Easy? No, it wasn't, but truthfully, it was easier than telling Da. But I nodded anyway. "I'm not ready to settle down. Get married, have a family." I couldn't look into his eyes. "Don't have any money, no future…" I managed to glance at his face. "Except what you've given me here."

"It's a start, Tate." Mr. Carmichael held his cup. "You intend to make her an honest woman? Marry her?"

Shrugging, a knot blocked my chest. I couldn't breathe. "Not sure. It's the right thing to do, I guess, but she's not insisting on it." I blinked harder than usual. "Mr. Carmichael, I don't even know her. Not really."

"We're not the same people at fourteen that we are at twenty-two. You're right." He stood. "You have a lot to consider." He walked around the desk and gripped my upper arm as I stood.

Once again, I nodded. Words difficult to form.

He opened the door, then stopped. "You've been rubbing your shoulder quite a bit. Hurts?"

"Deputy Wagner yanked my hands behind me. Hard. I think it pulled the stitched-up place open."

"I'll have Miranda look at it. Mrs. Carmichael's already retired for the night." He lightly chuckled. "Must be exhausted from all that gossip and tea drinking."

I gave a grin I didn't feel.

Sure enough, my shoulder had been bleeding, but not much. My shirt was stained but the blood hadn't gone through to my vest. While she worked on my shoulder, Miranda clucked about having too many people tomorrow, part of the rant in Spanish, and how dare the deputy treat me so roughly. She smoothed a salve over the incision, bandaged it and helped me slip on my shirt. All this in the warmth of the kitchen where aromas of cooked steak and potatoes still lingered. Despite the pain, I smiled at the sense of security it provided.

I thanked her, helped her put the medical supplies away, then slipped out the front door. Maybe Smitty would have the dishes done by the time I returned.

* * *

I TOSSED and turned all night. Sleep evaded me like a mutt I'd thrown rocks at. Visions of Imogene and Louisa haunted me. Not once in these past eight years had I imagined the consequences of my teenaged activities. A baby? How was that even possible? It wasn't. I'd been so young. And why did *that* have to happen? Immediately, I regretted thinking of Louisa as a "that." What kind of low-down skunk would think that way? Apparently, I would.

And what about a future? Should I offer to marry her? With what? All I had in the world, money-wise, was seven dollars left from the robbery, unless Joe spent it. Seven. I had no place to call my own, no money, no gun. What *could* I offer? Love? Like Ma and Da? Like Joe? No, not yet. But I could offer respect. And what about Louisa?

I got up, stumbled into the bunkhouse kitchen, bumping into only one table, found a coffee cup, and poured what was left from last night's supper. I sat at the long table, head in hand, and sipped the cold, brown brew.

I'd sat maybe an hour, with no answers, when Smitty wandered into the kitchen. I glanced through the swatted-fly-streaked window and spotted wisps of yellow and gold in the east. Time to make breakfast.

Smitty grunted orders and I did what was asked, but mainly kept quiet. Nothing I could do would please or appease him right now. I'd been depressed before, but nothing compared to the way I was feeling now. Maybe I could simply ride away during church service this morning. No. I didn't own a horse and as I'd learned, stealing —or *borrowing*—one brings jail time, or the noose. Could I walk away?

Now that held possibilities. I examined the soles of my boots. Sturdy enough to get me out of here.

What was I thinking? Was I the kind of man who ran away from problems? Wasn't I man enough to face what I'd done? The three-year-old inside me screamed *run away*. The adult inside demanded I stay and figure this out.

I hated being an adult.

Breakfast over and cleaned up, I helped set up chairs and tables under a wooden shade cover that seemed to stretch forever. In reality, it was at least twenty by thirty, plenty of room for everyone to get out of the sun. In the four weeks I'd been at this ranch, I'd seen it used for church services and Sunday chicken. Today would be a special day, what with Joe announcing his engagement. Or so I hoped. Maybe I'd be announcing mine, too.

I shuddered and rethought.

At the communal washstand in the bunkhouse, I scrubbed my hands and face, shaved, and splashed on Rowlands' Kalydor aftershave. Feeling like a new man, or at least a clean one, I slipped into my Sunday shirt, the one Ma had made, tucked it in, then stepped into sunshine.

Most of the ranch hands were already mingling under the shade, smelling chicken cooking on a grill. Miranda marched back and forth in front of it, turning the fryers side to side.

"Smells delicious!" I gave her my best smile. "Some secret ingredients in there?"

"*No sé.*" She shrugged and waved a fork under my nose. "*Voy a nunca contar.*"

Before I could ask what she'd said, Ma and Da drove into the yard, Joe and Frieda in the back of the rented buggy. Eagan, shoulders held back, rode Da's horse right behind.

We gave hugs all around before Mrs. Carmichael greeted them. "So happy you could come," she gushed.

Mrs. C., as I'd started to think of her, ushered the five into the shade and pointed at chairs.

"Please make yourselves comfortable. I've got lemonade in the house."

"I'll help." I bounded up the steps, leaving my family to choose where to sit. I met Mrs. C. in the kitchen. I picked up a tray with filled glasses, then stopped when she put a hand on my arm.

"Thank you for yesterday. Again. I'm sorry there was some misunderstanding and unpleasantness. But I hope you can drive me into town again—maybe in a few months."

I about dropped the tray. She asked me to drive her again? That was quite the compliment, but would Mr. C. feel the same way? Probably not since I'd spilled my guts to him last night. Shouldn't have told him. What was I thinking?

But that darn Becker. Would he ever leave me alone? Somehow, I'd take him down. Somehow, I'd show him to be the bully he really was. Somehow—

"Tate? You're a bit pale." Mrs. C. picked up another tray. "You coming down with something?"

"I'm fine, ma'am. Maybe my shoulder, a bit." I headed for the door. "But really, I'm fine."

Feeling like one of those fancy, towel-covering-the-arm servers, I extended the tray to each of the guests. Glasses distributed, I headed back to the house for more when another buggy drove into the yard. Mary Beth Anderson at the reins and Imogene next to her. In back, sat little Louisa. Thank goodness the tray was empty. I dropped it in the dirt, scrambled to retrieve it while waving at them.

In the back of my mind, I'd hoped one, if not both women, would suddenly have "other plans" and not be able to come. But no, here they were. I trotted over to help them down, having to choose which one first. Imogene won since she was already halfway out by the time I gathered enough wit to extend a hand. Mary Beth looped the reins around the brake and allowed me to put my hands around her slim waist and set her on the ground. Louisa jumped out all on her own and, wide-eyed, gazed around the ranch.

"This where you grow horses?" She started for the stable, then peered over the fence at horses in a distant pasture.

I chuckled, seeing the world for the first time through a child's eyes. "We sure do. Not only do we have horses, but we have cows and chickens and dogs and cats."

She turned to her mom. "Can I go see them now? Pretty please?"

Like a savior from heaven, Eagan appeared, thumped my good shoulder. "Who you got here, big brother?" He kneeled by Louisa. "I'm Eagan. What's your name?"

She glanced at Imogene who nodded. "Louisa Margaret Daley." And immediately continued, "Are those horses yours? Do you live here? My papa died and he said I can ride a horse, but he never let me and now he died, but I still want to ride a horse…"

She droned on, giving Eagan her full attention. I tied the horse to the rail and pointed the ladies toward the shade. "I'm on lemonade duty. Be right back."

I bolted into the house, safe for the moment. When I ventured outside, to my chagrin, I found my mother chatting with Mary Beth and Imogene—together! The women in my life were surely ganging up on me, plotting how to get even for me being so darn dumb.

Tray in hand, I offered lemonade to Mary Beth and then Imogene, both smiling. Ma held her glass and the three continued talking as if I weren't standing there. I passed among the other attendees, made sure to speak to Frieda and Joe and Da, then took the last glass and found an empty chair.

An iterant preacher stood in front of the assembled group waiting for everyone to take a seat. Without warning, Mary Beth sat on my right, Imogene on my left with Louisa next to her, and Ma right behind. Surrounded!

I got through the rambling, preaching, amens and two songs. The knot in my stomach took its time rising to my throat so that by the final "amen," I was speechless.

Mary Beth turned to me. "That was wonderful, Mr. Nolan. I've had the best time. Thank you for inviting me."

"You're welcome." A thought crossed what was left of my mind. "You're not leaving so soon, are you? You haven't eaten yet." Maybe she had to scoot back to town right away. As much as I'd wanted to spend time with her, today wasn't the day.

"Leave?" She leaned back like she was offended, but her blue-green eyes told me otherwise. "Not until I've eaten all the chicken and mashed potatoes around here. Smells heavenly, doesn't it?"

I pulled in a long sniff and nodded. "It does at that."

Imogene tapped my arm. "Would you mind if I took Louisa to the stable? She's dying to see the horses."

"Kind of stinky in there." I wrinkled my nose at the youngster. "Should be fine. The cats don't like to be touched, but those two dogs are friendly."

Standing, Imogene offered her hand to her daughter and the two headed for the animals. Alone now with Mary Beth, I stuttered and stammered. "I apologize for Sheriff Becker yesterday. He's determined to see me behind bars or at the end of a noose." I shrugged. "Don't know why." Would I be struck by lightning for lying?

"You seem like an honest, responsible man." She looked over her shoulder toward Joe and Frieda. "Like your brother. I know him from the telegraph office."

"You do?"

She nodded. "And your father and other brother from the butcher's." Her face lit up. "It's a small town and we all know each other. Especially when women come shopping, I hear all the town gossip."

That meant she'd heard of me. But she'd come out here anyway. I guessed that said

something. I touched her hand. "I'd like to take you to supper or for a buggy ride or something like that. But I have to stay here at the ranch."

"I know."

Of course she would. Small town and all that. "But next month, when I get paid, I'll come by and maybe we can get dessert at that pastry shop."

A smile lit up her face. "I'd love that." She eased to her feet. "I'm already looking forward to it."

Joe and Frieda walked up to us. Out of habit I introduced them, but Mary Beth and Joe said they had met already. Frieda kept a tight grip on Joe's hand.

"We have news." Joe lowered his voice and leaned in. "Frieda said yes."

"Hooray!" I shouted but then realized it wasn't for the public to know. "Set a date?"

Frieda gazed at Joe, a good foot taller than her. "I'm going with my family in nine days. Moving to Denver."

"At least that's better than California." Joe eased an arm around her slim shoulders and pulled her close. "We decided...that in six months I'll go up to Denver. We'll get married there. Then we'll come back here."

"Six months'll give you time to make arrangements." That was good news, indeed. "Well, congratulations you two." I hugged Frieda even though I probably shouldn't have been quite so forward. But I hugged Joe, too. "Ma and Da know?"

"Not yet. But soon."

Mary Beth shook hands with both Joe and Frieda. "Six months. That'll be, let's see—"

"January first." Frieda leaned into my brother. "Thought we'd start the new year as newlyweds."

I thought for sure she would melt right into his arms, or he into hers.

CHAPTER NINETEEN

STOMACHS FULL, EVERYONE HAD WANDERED OFF either to the bunkhouse for a much-deserved nap, or to rearrange the chairs and sit together in the shade, enjoying the slight, cooling breeze. Unusual for a July day, there was not enough wind to kick up dust and dirt, but the right amount to make staying outside rather pleasant.

As expected, my folks were delighted to hear Joe and Frieda's good news. Under the shade, we stood in a circle as a family of six now, Frieda included, all talking at once. Ma and Frieda plotted details and beamed at each other, while we four men bobbed heads, studied the sky, and hemmed and hawed about nothing. Eagan, the most animated of the group, thumped Joe on the back, then the shoulder, then the head until the two of them got into a wrestling match. Just like when we were kids.

Da and I stood back watching the antics. Although my shoulder was about healed up after yesterday's run-in with Deputy Wagner, it needed more time to mend.

However, if Joe or Eagan pulled me in, I'd have to do my share of wrestling. But fortunately, they didn't.

They stopped when Mr. C. strode over and joined our group. He shook hands with Da. "Glad you could come today, Ciernan. This is much more pleasant, under better circumstances, than the last time you came."

Da turned his green eyes on me. "It's the truth you be speakin'. Good to see Tate is well again."

Mr. C. nodded, then pointed at Joe and Eagan now both upright, brushing off dirt. "I see where Tate gets his spunk from."

"The lads have always shown gumption and pride." His Irish accent was thick today. Or maybe I hadn't been around him long enough lately to get used to it. "But," Da went on, "they're hard workers, they are. All my boys." He hooked his thumbs into his suspenders. "Take after their ol' da, they do."

Mr. C. laughed. "I can see that." He cocked his head toward me. "This one's a fine hand around here. He works hard and doesn't cause trouble. Or too much trouble." He glanced at me then back to Da. "But he keeps me on my toes."

"That he does!" Da's smile reached his eyes. "That he does!"

Mr. C. shook again with Da and then my brothers. He turned to me. "Need to see you before you turn in tonight."

"Yes, sir." I wondered what I'd done this time or maybe not done.

Before I had time to truly think, Imogene and Louisa wandered over. Da and the boys went in search of more lemonade. On the far side of the shade, Ma, Mary Beth, and Mrs. C. sat in deep conversation, which left me alone with Imogene and her daughter. Why did I feel cornered?

Because I was. This was the time now to have a conversation with Imogene. But I didn't want to have it with the little girl right there.

And like an angel again, Eagan, glass in hand, walked up. He handed the lemonade to Louisa. "You ever go bird nest hunting?" He pointed toward cottonwoods near the stream.

"Uh uh." She shook her head, sipped the cool liquid. "What's that?"

"We look up in the branches and count the nests. Haven't you done that before?"

"Uh uh."

Eagan held out a hand. "Then it's time you did." He turned to Imogene. "You mind?"

"Not at all. Have fun."

How did my brother know when he was so needed? I didn't take long to think about that. Imogene and I had matters to discuss. I led her to chairs in a corner of the shade and we sat, knee to knee. What to say? How to say it? We both started and stopped, smiled, frowned, gazed at the sky, a bird flying past, a horse whinnying. Anywhere but at each other.

Imogene gathered her courage sooner than I could. She leaned in close. "As I told you yesterday, I don't need anything from you. I'm not looking to make you marry me or anything like that." She straightened her skirt now bunched under her shoes. "I simply wanted you to meet your daughter."

"Does she know?"

"No. She's asked about a pa once in a while, so last time I told her he was gone. She thought that meant dead, and I left it there."

It struck me that letting her go on believing her da was dead wasn't right. But telling her about me, maybe wasn't right either. At least not yet. But soon. As she grew older, she had a right to know the truth.

"Been doing a lot of thinking about this." I almost reached for her hand, then thought better. "I have nothing to offer you. No worthwhile income, no home. I don't even own a horse." Or a gun.

"And we don't know each other." She blinked hard at me. "Not really."

I let out a hard sigh. "My thoughts exactly." At this point I needed to come clean about my past, the trouble I'd been into. "I came to this ranch—"

"I heard. You stole a horse—"

"Borrowed."

"*Borrowed* a horse, went to prison, got out, worked at the livery stable, got accused of murder, acquitted and now you're here." Her entire face showed concern, empathy, and humor all at once.

"That's about it. How'd you know?"

"Small town. I asked around." Imogene lowered her voice. "You've got quite the reputation. Not good, I'm afraid."

That piece of gossip wasn't what I needed to hear. "Becker's determined to see me at the end of a noose."

"And just for borrowing his horse." She chuckled a smile lighting up her eyes. "Some men are so unreasonable."

I relaxed. Maybe she wouldn't judge. "All that doesn't bother you?"

She took time replying. "Honestly? It does, but I saw how Becker treated you. It's clear how he feels."

The question on my mind couldn't wait. "So…" And this was a big question. "What now?"

"I'd wanted to go to California, but when I talked to Frieda, thought I'd go with them to Denver."

"Nice place, I hear. But cold."

She continued like I hadn't interrupted. "But then I talked to Mary Beth and your ma."

Great. Well, despite what she'd said, I heard church bells in my near future. "And?" My heart thudded against the rib cage.

"Mary Beth said I could probably get a job at the mercantile and your ma said she'd heard talk of another dress shop opening up. I can sew. Fact is, I'm pretty good. Made this dress myself." She stood and twirled. For the first time I noticed the twilight blue color with tiny flowers all over. Neckline was modest and the waist tucked in well.

"Quite nice!"

"Thank you." She remained standing, so I pushed up to my feet too. Should I kiss her, shake hands, bow?

Imogene turned toward the trees where Eagan and Louisa were gazing upward. "I think we'll stay here in Blanco Hill for a while. Mary Beth says we can stay with her until I find a house to rent. Says there's one coming up soon. I'll see about a job, and you can get to know your daughter."

I gulped. I didn't mean to, it just happened. "Fine," I warbled. "I won't be coming into town for at least a few months."

"I know." She flashed a quick grin. "Small town."

Unusual for me, a thought sprang to mind. "How about you and Louisa come out next Sunday for church? I can show her more horses and maybe, just maybe, let her ride one. Would that be all right?"

"If I can arrange things, we'll come. Assuming the Carmichaels don't mind."

"I'm sure they won't."

* * *

IN THE BUNKHOUSE, I dried the last pot, folded the towel over a chair, and headed for my bunk. It crossed my mind I'd almost forgotten Mr. C. asked to see me. Hopefully, it wasn't too late. I grabbed my hat and marched over to the main house. Lights were still ablaze, so I knew at least someone was still awake. I knocked. Miranda answered the door.

She nodded toward his office where he met me at the door.

"Sit down, Tate." He pointed to the chair in front of his desk while he took the one behind it.

I stifled a yawn. No sleep last night and a full day today was taking its toll. Twelve hours in the bunk would be welcomed. If only...

Mr. C. sat up straight although his shoulders slumped a bit. "Got word today that three men from Stinson's ranch have been arrested. Sheriff Samuels would like you to go into town, San Antone, and see if you can identify them."

He paused, waiting for the news to sink in, I guess. Or maybe he was figuring how to give me really bad news. Was I going to be arrested? I studied his face for answers, but the only thing there was fatigue.

When he didn't supply more information, I pressed on. "Of course. Happy to." And I was more than happy. Ecstatic wasn't something I would say aloud. But finally, justice would win. "You'll be going, too?"

Nodding, he rubbed both eyes and stifled a yawn behind the back of his hand. "Think I'll take José too. No telling what Stinson has in mind or who'll be there. The sheriff can only be in one place at a time."

That sounded ominous. "Expecting trouble, sir?"

A shrug, another yawn, then Mr. C. stood. "I hope not, Tate. But Stinson wants you arrested. Hopefully he doesn't know we're coming in tomorrow."

"It could get ugly." That wasn't a question. I knew it could.

* * *

THE RIDE into San Antonio was long, dusty, and the closer we got to town, the more my stomach clenched. I drank my canteen almost dry before I spotted the first outbuildings. José had been quiet with only an occasional comment about the prairie or streams or antelope. No doubt he was anxious. But surely not as much as me.

Mr. C. slowed as we passed the first house. From there, traffic picked up and people scurried down the boardwalks or darted into traffic to cross the jam-packed road. Buggies navigated holes and manure. Horses and wagons clopped down the middle, clogging Alameda Street.

I hadn't seen this many people, or wagons for that matter, ever. I couldn't remember seeing people who were merely trying to cross the street having to jump out of the way of horses and wagons. It was chaos. Pure chaos. Immediately, I craved the simplicity, the calmness, of the ranch.

Halfway down the street, we tied our mounts to the closest hitch rail, hoisted up our trousers, reset our hats, brushed dust off our vests, took deep breaths and opened the sheriff's office door. Eyes adjusting to the dim interior, I spotted Sheriff Samuels at his desk. He whipped out of his chair and shook hands with us three. Mr. C. introduced José and explained why he'd come along.

"Excellent idea." He nodded at the ranch foreman.

"Sure hope nothing goes wrong and we need a fourth gun."

Feeling like a little kid, I reminded both Mr. C. and the sheriff I didn't carry a gun. I left out the part I didn't own one. I would soon, but not now.

"My deputy's due back any minute, Mr. Nolan." The sheriff raised both eyebrows. "*He's* got a gun."

No doubt my sigh and embarrassment were heard clear down to the Alamo, about ten blocks away.

We waited only a few minutes until Samuels's deputy came back. A burly fella, had to stand six and a half feet tall by about that wide, shook hands all around. The grip wasn't as strong as I'd anticipated. Firm, but gentle.

"If you're ready, Mr. Nolan, let's go see those prisoners." Samuels pointed behind a closed door. "By the way, thanks for coming."

I raised one shoulder, my good one. Smiling, frowning, nodding...nothing seemed the right response. "I hope it's them, Sheriff. Tex got killed. For no good reason."

Samuels unlocked the thick wooden door, swinging it wide open. Both cells stood full. Grayed images of my own experiences behind bars threatened to cloud my vision. Too many days, weeks, months spent on the other side flew back in my face. That closed-in, too-crowded, near-panic feeling swept over me. Heart beating hard enough to block any breathing, I stepped back until Mr. C.'s hand on my shoulder stopped me.

"It'll be fine, Tate. Just see if you recognize anybody." He squeezed and let go. "You're safe."

Not believing him, but nodding anyway, I pulled in a big breath and moved into the room. I stood close to the bars and peered into the first cell. Five men of various sizes and clothing stared back. Nobody I recognized right off, but certainly smelled them. A bath would be in order. Today.

Three men sat in the next cell, all glaring at the sheriff, Mr. C., José, the deputy, and me. The first man squinted, rubbed his nose, and spat. Toward me. He may have been one of the men, but I couldn't be sure. I moved to the second sitting on the cot next to the first man. Something about him...and then I knew. It was him.

The man who shot me sat right there. If my arms were longer, I could have touched him, wrung his neck. If I'd had a gun, I would have shot him. Good thing I didn't.

"That's him, Sheriff. Right there. The one who put a bullet in my shoulder."

"You sure?"

"That's the Simon pure."

A quick look at the third and, as they say, my blood ran cold. That surly scowl, that cocksure tilt of his head, that way his shoulders were thrown back...there sat the ringleader, Larkin.

I wouldn't, couldn't, let Larkin see me afraid. Icy jolts raced up and down my body, my hands shook. Breathing was optional. Mustering every ounce of courage I could find, I turned to Sheriff Samuels. "That's him. Larkin. The leader."

Apparently, the words came out because Samuels nodded, looked at his deputy, then me. "You're sure?"

"Yes, sir."

Larkin pointed a finger-gun at me and pulled the trigger. I knew there were no bullets, but certainly one tore into my chest, knocking the wind out. It hurt like Satan's fire.

Samuels led our group back into the outer office.

"Thank you, Mr. Nolan. You'll need to sign a couple statements."

The deputy locked the wooden door to the cell door, and I finally breathed. "Of course." Was I shaking hard enough for the others to notice? I plunged both hands into my vest pockets.

"I'll draw up the paperwork right now." Samuels turned to Mr. C. "Can you stay in town, say half an hour? He can sign then and you three be on your way."

"Fine." Mr. C. shook hands with the sheriff and the deputy. "Take your time. We'll go get coffee and another breakfast."

The deputy pointed up the street. "Maria's Cocina. Best huevos rancheros around."

My mouth watered, and my stomach rumbled. Plus, the rest of my body wanted to get gone, anywhere else but here. Law offices were definitely not my favorite places.

CHAPTER TWENTY

EXPECTING TROUBLE, WE ALL KEPT ONE EYE ON the door while we shoveled in the best huevos rancheros I'd ever had. Corn tortillas swimming in red enchilada sauce topped with two eggs barely over easy was heaven on a plate. Sprinklings of chopped onions, *cebollas* as most called them, along with grated cheese made the most perfect meal *ever*. Despite my still-knotted stomach, I managed to clean my plate, wiping egg remnants with a freshly made flour tortilla.

Feeling like a new man, I stood and hid a belch behind my hand. It didn't stay hidden well. But I wasn't alone. My dining companions produced good ones too.

Mr. C. checked his pocket watch. "Plenty of time to have the paperwork done by now." He snapped shut the case. "Let's sign and head home."

We crossed the street, somehow dodging wagons and horses. If this was big city life, no thanks. I much preferred the wide-open prairie with only a few dozen jackrabbits jumping out at me.

I wouldn't draw an easy breath until my mount

stepped onto Carmichael property. Even then, I'd probably cringe at sounds unexpected...or expected. Admittedly, I was a ball of nerves and couldn't wait to get back.

Few more minutes I kept telling myself. Then, would all be behind me and the next time I saw these men, it'd be in front of a judge. I'd come to their trial and give testimony. Then I'd watch Larkin hang. Few more minutes.

Mr. C. stepped into the sheriff's office, José right behind. I glanced left and right, looking for what, I didn't know. Spotting nothing but bustling people, I pushed inside and froze. Mr. Stinson, along with another man, stood in front of Sheriff Samuels's desk. The ranch owner had one hand on a pile of paperwork. He spun around when I closed the door.

Stinson speared a glare and hand at me. "Why the hell isn't he arrested? I told you to. Told you he tried to murder my men." He stood up straight. "Why the hell is he loose on the street?"

"Don't have to explain myself to you." The sheriff pushed off from behind his desk, held up a hand. "Calm down or I'll toss you out of my office."

"Calm down?" Stinson's face turned the color of sunsets—red, purple, yellow. "Lock this man up at once!" He stared at me but cut his eyes toward a man I didn't recognize. He had to be with Stinson. "Buck," Stinson growled. "Keep your gun on him. If he moves, shoot."

The sheriff raced around his desk and pointed at Buck. "You shoot and I'll arrest you. Both of you. Gimme your gun belt."

Samuels turned to me. "Yours, too."

I shrugged, arms out to my side.

Stinson nodded at Buck who took his time unbuckling the rig. He tossed it to the sheriff.

"Now," Samuels said. "There'll be no shooting; no fighting in here." He locked eyes on each man. "Understand?"

We nodded, but I don't think Stinson or Buck did.

The seven of us, squeezed into an office built for no more than five, sized up each other like one of us was about to become dinner. Tension soaked up every drop of air.

Stinson moved closer to me and then turned on the sheriff. "I'll ask again. Why is this man-killer not behind bars?" His long arm about brushed my nose. "And what is he doing here if he's not in front of a judge?"

Wedging himself between me and Stinson, Mr. C. lowered his voice into a deep snarl, like a mountain lion ready to attack a horse. "It's clear to me your men are responsible for attacking Tate and killing Tex. Rustling my cattle." He nodded toward a document on the sheriff's desk. "Tate just swore it was two of your men."

Stinson exploded. "Swore? Swore? On paper?" Eyes narrowed, lips curled into a sneer, he glowered at me. "You sign it?"

Breaths froze in my chest.

Sheriff Samuels pushed the papers to one side, pointed to the door. "Leave my office right now, Stinson. I'll let you know about bail for your men. *After* you pay damages for their little 'party' at the Lone Star Saloon last night."

Buck reached across the desk, grabbed the papers I was supposed to sign, and ripped them in half. Samuels, Stinson, Mr. C., and I all dove for the scattered pieces.

I landed on top of the desk, Stinson on my back. With fists like rocks, he pounded my head, cheeks and anywhere else he could reach. I tried bucking him off, but darn, he was solid. Someone grabbed him around the chest and suddenly, four of us were on the floor, me on top. Out of the corner of my eye, I spotted Buck go for his gun belt hanging on a peg.

His hand pulled the gun from the holster, but the deputy buffaloed him with his Colt. Buck went down like a sack of road apples. Before I could manage to roll off, the deputy grabbed the back of my vest, hefting me off the pile of arms and legs underneath. I rolled to a thudding stop against a wall.

By the time stars cleared from my vision, Mr. C., José, Samuels, and Stinson were standing, glaring, chests heaving. Each one sported a glowing red mark on a cheek. José had two.

Sheriff Samuels regained composure first. "Deputy Tucker"—he pointed at Buck—"lock him up. Charges are assault, destruction of property, disorderly conduct." He stared at Stinson. "There'll be more later, but enough for now."

Stinson jumped in between the deputy and Buck. "Take him in there and I promise you, *Sheriff* Samuels, I'll have your badge. I'll make sure the town council yanks you out of office."

Samuels nodded at his deputy. "Go ahead, Tucker." He glared at Stinson. "You might get my badge, but until you do, he'll stay locked up, right alongside your other men."

I couldn't hide a grin. Justice would be served after all.

* * *

WE DIDN'T STAY in town long enough for more papers to be drawn up and signed. Before we left, old man Stinson had marched off in search of a town councilor to hound, but not before throwing more threats, accusations, and warnings my way. He punctuated his rant with a hefty door slamming. Windowpanes rattled. I was impressed.

Sheriff Samuels had promised to get new sworn statements delivered to the ranch in the next day or two. Which was fine because after Stinson had threatened havoc and mayhem, Samuels said I was officially under house arrest, confined to Mr. Carmichael's ranch until this business was cleared. That was fine by me. I was safe doing my chores. Suddenly, washing dishes had great appeal.

Although I should have been jangled from my trip to town, I slept like the dead that night. Smitty's tug on my foot roused me enough to recognize the sun barely hitting the horizon. Time to make breakfast. I sat up, rubbed my eyes, yawned as wide as the Palo Duro Canyon.

I slipped on my vest, then boots, thought about what Mr. C. had told Da about me. "He always keeps me on my toes." Stifling a chuckle, I agreed. Seemed like nothing but trouble followed wherever I went.

At breakfast, a couple of the men good-naturedly complained about having to do my chores yesterday, but I assured them I'd make up for their efforts. Wasn't sure how I'd do that, but undoubtedly something would come to mind.

Dishes dried, I headed to the barn wondering if anybody mucked stalls as thoroughly as I did. This morning, most of the men were out with the cattle on what they called the Big Blue, a pasture at the eastern edge of

Carmichael property, a couple hours' ride from here. That left Smitty in the bunkhouse and me in the barn. I assumed Mr. C. was busy in the house doing whatever it was he did. Miranda was undoubtedly starting to fix a mid-day meal for the Carmichaels.

The barn inside was always darker than I preferred. On sunny days, I had to wait a bit until I could see the horses, harnesses, and tools. Today, leaving the wide door partially open, I recognized the usual five horses busy munching on hay. Just what they did every day. Today they'd get a good helping of oats too.

I selected a rake leaning against a stall's short wall, then, in search of fresh hay, walked toward the farthest part of the barn. Without a sound, like a phantom of my nightmares, a dark figure grabbed me around my chest, blocking any air coming in or out. Fighting for my life, I clawed at a hand clamped over my mouth. I swung the rake, hoping the weapon would loosen the man's grip. Metal tines connected with a head.

A grunt and he let go. Rake still in hand, I spun, jumped to one side, raised the tool for another strike, but he was faster. He headbutted me backward into a small hay pile. Wind knocked out, lying like a turtle on his back, I flailed my hands and released the rake.

Anger and fear collided. His face near mine, I recognized Buck from yesterday. Bigger than me, he grabbed my vest and shirt, hauled me to my feet and pounded. Head, face, stomach, legs. My entire body took the brunt of his wrath. I hit back, but I wasn't as strong, or as big.

Refused to be beaten any more, my fear turned into fury. Fists knotting into hammers, I swung, connecting with a chest, then face. He grunted and kept on pummeling me.

Wind completely gone, I laid on the ground, head thumping, chest struggling for air.

Buck stopped and glared down at me. "Stinson says you sign those papers, you'll never see daylight again." A sneer pushed up a bruised cheek. "If you do, your pretty little daughter'll have a dead daddy this time for sure."

How the hell did he know?

He fished a piece of fabric out of his vest pocket and tossed it onto my chest. I picked up the material. Sky blue with tiny yellow flowers. Imogene's dress!

"Sign that statement and we'll make sure she's a widow. Your ma, too."

Lips swollen, eyes almost shut, chest and stomach on fire, all I could do was breathe.

"Understand? Get the message?" Buck straightened his hat.

I nodded, words refusing to form.

He stepped back and kicked me in the ribs. I rolled over and over landing finally against a horse's leg.

Buck chuckled and pointed a meaty finger at my face. "You ever, *ever*, set foot on Stinson property again, *ever* testify against us, your entire family, even pretty little Frieda will be pushing up tumbleweeds." He waited. "Understand?" A kick to my face. "Get it?"

I did. Loud and clear.

* * *

I LAID on that pile of hay until the world stopped tilting. Pushing myself up, immediately I thought better of doing that, but not before breakfast found its way up and out. Stomach roiling, I threw up again until nothing was left. I'm not sure how long I sat there, swatting flies, petting a dog that came wandering past, but eventually the sun stood overhead. Noon. I could tell by the sunlight no longer streaming through the east-facing door.

Wobbling up to my feet, I wandered outside to dunk my head into a horse trough. The cool water felt good on my face and head. A second dunk, then I pushed back hair plastered over my eyes. I studied the ranch house and thought long and hard about telling Mr. C. what happened.

If I did, undoubtedly, he'd go to Sheriff Samuels and then Stinson would kill me and everyone I ever loved. I took Buck's words to heart. Would I keep quiet? Who should know what happened? I had no answers, simply more questions.

I saddled Sparky, a fifteen hands high gelding, then groaned and grunted into the saddle, reined him west. I wasn't sure where I was going, just knew I had to get away, have time and space to think. Fortunately, Mr. C.'s land was extensive. I could ride a day or two and still be on his property.

A full-out gallop was what I desired and was what Sparky gave me. His solid, steady gait proved easy on my sore, aching body.

Westward I rode. Down gullies, up swales, across open prairies and meadows, over meandering streams, past herds of antelope, pockets of prairie dogs and oodles of rabbits. Sun, occasionally filtered by white, puffy clouds, did its best to lighten my mood. True, it was warm, bordering on hot, but a mild wind cooled the sweat under my arms.

I rode.

More gullies, more swales, more animals.

Sun on the horizon blinded me. It was then I realized how far I'd come. Even if I turned around right now, which I didn't intend to do, I wouldn't make it back to the ranch until at least midnight. And that was if I knew where I was going. Hopefully Sparky knew.

No good solutions had sprung to mind while I nursed sore ribs and pounding head across the landscape. I sure couldn't tell Mr. C., nor Da. Maybe Sheriff Samuels, but he'd go running to Stinson and then...

A line of cottonwoods marched up and down a stream wide enough to grow trout. My stomach rumbled while we stopped long enough for Sparky to get a good, long drink. I looked around. Still on Carmichael property, I was sure. Was this water the line between ranches? Taking no chances, I decided to make camp here under the trees, on this side of the stream. I'd catch dinner, cook the fish over a big fire, and figure out what next to do.

I unsaddled Sparky, rubbed her with the saddle blanket, then realized I had nothing to sleep on. In my haste, I hadn't brought a canteen, bedroll or even matches. What kind of thinking had I done? None, apparently.

While I could still see, I plunged into the stream hoping to catch a trout with my hands. Minutes later, I realized there was little chance of that happening, but darn, I was hungry. Maybe a rabbit? I laughed out loud at that idea. What? I'd chase it down, wring its neck? I needed a gun.

Although I had no matches, I did know how to start a fire using sticks and flint. It took a while, but eventually, about the time it got true dark, little sparks caught dried leaves and twigs. In no time, I had a bonfire going. At least something went right.

I sat by the fire, warming my hands. While it was hot during the day, the desert cooled at night. Flames relaxed my entire body. Making sure firewood was stacked for the night, I laid back on Sparky's saddle blanket, used the saddle for a pillow, and stared up at the stars.

What to do? I could run. Leave everything and everyone behind. Start fresh somewhere else. That idea had possibilities.

I could sign the papers and be sure the sheriff and Mr. C. knew what Stinson said. No. I booted that idea immediately.

I could hide at the ranch, never straying farther than the bunkhouse and main house. And what would that get me? Not much. Probably a label as coward.

Besides running, the only option that held any promise was to do what Stinson said—don't sign the papers. I could continue working at Mr. C.'s ranch until I saved up enough to buy a gun. I'd rob a bank or two, like Jesse James, and then light out for parts unknown. Change my name. Cut my hair, grow a beard. Start life all over again. It wasn't technically "running." It was more like…reinventing myself. Yep, that was the plan.

Sparky snorted, skittered back and forth, and pulled on his tied reins. I blinked my eyes open, surprised I'd been asleep. The fire was now nothing but glowing embers. What had spooked the horse?

And then…a howl from south of me. Wolf? An answering howl. Definitely wolf. Hair stood on my arms. I stroked Sparky's neck and spoke soft. "It's all right, boy." I stroked harder, more for me than for him. "Just wolves talkin' to each other."

He settled a bit and I clung to his neck about half a minute longer. There was comfort in his body, though I saw no reason for wolves to attack. Plenty of game around and we had none in our campsite. They had no need to eat Sparky—or me, for that matter.

Thankfully, I'd piled armloads of wood close to the

fire. I built it up until another bonfire raged. We'd be safe now. I hoped.

I sat near the fire the rest of the night feeding sticks into the flames until light from the east let me see my hands. I walked the camp's perimeter. And not five feet away, there they were—wolf paw prints. Unmistakable impressions larger than my hand. Icy fingers clawed up my spine. That had been close. Too darn close.

Finally able to breathe, I let out a long sigh while my stomach reminded me it was hungry. In fact, it growled louder than I'm sure that wolf would.

Saddling Sparky, I thought about my actions with the wolves. I hadn't run. I'd logically thought about it. That's what I'd do about this Stinson issue. I wouldn't run away like a scared little girl. I'd take my time bringing down the men who killed Tex and shot me. But I wouldn't sign the papers. I had no right to put everyone in danger.

And what to do about Imogene? And Louisa? Since I was quarantined to the ranch, I wouldn't see them often. That would give us time to think and adjust. Until I bought a gun and started robbing banks.

CHAPTER TWENTY-ONE

FOR MOST OF THE RETURN RIDE I GAVE SPARKY his head. Along the way, I vaguely remembered a couple of meadows and gullies, but the world was pretty much a blur. Some strange sense of foreboding urged me to gallop, to hurry. I wasn't sure what was wrong. I'd never had this feeling before, but all I knew was I needed to get back to the ranch. I gave Sparky and me one short rest with a long drink of water, and then raced back until I recognized a hill behind the main house. A glance at the overhead sun told me all I needed to know. I'd been gone close to twenty-four hours, and now it hit me.

Mr. Carmichael would be furious, not to mention José and Smitty. I'd let them down and there would be hell to pay. Did I deserve it? Sadly, yes. My body ached, head still throbbed, but realizing what damage I'd caused hurt worse than all the aches and pains put together. I couldn't be trusted. I was a loose cannon, so to speak. A loser. Waste of skin.

Unless I did something to change my life, right now,

today, I'd end up a derelict like those Yankee soldiers who lived behind the saloons. And then it really, truly hit me. I was one step away from that life.

I needed to do something right now to help myself. But what?

I topped the hill and pulled rein. Down below in front of the main house, Mr. C., José and Smitty were busy cinching saddles. I wondered what had happened and then figured it was about me. Would I spend tonight in jail? Probably. Pulling back my shoulders, I set my hat on straight and rode into the yard, ready to face whatever consequences I truly deserved.

Mr. C. jumped and spun when Smitty pointed at me.

I reined up next to them and before I could swing a leg over the saddle, Mr. C. stood at my side, his gaze trailing up and down my sore body.

"Where've you been? What gave you the right to run off?" He reached out to grab my torn vest, then apparently thought better. He stood back, took a breath. "You all right?"

Right then and there I knew what to do. On the ride back, I hadn't thought much about answering questions, but now I did. No way could I tell him Buck pummeled then threatened me. So, I did the next best thing. I lied.

Both feet on the ground, I leaned against Sparky for support and security. "Sorry, Mr. Carmichael." I met his stare, then turned to the other men. "Yesterday, after chores, I decided Sparky needed a bit of a run since he'd been cooped up in the barn. We were about an hour out when something spooked him." Did this sound believable?

"Rabbit or snake?" José stepped closer.

I shrugged. "Probably snake. I saw hundreds of rabbits and they didn't bother him." I took another breath. "Anyway, he bucked, reared, and then bolted. On the way, I slid out of the saddle, boot caught in the stirrup."

Smitty shook his head. "Not a good place to be. I've been there." He looked around for confirmation.

"Hit my head, ran into more rocks, through a stream. Finally rolled out of the stirrup and he stopped." My entire body hurt, so telling that part of the lie wasn't difficult at all. "Didn't know where we were, couldn't stand up. So, I sat for a few hours 'til it got dark. Late last night, I built a fire and this morning...well, here we are."

Mr. C. gave me another onceover. I couldn't tell from his expression if he believed me or not. His shoulders sagged and he breathed out, long and hard. "All right. Sorry you're hurt. Again." Another long breath in and out. "Get yourself cleaned up, something to eat, then come see me." Without a glance, handshake, or nod, he turned and walked up the steps to the porch. The screen door squeaked open and slammed shut.

Before I could decide how much trouble I was in, Smitty took Sparky's reins and those of the other horses. He headed for the barn.

Which left José and me standing at the hitch rail in front of the main house. Something about the way he stood, or maybe looked at me and then the sky...something told me he knew what Buck had done. But how could he?

He cocked one hip and looked toward the barn. "Never seen Sparky get excited over anything, 'cept maybe a feedbag of oats. Surprised he got all quirly."

I nodded. Aches and pains roared up and down my body. And then my sore stomach reminded me it hadn't been fed for quite a while. I thumbed over my shoulder toward the bunk house. "Gonna get cleaned up, then eat."

"*Sí.*" José started off then stopped and turned back to me. "Kid. I was thinking yesterday you're healed up enough to do harder jobs." A smile pushed up his mustache. "Maybe in a few days you'll start helping with the herd. They could use another hand on the Big Blue."

Exactly what I was hoping to hear. Now I didn't even have to ask for the assignment. "I'll be fit in a day or two."

I certainly planned to be, whether I was or not.

Following a hearty helping of stew I found in a pot warming on the stove, I decided to take myself down to the stream where I could shed my ripped clothes and take a better look at what Buck had done. Before I left, a close inspection in the shaving mirror as I gathered soap and clean clothes had revealed a split lip, which I was well aware of, cuts over both eyes, one swollen, and a long gash across my forehead. Both eyes black made me look like a clown I'd seen in a picture. There was nothing funny about my face though.

Cool water on my sore, bruised body did wonders for my mood, for my soul. For the first time, I saw things clearly. A day after I'd healed some, I'd join the work crew out in the eastern part of the ranch and help brand, doctor, bring in strays, and do whatever needed doing. I'd stay on the Big Blue working as hard as the others until asked to do something else. Two things I knew as I inspected the blue and black markings on my ribs and thigh. First, I'd never sign those papers, that sworn document against Stinson. I was sorry about Tex, but it was a risk I couldn't take.

Second, I'd take down Becker. Him and that bootlicking, worthless deputy. Somehow. Either kill them outright or beat them senseless. Or maybe I'd figure out how to run them out of town. Someway, somehow, Becker would pay for the humiliation he'd brought on me, not to mention the nine months in prison he'd recommended when I was sentenced. He owed me almost a year of freedom. I'd see to it he paid.

I toweled off, donned fresh clothes, and felt like a new man, albeit an *old* new man. I creaked and groaned as I walked to the bunkhouse. At least I smelled better.

* * *

Mr. C. was at his desk when I rapped on the slightly open door. He looked up from paperwork, motioned me in and pointed to a chair across the desk from his. I vaguely wondered if anyone besides me ever sat here.

He tapped his index finger on a short stack of papers. "These came in yesterday. Need your signature."

"Sir?" Here we go. Now to perfect my innocence.

Dipping the stylus in an ink well, he held out the pen to me and pointed at a blank line on the top page. "I've read it. Almost exactly what you said. Go ahead and sign. I'll get this back to Sheriff Samuels tomorrow."

I hesitated, my hand starting for the pen, then pulling back. "Sign what?"

"Your statement, Tate." Mr. C. pushed the pen closer to me. "Hurry up. I've got things to do."

Shaking my head, I shrugged. "What statement?"

"For cryin' out loud, Tate. What you said about those two men of Stinson's. You identified the men who killed Tex and shot you." He lowered the pen. "Don't tell me you don't remember."

Both eyebrows raised for good measure, I shrugged again. "I remember being shot. That's for sure." I tilted my head and frowned. "Don't recollect seeing those boys again, though."

Mr. C. jumped to his feet, leaned over the desk. "What gotten into you?"

"I'm sorry—"

"Must've hit your head one too many times." He straightened up, marched to the window, and gazed out. He mumbled something sounding like "little shit," but I couldn't be sure.

Call me what he wanted, still, I felt guilty for putting him through this, but I told myself I had no choice.

A long silence echoed in the room while he stared outside. After what could have been half a minute or maybe half an hour, he sighed and turned to me. His eyes had narrowed, lips pursed together.

He pointed a shaking finger east. "You're healed up enough. First thing in the morning, ride out to the Big Blue, join the crew out there. They can use an extra hand. Got fences to mend, need to get ready for fall gathering."

I pushed my achy body to my feet. A muscle under Mr. C's eye twitched. I doubted he believed me.

"Be back here in a week." He pointed to the papers again. "By then I'm sure you'll remember. I want those men behind bars for a long time. Tex was a good hand and an admirable man, and I won't see his killers go unpunished."

"Yes, sir." I gripped the door handle. "I'll try real hard to remember."

"Make sure you do."

* * *

DAYS PASSED QUICKLY ENOUGH AND, thankfully, without incident. I thought long and even harder about not signing the papers. Would Mr. Carmichael sign them himself, claiming it was my signature? Would he do something like that? I didn't think so, but then again, he was awfully mad when I wouldn't sign.

The days and nights on the prairie turned into magical moments. At night, starlight poured down like summer rains. Refreshing, honest, warm. Days were mysterious too. Turquoise skies, dotted with cotton clouds could turn into purple canopies within moments bringing curtains of rain. And then, minutes later, the sun would brighten the world, leaving behind sparkling waterdrops on the cattle and grass.

Working all day stringing new or fixing broken wire, riding after stray cattle, even digging post holes, hurt my body in places other than what Buck's fists had done. I was more than likely one big bruise, but I wouldn't complain. I hadn't felt this safe in months and I enjoyed the banter of the other cowboys. These rough and tough men took joshing well and gave it even better. Once they started ribbing me about my black eyes and what they'd heard about me falling off Sparky, I knew I'd become one of them. Accepted into the tribe of ranch hands.

I liked it here.

Completely losing track of the days, I was surprised when Solomon, Big S we called him, drove back from the ranch in a wagon. Timbers for posts and boxes of various supplies and what hopefully was food, was packed into the back. We crowded around as if we hadn't seen anybody from "the world" in years. He'd been gone overnight.

"What'd ya bring us, Big S?" A fella I knew only as Charlie stepped next to the driver and pointed behind him. "Got anything ready to eat? Maybe Mrs. Carmichael sent something?"

I could taste it now. Miranda's fried chicken, mashed potatoes with lots of white gravy. Peach cobbler. My stomach rumbled.

Big S jumped down and stood against the wagon's side. "She ain't cooked nothin'. You got your imaginations runnin' wild again."

Mutterings about women's cooking and Big S eating it all and how could he come back without food, raced around the wagon.

One of the hands, wearing a Mexican sugarloaf sombrero, circled to the other side. He sniffed into the air. "Ah *sí. Verdad.* Miranda has been cooking all right."

That's all it took for the six men to rush the wagon. Two scrambled over the sides and pushed aside boxes to uncover the aroma's source. They lifted high two boxes, gingham covers on top. Even from where I was, near the horses, smells of apple pie and—was that chicken— wafted my way.

As much as Big S protested, saying it was all for him, the hands made quick work of the food. Sated for the moment, we sat around the campfire, some smoking, some napping. I sat thinking about how much I enjoyed being there. Also wondering if there were any leftovers.

Much to my disappointment, Ray, the foreman of this crew, pushed up to his feet. The others grumbled as they found their feet, too. Body still sore and muscles still tender, it took me longer to spring to life. Last one up, I headed to my horse when Big S spoke.

"Kid."

Something in his voice made me stop. Sounded serious. "Yeah?"

"Boss wants you back first thing in the morning." He

thumbed west. "Didn't say why. Just said for you to get a move on. Said 'it's been more than a week.'" He shrugged. "Whatever that means."

Bollocks. Would I see the sheriff's horse when I rode in? More than likely.

CHAPTER TWENTY-TWO

IT WASN'T THE SHERIFF'S HORSE TIED AT THE hitch rail. My shoulders relaxed a bit. But whose was it? As I rode in closer, I spotted brother Joe sitting on the top porch step, all by himself. He looked a bit forlorn as I swung out of the saddle.

He pushed up to his feet and stuck out a hand. "Wondered when you'd get here." He glanced behind him at the closed door. "Mr. Carmichael said you'd be along any minute. Jeeze, Tate. It's been an hour."

I took his extended hand which felt like an odd thing to do. If memory served, we'd never done that before. But things were different now. We shook, his grip firm.

"It's a far piece to the Big Blue and," I lowered my voice, "took my time riding back." Hopefully, my smile lowered his ire a bit. "If I'd known you were here, I'd of galloped."

And then it hit me. Maybe something was wrong with Ma or Da. Eagan? Why hadn't I been told sooner?

"Came to tell you—"

"Everyone all right? Anybody hurt? Sick?"

Joe held up a hand, his eyes shining. "Fine. They're all fine. Just a bit of town gossip, first." He pointed behind him to the porch. "Let's sit."

Joe plopped onto the top step, and I sat next to him. "I love gossip. What's going on?"

Hesitating, my brother studied the barn. I gave him space knowing he'd tell me when he was ready.

"You know that woman who came out here for the barbecue after church? The one with the little girl?" He shoulder bumped me. "You seem to know her." He shot me a look like he already knew our past dalliances. How could he?

"Imogene?" Did my voice quake?

Joe nodded. "Yeah, that one." He looked at me instead of the sky. "Well, I was in the mercantile this morning and she was there, working."

"Good. Ma said she could probably get a job there."

"But she was busy making eyes at the deputy. He was standing there looking like he was interested in buying oats, but everybody knew he wasn't. She smiled, then he smiled." He lowered his voice. "Think they're a couple."

No, no, no is what I wanted to shout. But then again, we weren't married. Until a couple weeks ago I'd forgotten about her. I sat up straight. "Which deputy?"

"That O'Sullivan fella." Joe frowned. "He's new in town. Well, new-er."

Lordy. A deputy. At least it was a good man, Tommy O'Sullivan. But how good could a lawman be? None of them were to be trusted. Not even him. What would she see in him? Maybe Imogene was a badge chaser. Someone who loved men of that ilk. I'd heard some women were attracted to men who wore badges, or uniforms for that matter. But surely Imogene was smarter than that.

Joe nudged my boot with his boot. "You're awful quiet. I say something wrong?"

"Nah." I shrugged. "Just wondering what she sees in him."

"Me, too." A sly grin flicked across Joe's face. "Got other news too."

"More? More gossip?"

He pulled in air, glanced around, straightened his shoulders. "I'm leaving town." He rushed his words. "But I'll be back. *We'll* be back."

"What?" A knot formed in my chest. "What?"

"As you know, Frieda and her family are moving up to Denver, starting tomorrow." A slight grin wrinkled a cheek. "Decided to go with them to help out. We'll be married in January, then come back here to Blanco Hill to settle down."

I sat there speechless. Somewhere in my brain I'd known his plans, but they hadn't hung right here on my nose. Right now. I stuttered and stammered, finally getting out, "What'd Ma and Da say?"

Joe's grin turned into a full-fledged smile. "Da says I've finally grown up. Thinks it's the right thing to do. I might get a job up there too."

"And Ma?"

He wagged his head. "She cried, sayin' her 'wee lad' had become a man. But she's excited to have us come back next year and have a girl in the family. Somebody who wears skirts besides her."

"What about Eagan?"

"He's thrilled I'm leaving. Says he'll finally have the room to himself now. First time, ever." Joe stood and stepped down to the hitch rail.

I pushed up from the porch, stood there with him, and studied my younger brother. We'd been through so much together the past twenty years and now...was it over? Would I ever see him again?

And then it hit me. If he and Frieda were in Denver, there was a good chance they were safe from Stinson's threats and Buck's fists. I was glad they were going, only for that reason.

"I'll miss you, brother." I pulled him into a ferocious bearhug. "You be safe."

Released, Joe gripped the saddle horn to swing up onto his horse. "Next time you see me, I'll be an old married man!" His smile lit up the world. Without another word, he mounted, fitted his hat down tight, tossed me another smile, and urged his horse into a trot.

I stood in the ranch yard, watching my brother ride out of my life. At least for a while. I wondered if he'd ever truly return. Part of me doubted it, the other part needed to believe. At the yard's entrance, under a cross-beam, he pulled rein, turned, and waved.

Waving back, I watched until he trotted out of sight.

I cleared my throat, then turned to go inside and face Mr. C. I didn't have far to go as he was standing behind me, also watching Joe. When he'd come outside, I didn't know, never hearing the door squeak open or closed.

Mr. C. breathed out low. "It's hard saying goodbye."

Nodding, I had no words that wouldn't sound hoarse. Joe's leaving hurt worse than I'd imagined. I'd bet Ma was in a state.

We didn't go inside, Mr. C. and me. Instead, we sat on the top porch step, just where Joe and I had been. Together we watched the few ranch hands go about their daily chores, birds flitting from tree to tree, a dog chasing chickens. I was sure we sat like that for ten minutes until he spoke.

"Tate." His voice was low, but hard. "There's something you haven't told me about not signing that statement." He waited, but I couldn't say anything yet. "I don't buy one word of you not remembering. Not one. It doesn't ring true."

Bollocks and double *bollocks*. With Mr. C. at my elbow, it was almost impossible to lie. I respected the man too much to keep up the charade. The past week had taught me that.

"What's going on, Tate?"

All my reserves crumbled. Something about this man made me trust him. But why should I? On the other hand, he'd always been fair and straight with me. Guess I owed him. Deep breath, I started.

On his part, he kept quiet as I related the incident, interrupting with only a couple of grunts and raised eyebrows.

"And Mr. Carmichael," I stared at my boots, "I don't want to see you, or my family hurt. I truly believe he'll carry out his threats." And then I was done. All the words were gone, all my pent-up worries now on his shoulders, too.

We sat on that porch step for what felt like hours and days. One of the hands brought Sparky out and put him into a fenced corral. Two of the dogs chased each other from the barn clear up onto the porch then off toward the stream. A flock of blackbirds crowded into the trees by the icehouse. And still, he remained silent.

My thoughts turned to Imogene and that deputy. Somebody needed to warn her. Tell her she could do better, even though I vaguely liked him. To stay away. Far away. And what about Louisa? She'd be around O'Sullivan. Would he be a bad influence? I had to warn Imogene. But how?

Maybe Mr. C. would let me ride into town, just for an

hour. No, that'd be asking for trouble, what with two sheriffs saying I had to stay here at the ranch. And no doubt that worthless Becker would find me. I'd be in jail before I could swing down from the saddle.

And then I had a thought. Mrs. C. had her monthly ladies' tea. In town. I brightened. She would be the one. Certainly Mrs. C. would go to the mercantile where they could speak woman to woman. Maybe Imogene would listen to her.

"So, for now, Tate," Mr. C. was saying. "That's what we'll do."

Caught! Not listening. Just like in school. "Sir?"

Mr. C. creaked up to his feet, stood looking down at me. His eyes were kind, yet hard.

"Said this'll stay 'tween you and me. For now."

"We—"

"As I said, you'll stay here on the ranch. Don't go anywhere except back over to the Big Blue. Maybe a month or so with the crew will be good cover. The men won't put up with any shenanigans from an outsider. You'll be safe enough there."

"Thank you, sir." We shook hands. "I'll head on back. But first, is it all right if I speak with your wife? I got a problem I think she can help me with."

Eyeing me like he wasn't sure, finally his head bobbed. "She's inside sewing. Go on in. I'll be there shortly."

Mrs. C. put down her needle and the shirt she was mending as I rambled on, telling her what I suspected. Then I felt compelled to explain the reason for my concern. She didn't seem too shocked—her eyes didn't bug out, and she didn't order me off the property. Both what I thought she might do. Once again, I realized, I'd underestimated the Carmichaels. They were decent people. And while I'm sure she judged me, she didn't let it show.

She took her time responding.

"I'm going into town next week, Tate." Mrs. C. eased to her feet while I stood also. "I'll make it a point to see Imogene and invite her to luncheon. We can have a nice chat then." She tossed me a grin that crinkled the skin around her shining eyes. "I'll let you know what she says."

I wanted to hug her, but I didn't. I still had plenty of problems, but now I had people to help me. How could I repay their kindness?

By working hard and staying out of trouble. Should be simple enough.

CHAPTER TWENTY-THREE

SOMEONE TOLD ME MR. C. OWNED 390,000 ACRES of ranchland. Was that all? Sure seemed the acreage was at least twice that. Everywhere I looked, in every direction, Carmichael ruled. He ran dozens of herds of Charolais, Angus, and Hereford cattle on land that could probably feed more. I had no idea how many cows, steers, bulls, and calves were in those herds, but I was sure it was higher than I could count.

I'd also been told his ranch had originally been a Spanish land grant in the early part of this century but had been parceled off and sold to a family named Jones. Mr. C. bought the ranch lock, stock, and barrel more than twenty years ago and had planned, Charlie told me, to have his son run it when Mr. C. got too old.

That was sad. Nobody to pass all of this on to. What would he do? Probably sell his holdings to somebody who had enough money to stay afloat. More than I wanted to handle.

Losing track of days was easy, what with getting up with the sunrise, mending fences and finding stray animals. Watching for coyotes and wolves—the four- and two-legged variety—kept me on my toes, even when I was napping by the campfire. I worked hard, didn't complain, and my bruises healed. Life was good.

Around noon one day, Charlie rode back into the group, most of us sitting near the campfire and enjoying seconds of beans. He secured his horse to the tie line, then sauntered over to the fire. He sniffed toward a pot of stew. "Ah. Heaven's nectar. Just what this poor cowboy needs."

And then I remembered I hadn't seen him since yesterday afternoon. And even though we shared a tent, his absence wasn't surprising since we got sent out in groups of two or more to do whatever needed doing. He could have been a couple miles away working.

He sloshed stew into a bowl, grabbed a spoon and sat beside me near the fire. Before saying anything, he shoveled in half the bowl, then paused. "Just what this man needed. Could've eaten a fence post if it'd had enough beans."

I chortled out loud. He spooned a big helping into his mouth, then handed me the bowl. He spoke over the food. "Here. Mrs. C. sent you a note." He dug around in his vest pocket and extracted a folded piece of paper.

The men immediately made all sorts of rude comments, mainly about Mrs. C. being sweet on me and in return I drove her to town. But their definition of drove was not meant for delicate ears. My face caught fire. Nothing I could say or do deterred these men from sniggers and guffaws.

Had it been almost two weeks already? I certainly hadn't forgotten about the Imogene-O'Sullivan affair, trying to put it in perspective. Truth be told, I hadn't been successful pushing it away. I had three nightmares every day and night—Imogene would marry O'Sullivan, Stinson would send Buck to make good on his threats, and Becker would arrest me again, or worse. I wasn't going back to jail. I'd kill myself first.

I opened the note and smiled as I read. Mrs. C. had written a cryptic note, I'm sure in case someone else read it. *Things are fine. Don't worry.*

That was certainly a relief, but on the heels of my relief came doubt. What if Imogene lied to Mrs. C.? What if O'Sullivan *made* her say she was happy with him? What if Mrs. C. was simply being nice? Didn't want me to worry since I already had enough on my plate, as they say. Maybe in the next few days I could ride back to the ranch house and talk to her myself. That should clear things up.

Charlie helped himself to another bowl of stew, polished it off almost as quickly as he did the first. This time, he added a tortilla for sopping remnant broth and beans.

Lost in thoughts as to my next move, I missed Charlie's announcement. "...it's at the house, all safe and sound. Says we don't need money out here, but since it's payday, said he knows how we like to play poker. That's why he's keeping it."

Was he talking about pay? Had it been a month since the last time when I gave most of the money to Joe? Must've been.

A couple of the men grumbled, but the mutterings sounded more like they were disappointed about no poker games of any merit. Having Mr. C. keep my thirty-five dollars was fine by me. I'd collect it next time I went back to the ranch. Or maybe I'd ask him to hold on to it for me. Surprisingly, my chest swelled a bit thinking of how much money I'd made.

Half an hour or so letting our mid-day meal settle, then most of the hands took off to do whatever it was they did. That left me, Charlie, and two other fellows in camp. My job this afternoon was to bring in as much firewood as I could find. We'd already felled several mesquite bushes and a dead cottonwood down by the stream. Today, I'd have to go farther out to get enough to last the next few days. I didn't mind this assignment. We all did our fair share of providing firewood, keeping the coffee hot, and cooking, although one hand did most of the meal fixing.

Generally, we worked in pairs, but on this afternoon Charlie, who'd become something like a partner to me, was tasked with rounding up strays spotted roaming west. After his long ride from the ranch house, he wasn't too keen on riding farther, but like me, he accepted the job without complaint. I recognized the furrowed forehead and slightly narrowed eyes when the foreman told him.

We both stretched up to our feet, downed the final swig of coffee, then put plates and cups into the pan on the end of the chuckwagon. Whoever was left in camp had the job of washing. I'd had my fair share of dishes and was glad all I had to do was hack down mesquite bushes and drag the spindly limbs back to camp. Easy enough.

And it was relatively easy. I had to go farther down by the stream than I had preferred, but other than a few deer and rabbits, no two-legged critters came within sight. Exactly the way I liked it. Doing this kind of labor allowed me thinking time. Although I wasn't firmly convinced the Imogene-O'Sullivan affair was all right, I pushed it to the back of my nightmares.

I cut off branches, tied them into a big bundle, all the

while considering whether to deal first with stupid Becker or stupid Buck. Two "B" words of the worst kind. Possibly old man Stinson would be a third nightmare. While thinking, guess I wasn't paying as much attention as I should. I grabbed a thin branch, yanked it toward the horse. The end of the stick cut across my cheek and forehead. That scratch brought stinging, blood, and several curse words.

Enough wood for now, I figured, I tied my stick bundle behind me, mounted my horse and followed a stream headed back to camp dragging a significant amount of mesquite behind me. That's when I noticed the fence, Mr. C.'s fence, running on the other side of the water. Must be the edge of his property.

A rustling sound caught my attention. I turned in the saddle and peered across the fence into stands of mesquite and cottonwoods. Combined with grass and last year's fallen leaves, I couldn't see much beyond. The sound—footsteps? Animal? Wind?

No wind. It was as still as a dead rattler. I listened harder but only my heart pounding and breaths coming in and out disturbed the silence. I waited a long minute, then wagged my head. Must have been my imagination or a squirrel heading for his nest.

On the ride back, I convinced myself the noise was a squirrel. Of course. Had to be.

* * *

NEXT MORNING, Charley and I were assigned to chase strays down near where I'd been the day before. One of the hands reported seeing five, maybe six steers drinking from the stream and munching on mesquite branches. Possibly that's what I heard yesterday, although I hadn't seen cattle there, nor signs of them. I shrugged thinking more than likely they strayed following the water. Our job, this morning, was to bring them back to the herd.

Last slurp of coffee down our gullets, we took off for the stream. I knew where to start looking and chose the spot I'd been in yesterday. We rode side by side for a bit and then closer to the stream, single file. Charlie was a talker, but not overly so. He'd finally opened up to me and he could spin a whale of a yarn. A few years older than me, but not much, he'd been all around this country. Virginia, Georgia, California, and now Texas. And he had stories for each state. He hadn't been in the war, being he had been too young, like me. But his older brothers fought, and he didn't mind sharing their stories. Which ones were true was hard to figure.

"Those Charolais hide durn well." Charley peered through a clump of mesquite. "You'd think with them being white, they're easy to spot. But no, them doggies hide better'n a rabbit in a fox hole."

I started to question the rabbit fox hole comparison, but he went on.

"Yep, these Charolais are not only big, but mean too. You ever been on the wrong end of the horns?"

"Can't say I have."

He spoke over his shoulder. "I didn't see it, but sure heard about it. This one ol' boy, sittin' in his saddle, just watchin' the herd, got rammed by a Charolais mama cow."

He had my full attention.

"That ol' cow, almost as big as the horse, well, she charged that horse and headbutted him and the fella. Horse pancaked on his side and that ol' boy ended up under the horse, both scrambling to get back up and get away from that crazy cow."

Now that sounded a bit much, but I hadn't been around cattle like he had. At any rate, whether true or not, I enjoyed his story. And his company.

We rode the stream bank for several yards to where the fence crossed into this side of the water, making sure to stay on Carmichael property. Then we spotted it. Cut fence wire. Chopped clear to the ground. No doubt. A long look left then right. I didn't see anyone around, much less cattle, whether they were white Charolais, the Angus, or a Herford, a basic cow color. Nothing of the four or two-legged variety.

"Think we should ride back and report in?" I turned to Charlie who'd stopped next to me. "I mean, I don't want—"

"How 'bout we go downstream a bit longer?" Charlie chin-pointed south. "Might find those cows moseyed back to this side."

I wasn't sure it was the best idea, but then I wasn't sure it wasn't. "Let's go a bit more, and if we see nothing, we'll head back to camp."

Charley nodded and spurred his horse forward. He stayed well ahead of me for a quarter mile or so until I lost sight of him. Little bumps raised on my arms and my scalp tingled at being alone, I guess. I hated to admit a tinge of fear edged into my chest. I urged my horse to catch up.

Up ahead, thick stands of oak, mesquite, and cottonwood cloaked Charlie. I wanted to holler for him to hold up, wait for me, but that felt silly. Instead, I plunged into the undergrowth.

Coming out, with only a couple of extra scrapes from mesquite branches, I looked to my left and spotted Charlie. Off his horse. Standing, arms above his head. He turned to me, eyes wide.

In front of my partner stood three men. Two I recognized. Larkin and the other man in jail. The third I didn't know. The leader's rifle was aimed at Charlie's chest and at that distance, he couldn't miss. The others pointed their guns at me.

"Off the horse, Nolan." Larkin waved the rifle.

If I was going to die today, I vowed to take at least one of them with me. All reason left me. "You're on Carmichael land. You need to get off."

"I said get off' the horse, Nolan, or I'll yank you off."

"And I said, get off' the property, Larkin." I took a beat. "Now."

Larkin rushed me and before I could lash out with a boot, he grabbed my arm and yanked me out of the saddle. I hit on my shoulder but managed to get to my feet without much trouble. Chest filled with anger, I fisted both hands and swung. I hit nothing.

"Wanna dance, cowboy?" Larkin unbuckled his rig, tossed the gun and belt onto the ground. "Now, it's just you and me, kid."

"Been waiting for this." I bent and rammed him in the stomach and chest. He *ooffed* and thudded onto his back. Quick as a cat, he sprang to his feet, grabbed me around the waist, and like intimate dancers, we headed for the water.

We splashed within seconds, and I tripped over a rock. I took him down with me. Locked in an embrace, we rolled back and forth, each gaining the upper hand from time to time. Breathing proved difficult as did gaining my feet. We tumbled and turned and bounced off rocks, each of us fighting for victory.

Larkin was stronger than he looked. He held me down in the water, on my back.

Struggling, I tried to keep my face above water, but he

kept pushing me under. Flailing like a madman, I pulled in what I hoped was air. Water rushed down my throat. I coughed.

Sitting on top of me with his hand under my chin, he'd make sure I'd drown. Lungs on fire, I had to breathe. And that's when my hand touched a rock. A fist-sized rock. I gripped it, swung up and clobbered him in the head. He let up.

I struggled upright, my head above water and took several deep breaths. Water gushed from my nose, dribbled down my chin. Coughing up more water and breathing real air, so glad to be alive, I looked at Larkin. He lay on his back, unmoving, water lapping over his face. Blood poured down the left side of his head and mingled with the stream water.

Was he dead? Most of me wanted that. Somehow, I found the strength to stand, despite water tugging at my britches. I toed Larkin. Like that rattler. Definitely dead.

CHAPTER TWENTY-FOUR

I STOOD IN THE STREAM WONDERING WHAT THE hell happened. One minute I'm minding my own business, looking for stray cattle, and the next, I'd killed a man. And it couldn't be just any man. Had to be a Stinson man. And Larkin at that.

I snapped back to the present. Two men still held guns on Charlie and me. Charlie's hands reached high, like trying to touch the sky. I brushed sopping wet hair out of my eyes and blinked at the surreal scene.

Stinson's man, on a black and white horse, cocked his gun.

I hit the stream bank, rolled into dirt.

Bang!

Why didn't *I* have a gun?

Bang! Bang!

I covered my head with my arms and dug my face as far into the ground as possible. Would a pebble stop a bullet? I prayed so.

Bang!

Hoofbeats echoed in my ears. I rolled left, hoping to

avoid being trampled. I lodged my entire body under a mesquite. Eyes squeezed tight, I drew up my knees to keep demons away, just like when I was three and it was thundering outside.

Death, horrific death, would descend any moment. I prayed it would be quick and painless.

I waited.

A full minute of silence passed before I uncoiled. Chuckling spread through the undergrowth. Was that me? No. I squinted only to discover Charlie, sitting against a cottonwood, laughing. A long look and the other men were gone.

Correction. Besides Larkin still in the water, another man lay face down by his horse. I supposed the other man had galloped off. Probably rushing off to tell daddy the men had been mean to him.

Finding my feet, still not sure where the other gunman was, I darted behind bushes until reaching Charlie. Kneeling beside him, I smiled at his smile. Unfortunately, blood trickled down the side of his head and he held his left forearm as if the entire thing was about to break off.

"You all right?" Of course he wasn't, but what else could I have said?

Charlie's brown eyes trailed up to me. "That sumabitch done shot me."

I pried his hand off his arm and pushed up a ripped sleeve. Blood coated the skin and dripped onto the ground. Sure enough. Looked like a bullet, probably a .36, had sailed right through that arm. If we looked hard enough, more than likely we'd find the bullet lodged in a tree.

"You're lucky, pard." I touched his head, but he jerked away. "Looks like you'll live to fight another day." I chinned toward his arm. "Glad you don't need that left arm to feed yourself. Otherwise, you'd get stinkin' hungry."

"He shot me." Charlie frowned, then spit. "Not fair."

"Yeah, but you shot *him*." I patted his shoulder. "And that *was* fair." I figured my friend didn't remember firing his weapon, but I did. My ears still rang from all the gunfire along with smoke clogging my nose. Sounded like what the Battle of Gettysburg must've been like. I thought ours would never end.

Charlie pushed up using his good arm. I helped where I could and examined his head closer this time. "Bullet came near taking your head off. Again, you're lucky."

His eyes cleared as he touched the caking blood. "This? Warn't no durn bullet. Hit a branch when I tried to take cover." He patted the wound. "Near took an eye."

I chuckled with him. "What should we—"

Bellowing and rustling turned us both to the south. I stepped closer to the sound, figuring the noise was those Charolais we were chasing. Sure enough, within seconds, across the stream on the other side of the fence, a white cow ambled past a mesquite, stopping to munch the hanging bean pods. An almost grown calf stood next to her and also pulled at the snack.

"Found two of 'em." I pointed with one hand and used the other to grip Charlie's good arm to keep him from swaying too much. And then like magic, another mama and her calves joined the first. The five appeared unconcerned that we were close enough to smell them.

Charlie wasn't in good enough shape to help me get those animals over to this side of the fence. The good news was they were right at the opening where Stinson's men had cut the wire. Should be easy enough to shoo them back to our side.

Before I could come up with a real plan, more rustling through the underbrush turned both our heads. Breath held, I wondered who was sneaking up on us now. More Stinson men?

I leaned back into the tree, probably figuring I could hide among the cottonwood branches. Charlie leaned too. The distinctive creaking of saddle leather and quiet talking between men tightened every muscle in my body. I pulled his gun out of his holster and gripped it tighter than I'd ever held anything before. I'd shoot first and ask questions later.

"Hey, Ray?" A voice I recognized sailed through the bushes. "Found couple horses here. Got our brand."

Had to be a fella named Big Mike, "big" being that he was well over six and a half feet with muscle to go with it. He could eat an entire pot of stew if allowed. I'd seen him pick up a half-grown calf, sling it over his shoulder and march across the pasture like he was on a Sunday stroll. He was about as kindly as he was substantial.

"Big Mike? Ray?" Figuring they should know we're here, so we didn't get shot by those two thinking we were rustlers, I called loud. "Over here. Charlie's hurt." I stuck my partner's gun back into his holster.

"Kid? That you?" Ray ducked under a cottonwood branch on our right.

He and Big Mike slid out of their saddles, tied all four horses to mesquite and joined us. Ray, being crew foreman and man officially in charge, nodded at Charlie. "What happened?"

Charlie looked from Ray to Big Mike to me as if expecting us to answer for him. When he frowned, I explained. In detail. Leaving nothing out.

"Well." Mulling over my story, Ray ambled to the water, toed Larkin just as I had done. Big Mike pushed the other fella over. Neither spoke.

Feeling guilty, but knowing I killed in self-defense, I rushed to explain further. I released Charlie and joined the two at the stream. "Didn't want to kill him. Tried to drown me." I'd already explained that part but felt the need to reinforce what I'd said.

Ray nodded, grabbed Larkin's arms. "Help me get him to the other side. Don't want him lying here. Cattle might get sick from drinking spoiled water." He looked at me with gray-brown eyes that danced in the sun.

We plopped Larkin next to the other man on Stinson's side of the stream. On his side of the fence.

"Well," Ray said. "This is unfortunate. Guess we'll leave 'em here and send word to Mr. Carmichael." He turned to me. "You and Charlie need to do it. We'll get him patched up, you cleaned off..."

I looked down at my shirt. Caked with mud and dirt. Pants, too. I swiped muck from my cheek and tasted mud. Who knows what was in my mustache. Now that I thought about it, I was wet clear through to my underdrawers and now itched all over. No doubt had water in my boots. With all the excitement over, I shivered. Wet, dirty, worried, I walked over to Charlie, now astride a horse, Big Mike standing next to him.

"We'll head on back and get him patched up." Big Mike swung up onto his horse.

I started for my horse and then remembered the reason we were here in the first place. "What about the cattle?" I pointed over my shoulder to the Charolais which had moseyed along the fence line, plucking at grass.

Ray let out colorful curse words, followed by a long

sigh. "I'll send a couple men to come get 'em. Think you've had enough fun for one day."

I agreed with him. One thing I'd learned—I definitely needed a gun.

* * *

MR. C. WAS NOT happy when Charlie and me told him what had happened. This late in the day, sun almost down, wasn't a good time to be talking about something so important. But here we were, in his office, standing there like two schoolboys who'd been caught eating the teacher's lunch. We hadn't done anything wrong. So, why did I feel that way?

Rubbing his stubbled chin, Mr. C. sighed, stared at me, swung his stare over to Charlie, sighed again and allowed his shoulders to droop. I hated like the dickens to cause him this much grief. I entertained the notion of simply walking out the door, hopping on my horse and riding away. Away from all the heartache I've been causing. If I stayed, there would only be more.

I stepped back from his desk and guessed my movement made him look at me again.

He rubbed his nose, took a deep breath, and spoke. His words were soft, not loud and harsh as I figured they'd be. "Maybe it'll be clearer after a night's rest, but I'm thinking the three of us need to ride down to San Antone first thing in the morning. Tell Sheriff Samuels what happened."

"But—"

Mr. C. held up a hand. "Way I see it, he'll either lock up both of you until an inquiry can be held or release Charlie to my custody. Tate, with your record, he'll probably want to keep you in jail."

"Jail? I haven't done anything wrong." I flapped my arms out at my side, almost smacking Charlie in the face. No way was I going back to jail. No way.

"The way you two tell it, it's a clear case of self-defense. But will Stinson see it like that? No. Not at all."

Charlie rubbed his arm and looked for a chair. His face was losing color and I figured he'd pass out if he didn't sit. I guided him to the chair I usually sat in since I wasn't using it right then. He sagged into it.

Mr. C. stood behind his desk and stared out the window into darkness. I could only guess what he was thinking and none of it was good. None of this was my fault, but the weight of the world pressed on my shoulders until I could hardly stand. I had no right to bring all this to such a good man and his wife.

He edged from behind his desk, and I backed a step thinking he might take a swing. Stopping within arm's reach, he reached out and I flinched. He patted my shoulder. "We'll figure something out. I've got a good lawyer in town. Before we see the sheriff, we'll go see him."

Was there a glimmer of hope? A lawyer? One on my side this time? Maybe, but I wasn't holding out much hope. My last lawyer, court-appointed and with whiskey on his breath, slept through my trial. He was no help. I could have done a better job defending myself.

He pointed toward the door while I helped Charlie to his feet. "You boys get a good night's sleep and after breakfast we'll ride into town."

I wanted to scream *I won't go*, but the adult in me muffled that. Instead, I said good night.

* * *

SLEEP WAS as elusive as me getting a gun. So close and yet, impossible to attain. The moon appeared, disappeared, the stars twinkled, then went out as the sun came up, and still, I deliberated about this predicament.

I wasn't going to jail. That was a given. But the rest was one red question mark. If I borrowed another horse, I'd be on the run as a horse thief and probably get myself hanged in the next town. I couldn't go into Blanco Hill because sure as anything, Sheriff Becker and his dumb-as-shite deputy would arrest me or shoot me for some trumped up charge.

If I went with Mr. C., I'd wind up in jail and, if Stinson had his way, I'd hang.

If I left and rode to Mexico, at least I'd be safe. Probably. I'd have to learn more Spanish than the little bit I already knew. But I could work in a cantina—pour tequila with the best of them—or muck out stalls in a stable. As long as I wasn't in jail.

And, if I made enough money to have some extra, I could send for Imogene and Louisa. We could rent a small *casa* and—

"Sun's up, kid." Smitty smacked my foot. "Come help with breakfast."

I jumped. I'd been sleeping? Sitting up, I rubbed swollen eyes I was certain were bright red. "Be right there."

Splashing cold water on my face, I felt more awake. Didn't look much better if my reflection in the shaving mirror was any indication. I examined fingerprint bruises on my neck and under my chin. Maybe those would keep me out of jail. I ran a hand over them. Nah. Nothing would keep me from gripping bars.

I cut up potatoes, onions, and bacon which Smitty fried together. The aromas tantalized my appetite until I figured if they weren't done soon, I'd eat the cast iron pan. Charlie, looking better than the night before, wandered into the dining area just as food was ready. We plopped down at the table where only two other hands were waiting.

Between shoveling in food and gulping coffee, the four of us caught up on events and gossip from the past month. Seems not much had happened around the ranch and even less in town. For that, I was grateful. Apparently, life was boring when I wasn't in it.

Still undecided about this next adventure, I reluctantly eased off the bench, stacked my plate and cup on the counter, and looked at the door. What if I ran the other way? The back door led to the privy and farther on to the stream. Maybe I could hop the stream and keep going. But somehow, I found myself standing outside by the hitch rail with Charlie and Mr. C. on either side of me.

Mr. C. fitted his hat down tight. "Might as well get this done, boys. Mount up."

I swung up onto a sorrel I'd ridden often before. Ol' Jasmine and I got along well. She was fast, an easy galloper, and never once tried to bite me. We reined away from the house where I spotted Mrs. C. on the porch waving goodbye. I returned the gesture figuring I'd never see her again.

We rode out of the yard, down the road to where it T'd. To the right was Blanco Hill, the other way San Antonio. I pulled rein. Charlie and Mr. C. stopped, turned in their saddles, and frowned at me.

"This's as far as I go." My words weren't rehearsed but certainly heartfelt. I had trouble making eye contact with my mentor, my friend. A man who'd saved my butt more than once. How could I do this to him? I had no choice.

"Mr. Carmichael." A frog caught in my throat. "I sure appreciate all you've done for me. I do. But…" I breathed deeply, glanced at Charlie then back to Mr. C. "I can't go to jail. I won't. I'll be leaving you now. You've got my pay coming to me. Consider that a down payment on this horse. So, it's not stolen or borrowed, but bought."

"What the—"

I held up a hand, the other gripping the reins so tightly I was sure they'd melt into one strand. "With me gone, you won't have any more trouble. Seems everywhere I go, trouble follows and I'm gonna take it someplace else."

I turned to Charlie, saddle creaking under me. "You're the closest thing I've had to a real friend in quite a while. Sorry you got shot and I hope Mr. Carmichael's lawyer can keep you out of jail."

"Wish you'd reconsider." Mr. C.'s words were soft. "Becker brought your parole release papers the other day. They're signed, on my desk." He looked at me, his eyes pleading. "You're a free man, Tate. But if you run, I have no doubt there'll be a wanted poster on you within a day or two."

Well, well, I hadn't considered that. But free? That was music to my ears and brought a smile to my face. "I'm gonna enjoy my freedom while I can, sir."

"Where you going?" Mr. C. looked beyond me.

"Not sure. Just know it won't be around here." I reset my hat and nodded. "Gotta go. Thank you again, Mr. Carmichael and I'm sorry. Please give Mrs. Carmichael my regrets."

And with that, I spurred Jasmine into a gallop,

leaving Charlie and Mr. C. behind. I dared not look over my shoulder. I'd probably change my mind.

I headed south and west with no destination in mind, simply away. From jail. From trouble.

Now at a trot, Jasmine and I covered hills, a wide valley, two streams and skirted a rock outcropping. I'd ridden over an hour and needed to stretch. A stand of Texas oak stood in the distance which would serve well as a resting place.

I sat in the shade appreciating a cool breeze and sipped water from my canteen while Jasmine pulled at grasses. I chuckled thinking that if someone came up on us, they'd probably think we were idling away our day, enjoying life. But in reality, I was trying like mad to figure my next move.

Could I simply ride down to Mexico without telling anybody where I was going? Had I turned into that kind of man? Maybe. Another sip. Selfish. That's what I was. Selfish. And scared. I was terrified of going back to jail and hanging. But still, could I just ride away without telling Ma and Da and Eagan how much I loved them?

Decision made. I'd sneak into town, say my goodbyes, and ride out—quietly. Nobody except my family would know. Then I'd hie myself to Mexico. I'd change my name. While I swung up into the saddle, I tried out different monikers. Tate James. No. Henry Baca. Nope. Seamus O'Brien. Well, Seamus was easy since that was my first name. O'Brien I simply liked. But was it too Irish?

Kid Texas. Tate the Texan. Blanco Kid.

I continued riding and thinking, putting on one name after another, then shedding them. Had Frank and Jesse James gone by aliases? Maybe. But they weren't in hiding like I was. If I moved to Mexico, I could be Pedro

Obreon. That worked. Otherwise, Seamus O'Brien it was.

* * *

I WAITED on the outskirts of Blanco Hill until lamps up and down Main had been lit. Circles of light on the boardwalk gave downtown a welcoming glow. But not for me. I wasn't welcome here, at least by a few people in town. Especially Becker. My face grew warm thinking of that scum-sucking man.

Fortunately, our house wasn't directly in town, more on the edge, so stabling Jasmine in the barn was easy. The next neighbor was a hundred yards away and they were old and hard of hearing. I relaxed at that thought. Undoubtedly, they'd gone to bed with the chickens and wouldn't hear the barn door squeaking open if it was under their bed.

I made sure Jasmine had enough oats to snack on and gave a big handful to Da's horse as well. Deciding I'd more than likely stay the night, if not in the house, then the barn for sure, I unsaddled my horse and rubbed her back with the saddle blanket, promising her a good brushing and combing first thing in the morning.

That chore done, I tiptoed to the house, glad to see a lamp lit in the front room. Somebody was up. After taking at long breath, I tapped on the door, which felt odd since I lived here. Or rather, did. Still, this was my home.

Da looked out the curtained window to see who was disturbing their quiet evening. The door flew open, and I was greeted with Da's warm handshake followed by a tight hug from Ma. Eagan peered out from the bedroom, then like a bull, bolted across the front room, knocking into me. I spun and held onto the doorframe to keep from tumbling back outside.

Words swirled throughout the room, bumping into each other like a school of fish trying to get at one worm. Ma fussed over my bruises and worried I looked like I hadn't eaten, lost weight, not been sleeping...a smile ached my cheeks. It was good to be home.

When we had worn out ourselves talking, we sat in the front room and discussed my situation. Tears rolled down Ma's cheeks when I told her I would be leaving, for a long time anyway. She wasn't one to get emotional, but with one son gone and now the next soon to be, she probably realized her babies were all grown up. Probably hard for any ma to see that. But I couldn't help it.

"I'll stay tonight, if that's all right with you." I looked at each one. "I'll leave first thing tomorrow."

"Where will ye go?" Ma wiped the final tear.

I shrugged. "Mexico maybe."

Eagan punched me in the arm, again. "Watch out for them señoritas, big brother. I hear they—"

I shot him a piercing glare. That would be a conversation for later tonight, after the folks were asleep. Knowing it was past usual bedtimes, I yawned and stretched, even though I wasn't tired. Or sleepy. Excitement of the unknown kept me on edge.

Finally, we said our goodnights and headed for bed. Eagan and I stayed up talking until the first rooster crowed. The sun wasn't even thinking of rising yet when I slipped out of bed. Eagan's soft breathing tugged on me to stay. One more day. Just one.

One more day would give me a chance to figure things out. I'd talk with Ma, always the voice of reason. Maybe Da could loan me money. Or Eagan, for that matter. All right. One more day.

CHAPTER TWENTY-FIVE

ONE MORE DAY TURNED INTO TWO. WITH JOE gone, chores had piled up. While Da and Eagan were at work, I chopped wood, carting in a couple armloads for Ma. Part of the barn's wall was warping, and I enjoyed the work of hammering it back into place, plus I was out of sight. I hoped. I fed the chickens, a chore delegated to Ma, but she was busy inside sewing me another shirt.

When we weren't working, Ma and I sat at the kitchen table sipping tea and talking. Discussing. A bit of lecturing too.

"Ye gotta face facts, Tate." Ma's stare bore an uncomfortable hole into my soul. "Ye're a wanted man, ye are. Ye shoulda gone with that kind Mr. Carmichael, ye shoulda." She finished her tea, daintily setting the cup on the table. "But ye didna, so we needa think this through."

A knife through the heart wouldn't hurt this much. What had I done to my mother? She deserved only happiness, not...this...not *me*.

And while I sipped tea wishing it was coffee, I wondered what had happened to my dream of robbing more banks and trains than the James boys. Had I side-tracked? Had Mr. Carmichael influenced me to stay on the straight and narrow? Absolutely. But I still needed money. If Da couldn't loan me some, I'd be forced to rob again. Hopefully next time I'd get more than fourteen dollars like I had from the telegraph office.

Da came through by handing me thirty dollars when he got home. Eagan added twenty. I was set. Fifty was enough to see me through for the next month. Maybe more. I'd heard living in Mexico was cheap. I'd find out soon.

The four of us sat at the dinner table and passed the time like we always had. Some discussions, some arguments, some agreements. Over roast chicken, fried potatoes—a staple in this family—cornbread and peas, we enjoyed each other's company. At least I sure did. A weight like I'd never known before sat on my chest and burrowed itself into my heart. I was leaving. For good. I hated myself for getting into this in the first place. But as Ma said, what's done was done.

I raised a forkful of apple pie to my mouth when a knock at the door made me recoil. Nearly dropping the fork, I immediately considered hiding under the table. I was too big for that. Da wiped his mouth, tossed the napkin onto the table, grumbled what I thought were curse words, but knowing Ma was sitting right there, he wouldn't dare.

I sat stock still while Da opened the door. From there, visitors couldn't see into the dining room. I thought about pressing myself against a wall, melting into the horsehair plaster. I'd be safe there. But that would require movement. Could they hear my heart beating? I sure could.

"Evening, Mr. Nolan."

"Sheriff."

Sheriff Becker! Immediately I recognized that surly voice. A glance at Ma and Eagan. Had they turned a shade lighter? No. Anger tinged Ma's cheeks. She glanced at me, rose, and marched off. I listened hard.

"Ah, Mrs. Nolan. Good evening. Mind if I come in?"

"I'm afraid I do. The house isn't picked up. We weren't expecting company." Ma's voice was polite, but definitive. "I'd prefer we stand on the porch. 'Tis a lovely evening."

"Yes ma'am, it is at that."

Footsteps told me they headed outside. I glanced at Eagan who stood, pushed his chair back, and walked to the door. Alone now, I prayed Becker simply wanted to come say howdy. Right. And I'm the queen of England.

Although their conversation on the porch was harder to hear, I made out all the words.

Becker started soft and soon grew louder. "Sorry to tell you this, but your son, Tate, has a wanted poster out on him."

"A wanted poster?" Da's words were laced with worry.

A pause. "Afraid so. Seems he killed a hand of the rancher Ira Stinson. Man named Larkin. According to the word I got, Larkin and your son had been feuding. Over what, isn't clear. But Tate killed him."

Ma gasped, loud.

Da cursed.

Becker continued. "Figure he hightailed it here. I checked in the barn and there's a horse with Carmichael's brand." A long pause. "Tate's here, ain't he?"

"No sir." Eagan spoke up. "That's my horse. Da said I could buy one, so I saved my money. Mr. Carmichael had this one for sale, so I bought her. Her name's Jasmine. She rides good too. Ask Mr. Carmichael. He'll tell you."

"Got a bill of sale for that critter, Eagan?"

"'Course I do." Eagan spoke with surety. "It's in my room. I'll go get it."

"No need. I believe you."

I wish I could've seen Ma's face. No doubt she was concerned her youngest son could lie with such conviction. Possibly a wave of pride washed over her too. I was a bit awed myself. Could I have faced down a badge like that? At my brother's age?

The screen door squeaked open, then shut. Within seconds my three family members regained their seats at the table. My shoulders relaxed, but that was the only part that did. We sat quietly, feasting on but not tasting Ma's apple pie.

Pie and tea finished, I helped Ma clear the table and wash dishes. Being an old hand now at drying, we had the kitchen spotless within minutes. Dish towel in hand, I gave Ma a tight hug. She hugged back.

"Ye're leaving first light, aren't ye, son?"

Nodding, my heart shattered. I didn't want to leave but staying was no longer an option.

Still in my embrace, she asked, "Where'll ye go?"

Truly, I wasn't sure Mexico was the answer, but I told her so, anyway. While drying, I'd decided on Denver. It was a fledgling little gold mining camp with plenty of horses and plenty of stalls to muck. I'd meet up with Joe and together we could build an empire. Or we could rob banks together, like the James boys. So, in case she told someone who told Becker I was in Mexico, I'd be safe in Denver.

Denver, it was. For sure. Unless I came up with another idea.

Before bed, I gave Da the heartiest, most heartfelt handshake I could muster. Eagan, I punched in the shoulder a time or two reminding him who was the older brother. Ma, I hugged again reassuring her I'd be fine and not to give up on me. I'd see them all again soon.

Last light extinguished, my heart went out too. All the joy in my soul seemed to vanish as fast as the flame. I hadn't carried much with me when I left Carmichael's, so I had not much to pack, just the shirt Ma finished. She had promised a sack lunch for my trip, but I wouldn't be there for her to make it.

I waited until heavy breathing and a snore now and then rumbled around the house. A half-moon provided the right amount of light for me to get dressed, tiptoe across the house, grab my saddlebag and, inch by inch, open the door. I stepped onto the porch, closed the door behind me and squat-walked to the barn.

Jasmine perked up when I touched her as if saying she was ready to run. Good to know *she* was because *I* certainly wasn't. She let me saddle her without being ornery like some of the other mounts. She didn't bloat her sides, kick at me, or try to bite. Luck had been with me when I bought her.

Leading her out of the barn, I halted, looked left then right. Nothing but shadows and an owl flying onto a tree branch. Quiet. So quiet my nerves tingled. Quiet like a monster lurking behind the tree, waiting for me to mount up. While peering into the dark, I rubbed the back of my neck like it was still mud encrusted.

Simply my nerves, I told myself over and over. No such things as monsters. I rethought. Becker's a monster. Stinson is, too. But not the big, hairy, four-legged variety of man-eating monsters. But, nonetheless, they were man-eaters.

I swung up into the saddle, gave the house one last look, then headed north. Denver, I knew, was north and a bit west. How far of each I wasn't sure, but along the way someone could surely point me in the right direction. And with fifty dollars jingling in my pocket, I could afford a hotel a night or two. Things were looking up.

While night cloaked us, I let Jasmine walk a bit, then trotted. While I wasn't in an all-fire hurry to get miles under me, I didn't want to tarry, either. But galloping in the dark was a certain recipe for disaster if she stepped into a gopher hole or fell down a ravine. No, better to take it slow.

Fredericksburg sat about twenty miles west and a bit north of Blanco Hill. The sun was bathing the countryside in rich gold and rose hues. We could see where we were going, and I considered heading straight for that town. I hadn't been there since I was a kid and hoped they had a grocer where I could pick up supplies. Eating at a restaurant was too expensive. That would be a treat I'd reserve for later.

It was almost noon judging by the sun when I rode into Fredericksburg, a town of distinct German influence. Signs everywhere were in what they called Texas German, a melding of English and the various German dialects. A church, its steeple soaring above the town, sat in the middle of shops and houses. Jasmine and I surveyed Main Street as we sauntered toward a mercantile I spotted at the far end. Before we got there, I noticed a store with a sign proclaiming *Krauskopf's Guns*. Gunsmith, huh? First thing I needed.

I tied the reins to the rail out front, sashayed in like I had no cares, and froze. At least twenty guns of various sizes, makes and models lay in the display cases. How could I choose the one for me?

An older man, long beard setting off hard blue eyes, came out from behind a curtain which I supposed led to a back room. He eyed me up and down, then nodded, I guess approving of what he saw.

I stuck out a hand. "Seamus O'Brien, sir."

Studying my hand, he reluctantly extended his. "Englebert Krauskopf. I own dis here gun shop."

I spent the next hour or so handling each one, running my hand down the barrel like I was caressing a woman. And like a woman, each felt different in my hand, the way the grip fit or the heft. Not wanting to spend more than twelve, fifteen dollars, my choices were a bit more limited. But still, the gunsmith displayed three that fit my needs. I'd always wanted a Colt and there lay one, right in front of me.

The price was right for a .36 Navy Colt, which left me enough for ammunition and a used rig. Krauskopf had one hanging on a peg. I tried it on, and the holster seemed to glue itself to my right hip. Perfect. I was sure my grin lit the entire room as it stretched my cheeks. And the Colt slipped into the holster like it was made for it.

I loaded the cartridges into the bullet loops around the belt of the rig, buckled it around my hips, slid the gun into the holster, and I was ready. Soon, I'd have a name bigger than Jesse James. Bigger than Frank. Bigger'n both of them, together.

Total cost was close to twenty dollars, which left me with thirty. If I was careful the next month, I would do just fine. I thanked Mr. Krauskopf for the millionth time, adjusted the rig once more, set my hat on straight and stepped into sunshine. Glorious, glorious sunshine.

With such a lovely day on hand, I chose to walk down the boardwalk to the mercantile instead of riding. I'd admit I swaggered a bit, like those pirates when they looted towns. But I finally had what I'd wanted for years. And a Colt, no less.

On the way, I tipped my hat to all the women, pretty or not, and nodded to the men. Was it my imagination, but did each one stop and stare? Could my shoulders go back any farther?

I passed an alley within sight of the mercantile. My focus on the store, I failed to see a man step out of the shadow, grab my arm, wrench it up behind my back, kick my knees. I landed face first in the dirt. He kneeled on my back with one knee on my left shoulder. I couldn't move. I could barely breathe.

"Gotcha!" The man's voice was familiar. "Thought you could run." Cackles flew into the air.

When the weight lifted, I rolled over. There kneeled Sheriff Becker, that sneer pushing up his mustache while his beady eyes narrowed. Speechless. For once, I was speechless. Hundreds of questions bombarded my brain. Nothing came out through my mouth.

He leaned back studying me. One knee kept my right shoulder pressed against the ground. "Knew you ran home. Your brother's a liar."

"Lying for a brother isn't a crime." Had those words managed to escape?

"It is when it comes to aiding a fugitive. He'll be in jail by day's end."

Bollocks! Not Eagan. What had I done? Next, he'd arrest Ma and Da. "No. Leave him alone." Rage filled me with an unknown intensity. If I could have reached my gun, I would've shot the man.

He eyed my body as if choosing which portion to cut off for supper. "See you bought yourself a gun." Becker pulled my weapon out of the holster, inspected it. "Nice piece. This new?" He turned it over then jammed it under his belt. "Who'd you steal it from?"

"Bought it fair and square."

"Uh huh. Just like Eagan and his horse."

"Bill of sale's in my pocket."

Still kneeling on my shoulder, which was turning numb, he riffled through my pockets. I grabbed at his sleeve with the only hand available, but that didn't keep him from finding my money.

He held up the bills and two coins. "Well, lookey here. Where'd you get this kinda money?"

"Mine." I wasn't about to tell him anything. That no-good, worthless road apple.

Releasing the pressure on my shoulder, he stood, thumbing through my money. "Well, well. Thirty...no, thirty-two dollars."

I sat rubbing my recently healed shoulder which hurt like a hot poker had gone clear through. Pushing up to my feet, I reached for my money. He held it at arm's length.

"How much's your brother's freedom worth?"

"What?"

"Aiding a fugitive'll get him five to ten." His eyebrows lifted. "That's a long time. Wanna keep Eagan outta jail? What's it worth to you?"

"What?"

The sheriff snickered. "I'm thinkin' thirty-two oughta do the trick." He stuffed the money into an inside vest pocket. "And this Colt should be enough to keep your pa at home too." He glared at bystanders who'd gathered to watch the spectacle.

Turning back to me, he added, "Oh. And your rig too. That's for your ma." He spun his forefinger at my gun belt. "Now."

If I headbutted him, he'd *oof* and go down. I could beat him senseless, but surely by now the local sheriff or town marshal, or even the mayor, knew what was going on. I'd go to jail in Fredericksburg. Probably hang for assaulting a law officer. Instead, I unbuckled my new prized possession and handed over the leather rig.

"You ain't as dumb as you look, boy."

Still standing in the alley, I had to know. "How'd you find me?"

"I take back what I said about you not being dumb. Figured you were heading for either Mexico or Denver, since that's where your brother is. I sent Deputy Wagner to watch the road to Mexico, and I came here, knowing you'd need supplies since you left before dawn." He pointed up the street. "Saw you ride in. I waited here." He shrugged, giving me the once over. "You walked right into my web."

Dumb. Yep. I was dumb.

CHAPTER TWENTY-SIX

ALL RIGHT. SURPRISINGLY, I WASN'T IN JAIL. Seemed to be a habit of Becker's. Whenever I saw him, he tried to toss me behind bars. So, this time I was free. That was the good thing. On the downside, he had everything I owned in the world. I had no money, no gun, no food. Fair enough, at least I still had a horse. Becker hadn't taken Jasmine. Which left me—the shirt Ma sewed the day before, my horse, and saddle.

Pretty much stranded in Fredericksburg, I sat on the bench in front of the mercantile and watched that dumb as dirt sheriff ride off with my belongings. He had the audacity to flash a wide smile and salute me as he rode by. I returned the salute but used only one finger.

I could sit there all afternoon and pray for someone to come by and take pity on me. Or, if I was going to be a bank robber, maybe this would be a good day to start. My stomach rumbled then complained loudly. Since I hadn't fed it that morning, I knew the noisemaker wouldn't let up until food came its way. From the bench, I glanced right, left and across the street.

And there it was. A German bakery. Right across from me. I pulled in air smelling what I was sure was strudel. Yep. Apple strudel bursting with hard-to-find cinnamon. Without thinking, I licked my lips and narrowed my eyes to where all I saw was that bakery. An idea flooded my brain. I could hold them up and demand nothing but food. Why not? A man's gotta eat.

Now I needed a plan. Surely, they had a back door. I'd tie Jasmine in the alley near the door. Go in the front, pretend I had a gun, have them put as much food and money into a sack as they could, and I'd scurry out the back, jump on Jasmine and ride.

Since Becker—I gnashed my teeth at that name— knew I was heading for Denver, I'd have to change directions. If I went south to Mexico, surely Becker and his crazy deputy would find me. East was back the way I'd come, so north it was. I'd head toward a cattle town I'd heard mentioned, Fort Worth.

I led Jasmine to the alley and sure enough, found the bakery's back door. I tied her to a wooden crate, patted her neck assuring her things would be fine, and made my way to the front. That heavenly scent of baked bread floated under my nose before I stepped inside. My stomach did a backflip knowing food was on the way. Nothing smelled better than pastries and bread baking... or perhaps a nice steak...or Ma's fried chicken...before I realized it, I was inside, standing there. At the counter.

A lady approached me from the kitchen as I stood, soaking in the smells. *"Willkomen."* Her German had a distinct Texas drawl.

She wasn't much older than me. A floury fingerprint dotted her pink cheeks and her smile reached ear to ear. She greeted me like I was long-lost kin. Round blue eyes peeked at me from under impossibly long eyelashes. Immediately, I was in love. Or lust.

Right then my stomach decided to interject itself into my infatuation. It rumbled louder than a dish being dropped on a hard floor. Thoroughly embarrassed, I pushed on my stomach hoping to silence the intruder.

Smiling, a chortle pushing through, she cocked her head. "*Hungrig?*"

How could I tell this lovely lady I'd come to rob her? I couldn't. Instead, my shoulders slumped until I propped them up remembering the young lady. "This all you have? Everything?" I pointed at a tray of two pastries and one lonely pie.

"*Ja.*" Her eyes and mouth curved down a bit. "All for today. We're about to close. Not much left, I'm afraid." Her English, strong German accent, sung a song I'd never heard. The tune flew to my heart and captured my entire soul. She purred, "Come back tomorrow morning. We have more then."

I put fingertips to my hat brim, nodded something unintelligible, and backed out through the door and into the street. I stood staring up at the sign, the building, the door. No way could I rob such a creature. If I had money, I'd invite her to supper. As it was, she'd have to invite me.

* * *

I SAT under a tree by a little stream on the outskirts of town. Shadows grew longer as I chewed on a dandelion while Jasmine munched grass. I envied a critter that had food all around. Closing my eyes, I let self-pity wash over me. What kind of outlaw was I when I couldn't even hold up a bakery? A bakery, for Pete's sake. At least I could've been fed for my troubles.

Boysenberry pie aromas wafted my way. I opened my eyes and sniffed harder. Maybe dewberry or strawberry? Whatever it was, reminded me of my predicament. I pushed up to my feet. I'd follow my nose and get something to eat or die trying.

Leaving Jasmine where she was, I sniffed my way up toward town. A house sat alone, neighbors half a block away. And then I spied the aroma's source. Sure enough, a pie sat cooling on a windowsill. A long look left, right, behind me and straight ahead revealed nobody in sight. Not to be denied this time, my stomach prodded me to that window.

Oh yes. Fresh out of the oven, a pie, its lattice crust with dewberries peeking out, beckoned me like a seductive temptress. My hands on the plate, I slid it toward me anticipating the rapture to follow.

"Excuse me, young man." A woman's voice from beyond the pie called. "That's mine and I'll not be sharin'. It's made special." She leaned out through the open window so close I could see lines jutting out from her dark blue eyes, creases across her forehead, white hair swept up into a bun.

"Ma'am." Was I stuttering? "I apologize, but your pie smelled so good, and I haven't eaten since yesterday."

She leaned closer, if that was possible. "Made this pie for my Karl. He's coming home today." She sighed. "Or tomorrow."

Something about this woman drew me in. Older than Ma by at least twenty years, she seemed like a nice lady. I had to ask. "Where's Karl? If you don't mind my asking."

Standing straight, she threw her shoulders back and stuck out her chin. "Fighting in the war, of course."

"War, ma'am?" I hadn't heard about a new war.

"War of Northern Aggression, of course. Last I heard he was in Mississippi, some place called Vicksburg." Her eyes widened. "Of course! I know you! Where are my manners?"

"Ma'am?" What was she thinking? That war had come to a horrible end over seven years ago. And who exactly did she think I was?

"Come on around to the front door. Come in and you can tell me all about my Karl. He said a fellow from his regiment was stopping by." She waved toward the dark interior. "You must be him."

All right. If it meant I could eat, I'd be whoever she wanted. She greeted me at the front door and hugged me. Standing back, she eyed me hat to boots. "Fine figure of a soldier, ya are." She nodded approval. "Just like my Karl."

She flapped her hands and fluttered like a biddy chicken. "Heavens, there. Of course, you're hungry from such a long journey." Pointing to another room, she waved me to follow. "Come sit. I've got a meat pie coming out of the oven."

Oh boy. Luck had shone on me this afternoon. I sat at the dining table already set with two forks, two napkins, two spoons on two embroidered cloth placemats. "Will your husband be joining us?"

At the stove, she froze, then slowly turned to me. "Poor Günther. He's now wit' God. Went to heaven yesterday."

"Yesterday, ma'am?"

"Ja. Yesterday." She turned back to the oven, extracted a cast iron skillet with meat pie aromas spiraling into the kitchen. She set it on the stovetop, closed the oven door and took down two plates from the shelf above. "Or maybe last week."

Ready to eat the table itself, I steeled myself to wait for another half hour until the pie was edible.

"Sorry to hear about your husband." I glanced around the kitchen where I sat at the table. Nothing seemed out of place, not like she'd had a funeral yesterday. Or maybe she was getting ready for one. "I didn't catch your name, Mrs...."

She tossed a grin at me and flapped a hand. "Mrs. Steinmaker. Gertrude Steinmaker."

I hesitated, then stuck out a hand to shake with her. "Seamus O'Brien, ma'am."

Her hand, soft, aged, knuckles thickened showing years of hard work, felt tiny in mine. She *was* tiny. Came up to my shoulders when we had stood at the door. As much as I wanted to know more about this woman, my attention drifted from the pie on the windowsill to the meat pie cooling on the stove. I picked up a cloth napkin, brought it to my mouth and chewed on the end.

"Oh, of course, you're hungry, Mr. O'Brien. Let me get you food."

Music to my ears and my stomach, she slid a plate of steaming meat and potatoes with a bit of crust under my nose. She served herself half that amount, then sat.

Before she started, she leaned across the table at me. "Tell me about my Karl. Is he happy? Is he all right?" She gazed longingly at the door. "Will be wonderful to see him again. Bet he's grown."

Waiting a bit more for the food to cool, I gave general descriptions of her son's actions. He was brave. True to the cause. A good man to fight alongside with. Even went so far as telling her he'd saved a few lives. No use saying anything bad about the man. I hated like the blazes to lie—maybe I wasn't, maybe he really *was* the saint I'd painted—but I didn't know for sure. I hated even worse telling her that more than likely, Karl hadn't survived Vicksburg. He would never come through those doors. But I couldn't. No way could I break an old lady's heart.

Although still too warm, the first bite of heaven slid down my throat without hesitation. My stomach rumbled its applause. I tried to eat one bite at a time, interspersed with sips of cold milk she'd brought to the table. Although my glass was still half full, the plate was completely empty. Not a crumb to be seen. I had to admit, I hadn't really tasted much of the meat pie. Surely, with a second helping, I could savor the meal better.

I sat waiting for Mrs. Steinmaker to offer more. One thing Ma had instilled in us three boys was manners. Part of me wanted to get up and help myself, but Ma's words in my ear kept me seated. So, I waited. And waited. My hostess ate like a bird, pecking at her food, tiny bits on her fork. I watched every bite go to her mouth.

We passed the time in small chitchat. She asked little of me, mostly about her son. Since I had been too young to join the Confederacy back in '62, my memory relied on what I'd heard veterans talk about. And that wasn't much.

She had one more bite to go when she studied my plate. "Of course, you're still hungry." She flapped a hand at me. "Would you like another helping?"

"Yes, ma'am, I surely would." I stood, plate in hand. "It's the best meat pie I've had in years." No way would I tell her ma fixed one two days ago. I pointed to the stove. "Mind if I help myself?"

"I don't mind. Take all you want. I know you're a growing boy." Her eyes misted a bit. "Just like my Karl."

My heart broke for this kind woman, but what could I do? Maybe in exchange for giving me food, I could do some work around the house. Now with her men gone, surely she had chores needed doing.

Over a second helping, I broached the subject.

She looked at me, those sad blue eyes taking in the kitchen. "That would be wonderful, Mr. O'Brien. But I know you've got your life to live. Somewhere to go. Something you're going to do." A partial smile pinked her cheeks. "But I'd be mighty grateful for a day or two of your strong arms. And company."

No way would I ask for pay, her cooking and a place to sleep off the ground would be recompense enough. I'd need to get a job—or rob the bakery—to put coin in my pocket for my trip to Fort Worth. Figured I'd need at least five dollars to see me there. And that was five more than I had now.

"It's no problem, Mrs. Steinmaker." I sipped my milk and smiled at her smile. "Happy to help out."

While her meat pie was unforgettable, the dewberry pie turned out to be delicious. Tart in the right places, sweet in others. And the crust melted in my mouth. Ma was a good cook, but this woman made pie like an angel. A second piece was better than the first.

After supper, I stabled Jasmine in the barn where I noticed a couple boards on the wall about to come loose. After finding a set of tools carefully stored in a box, I spent an hour shoring up the horse home, which turned out to house not only Jasmine but a filly in good shape. Looked like she hadn't been watered yet today, but she had hay within reach. Probably a good handful of oats for both horses was in order.

By the time I stomped off muck from my boots and entered the house, my body had decided it was bedtime. Like a wave washing over me, exhaustion set in. Thinking back, it had been one long, heckuva day. Left home before sunup, bought a gun, lost the gun, had my money stolen, tried to rob a bakery, met a crazy woman, finally got fed, decided I'd go to Fort Worth. Yep, a long day.

Mrs. Steinmaker offered me Karl's bed. I didn't check to see how old the sheets were and if they'd been changed since he'd marched off. I didn't care. I said goodnight, pried off my boots and hat, and eased into bed.

Boiling coffee aroma opened my eyes. Slivers of gold spread across the room and ran down a wall. Morning, already? Sitting on the edge of the bed, I thought back to the previous day, ran a hand through my hair, the same hand across my cheeks. Time for a shave.

A stand with a water pitcher and a small mirror stood against the far wall. Looked like Karl had been of shaving age. I tugged on boots, took the pitcher, said good morning to Mrs. Steinmaker in the kitchen, and went out back to the pump. By now, about half the houses had water pumps inside the kitchen. I wasn't sure what it would take to make the change, but I knew nothing about plumbing. I could dig a trench, but that was about it.

All shaved, mustache trimmed, face washed, I joined her in the kitchen. She handed me a porcelain teacup, way too small for my hands, filled it with coffee and pointed to a chair at the table.

"Breakfast'll be two shakes." She tossed me a light grin. "Hope you like bacon, eggs, and flapjacks."

My stomach jumped for joy. "Yes ma'am, I do. Fact is"

—this part was mostly true—"it's my favorite." Except for strudel, pastries with strawberries, even porridge on a cold winter day. I struggled to find something I didn't like. Guessed I wasn't too particular.

We sat at the table enjoying breakfast and coffee. She sipped, picked at her food, and talked. I ate and listened. A second helping quieted my stomach. I'd never really considered how much I ate until comparing myself to Mrs. Steinmaker. In thinking on it, Ma didn't eat much either. Maybe it was a "ma" thing.

I took my time drinking a third cup of coffee. These cups were way too small for my big hands, and besides, I was used to mugs back at the ranch. However, Mrs. Steinmaker's coffee was quite superior to Smitty's. She certainly could cook.

"What would you like me to do first today? After I check on the horses."

Leaning back, she set down her cup, looked at me, then around the room. "Well, if you don't mind, I need wood split and kindling brought in." She flapped a hand. "If it's not too much for you."

"Happy to." I'm sure part of a grin pushed up my mustache. "What else?"

Pinkness spread across her cheeks. "Oh, my lord, you probably won't want to do this."

"Ma'am?"

"Well, if you insist." She flapped a hand again. "I need to go into town. Pick up a few things for tonight's supper. I'd appreciate strong arms carrying the sacks."

Going into town? Not where I'd wanted to be for a while. Forever. Maybe no one would remember me from yesterday. Maybe. Probably. And then another thought hit me. When we were paying for the items at the mercantile, I could see about their money drawer. More than likely the mercantile had more money than the bakery. But would it be harder to rob? I'd have to see.

"No problem, ma'am. I'd like to go with you and help. Haven't seen much of the town yet."

"Of course! Then it's settled." She stacked the plates in front of her. "You go tend the horses, I'll clean the kitchen, then we'll go shopping." She stood, smoothing her apron. "We'll have a grand day of it."

I wasn't so sure grand was the right word and tried on others while I fed, watered, and curried the stock. Found a few chickens in a coop behind the house. Fed and watered them too. I spent time looking around the property, figuring out what needed doing. To my surprise, the wood was chopped into small logs, and I'd have no trouble splitting them into kindling.

Puzzled, it seemed to me her husband died recently, or someone had been helping out. Not much was out of place.

I walked in through the back door and spotted Mrs. Steinmaker untying her apron. Underneath she wore a light blue dress, tucked in at the waist. The color set off her eyes. She'd been a handsome woman in younger years.

Thumbing over my shoulder, I asked about the wood and lack of major repairs needed.

"Oh," she flapped into the living room. "Karl's other friends from the war come by to help." She stopped, bonnet in hand, and stared at me. "He's such a popular fellow. My Karl is. I'm a lucky ma." Fitting on the bonnet, she tied the ribbon under her chin.

Unsure what to say, I plucked my hat from the wall hook and gripped it. Finally, I plopped the Stetson on my head, opened the door and escorted her down the steps, across the walkway and into the street. She spent the few minutes telling me about the history of Fredericksburg and how as a young bride she and her husband had opened an apothecary. They'd sold it years ago, but still received residuals from the sale.

I half listened and half watched for a sheriff, town marshal, anyone with a badge. I wouldn't put it past evil Becker to be hiding again, waiting to ambush me. But we arrived at the mercantile safe and sound.

I stood on the wooden porch, questioning my sanity, when I noted a sign in the window. *Help Wanted*. So, if robbing didn't turn out well, maybe I could work for wages until I had enough money to relieve someone of their money. After all, I had no gun, and it wasn't a proper holdup without a gun. True, I'd stolen from the telegraph office but that was only because Joe worked there. Hadn't needed a gun for that.

While Mrs. Steinmaker shopped, I asked about the job opening.

"Need someone who can carry boxes," the mercantile owner said as he introduced himself as Joshua Anderson. "Sweep. Take out trash. Keep an eye on things. Stock the shelves. Take inventory." He eyed me up and down. "Need someone who can make change. Work the counter."

Oh, I could do that. Right up my alley. I stuck out a hand. "Mr. Anderson. I'm your man. When do I start?"

"Didn't tell you the wages." He peered at me then my outstretched hand.

I flashed my best smile. "I'm sure they'll be fair."

"Ten cents an hour." He took my hand, then we shook. "Come in this afternoon. You'll start then."

"Yes, sir." I did quick mental math. A dollar a day. Cowboy wages, except I wouldn't have to pull cows out of muck and mud in the middle of a rainstorm. Wouldn't have to brand, dehorn, and castrate terrified animals. No, I'd have to deal with people. Much harder than cattle.

Sack in one arm, Mrs. Steinmaker on the other, I told her about my new job on the way back. I hoped she'd let me stay and eat with her. "I'll still have plenty of time to help around your house. I'll get that wood brought in before I go today. Should be back before dark."

* * *

THE DAYS PASSED QUICKLY ENOUGH. Up before dawn, horses and chickens tended, a hearty, delicious breakfast consumed, and then off to the mercantile where I soaked up everything I could about the best way to rob the place. Along the way, I also learned about inventory, ordering supplies, treating customers with care, watching for children swiping candy out of the jars —a certain amount was allowed. I even learned the name of the lovely German miss across the street at the bakery. Hilda. Something about pronouncing that name rolled off my tongue and lolled around in my mouth.

And so far, nobody had questioned who I was or looked at me warily. They seemed to take me in stride, nodding, especially when I mentioned I was staying with Mrs. Steinmaker.

On day seven, using the few minutes allowed off for a noon meal, I untied my apron, hiked up my courage, crossed the street to the Reinstein Bakery. And there she was. Hilda. As beautiful as I'd remembered.

"*Wilkommen.*" She pushed back a wisp of blond hair escaping under her hat. Standing behind the counter, she pointed to strudel and what looked to be tarts. "What would you like?"

You, is what I wanted to say. Instead, I produced what

I hoped was my most disarming smile. "What do you recommend?"

She pointed to a peach tart. "These are my favorites. *Ja.*" A blush spread across her cheeks, highlighting her pretty nose. "But I do like them all."

I was sure I would too, but I hadn't been paid yet. There was no jingle in my pocket which I couldn't admit to. If she knew, I'd never get a chance to escort her to supper. Besides, I'd planned to save every penny to have enough to leave. Suddenly, that thought sounded flat. Harsh. Uncaring.

I stood there, the only customer in the small store, thinking about the past week. I'd kept my nose out of trouble and hopefully away from the sheriff's purview.

Mrs. Steinmaker certainly didn't draw attention to herself, except for being a bit addlepated. While I was at work, townsmen would stop by to check on her, do odd jobs, which made me feel lazy when I returned from my day.

Suddenly I realized I'd been standing, staring at the pastries, and not answering Hilda. Undoubtedly, she knew where I lived and probably figured I was as muddled as Mrs. Steinmaker. That would never do. Should I be brutally honest and confess or lie? I chose lying.

I patted my stomach. "Just finished my meal, but thought I'd see what you have. Tomorrow I might buy Mrs. Steinmaker a surprise."

She beamed. "So nice of you!"

Her smile caught the sun and I swear a halo glowed above her head. Deciding it was now or never, I chose a round-about method to find out more. "Does your husband help you cook?"

Was that a stupid question or what? Of course he didn't. But I'd find out if she was married.

Hilda frowned, wagged her head. "No. No husband. My *vater*, he helps clean up."

Wanting to jump for joy, instead I nodded. "Nice man to help like that. He washes dishes?" I thought about my stint doing the same thing. No shame in good, honest work.

"*Ja.*"

Thumbing over my shoulder, I stood up straighter. "I work at the mercantile."

"I know." She ducked her head, the flush returning to her cheeks. "I see you there."

"You do?" My heart leaped. "And you didn't say hello?" Would she see I was teasing?

"Next time, I will." Hilda glanced behind her at the kitchen. "Excuse me. I have much to bake for the church bazaar this Saturday."

Saturday? Coming up in two days? "I'd like to help. Afraid I'm working though."

She laughed. Actually laughed like a bird enjoying a tasty worm. "Thank you for the offer. My *vater* and I manage. But..." Hilda leaned close. "You can come buy a pie for Mrs. Steinmaker then."

Assuring her I would, I about skipped toward the mercantile. My luck had turned and now I was about to court a beautiful woman—one who knew how to cook strudel. How perfect was that?

More sweeping, more counting bolts of calico, more customers to help select the perfect pickax, the afternoon dragged by. Within the hour, Mr. Anderson would close and lock the front doors and shortly after that, I'd hang up my apron, say goodnight, and head back home. At least Mrs. Steinmaker's home, a place and person I'd grown fond of.

I was in the back room, moving a newly arrived flour barrel when Mr. Anderson stepped in and glared. "Sheriff wants to see you." He glared harder and pointed behind him. "What have you done?"

"Nothing." I shrugged. "I work. I go home. That's it." That all too familiar cold fist plowed into my stomach. Now what?

I wiped my hands on my apron, inspected them for wayward dirt, then walked into the store and to the counter. A man I hadn't seen before, turned at my footsteps. That badge on the left side of his vest sparked like it was on fire.

Drawing in as deep a breath as possible, I stuck out a hand. "Understand you're looking for me, sir?"

His narrowed brown eyes roved over my entire body, taking inventory like I did jars of pickles. Since he didn't offer a hand, inch by inch, I lowered mine.

Pursing his chapped lips, he narrowed his eyes and walked around me. "Huh."

Like daggers, his scrutiny pierced my body, my heart, my soul. "Sir?"

He moved in close, but not too close. I couldn't reach the gun in the holster on his hip. Not like I would do something rash. However, I'd never been accused of being overly bright. I chose to stand still.

"You Tate Nolan?" He spit my name like it was vile, evil.

Fortunately, I caught myself before I took a step back. Inside, I wanted to run, bolt out of the store, jump on Jasmine, and take off for Fort Worth. Instead, I stood, wrinkling my forehead, raising my eyebrows. "Nolan, you say?" Had I stuttered? "No sir. I'm Seamus O'Brien."

"So Anderson said." From his vest pocket, he pulled out a folded piece of paper. "Got this couple pays ago. Description matches you."

I swallowed hard.

"Says here," the sheriff read from the paper. "About six-foot, green eyes, dark-blond hair, about twenty-two. Name's Tate Nolan. From Blanco Hill." He refolded it and shoved the wanted poster in his vest. "Fits you to a tee."

"Yes sir." Surprised I could speak, I continued. "Except also fits about half the men here in west Texas. "Who's looking for this Nolan fella? And what'd he do?"

More scrutiny, more eyes narrowing, glaring at me. "Sheriff Samuels down in San Antone's looking for this murderer."

"Murderer?" I pushed down panic.

He nodded and refit his hat.

The sheriff turned his back on me, stopped, then turned back around. I still hadn't moved. "You. Seamus O'Brien. Don't go nowhere." He pointed to his eyes. "These are on you."

I nodded to the receding figure of the law, his warning strangely familiar. I considered. If I rode out now, he'd put two and two together and no doubt a posse would be on my tail within the hour. If I stayed around, Sheriff whatever his name was, would figure out sooner or later he'd got the right man.

The remainder of the afternoon passed by numbly. Chores done, just before I headed home, Mr. Anderson stopped me.

"Pay day, Seamus." He held out seven dollars. "You've done well. Glad to have you here. What'd Sheriff Driggs want?"

Gripping the coins like the lifelines they were, I

shrugged. "Thought I was somebody else." I dropped my pay into a vest pocket. "Guess it's an easy mistake."

My boss patted my shoulder, something he'd never done before. "Guess so. See you tomorrow."

I fitted my hat down tight and nodded as I closed the door behind me. A long look left, then right. Was that the badge standing at the far end of the street? Too far to tell. Nerves tingling and like a mouse in a barn full of cats, I scurried home.

CHAPTER TWENTY-SEVEN

THAT NIGHT I DIDN'T SLEEP. AT ALL. NOTHING I did made my eyes close long enough for them not to spring back open. Three glasses of milk and a piece of pie didn't bring lullabies to mind. I tossed and turned until gray lit the room.

Nothing mattered what I did or didn't do. I stayed out of saloons, out of trouble. I didn't go anywhere, do anything, didn't threaten anyone, didn't even say mean things to children who liked to steal licorice whips at the store. "Scat" never once left my lips. But here I was, again, deciding between running for my life and taking a stand. What had I ever done to deserve this?

Me? A wanted man? A murderer? All right, so technically I *was* a murderer. I shuddered at the sound of that word. Should I go back to San Antonio, back to Sheriff Samuels and turn myself in? Would Mr. Carmichael hire that lawyer he'd talked about? Would he even speak to me?

And what about Becker? Surely by now he'd also received the same wanted poster as this town's sheriff.

Becker knew where I was and the question at the top of my mind—why hadn't he ridden into town already? Why wasn't I dead? Or, at least behind bars? What kind of game was Becker, the *shite* sheriff, playing?

At my room's washstand, I scrubbed my face—hard. No amount of soap and water gave me an answer. With seven dollars now in my pocket, I probably had enough to get me to Fort Worth, or some other cattle town big enough to rob. Did Jesse and Frank have this much trouble preparing for a holdup? At least they had each other. I'd wanted my brother to join me, but he seemed on a different path. Guess it was up to me now.

How about Eagan? His face popped into view as I stood at the shaving mirror this morning. No. He was too innocent, although certainly old enough to go on the owl hoot trail. Eagan simply didn't seem to have whatever was needed to be an outlaw. I'd leave him out of my plans. Maybe after I'd robbed a bank or two, Joe would want to join me. After all, how much money could he make as a telegrapher in Denver? Especially with a wife to feed and shelter.

Could I get word to Joe to meet me in Fort Worth? Not from here. No doubt that Sheriff Driggs—I'd asked Mrs. Steinmaker his name—would be watching the postal and telegraph office for cryptic messages.

Sitting at the breakfast table, hot flapjacks, eggs, and ham in front of me, I lifted the dainty coffee cup to my lips and decided. I'd stay here a day or two longer, stop by the bazaar, and buy a pie. Then early Sunday morning, I'd say goodbye to Mrs. Steinmaker and light a shuck for Fort Worth.

Would those simple plans work the way I wanted them to? I hoped so with all my being. Meanwhile, I'd keep an extra low profile.

Working to do exactly that, Friday at the mercantile passed like all the other days before. I stayed in the back storeroom most of the day, busy with an inventory list that I took my time reconciling, trying like the devil to keep out of sight.

Sitting on the floor in the storeroom, back against a barrel, I munched on a sandwich Mrs. Steinmaker had sent along for my mid-day meal. She was a fine cook and, if circumstances had been different, I'd have stayed indefinitely. I pushed an errant piece of beef from the sandwich into my mouth, chewed and thought. About the time I'd decided to stay another week or so, take my chances with Becker, one of the female clerks ventured into the storeroom.

"There you are, Mr. O'Brien." The woman, who I suspected to be in her early forties, placed one hand on her hip. "We looked all over for you."

I looked up at this woman who worked mainly in the cloth and sewing section. "You did?" I noticed she used "we," but figured she really meant "I."

"Yes, we certainly did." She brought her other hand from behind her back. "Hilda and I searched every aisle, every back room except this one."

Hilda? Did she say Hilda? I sat up straighter. And was the clerk angry? Her words were sharp and clipped. And then I saw what she had in hand. One of those peach tarts from the bakery. My heart leaped and my mouth watered. "Well, here I am. Glad you found me." I glanced around for Hilda.

She handed me the pastry. "Hilda wanted to give this herself but had to get back to the store." One raised eyebrow wrinkled her forehead. "Seemed disappointed, she did."

Aromas of peaches and cinnamon wafted under my

nose and around my head. "Thank you for finding me."
Ma's rules of etiquette roared in my ear. "Would you like
some of this?"

The woman shook her head. "No, thank you. I've just
finished my own meal."

Music to my ears. This tart was mine, all mine. I held
it under my nose, then realized the clerk remained standing. I looked up again, probably a sappy smile on my
face.

"Said she'd see you at the bazaar tomorrow." Both
hands on her hips, the woman, whose name I couldn't
remember, looked around the storeroom and then at me.
"Hilda's a sweet girl. Treat her right." And then she did
an about turn and marched into the store.

Of course, I'd treat her right—if I was staying. And
then it hit me. This living the outlaw life sure had its
downside. I couldn't find a good woman, settle down
with kids. Not in good conscience. If I had a wife, I'd
need to be home at least most evenings. Couldn't ride off
and be gone weeks at a time robbing banks and trains.
No self-respecting woman would put up with that.

Then again, I thought as I took my first bite of
heaven, if I did take a wife, I'd be tied down and either
work for somebody, like I was now, own a business
which I figured took a lot of work and dedication, or find
a field to plow. None of that appealed to me. Another
bite closed my eyes. If her peach tart was this good, what
was her strudel like?

I passed the rest of the day whistling, catching myself
smiling as I counted canned tomatoes. It was all Hilda's
fault. Sorry I'd missed her, but happy she'd brought the
tart. The bazaar was the next day, and I planned to spend
the time allotted for mid-day meal to attend the church
festivities—the only part of church I truly enjoyed. I'd

visit with Hilda and buy a pie for Mrs. Steinmaker. She'd mentioned attending as well, but even if she bought a pie herself, having two at home would not be too many.

* * *

EARLY SUN RAYS spread joy over the entire town of Fredericksburg. Maybe not the entire town, but my little piece of it at any rate. Mr. Anderson had asked me to come in early on Saturday, expecting a larger than usual crowd. He said he always enjoyed the bazaar because people from outlying areas came in and spent money. I was sure the restaurants and other businesses felt the same way.

Up and ready to go by daybreak, Mrs. Steinmaker had breakfast on the table. Freshly washed and shaved, I came into the kitchen, helped myself to coffee, and sat. She slid a plate of potatoes and eggs under my nose. My mouth watered. She was an amazing cook.

"When you're in town today," she hovered beside me, coffeepot in hand. "Be sure to watch out for my Karl. He may want to go by the mercantile before coming home." She topped off my cup. "Or he'll stop at the bazaar and buy me flowers. He's so wonderful like that."

"If I see him, I'll tell him to skedaddle on home." How could I not lie to this woman?

After breakfast, I checked on the stock, chuckling at thinking of chickens as stock. Fed and watered, the horses seemed content to be idle and do nothing but eat all day. I'd have to ride both tomorrow, just to keep them fit. Then it hit me. Of course. I'd be riding Jasmine out of town and up toward Fort Worth. *Was that tomorrow? Already?*

I dragged into the house, sad thinking of leaving. I

hadn't been in town two weeks, and already thought of it as home. Throwing my shoulders back, I chided myself. *Shite*, I was a wanted man, and wouldn't do anything to shame Mrs. Steinmaker or Hilda...Mr. Anderson for that matter.

No. I'd do what needed doing. I'd leave. Or was it running? Yep. Running like a coward. Or was it running like a smart man? Hard to tell. I hated not knowing which I was. Maybe it was time to grow up and accept responsibilities. Then again...

I walked to town mumbling and passing a few people I recognized. No names, but familiar faces. From the steps of the mercantile, conversations and bits of hammering sailed to my ears. Plenty commotion coming from the other end of town. As it should.

Busy all morning, I hadn't had a chance to think much about Hilda, the pie, my leaving...any of it. Mr. Anderson and customers kept me hopping. I must've walked into the storeroom and back into the salesroom a million times. Who knew canned green beans were so popular?

Stomach growling, reminding me it was past my usual lunch time, I wound my way through customers to find Mr. Anderson behind the register. Normally, I'd be watching exactly how much money was there, but right now, all I needed was half an hour off. I had pie to buy.

Without missing a beat talking to a man, Mr. Anderson nodded as I pointed to the door. Not bothering to untie my apron, truthfully forgetting I had it on, I bolted outside, glad to have a bit more elbow room.

Finding the bazaar was not difficult. I simply threaded my way through the crowd headed for the Holy Ghost Lutheran Church at the west end near Main Street. I'd heard rumors that the catholic church would have a bazaar next month and wondered briefly if Hilda would sell there as well. Didn't matter. I'd be long gone by then.

Swept along with the throng, I found myself on an expansive grassy field, tents appearing like gigantic mushrooms. Smells of cooking wafted overhead, under my nose. Off to one side, children ran pushing wooden circles, others hopping around in burlap bags. And yet others simply ran and chased, laughing.

For the adults, men stood in wagons laden with hay bales, offering tastes of "Fredericksburg's Finest Whiskey." One or two others countered with the "Finest Dewberry Wine." It all sounded delicious. Another time, another place and I would've been the first to sample. But not right now.

Right now I had to find Hilda. Thank her for the peach tart. Buy a pie. Take the surprise home. Rush back to work. All within half an hour.

On the far side of the field, two women and one man stood, their backs to me, in front of a tent. I followed my nose and there she was. Hilda flashed a wide grin when our eyes met.

I smiled back, feeling the fool, but couldn't help myself. Something about her mesmerized me. Her creamy pink skin, round blue eyes, long fingers on delicate hands. I wasn't sure about her hair as it was always up in a bun, tucked under a cap. She wasn't as tall as me, but definitely taller than most women. My cheeks ached with a grin.

A man, strands of white hair peeking from under a hat, moved in beside her. Had to be her da. They had the same eyes and nose. Was I ready to meet the da? I'd known her less than two weeks, but my heart thumped louder, and my mouth dried when I was around her. Was

I in love? Maybe, but I was definitely in 'quite interested.'

The customers selected their pastries while I waited. I peeked over their shoulders trying hard not to push my way in. But I had to get back to work. The three paid for two strudels and one round pastry item I couldn't name, but the smell was divine.

I stepped up to the table and attempted to say something intelligent. Instead, noise came out. She laughed that captivating laugh again and turned to her da.

"This is Seamus." She pointed at me. "The man I told you about."

Regaining enough sense to respond, I stuck out a hand. "Seamus O'Brien, sir. I've heard good things about you."

"Have you now?" He stepped back, eyeing me like I was the enemy, complete with sword and shield.

I kept my hand extended, hoping he'd relent and grip it. "Yes sir, I have." I stretched across the table. "Understand you're in charge of washing dishes." My smile reached ear to ear, I hoped. "Done my fair share of dishes myself. I admire a man who does."

He let out a long laugh, much like Hilda's. He reached for my hand, and we shook, his grip bull strong, taking me almost to my knees. "Think I'm gonna like you."

I squeezed back and nodded.

Hilda moved in, her timing perfect. "I told *Vater* you work at the mercantile and live with Mrs. Steinmaker."

"Yes, sir, I do. On both accounts." I wasn't about to give any more information. No one needed to know. But if asked, I'd be sure to concoct a trustworthy previous life.

She stood looking at me looking at her. Hilda's father

cleared his throat, bringing me out of the trance. I shook my head. "Uh...I'd like to buy a pie for Mrs. Steinmaker." My gaze roved over the only one left. "What do you recommend?" I was teasing, since I had no other choice.

She produced that smile I'd come to love. "Mrs. Steinmaker came by early and bought an apple pie and strudel."

"Apple?" My favorite. Unless it was blueberry. Or...

"How about this sweet potato pie? It's my last one." She pointed to a round delight, a golden custard surrounded by crust.

"Sold!" I'd never had one, but no doubt it was delightful. I pulled out a dollar coin, remembered to thank her for the tart.

She blushed, glanced at her da, back at me. "You're *wilkommen*. Did you like?"

"Too good for words." I gave her the coin and she handed me the pie. "Thank you again."

I stepped back ready to go, but her da nudged her. She looked down, then at me. "Tomorrow. Sunday." She hesitated, then continued. "After church, Vater and a friend and I are going on a picnic. We would like you to come too."

What? She was asking me out? Surely blinking more than humanly possible, I gripped the pie, hard. No telling how many hours, days or years passed before I could nod. "Of course. I'd love to. I'm honored."

"Wonderful, Mr. O'Brien." Her da stuck out a hand. "See you after church."

I nodded like a fool, smiled like an idiot, turned with the pie in hand, and walked on air to Mrs. Steinmaker's house. I set the pie next to the other one on the table, visited the privy, then set out for the store. Certain I was late, I about ran.

As I pushed through the people, I realized I'd planned to leave first light. No way should I stick around for some picnic. But it was with Hilda. Maybe I'd leave Monday.

A block from the store, lost deep in thought, a voice from behind froze me. "Tate? Tate Nolan? That you?"

I spun and nearly crashed into my friend in crime from Blanco Hill. There stood Wink Tannen, the man I'd "borrowed" the sheriff's horse with. He'd served six months in prison. After all, he hadn't stolen the sheriff's horse like I did. His sentence was half of mine, which was nine months in prison plus three on parole. Part of me hated him for that, the other was glad his was reduced.

"Wink?" Surprised a word came out, I moved in until we almost touched noses. "I'm Seamus O'Brien now. Don't call me Tate."

"Fine." He held up a hand like I'd offended him.

Truly confused, I glanced behind him like he had a whole passel of people with him. "What're you doing here?" I thought back to the last time I'd seen him. Months ago. "Where've you been? You kinda vanished."

Wink chuckled and toed a clump of dirt on the boardwalk. "Followed a gal down to El Paso." He shrugged. "Let's just say, she didn't work out."

"You stayin' around for a bit?"

Glancing up and down Main, Wink shrugged. "Nah. Day or two. Decided I'd take a ride up north, toward Denver. See what kinda trouble I can get into." He raised one eyebrow, like he always did when he was concocting a scheme. "Wanna come?"

Shaking my head and not believing I was doing so, I pointed toward the store. "Not today. Got a job. Place to live. Maybe even a girl. I like it here."

Had those words actually come out of my mouth? What made Fredericksburg better than Blanco Hill? Couldn't put a finger on it, but I truly did like it there.

Wink stepped back a notch. "What's come over you, Tate?"

"Ah!" I held up a finger, lowered my voice. "Seamus."

"Sorry, forgot." He leaned back in close. "Thought up in Denver's more money than here. Heard there's gold... silver, too. Lots of prospectors who don't need all that money."

There was a time when I'd have hung up my apron, jumped on a horse and beelined with him to Denver, or anywhere there was money. But something inside me made me want more. Not more, exactly...different.

I didn't want to turn my back on my friend. Since childhood, we'd been through some thick and thin times together and I owed him. He'd stood up for me at school when a bully decided to bloody my nose with his fists. Also, when the teacher chose to make an example of me when I hadn't been able to read as well as she liked. And the time...

All right. I stood there looking at him. We'd changed. Maybe I'd changed. But he deserved my time. But not right now. I realized, as I stood, I was late getting back. Mr. Anderson might dock my pay and I couldn't have that.

"Listen, Wink. I gotta go. I'm working at the mercantile. Get off around six. Meet me there and I'll introduce you to the sweetest woman this side of the Mississippi."

Nodding, he flashed a wide smile. "Bet she's a beauty, too. Can't wait to meet her."

I started off at a trot and hollered over my shoulder. "See you then."

* * *

FORTUNATELY, Mr. Anderson had been too busy to notice I was late getting back. If anything, he seemed relieved I showed up at all. He nodded as he spotted me walking out of the storeroom, more canned tomatoes in hand.

Long shadows stretched through the west-facing windows, and I knew it was about time to go home. Would Wink be there waiting? I hoped so, although I figured, then again, he might have moved on toward Denver.

But no, he was standing on the porch when I stepped outside, Mr. Anderson closing and locking the doors behind me. Wink and I shook hands while he slapped my shoulder with his free hand.

"Good to see ya again, ol' boy. Good to see ya."

I pointed east, toward Mrs. Steinmaker's house. "I'm this way." He kept his stride even with mine, something he always did. A sly smile slid up my cheek. "Think you'll like the little lady. She's pleasant and a terrific cook. Keeps a good house, too."

A hearty slap on the back sent me two steps ahead. "You sly dog, you." Wink pushed me into the street. "Got yourself a girl. Sounds serious. She pretty?"

"Got the bluest eyes and softest skin around." I was having way too much fun at Wink's expense. "Not real tall, but..."

"Tall's not important in bed." Wink nudged me.

"Guess not." I tried not to snicker.

"She got a sister?"

The side street where she lived was coming up. "Sister? Hasn't mentioned one. Maybe."

Wink rambled on and on about sisters and women

and what he could do with them—together and sepa-rately—images I found hard to picture. I couldn't wait to see his face when he met Mrs. Steinmaker.

And then there we were, at her front door. I bounded up the three steps, rapped gently on the door, like I did every night, and opened it. "I'm home," I shouted. "Brought a friend."

"How lovely!" she called from the kitchen.

Aromas of roast beef, potatoes and something frying sailed into the living room. A smile blossomed on my face and about tore Wink's off. I hung my hat on the peg near the door, indicated for him to do the same. "Come meet the little woman." This was too grand.

We walked into the kitchen and there stood Mrs. Steinmaker at the stove, as usual, stirring something in a fry pan. She held up a fork, turned to us and smiled.

"Oh my, Seamus! You've brought a friend from Karl's regiment." Fork in hand, she hugged Wink. "So good to meet you. Bet you're hungry from your long trip." She turned to the stove, then spun back around. "Did you see Karl on your way here? How is he?"

Poor Wink. He stood, mouth open, blinking, shifting his weight from one foot to the other. That look of bewil-derment—eyes wide, swallowing so hard his Adam's apple danced up and down his throat—was the funniest thing I'd seen in years.

Deciding to rescue him, I jumped in. "Mrs. Stein-maker, this is Wink Tannen. He told me today he hasn't seen Karl for a while. Thinks he may have transferred to another regiment."

Her shoulders slumped and for a moment I was ashamed of my lie. All I wanted was to protect her.

She stood up straight, shoulders righted. "Well, I'm

sure when he's able, he'll write to let me know where he is."

"Yes, ma'am." Wink and I spoke in unison.

Cooking smells about sent me to my knees. If I didn't eat soon, I'd surely dry up and blow away. Wink licked his lower lip, obviously thinking what I was.

I pointed toward the back. "We'll go get washed up, Mrs. Steinmaker. Then tell me how I can help."

"All right, Seamus. Be sure to wash behind your ears."

I loved that about her. She was the kindest, gentlest woman I'd ever met. Ma was a close

second.

Out back at a bench with the water pump, Wink and I took turns dousing our heads and scrubbing faces. Standing like two half-drowned barn cats, we dried off in the setting sun.

Wink peered out over a towel. "So, where's this beautiful woman I've been hearing all about? She in the bedroom waiting for you?"

I burst out laughing. I knew he'd be embarrassed, but I couldn't help myself. I didn't get the chance to pull wool over eyes often.

"What's so funny?" Wink stared at me, at the back door, at me again. He pointed. "Don't tell me...she's... your?" One hand bunched the towel. "And who's Karl?"

CHAPTER TWENTY-EIGHT

I DIDN'T REALLY WANT WINK ON THIS PICNIC with me and Hilda, but I wasn't sure he'd want to hang around Mrs. Steinmaker's all day, waiting for me to return.

Not sure what to do about him, the next morning, we sat on the front porch in two wooden rockers, coffee cups in hand and watched the sun spreads its glory across Fredericksburg. Birds flitted from mesquite to pine, back to mesquite, a roadrunner dove into a bush attacking something that was too slow. A coyote howled in the distance, its call fading. Not many people were out and about, but within a matter of hours, the town would be busy with piety headed for church.

Wink sipped from the flowered China cup, his big hands wrapping completely around it. He looked at the liquid, then over at me. "You gonna stay here?"

I shook my head. "Had figured on leaving today, but got invited to a picnic and Hilda's a good cook, and it was her da's suggestion I come, and Mrs. Steinmaker likes having me around, and I got a good job—"

"You're not going anywhere. At least for a bit." Wink held up a hand. "If I get clear up to Denver, I'll find that brother of yours and tell him what you're doing."

"You do that." I peered toward Main. "But there's a wanted poster on me and Sheriff Becker knows where I am." I stared into my minuscule cup. "Wondering why the hell he ain't come to get me yet." A look into Wink's clouded face brought a knot to my stomach. "Figured I should leave before he comes looking."

"Won't come looking for a good long while, Tate." Wink shook his head. "Seamus."

"Why's that?" What was Wink not telling me? Did I dare hope?

He pointed his cup east. "Guess you ain't heard." He pulled in a long breath. "Last week…no, now about eight, ten days ago, there was a fight down at Sam's Emporium."

"And?"

"You remember Hershel Robertson and Big Dan Bigelow?"

Wink could be so vague, frustrating, at times. "Course I do. What's that got to do with Becker?"

He stood, scratched his rear, sipped his coffee, and turned to me. "Well, Hersh and Big Dan got into one hellacious fight. Before you knew it, 'bout six, seven other men were swingin' fists, throwin' chairs and tables —even whiskey bottles." He finished his coffee, turned, and disappeared inside.

"And?" I called after him once not wanting to wake the neighborhood, although Mrs. Steinmaker, and probably most other women, were already up and fixing breakfast. Heart beating a bit harder, I wiped my mouth, sipped coffee, tapped my boots which echoed against the wooden floor.

A minute or two later, he reappeared, cup brimming, steam spiraling upward. He sat. "Well, that fight, Tate. It was grand." His arms flapped. "Bottles breakin'—*crash, tinkle*—women screamin'— *ooohhh*—men shoutin." Tate, it was better'n any party I *ever* been to."

No way could I control myself. "Wink, what the hell happened to Becker?"

He leaned back like I was about to wallop him. "I'm gettin' to that." Wink shifted his weight and gazed out over the prairie's rolling hills. He pulled in a deep breath. "There's all this fightin', hollerin', screamin' and then somebody decides to up the ante. Pulled out a gun, they did. Started shootin' up the place and that's when Sheriff Becker, Deputy Wagner, and that other one, O'Sullivan, come rushin' in."

Now on the edge of the chair, I sat glued to Wink's words. My life might depend, literally, on what he said next. I wanted to wrap my hands around his throat to get the words out, but instead, gripped the cup. "And?"

"Gunsmoke everywhere, bottles and now women bein' tossed about, men runnin' up and down those stairs. I tell you, Tate, it was a spectacle." Wink stopped, looked left and right. "Becker waded into the middle of the ruckus right as somebody fired. Hit that ol' sheriff in one side, come out the other."

Air froze in my chest. "He die?"

"No, but he might as well of." Wink leaned back and looked at me. "And that Deputy Wagner? Got grazed in the head. Ain't been right since."

I turned numb for a moment before curiosity and shock raced up and down my spine. Hallelujah and Glory Be! Could this day get any better? "What about O'Sullivan?" I gasped in a quick breath. "He get hurt?" That deputy, I searched for a first name and finally remembered *Tommy*, was the only law dog who'd been half decent to me. And he was courting Imogene. If such a thing were possible, I rather liked him, especially since he was Ireland-born, like me.

Wink kept talking, but was I listening?

"Yea, that deputy got hit, too. Just in the leg, so he's hobblin' around now, actin' like a big-town sheriff. Not as timid as he used to be." Wink finished his coffee. "Considerable reason I lit a shuck for Denver."

"Think O'Sullivan knows I'm here?"

"Maybe. But he's too busy worryin' about the town to worry about you." He stood,

sniffing toward the open door. "But I imagine he'll come lookin' when he's a mind to." He

sniffed again. "Reckon she's got breakfast ready?"

* * *

A BIG BREATH OUT, I relaxed and tried to hide a grin when Wink announced he'd stay around the house and help Mrs. Steinmaker with whatever she needed today. My one day off would prove to be eventful, but relaxing, I was sure. Maybe, somehow, I could steal a kiss from Hilda. Wouldn't tha' be grand, as Ma would say.

I met Hilda and her da in front of the church. Hilda was more beautiful than ever. Her pink flowered dress, nipped in at the waist, set off her pink cheeks like they were painted to match. Two pink flowers adorned her straw bonnet. She was as close to picture perfect as I could have imagined. And *I* was with *her*. How amazing was that?

Her smile reached both ears when she spotted me waiting on the grass. Her da reached out a hand to shake, and again, his grip about took me to my knees.

She slipped her arm in mine and nodded toward a buggy on the far side of the field. "There's plenty of room in our carriage, Mr. O'Brien." She nudged me that way.

Mr. Reinstein—I'd asked Mrs. Steinmaker for Hilda's father's last name—pointed over his shoulder. "I'll wait for Emily Anne." An eyebrow lifted. "Uh...Mrs. Coogan. She'll be joining us today."

So, just as I suspected. He had a lady friend and was hoping his daughter would find someone too. Why not?

I helped Hilda into the back seat of the buggy where I spotted a woven basket covered with a red checkered cloth. Was that big enough to hold food for four adults? I hoped so because although Mrs. Steinmaker had made a large breakfast, my stomach was restlessly anticipating sustenance. In fact, it thought my throat had been cut.

Hilda and I sat there making small chit chat until Mr. Reinstein and a woman I vaguely recognized walked up to the buggy. He introduced us and I froze. Once I thought hard, I'd met her at Mr. Carmichael's ranch, one of the big after-church to-dos. A sizable knot fisted in my stomach, slid up to my chest, lodged itself in my throat.

She stuck out a dainty hand. "Mr. O'Brien. So good to meet you."

Maybe she hadn't recognized me. After all, I'd been busy with the other women in my life to pay much attention to others. But I did remember her. I silently cleared my throat.

Mr. Reinstein stepped up into the buggy, rocking us side to side. He wasn't a fat man, but certainly had enough muscles to probably carry this buggy on his shoulders. No way would I pick a fight with him. Hopefully, I wouldn't need to. But now with this woman, his daughter, in close proximity, I'd definitely have to mind my Ps and Qs and stay far away. I tugged my hat down farther on my forehead.

He flicked the reins and we trotted effortlessly out of town. I half listened to Hilda who pointed out the scenery. Nodding, I grunted what I thought was intelligent conversation. Hopefully, wherever we were headed, there was a stream where Hilda and I could spend most of the afternoon—far away from this Mrs. Coogan.

We traversed several wide hills, not steep, simply wide, down a few valleys and finally pulled up at a stream, water jogging over rocks. Its blueness shone in the sunshine while the creek gurgled a happy tune.

I helped Hilda down from the buggy, my hands enjoying the slimness of her waist. She handed me the basket and set out for a towering Texas oak, its branches spreading for what looked like miles and providing enough shade to cover half of Fredericksburg. If I hadn't been so nervous, I would have reveled in the serenity, beauty and being with gorgeous Hilda.

But I was worse than a cat in a roomful of rocking chairs. I jumped at every word and Mr. Reinstein's tap on my shoulder about sent me to the moon. I helped Hilda spread a blanket and arrange the food. Ham sandwiches, boiled potatoes with a small block of salt nearby, and a pie of unknown contents kept my attention. My stomach thanked me, even though not a bite had gone into my mouth.

Like a newborn foal, I folded my legs under me awkwardly which caused me to plop down next to Hilda, now busy piling sandwiches on plates. I helped with napkins while her da uncorked and handed out beer bottles. Now he was someone after my own heart. We'd get along just fine.

Emily Anne Coogan tucked in her skirt and floated to

the ground like a big butterfly. She was graceful, I'd have to give her that. Her gray-green eyes traveled over my face, which I hoped remained half hidden by my hat.

We passed the next few minutes with small talk and then after several sips of beer, Mrs. Coogan pointed a finger at me. "You certainly look familiar, Mr. O'Brien. Have we met before?"

Everything in me wanted to get up and throw the blanket over her face and run. Instead, I leaned back, shook my head. "Don't believe I've had the pleasure, ma'am." And that much was true. We'd never been formally introduced.

"You certainly look like someone I've met." She eyed the pie. "Is this dewberry?"

Hilda flashed a picture-perfect smile. "*Ja*. Dewberry and apple."

Yum. I could almost taste it if it wasn't for the iron coating my mouth.

I kept one eye on Mrs. Coogan and the other on my food with an occasional glance at Hilda. Would this meal ever get over so we could spend time at the stream? I assumed the sandwich was delicious and the pie heavenly, but I didn't taste a thing. My heart pounded too hard, and my mouth had turned so dry a second beer was needed to wash down the meal.

About the time I figured that woman had forgotten about me, her blinking eyes and fluttering eyelashes having turned to Mr. Reinstein most of the meal, I made the mistake of relaxing. I leaned back ready to invite Hilda to the water when Mrs. Coogan pointed directly at me and smiled. It wasn't a regular smile—lips curling upward producing dimples—but more like a Sabretooth tiger about to gobble up a deer. I leaned back, bumping into Hilda.

Mrs. Coogan chirruped. "Ah ha. That's where I've seen you." She glanced at Mr. Reinstein and made sure he looked at me too. "Outside of Blanco Hill. Mr. Carmichael's ranch. One of his after-church Sunday socials."

"Ma'am?" Maybe if I stalled long enough, she's forget, or drink another beer, or...something. Anything.

"You're from Blanco Hill, right, Mr. O'Brien?"

Breaths clotted in my chest. "Been through there once or twice." I turned to Hilda hoping, praying she'd rescue me. "Shall we take a walk by the stream?" I held out a hand.

Hilda nodded.

I scrambled to my feet, helped Hilda up, but Mrs. Coogan proved relentless.

"I *know* I've seen you before. I'm sure it was there."

Some sort of sanity returned to my brain. I snapped my fingers. "I know what it was, Mrs. Coogan." I glanced at the two Reinsteins. "My brother Joe took his girl there one Sunday. He said Mrs. Carmichael had invited them since she knew him from the telegraph office."

And part of that was true.

"Joe, you said?"

Mentally kicking myself for giving his real name, I nodded. What else could I do?

"Joe, down at the telegraph office?"

Rats and double rats! Of course. How stupid of me. If she'd been in Blanco Hill more than a week, she'd probably have met Joe.

"But his last name—"

"Different fathers."

"Ah." All three chimed in like a Greek chorus.

"Although, we're technically half brothers, less than two years between us. My brother and I...we look a bit alike." I shrugged. "Happens all the time." All right, it *never* happens, but she didn't need to know.

Mrs. Coogan held up a hand for Hilda's da to help her to her feet. "Well, Mr. O'Brien. I guess you and your brother certainly do look alike. My mistake."

"No harm done, ma'am." But I was still quaking inside. Would she buy the lie?

I helped Hilda repack the plates and napkins, then we wandered down to the stream. Relaxing, but still on guard, I tossed pebbles into the water, its gurgling causing my eyes to close.

Hilda sat, unlaced her button-up shoes, slipped out of them, and pulled her dainty feet out of stockings. "Let's wade." That smile, her beauty, charm, lit up the entire world. How could I say no?

She was being so forward, not like women in polite society today. Was she like this with all her beaus or just me? Hilda actually showed a bit of ankle when she removed her shoes. Not that I was watching, but her bold, uninhibited actions gave my stomach a twist. I licked my lips not realizing I had done so until water hit my face.

Hilda stood calf-high in water, giggling like a school-girl. She splashed me again before I could tug the left boot off. It had always been a tad too small and I was sure my foot was swollen—simply out of spite. I needed it off and now. With a hefty tug and pull, my foot wrenched itself out and I sailed backward onto my back. Hilda laughed louder and doused me with cupped hands of water.

All right. Two could play. I jumped to my feet, wiped water from my face, and growled like a tiger ready to attack a princess. I crouched, continued growling while Hilda twittered and pretended to be afraid. My brothers and I used to play this game when we were younger, but today it was so much better with Hilda. She backed away, continuing to giggle and splash, this time with her bare feet.

We chased as best we could over smooth rocks until I finally caught her. So far, we remained dry, but with her in my arms, I hit a rock and went down, taking her with me. We both went under, came up laughing, sputtering and seriously wet. I definitely hadn't had this much fun in ages.

"I'm sorry. You all right?" I held her at arm's length and surveyed her entire body, bonnet to bare feet. My concern for her was overridden by my chortling. Her giggling kept my laughter at full strength.

She looked over my shoulder toward our picnic area. Her da stood on the bank. "Hilda? Are you hurt?"

Chuckling dwindling to tittering, Hilda shook her head. "Fine, *Vater*. No harm."

I turned to look at him full on. This was no good first impression. No doubt he'd make me walk home from here. And I couldn't really blame him. After all, I had made Hilda trip—and quite wet.

Mrs. Coogan appeared at his side. She stood grinning, looking like part of her wanted to join us, the other totally outraged. Finally, she took a cue from Mr. Reinstein who stood smiling.

"You two"—he waved a pointed finger at both of us—"behave yourselves." He turned and then spoke over his shoulder. "Don't get too wet. Hilda, you already had your bath this week."

With that, he and Mrs. Coogan walked away.

Hilda and I splashed a bit more, at last choosing to sit on the stream bank and dry. Or try to. We sat, shoulder to shoulder, and all I could think of was kissing her. She rambled on about something, a bird maybe. Or a new recipe? I heard words but they didn't connect. I reveled in her beauty, in the melodious way those words formed from her spectacular mouth. Courage gathered, I moved in close and kissed her cheek.

She recoiled, smiled, and then kissed me. Full on the lips. Stunned, shocked, and my entire body tingling, we kissed and kissed until I was sure my lips had fallen off. I couldn't feel them but didn't care.

If her da and that woman hadn't been around, I'd have tried to take our kissing to the next level. But they weren't far away, and I'd vowed to be a gentleman. Look what had happened with Imogene—we'd produced a daughter. And one surprise child was enough.

We laid back on the bank and held hands. She counted the leaves above us while I plotted how to kiss her in places besides her lips.

We'd been like that only a few minutes, I was sure, until her da called us. Time to pack up and leave, he said. This had been one of the best days of my life and I sure hated to see the end.

Back in the buggy, Hilda and I held hands while she grinned sideways at me. I smiled back but underneath were questions—*do I stay, do I go?* What do I do? And then Mrs. Coogan made the decision for me.

She turned sideways from the front seat. "Mr. O'Brien. I've been thinking. My best friend has lunch with Mrs. Carmichael once a month. I'm sure my friend can ask Ellie about your brother." She pulled in air. "I'm simply curious, you know. But I'm sure it was *you* I saw."

Time to pull out and head for Fort Worth. If Mrs. Carmichael explained who I was, no doubt Mrs. Coogan would come running back to Mr. Reinstein, who of course, would tell Hilda. Somebody would go to the sheriff and then, if I made it that far, I would stand on the gallows looking up at a noose. Soon.

No, time to go. But I'd have to leave Hilda and Mrs. Steinmaker. Well, couldn't be helped.

We rode back into town as the world grayed. Hating to see a marvelous day end, but knowing it must, I thanked Mr. Reinstein, tipped my hat to Mrs. Coogan, and promised Hilda I'd see her tomorrow. Like that would happen.

They dropped me off in front of the mercantile and I started for home mentally listing everything I needed to do before tomorrow morning. I waved to Hilda as they turned a corner. Ambling down Main, I slowed. Maybe I wouldn't leave tomorrow. Maybe I could give it another few days, a week. Then I could truly plan.

Footsteps behind me made me turn. The town's sheriff stood there, .45 stuck in my chest. "Hands up, Nolan."

CHAPTER TWENTY-NINE

"NOLAN?" HAD THAT WORD COME OUT AT ALL?

"Don't play games with me." Sheriff Driggs pushed the gun against my breastbone. "I know who you are."

"Sir?" I stammered and hated myself for doing so. "I'm Seamus O'Brien. Don't know who this Nolan person is."

Without warning, he backhanded me with his .45. Cheek on fire, I spun, somehow keeping on my feet. Doubled over, I held my throbbing face.

"Let's go."

I straightened in time to spot his upraised arm, gun in hand. Instinctively, one of my hands went up to grip his. My other hand grabbed his vest. Locked in a grotesque dance, we stepped right, then left. Although I was taller, he was stronger and had more weight.

Breaking my hold on him, he shoved me back so hard I splatted to the boardwalk. From there, I looked up into the .45's barrel, now resembling a cannon. Head throbbing, cheek on fire, stomach churning, I rolled to my left about to lose supper. A grip on my arm pulled me to my feet.

"That little shenanigan just bought you ten more years. Hard time." He yanked me toward his office half a block away. "Don't matter, though." Driggs stopped, studied my face, and laughed. "You'll be hanged long before that."

Pushed and pulled to his office, I stepped through the door and that old feeling of entrapment flooded back inside me. I couldn't, wouldn't be locked up. No way would I stand behind bars, gripping them, waiting, hoping for release. No way.

I spun, knocked into the lawman, and bolted into the street. Not caring where I was going or who I'd run over, I simply ran. Down the street. Across to the other side. I leaped up onto the boardwalk.

Bang!

My side caught fire. Gripping the soggy shirt, I ran bent over, watching my boots take me away. Running, stumbling, I made it to the end of Main, jumped off the boardwalk and bolted into the underbrush. Any second I expected another shot, more excruciating pain, and my face plowing into the ground.

I ran.

Mesquite branches clawed my face. Elbow bushes taller than me blocked my way until I crashed through. Sage slowed me some, but I managed to go around. I stumbled. Ran. Scrambled into the thicket.

A stream gurgled ahead if I remembered right, and figured if I got there, heading upstream would get me away. I ran harder. Closer now, I spotted blue. Water. Side slick with blood, I didn't dare look down or I'd lose my footing for sure. Instead, I concentrated on putting one boot in front of the other.

Were those hoofbeats behind me? Maybe, but possibly it was the stream's noise. Keeping my eyes on the water, I headed there.

Whoosh. A sound slashed overhead. I wanted to look up, but before I could, a rope encircled my chest. It pulled tight. Jerked to a stop, I sailed backward, hitting the ground, knocking out my breath. Rocks poked me. My head hit something hard. Entire body on fire and wriggling like a hooked fish, I opened my mouth to scream.

* * *

PRICKLY PEARS RATTLED around inside my head. One cactus pad folded itself in two, scratching as it slid side to side. I gripped my skull, tears cascading down my cheeks. I breathed deep, hoping extra oxygen would help. A few breaths later and my head was reduced to being merely on fire, burning from the inside out.

Forcing my eyes open, I fought to make sense of my world. Turning my head only served to multiply the throbbing, the agony that used to be my brain. Side pinching, hammering in time to my aching head, I clutched my ribs with both hands. What in tarnation happened?

Focusing, or trying to, I made out a dim outline of a window far above me. Not much light came through. Must be night. Or maybe I was dead. No. I hurt way too much for that. Then where was I?

I used one hand to pat next to my body. Hard. Wooden hard. A floor. Next question. Whose floor? Too dark to figure that out, I turned to listening. Was that a snore or heavy breathing? Whose? Mrs. Steinmaker didn't usually snore. Head demanding attention, I released my ribs to clutch the brains pushing their way out.

And now my stomach decided it would reject anything I'd eaten in the past year and a half. I needed more hands to grip my head, stomach, side.

I groaned. Loud. Didn't mean to, it slipped out. Then a moan. Apparently, I was a one-man band. Another groan. All mine.

"You finally awake?"

That voice wasn't mine, I didn't think. Maybe it was. Probably not. Why would I ask myself if—

"Tate. You awake?" A pause. "Thought I heard you say something."

All right. That definitely wasn't me. The voice came from somewhere in the dark, off to my left. Maybe from the window. I couldn't tell for sure since this brass band parading in my head wouldn't let up. It had added more tubas and trumpets, a bass drum rounding out the ensemble. I grabbed my head while another groan escaped.

That voice. The words. Familiar. In between the pounding in my head, I asked, "Who's there?" That in itself was harder than I ever thought possible. Squeezing my eyes tight, wet dripped down my cheeks.

Rustling, like someone turning over on a cot, came from my left. Definitely someone there.

"It's me. Wink. Wink Tannen."

More rustling nearby. Wiping the tears from my face, I spoke into the inky darkness. "Wink? Where are we?" I wanted to ask more questions, but none escaped. If I could simply elbow my way up to a seated position, maybe, possibly, hopefully, my head would allow me to think.

Chuckling from Wink. "Where? Jail, *mi amigo*. Jail. Just like the good ol' days."

Well that certainly wasn't what I wanted to hear. And then, while I mulled over his answer, vague images floated in. Me running. My side hurting. Something about falling. Had I been lassoed like a renegade steer? But why? I managed to roll onto my left side, the one not on fire. From there I pushed up, gripping my blood-encrusted right side. Deep breaths allowed me to make out bars in front of my face.

Jail. Again. He was right. "Wink? Why're you here? Thought you were leaving town."

A low chuckle erupted from the dark. "I was. Stepped into that saloon down the street to have a beer or two for the road."

He'd done something like this before, so I knew what he'd say next. Somebody took exception to him for whatever reason and took a swing. Surely a ruckus broke out. I vaguely wondered if he'd say anything new.

"Next thing I knew, I was up there laying on the bar, that old saloonkeep 'bout ready to clobber me with a beer mug when that ol' sheriff comes blusterin' in, wavin' his twelve gauge like he was God himself."

Uh huh. My head and side couldn't take much more. I needed laudanum or at least whiskey to ease my misery. Knowing I couldn't shout, call for help, it would hurt too much, I curled up like a baby. Could I sleep? Gripping my head, I mumbled for Wink to stop talking. I was beyond irritation and between my head, my side, my whole body, and now Wink jabbering, I knew I'd explode.

Somehow, I laid there until the room grayed. Sure enough, in the next cell lay Wink, sound asleep, lightly snoring. How soon would the sheriff or deputy come in to check on prisoners? I shuddered. Literally. There was that word. Prisoner. Not again. When I could think straight without this brass band marching in circles—at least the prickly pears were gone—I'd plan an escape. May not be today. Maybe not tomorrow. But soon. I'd get out of this one-horse town and head to Fort Worth.

And rob a bank.

Maybe a train.

How about both?

Yeah, that was the ticket. I'd do both. Better than the James boys. I'd show them and the world I was the best outlaw this side of the Rio Grande. And then after that, I'd ride west across that wide bit of water and rob banks and trains over there. I'd be—

The door separating the cells and the office creaked open. A voice over my head roared. "Got cha this time, Tate Nolan."

Bootsteps made their way to my cell. Somehow, I managed to roll onto my back where I stared up into the face of Sheriff Driggs, that shite-eating grin taking up most of the surly mug. My mouth opened and closed, words stuck in my too-dry throat. I squeezed out, "Water."

He kneeled next to me, my body now uncurled, still on the floor. "What's that?" He cupped an ear. "Can't hear you. Oh...you need water?" Chortling, he stuck a hand between the bars and pushed on my injured side, like squeezing a tomato to see if it's ripe.

Unwelcome tears clouded my vision. I imagined ripping off the entire arm at the shoulder and beating him with his own club. But all I could do was force down sobs. My head, side, entire body ached like I'd never hurt before. And I'd been in my share of darn good bar fights where days passed before I could clench my hands again. This...this was different. I was dying, I was sure.

The sheriff poked again and glanced at Wink now sitting on his bunk. The lawman turned back to me, pointing. "Get up on that bunk, boy. I'll fetch the doc." He eased to his feet and stood, towering over me. "Try anything stupid, boy, you won't need one. And the undertaker don't deal with scum outlaws like you. We'll toss your carcass to the coyotes."

With that, he sauntered through the wooden door, closed it. The lock clicked loud.

"He's a pleasant individual." Wink stood, walked closer to me, and gripped the bars separating us.

I groaned up to my knees, crawled to the bunk, using the side to steady me as I got to my feet. Holding onto the bars, I stood upright, turned around to Wink, still standing there. We'd been behind bars too many times and I told him so.

He shrugged. "Not my fault. That other fella took a swing at me. How was I supposed to know Delilah was his gal?"

Energy draining out through my scuffed boots, I eased down to the bunk and the cotton tick mattress. I could only guess how many bedbugs and lice resided in there. But at this point, I didn't care. I needed off my feet.

I lay back, forearm over my eyes, blocking out happy rays of sunshine streaming through the window. I couldn't decide what to hate more—the sun, Wink, or getting caught. And then it hit me. How did the sheriff know for certain my identity? Had to have been Wink who'd told. My friend. Former partner. I gritted my teeth thinking as soon as I could make sense of things, I'd see who else he told...and why.

* * *

HANDS UNBUTTONED MY SHIRT. I recoiled, thinking a monster was eating me. And then my world came into focus. A man I didn't recognize sat next to me, his butt on the edge of the bunk, the front of my bloody shirt in one hand.

"Hold still now. Not gonna hurt you more than you already are."

"Doc?" Did that word come out? Poking, prodding about sent me to the moon.

"Hold still." Doc pushed one shoulder against the mattress. "This might hurt a bit." He looked over his shoulder. "Sheriff? Hold him down, right here. Yours, here."

Great. The sheriff's meaty hands gripped my thighs and pressed my lower body against the bunk. Hands I didn't recognize held my shoulders and forced my chest back. How many hands did this doc have, anyway?

His face now in mine, I detected a hint of eggs and bacon on his breath. Definitely coffee. "Lie real still and I'll get that bullet outta there. Already causing an infection. If it doesn't come out soon, I'm afraid you'll die."

Nodding, I squeezed my eyes shut and prayed for laudanum or a snootful of whiskey. Neither came my way.

"Hold him now."

Prickly cactus, on fire, doused with kerosene, thorns a foot and half long, sawed at my side. I screamed until a hand shoved a cloth into my mouth.

I shook harder than the time my brother jumped out from the dark barn and scared me. Thinking about that and good times with Joe and Eagan got me through the roughest part of this bullet removal. Doc poured stinging liquid over my side then wrapped cloth around my entire chest. Four hands released me. A long, relieved sigh escaped my lips, and I opened my eyes.

I expected an old, white-haired grizzled man, needing a shave, with kind blue eyes staring at me. Instead, a man who looked to be a few years older than me, long dark hair pulled back with a bandanna, dark eyes, neatly trimmed mustache, blinked at me.

"If it doesn't get any more infected, your side's gonna be fine." He pulled the sock from my mouth. "How're you feeling? How's the head?"

"Right as rain." But those words came out a croak. A cup of water slid down my throat and I was able to tell him again.

Doc poked at a knot on the back of my head. "Gonna have a headache for a few more days. Should get better soon." He stood, turned to the sheriff standing outside my cell. "Keep the bullet wound clean." He looked down at me. "See you tomorrow."

Tomorrow? I didn't plan to be here tomorrow, but instead of tipping my hand, I nodded and muttered a thanks.

Once the nameless doc, Sheriff Driggs, and man I assumed to be deputy, closed the door to the office, I relaxed. For now, it appeared the worst was over.

Wink stood again at the bars. "That was ghastly, my friend. Blood everywhere. You screaming. Hope *I* never get shot."

I nodded, closed my eyes. Shot twice now within a few months. Was that how my life would go, until a bullet found my heart? Maybe I should rethink this owl hoot trail life and settle down with...Imogene? My first conquest. Mother of my daughter. I cringed. Or Mary Beth, that lovely creature from Blanco Hill's mercantile?

Hilda? The sweets baker? I liked her a lot. A whole lot. Her and her pastries. I even liked her da.

While deciding which of the three I'd settle down with, the door creaked open again. The Sheriff stepped in, held the door. "Nolan. Doc says you can't ride for at least five days. I'm sending word to San Antone I've got you in custody. Hopefully that sheriff over there'll come here in the next day or two." He chuckled. "Save me a trip."

He turned to Wink and pointed. "Your hearing's at one this afternoon. Be on your best behavior or you'll be heading for federal prison."

Wink gulped so loud I could hear it. If I were him, I'd hold doors and help old ladies across the street. Anything to stay out of there. I'd been there. I knew.

* * *

WHILE I SPENT most of the day on my bunk, Wink was gone half of that time. At long last the door opened, and he stepped in, a deputy on his heels.

"Just came by to say goodbye." Wink offered to shake hands, but I wasn't getting up for anybody. "Hope you get to feeling better."

"You going somewhere?" I managed to turn onto my side—the good one.

Wink thumbed over his shoulder. "Judge gave me six months' probation. But...I also gotta do three months' community service. Pay for damages." He hesitated. "Since now there's an opening at the mercantile, judge says I gotta work there, then scoop up road apples from Main, and help build more boardwalks. And whatever else needs doing."

"The mercantile? That's *my* job."

"Not no more." Wink cocked his head to the right. "Once Sheriff Driggs told your boss about you, you got fired. Guess he hasn't told you yet."

"Guess not." Of course. What did I expect? "Wink?"

"Yeah?" He turned back from the door, deputy waiting in the outer office.

"You tell Driggs my name?"

Wink hung his head, studied his boots. He nodded. "Slipped out. He asked what brought me to town and, well, with my head all fuzzy, I told him I'd come to see you." A sigh. "Sorry."

Some friend. But then again, I wasn't surprised. Disappointed, yes. But surprised, no. "Guess it couldn't be helped."

"Be seein' you around, Tate."

I laid back onto the lumpy mattress and pondered my life. Something had to change. This time. For real.

Voices from the office penetrated the wooden walls. I listened hard. A woman's voice. One I recognized. Mrs. Steinmaker! My savior!

"...a good boy. Sheriff, he served with my Karl at Vicksburg. Said so himself. So, see? He can't possibly be this Mister Nolan you claim he is."

The door started to open. More voices, this one from Sheriff Driggs. "Ma'am, he's been identified. He also fits the wanted poster description."

"I don't care. Please, let me see him."

The door opened fully and in stepped Mrs. Steinmaker. Her face radiated sunshine and pure joy at seeing me. Then she frowned. "Oh, poor Mr. O'Brien. You're hurt." She rushed to the bars.

"Mrs. Steinmaker." I smiled despite the movement making my head thump. Somehow, I swallowed groans and pushed to a sitting position. "I'll be all right."

She turned to Driggs standing next to her, the top of her head at his shoulder. "What did my boy do? My Seamus O'Brien? That's him, Sheriff. That's Seamus, not this so-called Tate Nolan."

"Like I said, ma'am, he's been identified."

"Yes, by me!" She pointed a gloved hand to her chest, something I'd never seen her do before. There was fire in her eyes I'd never seen either. "And this is Seamus O'Brien. Sent by my Karl. O'Brien is a friend, and he shouldn't be behind bars. I want him freed."

"Ma'am, sorry. Can't do that." Driggs shrugged. "He was wounded trying to escape and an innocent man wouldn't have run."

They were speaking as if I wasn't in the room. Maybe there was a chance Mrs. Steinmaker actually could help. "Ma'am?" I waited for her to turn her blue-bonnet eyes on me. "Maybe if you could talk to Hilda and her da. Over at the bakery? Ask them to come, they could tell Sheriff Driggs who I am."

She swiveled to the sheriff and craned her neck. "Would that help, Sheriff? Could I do that?"

He shook his head. "I don't think—"

"Yes, ma'am. It would help a lot." I eased off the bunk and placed my hand over hers. "And maybe Mr. Anderson, my boss over at the mercantile. That might make the difference between life and death." I hated to be dramatic, but it seemed the thing to do.

"Of course, Mister O'Brien. I'll go there right now." She patted my hand on top of hers. "You'll be out of here in no time."

Like a woman on a mission, she spun, head held high, marched out of the room. The sheriff started to follow, then turned back to me, pointed a long finger at my nose. "This isn't over." He slammed the door. Hard.

CHAPTER THIRTY

FEELING WELL ENOUGH TO PACE IN MY CELL—
actually, I didn't pace—I eased from bar to bar, gripping
the iron like I was on a ship going down for the third
time. I managed to sidestep ten feet over to the window.
Warm air pushed in which brought sweat to my forehead. Maybe it was the effort of being on my feet and
moving. Maybe both.

Through that window I heard wooden doors being
closed, women calling to children and husbands about
supper. With that my stomach rumbled, lightly, as if
reminding me I hadn't fed it recently, but don't put too
much down there. It might all come right back up.

That in mind and the fact my legs were shaking, I
made my way back to the bunk. This had been one long
day, an exhausting one, and all I wanted right now was
something to eat and a long sleep. Whiskey wouldn't be
unwelcomed, however.

Easing down to the bunk, I sat gripping my side and
then my head. The brass band from earlier this morning
had kicked out a few trumpets and one tuba. They still

oompahed in my head, but they didn't upset my stomach as much.

The outer door opened and in stepped Sheriff Driggs, followed by Hilda, her da, and Mrs. Coogan. Groans, loud and long, slipped from my lips before I could reel them in. Mrs. Coogan, Emily Anne Coogan, would certainly tell the sheriff that for certain I was Tate Nolan. Which meant I'd be hanging by next weekend.

Hilda stood at the bars and reached out a slender, flour-dusted arm. "Are you well, Mr. O'Brien? I hear you've been shot." One big tear rolled down her cheek. She sniffed back more.

"This's a travesty." Mr. Renstein hooked a thumb into his vest pocket. He used the other hand to sweep around the holding area. "Locked in here like a common criminal. It's a disgrace." He moved next to Hilda. "We'll get you out of here. Soon."

Sheriff Driggs crowded in. "Can you definitely identify this man, Mr. Renstein? Miss Renstein?"

Both nodded. "Yes, sir." They spoke in unison.

Emily Anne Coogan, quiet up until now, slid a smile up the right side of her face. She turned to the lawman. "I know exactly who he is, Sheriff. I knew him in Blanco Hill."

Icy water filled my veins, rolled down my back, across my chest. I couldn't breathe.

"Who is he then?" Driggs asked with confidence.

She eyed me. Was that a wink? Her scrutiny ran over my entire body and pierced my soul. "No doubt, Sheriff. I knew him and his half brother in Blanco Hill. They look alike, but this is definitely…"

She left me dangling, like a trout on a line. I opened my mouth to urge her on, but she didn't need prompting.

"Seamus O'Brien." Mrs. Coogan nodded and placed one hand on a hip. "I'd know him anywhere. And yes, before you ask, Sheriff, I've run into him socially. No doubt in my mind he's who he says he is."

Heart pounding, the world stood still. Had she just exonerated me? *Why* crossed my mind, but right now I didn't care the reason.

"Told you, Sheriff." Hilda spun toward the lawman. "Told you he was innocent. You've got the wrong man. *Shot* the wrong man."

"Release him right now." Mr. Renstein nodded at me. "I'll see to it he goes back to Mrs. Steinmaker's. She's waiting for him."

Driggs held up a hand. "Before I let him go, Mrs. Coogan you mentioned someone who looks like him."

"A half brother. Same mother." Mrs. Coogan clutched her purse. "Resemblance is rather uncanny."

Driggs raised both bushy eyebrows. "This uncanny man have a name?"

I held my breath, again.

"He does. Tom Dugan. That's with one g."

"Hmmm…never heard of him." The sheriff shrugged. "Thanks, Mrs. Coogan." He pointed toward his office. "Now, if you'll all wait out there, I'll take care of Mr. O'Brien." He said O'Brien like it was a dirty, filthy word, one he was forced to say—like *please* and *thank you*.

When the throng was reduced to the two of us, Sheriff Driggs unlocked the door, swung it open. "Let me be clear, Tate Nolan." He stared a hole into my eyes. "I don't believe them, and I don't believe you. Don't leave town until I get this settled. Until I tell you."

I gulped louder than I thought possible. Air stuck in my chest preventing me from verbally agreeing to the conditions of my release. A nod would have to do.

Freedom, sweet freedom waved a seductive arm at me. She crooked a finger, and I followed her into the outer office, past a puzzled deputy, then farther out into pure sunshine. I stood swaying, my head still throbbing and my side now bleeding. Warm moisture soaked through the cloth bandage. I'd need to lie down soon.

Hilda took one arm, her da the other and they led me to the buggy parked nearby which yesterday had taken us to picnic paradise. I eased into the back seat, Hilda tucked in beside me, Mr. Renstein took his place behind the reins and Mrs. Coogan stopped by my shoulder long enough to flash a quick smile. She climbed in next to her beau and off we went to Mrs. Steinmaker's.

That lovely woman met us at the door where heavenly scents of roasting beef and potatoes floated out behind her. "You poor dear, Mr. O'Brien." She hiked her skirt and sailed down the two steps. "Here, let me help."

By the time she arrived at the buggy, I was already out and swaying, hanging on to the seat back, desperate to keep on my feet. Mrs. Coogan gripped an arm, Hilda the other, and up the steps we went, then inside.

I eased to the couch afraid my weeping side would stain the brocade fabric. Holding my ribs and side, I waited to release them while Mrs. Steinmaker went in search of a towel. I held it against the wound until I figured the bleeding was done.

The women gathered around, clucking like old chickens, each one declaring they were the most concerned about me. Before I could actually lie on the sofa, Mr. Renstein hoisted me to my feet.

"Let's get that bandage changed, Mr. O'Brien, then I'd suggest a long nap would be in order." He tugged until I took a few steps. "I'm assuming your room is this way?"

Mrs. Steinmaker led the way, the other two women

trailing behind. My room wasn't large enough to accommodate everyone, which left all three women standing outside the door watching Mr. Renstein peel off my shirt.

"Oh heavens." Mrs. Steinmaker flapped a hand. "Let's give them some privacy. I could use help in the kitchen."

And with that, the women disappeared, fussing their way elsewhere.

I sat long enough for him to clean my side, wrap more white cloth around my chest, covering the wound. I had no idea where he got the material, but at that moment, I didn't care. All I wanted was to lie back, close my eyes, and forget the last several hours.

* * *

Crash!

Startled awake, I stared into piercing sunshine. Where was I, anyway? I looked for jail bars, but instead, found four wooden walls, my clothes neatly hung on a peg by the door. Must be at Mrs. Steinmaker's.

Events of the past flooded in, partly thanks to my throbbing side and head pain now reduced to merely intense aching. Apparently, the brass band had gone home, tired of making enormous amounts of racket. What had broken? I listened to Mrs. Steinmaker grumble and then what sounded like a broom sweep across the floor, followed by crockery into a dustpan.

Pushing up, I sat and gripped my side. No new blood leaked from the bullet wound. My stomach decided it had been neglected and chose now to rumble and complain. It *had* been a while since I'd eaten and right about now a cup of strong coffee and a hearty breakfast sounded better than Hilda and me on a picnic. Although I had to admit, that image ran a close second to coffee.

Dressed, I managed to make it to the kitchen without a grunt or groan. My side felt better and as soon as coffee made its way down my throat, my head would be fine.

"Good morning, Mrs. Steinmaker," I said to her back as she stood by the stove.

"Eek!" She jumped and spun at the same time. I smiled.

"Sorry, didn't mean to startle you."

Fork in hand, she turned and gave me a gentle hug, a tear running down her cheek. "Oh, Mr. O'Brien. There for a moment thought we'd lost ya." She let go and stood back, eyeing me top to bottom. "Sit there. I'll fetch ya breakfast."

"Coffee would be nice." I reached for the pot on the stove, but she swatted my hand.

"I'll be getting it for you." She used the fork to point to a chair at the table. "Sit."

"Yes, ma'am." Watching her, I realized what a gem Karl must've had for a ma. And I speculated if he loved her as much as she did him.

Two cups of coffee did wonders for my head and disposition. While I wasn't ready yet to take on the world, I was ready to make sense of it. Eggs, bacon, sliced potatoes, and cornbread in front of me, I dug in. Mrs. Steinmaker took a seat across the table. While I ate, we discussed the picnic and the fact I was now jobless.

"It's terrible what they did to ya." Mrs. Steinmaker shook her head and took a dainty sip of coffee. "But don't you worry. Stay here as long as you want, and I'm sure another job will come along—when you're well enough."

Always the optimist, she was. Before we talked much longer, a knock at the door startled both of us. She shuffled to the door and let in Mrs. Coogan, alone.

Breakfast stuck in my throat. What was *she* doing here? If we had to have visitors, I'd have much preferred Hilda. I eased to my feet when Mrs. Steinmaker offered our visitor coffee and a seat at the table.

I'd been around long enough to know such kindness comes with a price. I wondered what hers was. Undoubtedly, she saved me from a certain neck-stretching and the cost would be high. The *why* ran a close second.

More coffee was poured, small talk ensued, then Mrs. Steinmaker excused herself, citing a need to check on her laundry hanging out to dry. I figured she needed the privy but that was never discussed in front of company.

Mrs. Coogan waited until the screen door closed when she turned her light brown eyes on me. We'd already run down the litany of how I was feeling, too bad about my job, and all the details of being arrested. Now, we'd get down to business.

I jumped in before she could start. "I'm grateful for what you've done, Mrs. Coogan. I truly am. But I have to ask why." I picked up my cup, set the crockery down without sipping.

She cocked her head to one side, a coy smile claiming half of her face. "I don't like authority, and...thought I may need a favor."

"But even back at the picnic—"

"Even back then. I enjoyed putting you on the spot. I guess that wasn't very polite, but the half brother bit made me laugh." She leaned closer. "You've got a sharp mind. You entertain me."

This time I drained the coffee. Had I been complimented or insulted? Hard to tell. I didn't know her well enough. I ran a shaky hand over a rough chin, a shave being in order. "What do you want from me?" Did that come out the way I'd wanted?

She leaned back studying my face like it was a map of the moon. "Nothing yet. Thought I'd be nice." One shoulder rose. "If you'd rather I not, I'll be glad to—"

"No ma'am, nice is fine." My own grin pushed up sore cheeks. "I'm curious though." I checked the back door. No Mrs. Steinmaker. "Who's Tom Dugan, with one g?"

This time she laughed out loud. "Oh, him? That was good wasn't it? He's my ex-father-in-law. From my first husband."

"He a wanted man?"

More chuckling. "Not anymore. He's dead. So even if Driggs tries to find him, he'll find nothing." She finished her coffee, pushed back her chair and rose. "I have to go to Blanco Hill next week. I'll visit your folks, tell them you're alive and doing fine. I'll tell them you're—"

"On my way to New Orleans. They'll believe that." I stood also and extended a hand just as Mrs. Steinmaker stepped inside. "Thank you, Mrs. Coogan."

"You have to be going?" Mrs. Steinmaker patted the side of her rosy face. Summer heat was in full force today.

"Afraid so." Mrs. Coogan gave her a quick hug. "Wanted to see how Mr. O'Brien was doing. I'll be pleased to tell Hilda and Günter he's up and doing well."

We followed her to the door, waved as she made her way to the street. Energy drained, I eased to the sofa. Pondering on what had just happened, I leaned back, eyes closing despite my insistence they remain open.

A hand on my shoulder shook me, hard.

"Mr. O'Brien. I'm afraid you're snoring rather loudly." Mrs. Steinmaker leaned close. "You'll be more comfortable in bed, I'm sure."

* * *

ONE DAY FOLLOWED the next and I grew stronger with each passing hour. Food was hot and plentiful, conversations insightful and enjoyable. After supper, my hostess and I sat on the porch, swatted at mosquitos still hoping to munch on us, and chatted until we couldn't see hands in front of faces. I found Mrs. Steinmaker to be a most pleasant companion and her stories of her homeland, before she immigrated as a young teen, totally fascinating. In many ways, I wished my parents and I hadn't left Ireland when we did. At six months old, I had no experiences of my own to refer to. I related some of my parents' lives but gave most of my attention to my benefactor.

Hilda stopped by every day to bring strudel and apple tarts. Her visits got longer while our conversations became more intimate. Between Mrs. Steinmaker and Hilda, if I'd known my life would have been this wonderful, I would've tried sooner to get shot. Aches and pains still kept me up at night, but they were tolerable thanks to laudanum and whiskey. I tended to alternate them which kept me in a numbed, cushioned world.

I pulled a laudanum bottle out of my vest pocket while sitting next to Hilda. We were on the porch and aromas of cooking pork chops sailed out and around my head. Corn was now coming in from the fields and I hoped we'd have fresh corn on the cob. My stomach rumbled at the thought.

Tipping the bottle to my lips, I anticipated the elixir numbing my throbbing side. Instead, Hilda grabbed my pain killer.

"Your eyes are glassy, and your speech is slurred. I'm

afraid you've had too much." She held it up to the fading light. "You're well enough not to need this anymore."

"I'm not done with it yet." I lunged for the bottle she held at arm's length.

"Yes, you are."

And then it hit me. I'd gone through this before back at the ranch house after being shot. Joe and the bunkhouse boys had set me right. I remembered staying in the barn, throwing up in the barn, shaking in the barn. No way would I go through that nightmare again.

Letting out a long sigh, I wilted. "Thank you." My gaze took in another savior. "Pour it out, keep it. I don't want it." No more laudanum or whiskey. I'd power through the pain.

And then she asked a question I couldn't answer, one I hadn't given any rational thought to, but simply emotional attention.

She leaned against my shoulder and stared into the encroaching night. "What are your plans for the future?"

Mouth opened and closed at least a hundred times while I thought how to answer. I had no answer, was the problem. Her tiny but strong hand in mine did nothing to alleviate the conundrum rattling in my entire being. How to answer?

Sitting up, she gazed into the distance, now turning silvery gold highlighting flowers in the field beyond. Two butterflies fought over a single red flower while crickets tuned their bows. This evening would be heavenly—if she hadn't asked that question.

"You're awfully quiet." She nudged me with her delicate shoulder. "Did I say something wrong?" She sighed. "It's simply that—"

"I'm not sure." There. I said what was in my heart. Deciding time was at hand to pour out my heart, I breathed deeply and coughed. Not what I'd planned, but the action was hard enough my ribs immediately complained. I gripped them and as if on cue, my head thumped.

I swallowed pain and continued in fits and starts. "I've always dreamed of being better than Jesse James and his brother Frank. Thought I wanted to rob banks and trains." The setting sun held my interest, but I felt her gaze on the side of my head.

"Banks?"

"Growing up, there wasn't much money. Figured the fastest way to get some was to rob a bank or train." So, this was where I'd have to lie. "Never did, of course. Robbing people doesn't solve problems—or really make you rich."

"I'm relieved to hear you say that." Hilda flashed a world-stopping smile. "I couldn't hold with anyone who would steal people's hard-earned money."

And with those words, my stage-robbing, bank-robbing, train-robbing ideas were put to rest. For the moment. I wanted Hilda. I loved Hilda. Loved everything about her. And then like a bolt of clarity from heaven, I realized what I wanted. What I would do.

I'd marry Hilda. Settle down. Get a job. I shuddered at that word but continued. We'd have a family. We'd grow old together. Like a soft blanket, the idea threw its comfort around my shoulders and hugged me. All was right with my world.

Except it wasn't.

"Are you feeling all right, Seamus?" Hilda squeezed my hand. "You've turned a bit pale."

I looked down at our entwined fingers. I wanted her. Bad. If I wasn't a gentleman and sitting on Mrs. Stein-maker's porch swing right now, I'd take her to my room

and make her mine. Images brought sweat to my forehead. I could feel it.

"Seamus?"

Jolted back to reality, I squeezed her hand, lightly.
"Sorry, Hilda. I was thinking." Testing the water, I asked,
"What are your plans for the future?"

She giggled, shot me a coy glance sideways. "I've
thought a lot. I enjoy running my own business. Not
many women get the chance. But I'd like to settle down,
raise a family, but keep my business. Maybe bring in a
partner so I don't have to work so hard."

"What about your da?"

Wagging her head, she studied the tree near the
porch. "He's slowing down, getting older. He'll help, but
I think if someone would take over his duties, he
wouldn't say no."

So, I'd found me a job too. My life's plans took on a
life of their own and I couldn't stop the words from
pouring out of my mouth.

"Listen." I gazed into her baby blue eyes. "I've got
loose ends that need tying, but when that's done, I'd like
to come back. Here, to Fredericksburg. And if you're
willing, we can get married. I can take your da's place at
the store."

She sat still, blinking at me. Finally, she tilted her
pretty head. "Are you proposing, Mr. O'Brien?"

When she put it that way, I panicked. Was that really
what I wanted? Could I back out now? Deep breath.
"Guess I am, Hilda." Another deep breath. "Will you?"

Leaning over, she kissed me. Hard and deep. "I will."

Panic, lust, fear, wonderment, love, hope all bundled
themselves into one emotion. I wrapped my arms around
her shoulders and pulled her close. If this was heaven, I
was glad I'd died and gone there.

She kissed me again and my world melted into hers.

"Oh! Excuse me!"

We broke apart and turned to see Mrs. Steinmaker standing in the doorway. A half grin, half radiant beam took up her face, highlighted by her sparkling round eyes.

"Mrs. Steinmaker." I eased to my feet, helping Hilda up also. "We've got an announcement." I looked from my love and then to the woman who'd saved me. "Hilda and I are getting married."

"Ohhh!" Mrs. Steinmaker squealed, literally. She jumped up and down and for a woman her age, that must've been hard to do. Running to us both with outstretched arms, she hugged Hilda and me until I couldn't breathe.

"Thank you, ma'am. Thank you." I croaked until air flooded back into my chest.

Mrs. Steinmaker flapped her hands at Hilda. "Hilda, you simply must say for supper. We're having pork chops." She flapped at me. "When will you ask her pa for permission?"

I stepped back. Ask permission? What kind of racket was that? Did I need to bring him gifts before asking? And why should I? Apparently, the shock and then myriad of questions wallpapered my face. Both women smiled.

The older woman explained first. "It's customary to ask a woman's father's permission to marry his daughter. You must prove you can provide for her and...children, should you be blessed with them."

"I'd like many children." Hilda's face pinked into rose. "Boys and girls."

"You get either one or the other, don't you? Or is there a third choice?" I couldn't believe I'd blurted that out. Nerves were to blame. Both women froze and glared. Now I knew how Da felt when Ma's eyes focused in on him. I squirmed. Shrugged.

Thawing, Hilda giggled. "Of course, silly. One at a time."

Whew. Now to tackle the problem of her da. I turned to Hilda. "I'll go see your da first thing tomorrow."

CHAPTER THIRTY-ONE

THE WHOLE EVENT WASN'T ANYTHING I'D planned, schemed, or thought. While her da sat, I stood in front of him, alone, dumbstruck, by myself, without Hilda's sweet breath and encouragement to prop me up. What could he be thinking? Surely, he knew what I wanted. But then again, maybe he didn't. Mr. Renstein sat, shoulders back, in his green brocade wingback chair in his front room, and stared up at me standing there, hat in hand. I rethought that look in his eyes. Did he know? Based on that nerve-jolting twinkle, added to a silly smirk-grin-grimace on his face, he knew.

"Can't think of a finer man to marry my daughter, Seamus." He nodded and pointed to a photo perched on the edge of a table. "Elsie would approve too."

"Elsie?" Was she like Mrs. Steinmaker's Karl? Gone, yet always there.

"My wife." He reached for the framed tintype of two young people looking stern into the camera lens. "Thirty years. I was lucky enough to have her with me thirty years." Looking up at me, he added, "Those were glorious years. I hope you and my Hilda have glorious years also."

I didn't want to push the subject, but my side was aching along with my head. However, I couldn't show weakness. "So, you're giving me permission, sir?" I gripped the hat brim tighter like it would fly away.

A long pause then his eyebrows rose as he eased up from his chair. "I suppose I am, Seamus." He extended a hand, gripped mine like I would run away. "Promise me one thing."

"Of course, sir." Why was my heart in my throat?

"Love her. Treat her with the respect she deserves." He released my hand only to place his on my shoulder. He squeezed. I wasn't sure whether that was on purpose, or his nerves. Whichever, the pressure was similar to the handshake. My knees threatened to buckle. "Can you do that, son?"

I swallowed. "Absolutely. Always." And meant it.

He walked me to the door, held the handle. "So. This Saturday? You're thinking maybe around early afternoon?" Mr. Renstein chuckled. "Figured you'd want to tie the knot as soon as possible."

Saturday? This Saturday? Fear raced up and down my spine, pirouetted in my brain. "Today is Tuesday, right?"

"Want to get married tomorrow?" He tilted his head. "Guess we could arrange that."

I held up a trembling hand which happened to have my hat clutched in it. "Saturday won't work, I'm afraid. I've got a bit of unfinished business to...uh, finish... before we can get married."

Married. There was that word. Suddenly, *married* and *noose* sounded the same.

"What kind of business?" He pointed toward the jail. "You're not really wanted, are you?" His eyes narrowed.

Shaking my head, hoping to loosen the stuck marbles, I stuttered. "No. Just some fam—"

"Good." He opened the door, walked with me onto the porch. "How about two weeks from this coming Saturday then? Give you enough time?"

Not really, but my head bobbed without doing any thinking. Two steps down to the street, I stood and turned, looking at him. "Thank you, sir." I headed for the sanctity of Mrs. Steinmaker's.

* * *

LYING ON THE BED, thoughts paraded across my chest and through my head. Did I really intend to marry Hilda? Settle down? Be a respectable husband? A well-thought-of citizen? How would I support her? And then it hit me. She'd support *me*. That was no way for a marriage to work. The man provided for the woman. The woman made the man happy. Cut and dried. Pure and simple. Black and white.

That was the way things worked and who was I to change society? True, a few women worked outside the home. Ma sewed, but only because she wanted to bring in a bit of extra "spending" money, she called it. And she did that at home. But usually, they were widows or women too homely to catch a man. Hilda wasn't either of those, and come to think on it, neither was Mary Beth Anderson at Blanco Hill's Mercantile.

All that aside, unusual for a woman, Hilda owned a business. More than likely though, her da owned it and she ran the store. If we did marry, I'd want to own the business and give her da a sizable monthly allowance.

She'd be gone all day baking goodies for the town.

Wait. If she worked all day, who cleaned the house?

Cooked supper? Took care of the children? Changed dirty diapers? Would that be me? Did men *do* that? I mean... what if Da found out? Or Joe and Eagan? I couldn't show my face in Blanco Hill ever again.

That line of thinking changed everything.

But to the present predicament. What about Imogene? Did I owe her anything? Yes. And little Louisa. Should I be the da she's never had? Maybe. Somehow, however, I needed to give Imogene and my folks the news. I couldn't ride into Blanco Hill during the day, show my face in town. I'd be locked up before I could say howdy.

Should I tell Hilda my real name? If she married Tate Nolan thinking he was Seamus O'Brien, was she legally Mrs. Tate Nolan or Mrs. Seamus O'Brien? My head throbbed. How did I get myself into these predicaments? I punched the pillow. All I'd wanted to do was rob a bank. Be more famous than Jesse James. Now I'd be famous as the only "kept" man in Fredericksburg.

Dark blotches on the wooden ceiling grew darker and larger. I rubbed my eyes and realized the light normally flooding my room had turned dim. Clouds? Rain? A sniff and nothing but evening penetrated my nose.

Following that same nose to the kitchen, I found Mrs. Steinmaker sitting at the table alone, a plate with one of her famous blackberry pie slices in front of her. A half-empty cup of coffee was gripped in her sturdy hand.

"There you are, Seamus." Her smile lit up the dim dining room. "Thought you'd sleep all day and all night." She set her cup on the table and scooted back her chair. I held up a hand and she stopped.

"Don't move. Don't mean to interrupt your dessert." I yawned, stretched, and headed for the always-full coffee pot. "Didn't intend to sleep. Guess I was tired."

"Big day, I understand." Her eyes sparkled, rose colored her cheeks. "What'd he say?"

Had I told her what I had planned? I guess she knew my questioning look.

"News like that gets around a small town." A chuckle erupted from her chest. "Hard to keep secrets here."

"Yes ma'am." I wanted to strangle whoever spilled the beans because now I wasn't sure it would happen. So many uncertainties clouded what little sense I had. What I needed was an impartial third party—not anyone in Fredericksburg, not my family—to help me figure this out.

"Seamus?" Mrs. Steinmaker tapped my shoulder. She had stood? "I don't know where you go when you stand there staring, but I hope it's somewhere fun."

"Just thinking. There's a lot to think about." There. I'd used the word "think" twice in two sentences and no doubt hadn't done any at all when proposing to Hilda. Something about her was irresistible. But did I love her? Would I forever? Second, third and fourth doubts bombarded my entire body. Feeling more like one of those rabbits trying to figure out which way to escape oncoming buggy wheels baring down, I numbly found a cup, poured dark brew, and plopped down at the table.

Mysteriously, a slice of pie appeared in front of me. A fork too. I looked up at my host who stood smiling like she'd won the "World's Best Person" trophy. Could she beam any wider or brighter? She stepped back closer to the stove. "Two weeks, Seamus. I'll have time to sew you a proper jacket and shirt. Not sure about trousers, though."

Before I could tell her not to bother, she continued. "I've got the perfect material saved for Karl, a nice wool, but I think you'll need it sooner. I'll start first thing in the morning." She took a quick breath. "And I can't wait to wear my yellow dress for the wedding. It's been years."

With that declaration, she put her plate and cup in the pan on the counter, and flapped her way out of the room, quietly muttering about pins, thread, and buttons until the words died away. I sat brooding, alone.

And then it hit me. Mr. Carmichael. *He* would know what to do. But could I trust him not to turn me in to the law? I'd have to. No one else, besides my family, would I trust. For the first time in days, I relaxed. My world brightened, the pie was tart and sweet, the coffee a perfect bitter, and Mrs. Steinmaker's quiet humming filled me with love and contentment. If this was married life, then yes, this was what I wanted.

I could rob on the side. Maybe take a few days off and hold up a mercantile and work my way up to a bank. A train would take longer to plan since I'd never been on one, but with more robbing experience, I could rob a train.

* * *

MRS. STEINMAKER STOOD on the porch shielding her eyes from early morning rays and waved good-bye. I'd told her I had to muster out of my unit, but I'd be back within a week. She had wished me a safe trip and said she'd have my shirt finished by then, ready to try on, and part of the jacket as well.

I skirted Blanco Hill, taking my time riding through brush, mesquite and stands of Texas

oak. I stopped under a thick stand, pulled out the sandwich Mrs. Steinmaker had given me before I'd left. First bite and flies and mosquitos buzzed around me, swarming like I was dead and rotting. A perfect meal for those pests. I swatted, cursed, swatted, and spewed out all the curse words I knew, especially the colorful ones I'd learned in prison. Nothing helped. The thickets turned into a perfect breeding ground for all critters that slither, bite, or sting. And we'd had plenty of rain lately which added to the mess.

Sandwich quickly consumed, I swung up into the saddle, my body a knot of nerves and spurred my horse into a gentle lope.

Knowing I couldn't simply ride up to the front of the house, knock, and step in like I used to, I reined up a quarter mile away. Tying my horse to an oak branch, I reset my hat, hitched up my britches, straightened my shoulders and sneaked to the back.

As it happened, Carmichael's cook, Miranda, loaded down with an armful of firewood, was headed for the back door.

"Miranda?" I called softly, not wanting to bring any more attention to myself than necessary.

She froze, then turned at my voice. Frowning at first, her mouth changed to a smile. "Mr. Nolan! Is that you?"

I walked up to her taking most of the wood from her arms. "Yes, ma'am. It's me."

"*¡Mi hijito!*" She started to hug me then, but with both our arms full of cut wood, settled on beaming. "You're back! *Bienviendo.*"

"Just visiting." I kept my voice low, hoping she'd do the same. A long survey of the grounds revealed no ranch hands working outside. I peeked around the corner. No visiting horses tied at the hitching rail out front. Relieved, I stepped up the two creaky steps into the kitchen, holding the door for her. I set the wood in its usual spot by the stove. She did the same then gave me a rib-shattering hug. I winced and groaned.

"I'm sorry. You're hurt?" Miranda put a hand out to pat my side then withdrew, I guess remembering we didn't know each other *that* well, although at one point, not too long ago, she'd undressed me when I'd been shot.

I held her hand away from my side. "Recovering from a bullet wound." I rushed my words. "*Another* one. But I'm fine. Just a bit tender."

If eyebrows could rise onto the top of a head, Miranda's would have done so. "*Another* bullet? *¡Aye, señor!* Your luck." She tsked, shook her head, tsked louder.

No time to waste, I glanced around the kitchen and through the open door to the dining room. "Mr. Carmichael around? I need to talk to him."

"*Sí*. He return this morning from San Antonio."

"Could you please ask him if he's got time to talk to me? It's real important." I peered into the dining room again. "Mrs. Carmichael? She around?"

"No. She go into town for time with her friends."

Good. I didn't need her interfering. Then again, maybe I'd need female advice. I waited for Miranda to return.

Three minutes later, I found myself standing in Mr. C.'s office, his hand in mine, grasping like we were old friends. Maybe we were. Released, I sat in my usual chair.

A minute or two of chit chat then I got down to the reason I was there. Mr. C. listened intently, never interrupting as my words burbled forth. It wasn't until I finished that I realized just how much of a mess I'd gotten myself into. And it was a mess.

Mr. C. sighed, sat back, steepled his fingers and

peered at me. At long last, he smoothed his mustache, sighed again. "I don't have answers to many questions, but I'm gonna give you one piece of advice."

"Yes, sir?" I leaned forward.

"Building a marriage on a lie is no good. You gotta come clean with...Hilda?"

"Hilda, yes." My stomach tightened and I couldn't breathe. "That means I gotta tell her all about me. About my past. About who I am?"

"It's advice, son. Keeping a marriage, any relationship, on solid footing is tough enough." He stared out the window. "But when it begins on a lie, I don't see much success. You're in for heartache and disappointment. And what if you have children?"

He droned on, but I'd stopped listening. Everything was wrong. Everything. No glimmer of hope for my future. Nothing but blackness, an endless abyss of pain and suffering. Kinda like being adrift in the night sky with no star to hang on to.

All because I was stupid. In love and stupid.

Mr. C. sat still, fingers steepled while I inspected the world. I studied the papers on his desk, the view of trees through his window, and the fact my boots, firmly planted on the floor, were dusty, scratched and wouldn't do for a wedding.

Like being jabbed by a bee, Mr. C. jerked, looked at me instead of his fingers. "Forgot I had this." He pushed aside papers. "You'll want to see this." A creased newspaper hid under a stack.

Holding it up, he turned the paper around so I could read the banner. *San Antonio Express. Sunday...* The rest I ignored because the headline screamed at me. *Texas Kid kills Rancher Stinson's Foreman.*

What in the world was going on? Who was Texas Kid and why was Mr. C. showing me this? "Sir?"

He rattled it at me, pointing at the words. "This is you. They've declared you the Texas Kid and made you into a killer. Says later on you've shot five men. In cold blood."

"And you think this is me?" No amount of swallowing would push down the rock that was stuck in my throat.

"I do. Perfect description. Eyewitness account of when you were shot, Tex killed, and then more recently when you killed Stinson's man."

"But I didn't kill five men. Hit one in self-defense." Completely at sea with this latest piece of news, I fought for understanding. "This writer thinks I'm a cold-blooded killer?"

Mr. C. shrugged. "Look at it from his point of view. What sells more papers? One killing or five?"

Obviously five. But still. Could life get any worse? Or more complicated? Apparently yes because, like a well-scripted play, right then Miranda tapped on the door and opened it.

"Mr. Carmichael?" She pointed over her shoulder. "Sheriff Samuels from San Antonio is in the front room wanting to see you."

The sheriff? Icy apprehension rippled down my back.

Mr. C.'s eyes widened, eyebrows arched. He whispered to me. "Suppose he knows you're here?"

I shrugged. If I could evaporate, turn into a ghost right now, I would. Maybe if I hid under the desk…

"Sir?" Miranda glanced behind her.

"Be right there. Keep him in the front room."

She shut the door while Mr. C. stood. "Don't move. Stay quiet. I'll see what he wants." He walked around the desk, then looked down at a frozen me. "I won't tell him you're here."

And with those words, he stepped out of the room like a man on a mission. Did I trust him? Absolutely. But had that sheriff spotted my horse? Had someone seen me and pointed to the house? Maybe if I listened hard, I could tell what they were saying. Unfortunately, my beating heart thudded in my ears until all I heard was drumming and a whine until I cracked open the door wide enough to catch most of the words.

"What can I do for you, Sheriff?"

"On my way up to Fredericksburg, thought I'd stop by."

"Fredericksburg?"

"Got word Texas Kid's livin' there now." Some sort of expletive erupted from the baritone voice. One too low for me to make out. "Idiotic sheriff there had him behind bars but let him go. Seems a couple influential towns-people thought he was an ace-high kinda fella. Insisted he was innocent."

"Maybe they got the wrong man."

"Got the *right* man. Know he used to work for you. Thought maybe he'd come back or at least stopped by."

Mr. C. muttered something. Sheriff Samuels's baritone rumbled down the hall. "Rancher Stinson's added another five hundred to the reward. Makes it a thousand now. "

Mr. C. whistled.

The sheriff continued. "Stinson's a big man around town and he won't stop 'til Nolan's dead. Said he'd hang him himself when he found him." A pause brought my ear closer to the door. "Thought *I* better find this fella before a mob does."

A mob? Why? What had I done to deserve a mob? My stomach knotted after sending a rock up to my throat.

Silence. Footsteps toward the front door relaxed me only a bit. Mr. C.'s voice was definitive. "No need for him to be here. But I'll keep an eye out. Thanks for stopping..."

My heart returned to its regular beating a minute or two later about the time I heard close bootsteps and then the squeak of the door. Mr. C. stepped in, closed the door, and wordlessly plopped into his chair behind the desk. I waited for him to say something. Anything. Instead, he stared at me. Simply stared. Didn't even steeple his fingers. He stared at me until I squirmed.

"You speak Spanish?"

I shook my head. Odd question. Then I realized what he was saying. I needed to head south right now. Today. Within the minute. Leave everyone behind.

A long sigh followed another sigh. "Here's the thing, Tate." He leaned in close. "You're in a mess bigger'n I could've imagined. Besides Samuels, Marshal Becker's got it in for you."

"Becker? Marshal?" I searched my brain for who he was talking about.

Mr. C. leaned back. "The deputy that harassed you when Becker was sheriff? Walter Wagner? He's now sheriff."

"Becker's not sheriff anymore?" I prayed he wasn't. Had he died like I thought I'd heard?

He wagged his head. "No. After he recovered, got appointed Deputy US Marshal." Mr. C pointed toward town. "Got a big office and everything in Blanco Hills. Even hired himself three deputies under him."

Dark blobs swam in front of my eyes. Closing them, I rubbed. Harder. My head throbbed while my side reminded me of the latest shooting. Stomach threatening to bring up whatever I'd last eaten, I choked down rising bile.

I'm sure I stuttered. "You mean to tell me, I got that San Antone Sheriff Samuels, Blanco Hills Sheriff Wagner, Deputy Marshal Becker, and the Fredericksburg Sheriff Driggs, all lookin' for me? All of 'em?" My hand ran across the top of my head, across my mouth. Again, what had I done to deserve this?

"'Fraid so. But good news…Tommy O'Sullivan's still the deputy here in Blanco Hill. He was good to you, right?"

I nodded.

Part of a thin smile slid up one side of Mr. C.'s face. "When you make a mess, you make a mess." He chuckled. "And that doesn't even take into account all the women you've…well…*influenced*."

Now it was my turn to sit and think. Contemplate. I could run down to Mexico. Lose myself in tequila and women. But with what money? Plus, that was the coward's way out. I had more decency and pride than to abandon them. Maybe I wouldn't marry Hilda, or Imogene or even Mary Beth Anderson for that matter, but I wouldn't leave them without an explanation. I *did* have my standards. And poor Mrs. Steinmaker. No way would I simply ride off one day like her Karl, and never return. I couldn't do that to her. Ma, either.

No, I'd rather die standing up.

"I'm not running. Not moving to Mexico, Mr. C." My shoulders straightened and I sat up tall despite my burning side. "I'll turn myself in."

CHAPTER THIRTY-TWO

"TURN YOURSELF *in*?" MR. C. SHOUTED DESPITE my being two arm's length away. "Turn your...what kinda crazy fancy you got rumbling around in your head, Tate?" He huffed and puffed, mumbled, more to himself I believe than to me. "Turn yourself in. Good Lord. What'll happen next? He'll open those cell doors, march right in, lock himself up. Probably even put the noose around his own neck. Hmmpfff."

I wondered if he even knew I was still in the room, still sitting there, holding my side which burned like Lucifer had just poked me. Then realization hit. He was truly on my side. A lot. Thinking back, he had picked me at the livery stable what seemed like years ago, why, I don't know. And now, here he was, trying to figure out how to save my life. So much I owed him.

He bolted out of his chair, paused in front of the window, and stood watching clouds skitter past. I saw them too, but the fluffy white didn't mean much. I'd pushed it too far today and my world was spinning. I grabbed at the desk but ended up with my head between my knees, waiting for my boots to come into focus. A hand patted my shoulder.

"We'll figure this out, Tate." The voice was hard, firm, and soft at the same time.

I nodded and grunted. My long-ago sandwich threatened to rise, but I pushed back the sourness. The voice from above relaxed me.

"Think it's best you stay here tonight, son. First thing in the morning I'll send a hand into San Antone, get my lawyer. He's ace high."

Sitting back, boots and desk now in focus, I wiped my mouth. "I'm sorry, Mr. Carmichael. Didn't mean to bring you any trouble. Just needed advice. I can't have you pay for a lawyer." I wanted to add "I'm not worth it," but figured I'd get a diatribe about how I was always putting myself down but I *was* worth it, and so on.

He eased back into his seat and again looked at me. "Tate. I've told you before. You're the closest thing I have to a son. Especially since my own took the wrong path and died. I don't want your life to end like his." He pulled in air followed by a long sigh. "If I can help, I'm happy to do so."

"Thank you, sir."

Chuckling, he picked up a stylus and found a blank piece of paper. "Besides, I'd like to have grandchildren riding my horses around here." He pointed the writing utensil at me. "Can't do that if you get yourself hanged."

I threw myself back against the chair. Grandchildren? He was serious.

And I hadn't thought about it from his perspective. For the time being, however, I had to figure out how to get out of this heap of trouble I'd managed to create. I rethought. It wasn't all my doing. No siree. Somebody had written about me. Written lies and falsehoods which only got me into more trouble. Could this lawyer untangle the Gordian knot I'd created of my life?

Mr. C. finished writing, reread, folded the paper, then stuck it into an envelope. "There's still enough daylight to get this to Efron." He glanced at me. "Efron Efronton." He held up a hand. "I know. I know. Whoever named him should be scolded. But...that's his name. And he's a crack lawyer."

I shrugged. Who was I to scoff at silly names? Maybe he'd made it up like I did with Seamus O'Brien. The name had begun to wear well on me and on the ride here to the ranch, I'd thought about keeping it—assuming I stayed alive.

"You're looking peaked, Tate." Mr. C. pointed toward the door. "I'll ask Miranda to make up the guest bedroom and I'm sure when my wife returns, she'd enjoy spending some time talking to you."

"I'd enjoy that, too." I wobbled to my feet like those wooden tops I used to spin as a boy. I followed him out into the front room just as Miranda hurried from the kitchen. Mr. C. spoke with her for a bit while I stood, feeling the fool, like a child needing a blanket or a parent to soothe a skinned knee. I was old enough to handle this myself. But...I wasn't handling things at all.

"I'll get this to one of the boys at the bunkhouse." Mr. C. held up the envelope and turned to me. "You go with Miranda." He stepped toward the front door. "See you at supper."

* * *

SUPPER WAS MORE than I'd remembered from past meals. Cornbread, fried chicken—Miranda's specialty— fresh green beans and dewberry pie for dessert. Was her pie better than Mrs. Steinmaker's? Not better, but as good and definitely appreciated.

Even better than dessert was a pleasant conversation with Mrs. C. Always a delightful person, she seemed truly concerned about me. She mentioned chatting with Emily Anne Coogan from Fredericksburg, Hilda's da's special friend. I had a feeling they were plotting something, but I couldn't be sure.

Dark blue replaced the purple-filled sky while Mr. C. and I sat on the porch, both of us enjoying a cigar. I'd never smoked one and now could see why it was done after supper. Smooth and calming. Perfect for a night like tonight.

Caught in the darkness, slow hoofbeats filled the silence. Sound coming from the south between the barn and bunkhouse, half of me relaxed thinking it was the hand Mr. C. had sent into town. The other half knew, just *knew*, a sheriff would put a bullet into my chest within the minute.

I bolted into the house, slamming the screen door, cringing at the sound alerting whoever to my location. Threading my way to the back door, I stopped in the kitchen. Like a terrified mouse, I scanned the room looking for a hiding hole. In the oven? Under the table? In the pantry? How small could I make myself? I stepped left, then right.

Miranda stood in the doorway, her eyebrows raised. "Are you all right, Mr. Nolan? Did you lose something?"

"Shhhh." I flapped my hand at her. "Somebody's come."

"Oh." She glanced over her shoulder, turned back to me. "Nobody's here."

But I didn't relax. I headed for the back door wondering where my horse was. Still tied at the tree if memory served. What was I thinking, leaving him out there this long? Well, as soon as I figured out who had ridden in, I'd either get on my horse and make a dead run for safety or put him up in the barn.

Waiting at the back door, hand on the knob, breath held, I listened for the sheriff's boots to clump across the front room floor. Nothing. Yet. A deep breath in and still I lingered, knowing I was making a mistake by not running. But I wasn't a runner. Or was I? I'd run to Fredericksburg, intending to get to Denver. But still, that was running wasn't it?

I would no longer be that man, I vowed. The man who ran. Like I'd told Mr. C., I wouldn't run to Mexico... then why was I standing at the door waiting to bolt into the night like a common thief?

Mrs. C. stood in the doorway, dining room behind her. "Tate?" She waited for me to turn all the way around and look at her. "One of the hands just returned from San Antone. The lawyer'll be here in the morning."

All the air ran out of my body while my shoulders slumped. "Yes ma'am. Thank you."

"Knew you'd want to know." She flashed a heart-stopping smile.

"Yes, ma'am."

"Good night, Tate."

"Ma'am." Every single speck of energy slid out through my toes and lay in a puddle on the kitchen floor. I glanced at Miranda who shot me a smile and a wink. Without a word, I knew what she was saying. I grinned back, opened the back door, and stepped into a warm Texas evening.

* * *

"THINK THAT'S ABOUT EVERYTHING, Mr. Efronton." I sipped from a clear water glass and placed it on Mr. C.'s desk. Would this lawyer stand up for me? Would he figure out how to get me out of this predicament? All I knew for sure was he was my last hope. Lying in bed, I rethought my vow not to run. On the other hand, maybe hightailing it was something to reconsider. How badly did I want *not* to swing at the end of a rope? To live? Pretty bad.

Despite the sun's glow bouncing off the lawyer's bald head, I was fairly certain a huge brain lay under the skull. He'd greeted me warmly, shook hands even. Then asked a couple questions, listening, taking notes while I poured out my heart. After what felt like an hour or two, I ran out of words. From my point of view, my situation looked bleak and hopeless.

Mr. C. cleared his throat, sipped water, and sat up straight in his chair. "Efron, what d'you think?"

The lawyer picked up his half-full glass and downed the remainder in one long gulp. Water drops sparkled on his thick, gray-streaked mustache. He watched Mr. C. refill the glass, looked at his notes, stared out the window.

Great was the only word that came to my mind. Any second now he's going to tell me what a loser I am and how I might as well lead the way to the gallows. I was going there anyhow. Minutes, hours, days ticked by.

Mr. Efronton picked up a stylus, scribbled words...or maybe drew a picture...on a sheet of paper then sat back. His round eyes were magnified by the round glasses he wore on the tip of his nose. "Son."

"Sir?" My heart thumped so hard I was surprised a word came out.

"You got yourself a peck of trouble." His Louisiana

drawl came out thick as molasses. "So, let me get this straight." He held up one finger at a time. "You got yourself a daughter out of wedlock. Her and her mama's there in town."

I nodded, unwilling to put a voice to anything yet.

"Second." Another finger went up. "You took off for Denver but ended up in Fredericksburg under a different name."

"Sir."

Another finger appeared. "You're planning to marry a woman who thinks your last name's O'Brien."

Before I could nod or affirm, he went on, his pinkie now joining the others. "You killed Rancher Stinson's main ranch hand last month up on the Big Blue. Right?"

"No. I hit him with a rock. He tried to drown me. Self-defense. Pure self-defense." I shrugged and added almost under my breath, "I didn't shoot him. Don't own a gun."

"Says here there were two eyewitnesses. One has disappeared, fella by the name of Charlie Brennan. The other, Stinson's hired man, says you killed him in cold blood." Efronton raised both eyebrows and cocked his head. "This was *after* one of Stinson's men caught you and Tex on their property."

Mr. C. jumped in. "Rustling my cattle." He pointed to me. "Tate and Tex were trying to get 'em back."

"But you were trespassing, nevertheless."

How could I explain better? "Maybe we were. But they rustled those steers and all we wanted to do was herd 'em back across the stream. Over to our side. Those men of Stinson's killed Tex, shot me."

"Unfortunately, Mr. Nolan, it's your word against theirs."

Silence wedged itself into the room. The lawyer read

another paper then frowned at me. "Says here, you killed a fella here in Blanco Hill and when Sheriff Becker tried to arrest you, you resisted."

Not my finest moment for sure. "Somebody else killed him. I kneeled to see if he was still breathing, and that sheriff accused *me*. Wouldn't listen. So, I ended up in jail." I shuddered at that word.

I'd already mentioned Sheriff Driggs, but I figured repeating wasn't a bad idea. "I got back from an outing on Sunday evening, and for no good reason, that sheriff over in Fredericksburg shot me. In the side." I patted myself which made the wound throb.

Mr. C. lowered his voice as he leaned back. "I have full confidence Tate's telling the truth, Efron. He has no reason to lie to me."

It was the lawyer's turn to lean back. He glanced at papers held in his hand, stared out the window—again. A long, labored sigh escaped from his brocade vested chest.

He leaned forward as Mr. C. and I did. Mr. Efronton's gaze swept over me like I was a prized turkey to be won in a shooting contest. I felt like a turkey, for sure. "Tate, Mr. Nolan?"

"Sir?"

"You speak Spanish?"

I'm sure my eyes widened beyond the eyebrows. How could he imply I run? "No sir. Not good enough. I can get by with the men on the ranch, but not enough to live in Mexico." I sucked in a bucket of air. "You suggesting I run? Hide in Mexico?" I frowned at him. "I'm not running, sir. I'll face whatever happens, but I'm done with running."

In a perverse sort of way, I felt good. Good about myself and good about my decision. It was time I became a man and the moment had arrived. My shoulders brought themselves back.

A full-face smile blossomed on the lawyer's face. "I was hoping you'd say that, son. Proves what kind of man you're becoming. Good for you."

Mr. C. nodded approval.

Efronton nodded slightly, if his round head bobbing was an indication of thinking. "Here's what I think needs to happen." He pulled in air. "Tate, Mr. Nolan, you'll need to have a trial for both of these murders. Clear your name."

"But—"

"I know. It's a chance we'll have to take. It'll be up to your defense counsel, which is me, and a jury. The judge has to go along with what a jury decides."

A boulder landed on my chest. "You're suggesting I turn myself in, have a trial, and then probably swing?"

"Not if I can help it."

Mr. C. fell back against his chair. "There's no other way out, Efron? You think this is the best way to clear Tate?"

More head bobbing. "Not the best way. The only way, other than living in Mexico, it is. No telling how much more Stinson's going to add to the bounty." The lawyer looked at me. "It's already up to fifteen hundred."

"That's a lot of money." My gaze wandered from the lawyer to Mr. C. and then back. I knew this day would come and here it was. "All right, Mr. Efronton. I'll accept what you think. But before I turn myself in, there's some unfinished business I need to...finish." That sounded oddly familiar.

"Like what?" Mr. C. cocked his head.

Speaking over the lump in my throat was tough. "Gotta say goodbye to my folks. To Eagan. To Imogene and Louisa. Somehow get a note to Joe." Pressure built in my chest. "Then I gotta go to Fredericksburg and tell Hilda. But mostly, I gotta see Mrs. Steinmaker. Tell her I won't be coming home again. It'll kill her, I'm afraid. She's already lost Karl."

"I won't pretend to know who all those people are, Tate." The lawyer straightened his papers. "But I do understand needing closure." He shrugged. "Just in case." He pushed up to his feet. "I always say hope for the best, prepare for the worst."

Extending a hand, Efronton shook with me and then Mr. C. "You know where to find me when you're ready. Meantime, I'll dig around town, both Blanco Hill and San Antone. See what I can find."

The door shut behind him leaving Mr. C. and me in silence. We both sat, staring out the window, lost in our own thoughts. I owed it to Mr. C. to do everything I could to make this right, bring him grandchildren.

CHAPTER THIRTY-THREE

I HAD NO IDEA HOW LONG WE SAT BEFORE A knock at the door jarred me into the present.

"Come in," Mr. C. called.

Mrs. C. stood in the doorway, concern etching her smooth face. "Mr. Efronton left quite a bit ago. I was concerned about you two."

"We're fine. Just thinking." Mr. C. eased to his feet.

"Also wanted to tell you luncheon is ready, on the table." Mrs. C. turned her blue eyes on me. "We'd like you to join us, Tate."

Food? Now? "I'm not hungry, Mrs. Carmichael. But thank you."

Mr. C. skirted his desk and headed for the door. He clapped me on the shoulder. "Nonsense. Young man like you is always hungry. Come."

We sat at the table discussing my situation. Would I have the strength, the endurance to go to two trials? Looked like I'd have to.

Mrs. C. put down her fork with the final bite of ham, patted her mouth with the corner of a cloth napkin, then raised her concerned eyes to mine. "What would you think about inviting your folks, Eagan, too, for Sunday church and picnic in a few days?" She looked at Mr. C. for a nod, which he gave her.

"Don't forget Imogene and Louisa." Mr. C. pointed a fork at me. "They're important, too."

"Yes, sir." I pushed down the bit of ham stuck in my throat and regarded Mrs. C. Maybe one day I'd call her by her first name, Ellie, but today wasn't the day. "I'd like that very much, ma'am. That'd give me a chance to talk to them without going into town."

"Then it's all settled." Mrs. C. rose, taking her empty plate with her. "Sunday will be perfect."

* * *

WAITING three days felt more like three years. A soft rain ushered in Sunday. Not only did the moisture bring needed relief from the scorching days of August, but it brought my family.

Not willing to take chances, I stayed hidden in the kitchen where one by one Ma and then Da and Eagan were led in. The reunion was tearful on Ma's part, a hearty handshake from Da and Eagan. And then when Imogene and little Louisa appeared, I got two hugs.

Somehow, I explained in short, clear terms what was happening. Why I couldn't come see them. Why the secrecy.

Ma's tears tightened my throat. Da's eyes turned red. Eagan simply stared, open mouthed. I couldn't tell how he felt about his big brother. I'm sure there were hundreds of thoughts trooping through their heads. But all I hoped for was no one would say anything, at least until I was a free man. And that was a big *if*.

Imogene sent Louisa with Ma and Da to go pet the horses. Eagan dawdled and at last pointed outside mumbling something about a second helping of pie.

My first lady love and I stood in the kitchen, lingering smells of chicken and baked bread twirling under our noses. We stood, uncomfortable, not knowing what else to say.

She cleared her throat, stared at the stove as if it held a secret. She spoke to the appliance. "You need to know. I've been seeing someone." Imogene changed her gaze to me. "Deputy Sheriff O'Sullivan from Blanco Hill."

"Tommy O'Sullivan from Ireland? He was good to me if I remember right." I smiled, confirming what I already knew.

"One and the same." A slight grin crinkled her cheeks. "He's quite nice. Plays well with Louisa. Takes us both out to supper sometimes. Buys her toys."

"On a deputy's salary?" I'm sure that came out too harsh, but I couldn't imagine him making much money, especially that much.

"I'm still working at the mercantile. And Louisa's in school. Likes the teacher." Imogene started words twice, waited, then started again. "I don't want to hurt you. You've certainly got enough trouble as it is."

Where was this going? Suddenly, I didn't enjoy standing here with her. Panic clamped around my chest. Should I run? I chided myself and waited for her to continue.

"But Tate." She lifted a shoulder along with both eyebrows. "I really like him. We've become a...a couple."

That, I had seen coming. I pushed aside questions. "I'm happy for you." I gripped her arms and kissed her forehead. "I truly am." Should I tell her about Hilda?

This moment didn't seem the time. I'd save that gem for later.

"I know what you're thinking, Tate." Imogene stepped back. "But I won't tell Tommy about you. I promise."

"Thank you." I started to escort her toward the front door. We got to the dining room, and she stopped.

"Don't come closer to the door. He brought me here." She pointed over her shoulder. "Tommy's right outside."

* * *

THE MOMENT the last guest rode away, I saddled my mount, tucked a bag of sandwiches Miranda had made into my saddlebag, shook hands with Mr. C. and promised I'd be in touch. I explained to Mrs. C. standing next to her husband here in the barn, that I had to go back to Fredericksburg and somehow tell Hilda and Mrs. Steinmaker my decision.

Then...I'd turn myself in.

A bag of gravel sat in my stomach as I waved what I hoped was not a final goodbye. With sun spreading long gray fingers over the hills and valleys, I skirted Blanco Hill and aimed for a bit outside of Fredericksburg. Stopping that far away should be safe to tie up my horse and tiptoe into town.

My horse and I clomped through the night, stopping once or twice at a small stream where we drank, and I ate a sandwich. Ham, if the smell was right. Too dark to see much, I'd had to guess at the food. Not surprisingly, all of it was tasty and plentiful. A sky full of moon and stars would have been helpful, but since it'd drizzled all day and night, no chance of heavenly illumination.

I slept by the third stream until sun hit my face.

Fortunately, my mount was still tied to a bush not far away. Looked like he'd been munching on leaves and grass. He even looked a bit sleepy.

A hearty cup of tea would taste great about now, but I dared not make a fire, plus I had no cup or tea. I finished the rest of the sandwiches hoping I'd be at Mrs. Stein-maker's in time for luncheon. A quick glance at the sun. Maybe breakfast if she ate late this morning.

Judging by the bushes and rising hills off to my west, I figured I was less than five miles from Fredericksburg. Patting my horse's neck, I then leaned against her side, the saddle leather creaking. Instead of riding west and into doom, I could turn and ride south into Mexico. I *could*. But again, was that the man I wanted to be? Well, alive, yes. But not a coward.

And not a coward if I was ever going to be a real, honest to goodness outlaw. A famed outlaw like the James…I blew out a long breath, ran a hand across a face in need of a shave. Sandpaper coated my chin. Hadn't I shaved just yesterday morning before Mr. C.'s guests arrived? I shook my head. There I was facing my own death—probably—and I'm busy thinking about shaving? Loser. I was indeed a loser. Needed to keep my mind on the situation right now.

The saddle creaked under my weight as I swung up. I adjusted the reins, clicked my tongue and off we went. Just me and Jasmine riding into uncertain jeopardy. I sat up straighter, determined to be a man about all this.

I tied the horse to a low Texas oak branch in a thicket a couple blocks from Mrs. Steinmaker's house. I could almost smell her bacon and eggs cooking. Or was that pie? Whatever it was, my stomach rumbled. Pushing between bushes and a stand of brambles, I cursed and fought my way close enough to see that pie sitting on her windowsill. I knew it! Probably a blackberry pie since this was blackberry season. Soon, it would be apple time. And with apples in season, what would Hilda do? Make strudel and pies and cakes and—

"Hold it! Hands up!"

A baritone voice spun me around. San Antonio's Sheriff Samuels stood not ten feet away, shotgun pointed at my belly. He couldn't miss at this range. Arms reaching skyway, my heart caught in my throat. Throbbing in my ears kept me from breathing. Maybe I'd pass out or die.

Samuels cocked the weapon. Metal on metal echoed off the house. I tilted my head. "No need to shoot. I'm unarmed." And if I had a gun, would I use it?

He edged closer, the shotgun barrel growing into the size of a cavern. "Caught you." A few steps more and we stood a yard apart. So close, I could smell bacon on his breath. At least he'd had breakfast.

"Hands down. That's right. Now turn around." He spun his finger in a circle.

Arms now at my side and facing Mrs. Steinmaker's house, the sheriff grabbed my wrists, wrenching my arms behind me. That familiar sound of handcuffs being unlocked hit my ears. Within seconds I'd be bound.

"Why, there you are Seamus!" Mrs. Steinmaker appeared at the window and leaned over the cooling pie. "I wondered if you'd mustered out of the army yet." She squinted. "I see you did. And who's that nice young sheriff you brought with you?"

"Ma'am, go back inside." Sheriff Samuels yanked on my arms. My right wrist was now weighted down by thick iron grating as it locked. "This man's under arrest."

"Arrest?" Mrs. Steinmaker ducked out of the window and within seconds marched down the front steps and stopped in front of me. She narrowed her eyes at the lawman behind me. "What do you think you're doing?" She pointed an angry finger in his face. "This here's Seamus O'Brien. A fine, upstanding young man who's been off serving his country. I insist you leave him alone."

Was that a chuckle I heard coming from behind? At least he hadn't snapped the other cuff on yet.

"Ma'am—"

"Mrs. Steinmaker. Gertrude Steinmaker."

More chuckling. "Mrs. Steinmaker. This ain't Seamus O'Brien. No sir, not one whit. This here's Tate Nolan, a wanted man. Got a fifteen-hundred-dollar reward on his head."

She marched up to me, grabbed my arm and tugged. "I don't care if he's got a million dollars on his head." She tugged harder. "This is Seamus O'Brien and he's not the man you're looking for. Give him over."

Mrs. Steinmaker pulled so hard Sheriff Samuels lost his grip on my arm. I stumbled forward, bumping into her. She stepped backward. "Sorry," I mumbled.

"Who you got here?" A voice I recognized from Blanco Hill came up behind me. I wobbled around, one hand still behind my back. There stood Tommy O'Sullivan, now Blanco Hill town Deputy Sheriff and Imogene's current beau.

Most of me relaxed knowing a friendly lawman would take over. Maybe by noon I'd be a free man. O'Sullivan gripped my upper arm yanking me hard away from both Samuels and Mrs. Steinmaker. The four of us stood near the street, all glaring at each other. I didn't want Mrs. Steinmaker there. She might get hurt and I'd never live with myself if that happened.

Standing next to O'Sullivan, I lowered my voice to

softly concerned, betraying the loudly terrified I truly felt. "Mrs. Steinmaker." I leaned toward her. "Why don't you go back inside? After I talk to these fellas, I'll come inside and explain."

She stomped her small foot on the ground. "I'll do no such thing, Seamus. I'll stand here until these men release you." She turned to the sheriff from San Antone. "I insist you unlock that handcuff. He's no threat and you have no right to treat him like that."

Somehow her tirade hit me as funny. I chuckled out loud. "Don't worry, Mrs. Steinmaker—"

"Think this's funny, do you?" Samuels moved in close, fisted a hand and plowed it into my stomach. Another fist hit my left cheek.

Doubling over, I grabbed my jaw, now on fire.

"What d'you think you're doing?" O'Sullivan's voice rang above me. "He's my prisoner."

"Yours? He's mine. That's my handcuff on his wrist." Samuels's sharp words rolled down the street.

Deep breath dragged in, I straightened just in time to be jerked back by O'Sullivan. Blurry images danced before me; one resembled Mrs. Steinmaker. Then more images. Voices. Sounds. People shouting, moving around me.

I held my belly with my handcuffed hand while images came into focus. O'Sullivan tugged one way, his hand still on my upper arm, Samuels tugging the other way. Like a demon emerging from a deadly fog, in front of me appeared Fredericksburg Sheriff, his .45 leveled at my chest.

"What's goin' on here?" Sheriff Driggs moved next to Mrs. Steinmaker. He squinted at me. "Looks like you got yourself into more trouble. What's it this time? Another murder?"

"I didn't kill any—"

Fredericksburg's sheriff grabbed my vest and pulled until the other sheriffs released me. I sailed into him, knocking him backward. Staying on his feet, Driggs came forward and punched my other jaw. Stars winked as they swirled in front of my eyes. I grabbed at the pain, doubled over again.

"Oh my! Seamus!" A woman's screech rose above the three men yelling at each other. "Seamus! Are you all right?" I looked up. Hilda and her da. Great.

Now with seven of us circling each other, we migrated into the street. I tried telling the women to get away, to leave, but like petulant children, they stayed, talking, hollering, pointing...talking.

"He's *my* prisoner." San Antone's Samuels gripped my arm, wrenching it behind my back again. Surprisingly, he held up his shotgun. "He's mine and I'm taking him with me. That reward is mine."

Reward? How could I have forgotten about the bounty on my head? Fifteen hundred was a fortune, which made me a valuable catch.

O'Sullivan stepped up face to face with Samuels. "He's mine. I had him in jail first." He gripped the side of my vest and shirt and yanked me sideways. "I'll be taking him back to Blanco Hill."

"Now hold on just a minute there." Fredericksburg's sheriff pushed his way in. "This here's *my* town and he's in *my* jurisdiction." He knocked O'Sullivan's hand off my vest and gripped it in the same place. He pulled. "Prisoner's mine. That money's mine."

The three men squeezed in all around me. There wasn't room to scratch my nose if I'd wanted. Voices rose until my ears rang.

Then someone pushed. I didn't know who did what,

but someone pushed back. Then someone swung. Within seconds, the four of us were on top of each other like one of the fights in Sam's Emporium. I struggled to find a way out, but Samuels's grip on the handcuff kept me in the mix.

A boot to my ribs brought an *umphf* and new stars to my world. Someone heavy rolled on top of me, squeezing air out of my lungs. Dirt flew up my nose. One arm was jammed under two writhing men. If I didn't get out soon, I'd either be crushed or smothered. I wiggled to no avail.

Bang! "What in tarnation's goin' on?"

I cringed and jumped at the same time. The men froze, then like melting snowmen, oozed off of me, came to their knees and stood. I lay on the ground struggling for a breath and to figure out what just happened.

"See you found my prisoner." The baritone was familiar. I prayed it wasn't who I thought it was.

"He's mine, Marshal."

"Mine. Those're my handcuffs."

"*Mine.* This here's *my* town."

Pulling in enough air to make sense of the world, from here in the dirt I saw mostly legs and then farther up, heads, a couple sporting bloody lips. Grunting, I sat and looked up at the men. Icy cold flooded my body. The new voice? Fritz Becker, former sheriff of Blanco Hill, now US Marshal.

"On your feet, Nolan." Becker's .45, pointed at my head, made me scramble to get upright. Heavy breathing like raging bulls from the sheriffs stirred up the street's dirt. I fought a cough and sneeze.

Mrs. Steinmaker stepped toward me, then stopped at Becker's outstretched hand in her face. "He's a murderer, ma'am. Stay away."

"He's no such thing. That's Seamus O'Brien, just come back from the war." She eyed me head to boots. "A fine young man he is, too. He's best friends with my Karl."

By now, I had no idea what she was talking about, what with all the huffing and puffing around me, the noises coming from Hilda. I couldn't tell if those were gasps, squeaks, sobs or what. She stood off to her da's side, holding his arm. Shock, disappointment, disbelief cascaded over his face bringing his eyebrows together and up toward his hairline. His mouth had turned down almost to his jaw. He fisted one hand, and I was sure he'd deck me with it if he could get close enough.

For a brief moment, I was glad to be surrounded by lawmen.

As if coming out of long hibernation, the three sheriffs moved, mumbling and grumbling.

Fredericksburg's sheriff wiped blood off his lower lip and pointed up the street. "Let's get him down to jail and then sort this out." He lowered his voice, glanced around. "Listen men. There's plenty of reward money to go around."

That created more words than I'd ever heard, even from the priest's pulpit. Accusations, law "facts," finger pointing and grabs at me flew around my world. I was pulled, pushed frontward and backward until I figured both arms were bruised.

Bang! I jumped as did Mrs. Steinmaker who I was watching.

"That's it!" Fredericksburg's Sheriff Driggs held his .45 in the air, smoke wafting from the barrel. "I said we'll lock him up in my jail and discuss this like civilized men." He eyeballed each lawman, gripped my upper arm until I was sure there was no blood in my hand, and yanked me toward those dreaded iron bars. While I walked, I thanked whoever put the bounty on my head that indicated I should be taken alive. Who knows what this pack of animals would do if I were dead? Probably cut me up into pieces just for part of the reward.

The heart-stopping grating of a key locking up my life brought a new kind of terror to my chest. I gripped the iron bars and regarded the men standing in front of me. The women and Hilda's da stood in the outer office looking at me since there wasn't enough room for everyone to squeeze in.

I worked my jaw around until hopefully words would form and they'd make sense. Over the men's voices, I tried to make myself clear. "I'm innocent. No need for this."

"I tell you, as US Marshal, I *do* have jurisdiction here." Becker snorted. "I outrank you. All of you!"

That released a flurry of more accusations. For once, I was happy to be back here behind bars, out of reach of angry men. For the moment anyway. I slumped to the lumpy cot, held my throbbing head in my hands, and studied the dirt-packed floor.

CHAPTER THIRTY-FOUR

"BREAKFAST, NOLAN. STAND OVER BY THE wall."

Already standing, I turned from staring out the window. Stand by the wall? Where did he think I was? Oh, right. This was Deputy Dumb. A man who should've been locked up himself for being stupid. But I simply shrugged and waited. He slid the tray under the bottom bar, glared at me, then left.

Three days had passed since I'd been locked up. Three long days and endless processions of Mrs. Steinmaker who brought muffins and fried chicken; Hilda who would sneak in when her da wasn't looking. She brought day-old strudel. Sheriff O'Sullivan had visited yesterday before leaving for Blanco Hill. I recalled our conversation.

"How'd you know where to find me?" I stood at the bars, one hand on my hip.

Tommy O'Sullivan flashed a slight smile. "Louisa tipped me off."

"Louisa? How could she know?"

"I asked her that." He smiled again, this time wider. "She's such a sweet thing." He drew in a breath. "Said she'd heard Imogene talking to Eagan about you leaving, going clear over to a town twenty miles away. She couldn't imagine anyone riding that far."

Louisa. Yeah, real sweet.

O'Sullivan thumbed over his shoulder. "I gotta be going."

"Don't tell my folks—"

"I won't. Promise." He lowered his voice. "Listen, I think these charges are trumped up, but if I can get that reward money, I'm gonna ask Imogene to be my wife. I think she'll say yes."

"But—"

"I realize Louisa's your daughter." He cocked his head to one side. "Imogene told me. We have no secrets between us. I'll treat Louisa as my own. I will."

My forehead wrinkled. I could feel it. I stepped back and met his green-eyed gaze. "If you do get that money, I think she will. Treat them well." A rock in my stomach thudded. No more words would come.

"Promise." He stuck his hand in between the bars, and we shook.

Back to the present and thinking about that conversation, I wished the best for the three of them, even if he didn't get my reward money. He seemed to be a good man and he obviously loved Imogene. I picked at the ham and eggs on my plate. The coffee this morning tasted tinny, bland, dead. Like my life.

Finished, I pushed the plate under the bottom bar and returned to watching out the window.

"Hello, Tate."

I spun around at the familiar voice. Mr. Carmichael! Standing beside him was Mr. Efronton, the San Antonio lawyer. My grin hurt sore cheeks. I'd never been happier to see anyone. I rushed across the cell and stuck my hand through the bars. First, I shook with Mr. C. and then the lawyer. Somehow, a boulder lifted off my shoulders and I stood straighter.

When words could form, I started. "How'd you know?"

Mr. Efronton shook his head with a tinge of a smile. "Sheriff Samuels rode into town all lathered up about not getting reward money even though he'd been the first to handcuff you. Made it quite clear he'd been robbed."

Mr. C. continued for him. "So Efron came over to talk about you and we decided it was best for us to come see for ourselves."

What I wanted was to sit with these two men over a beer or two and hash out my predicament. Somehow bars in between brought my problems all too close. "Thank you, both." I then described how I'd been caught and the ensuing riot between the four lawmen, each believing they should get the reward.

"The only good part," I said with a shrug, "was they didn't shoot each other. No doubt they would've blamed me."

Mr. C. chuckled, actually chuckled. Mr. Efronton hid a smile.

The men located chairs in the outer office and dragged them up to my cell bars. I eased to the cot and like that, we sat for two hours, planning my defense. Nothing said made me feel better. I had no witnesses, only derelicts and dead men, and one man—the only live man who could help—was gone. Charlie, my partner on the Big Blue, had vanished like a ghost into the night. I wondered if he'd been threatened by Stinson. If so, he was smart to disappear.

For defense, all we could come up with was my good character. And my prison record certainly didn't help that aspect. No, I was a *melted willy*, as Da would say.

With no more words and ideas, Mr. C. and the lawyer stood, both rubbing their backs and stretching. I'd not seen two more downcast people in the past few months. They shook hands with me promising to be in touch. Soon.

I returned to staring out the window.

* * *

SUPPER CAME and went along with another visit from Mrs. Steinmaker who informed me that Karl would be home tomorrow. Finally. I truly wished that was true, but the roast she'd brought helped ease the stomachache I'd had the past three days.

She was standing at the bars watching me devour her wonderful meal when Sheriff Driggs marched in. He nodded at Mrs. Steinmaker and then turned his glare on me. "Just got word. Thought you'd want to know."

Of course, I wanted to know. Especially if it was about my imminent release. I nodded.

He pulled his shoulders back far enough the buttons strained. "Judge's decided to combine your trials, something about the court saving time and money, and hold them this Saturday." Driggs leaned in close. "Means you've got two days to live. After that, well, after your trial...shouldn't take more'n couple minutes...you'll be walkin' up those gallow steps, prayin' to meet your maker."

Not what I wanted to hear, but two days should give me time to either escape or write a will.

"Meet your maker." Driggs snickered. "Meetin'

Satan's more like it." He let out a rumble that sounded more like a bad windstorm than a laugh. Walking away, he rumbled again, this time softer.

I stood for a moment staring at Mrs. Steinmaker, whose eyes watered. Was she crying? "It'll be all right, ma'am." I knew I was lying, but what else could I say? "I've got a good lawyer and he'll help. It'll be fine." I reached through the bars and patted her arm. "Please don't cry. Please."

CHAPTER THIRTY-FIVE

THANK GOODNESS MR. C. AND THE LAWYER HAD stuck around town. Even though they'd visited a couple of times, we hadn't come up with much of a strategy. And now here it was, time for my trial.

A trial? Didn't I get a hearing first? Apparently not.

Breakfast was early—a hearty helping of scrambled eggs, ham, and cubed potatoes. The coffee was hearty as well. Strong and black, just the way Mrs. Steinmaker boiled hers. Half of me wondered what was going on, like the good food was a sign from heaven or, perhaps from Satan. The other half of me figured there was a new cook over at the restaurant.

Sheriff Driggs appeared at my cell as I slurped the last of my coffee. "Let's go." He motioned for me to stand back against the wall, under the window. I did and he unlocked the cell. Freedom, glorious freedom—at least for a few minutes. I hadn't been outside except to visit the outhouse in the last seven days.

The march up the street was long and painful. Although my ribs were mending well, the rest of me ached and groaned as the good citizens of Fredericksburg stepped aside from their Saturday shopping to watch me being paraded to my doom. At least my family wasn't here to see this spectacle.

Sheriff Driggs kept a tight grip on my right arm while Deputy Dumb walked behind, shotgun cradled in his elbow. I had no doubt he'd shoot me in the back if I so much as tripped, much less tried to run.

Up those courthouse steps we went, town folks murmuring behind me. Must not be something people saw every day. Down the hall, right turn and I froze at the courtroom door. Standing in front of the judge's bench was a man, riffling through papers. I squinted. The judge from Blanco Hill! The judge who'd first sentenced me to prison, and more recently to time with Mr. Carmichael. All sorts of curse words rattled in my brain, but none came forth. I couldn't speak, think, or move.

He looked over at me, frowned, huffed, and marched off into a room off to the left. The door slammed with a vengeance. Nudged forward, I wound my way past rows of empty chairs until Driggs pushed me into a wooden chair which creaked as I sat. He took his seat next to mine while Deputy Dumb sat directly behind me.

With three of us in this large room, my breathing bounced off walls. My heart pounded like a bass drum I'd seen when a circus paraded through town. About the time my breathing was normal, someone tapped my shoulder. Mr. Carmichael and Lawyer Efronton. Both nodded to me, the sheriff, ignored the deputy, and took seats next to me. Having them there was better than a warm blanket on a cold night. I knew things would be all right.

More and more spectators stepped in, their conversations muted. Rustling and throat clearing behind me indicated at least thirty people chose to spend their day in here with me. *Was Mrs. Steinmaker here? Hilda and her da?* I'd think not. She had a business to run, goodies to bake and besides, her da hated me. Couldn't really blame him.

One man caught my stare. Older, paunchy fella, gray hair at his collar, glasses stuck at the end of his nose, sat at the far end of my row, right up front. He pulled papers out from his vest making a show of straightening them, rustling them as loudly as possible.

Sheriff Driggs leaned close to me. "That's Old Man Andersen. County Prosecutor. Got a perfect record. Every case he gets...well Kid, they're all found guilty."

Kid? Had he read the papers? Swallowing was difficult until I glanced behind me and spotted that shite-eating Blanco Hill Sheriff Walter Wagner swaggering in. He pointed a meaty finger at me and sneered. Great. But what was he doing here? Again. This wasn't his jurisdiction. I turned back around just in time to see six men march in from a back door, then take seats on the side of the courtroom. Must be the jury. Studying each one, I realized they seemed to be ordinary citizens since they all had stoic expressions on their faces. Probably glad they weren't sitting in my chair.

Before I could contemplate further, I had to stand when the judge sailed in, his black robe trailing behind. A fella I assumed was a bailiff swaggered in, too, and planted himself slightly behind the judge. I half expected to see both sporting those white powdered wigs I'd seen in pictures from the English courts. Pompous snobs.

We sat after the judge took his seat. He adjusted the glasses on his nose, shuffled paper and then looked at me, the packed courtroom, then back at me. He sighed loud and long, leaned forward. He pointed at me.

"Once more, eh Mr. Nolan? Couldn't walk the

straight road? Couldn't be a contributing member of society? Had to go kill men?" He straightened his shoulders. "Stealing a man's horse wasn't enough? Robbing a telegraph office, hitting your brother, killing a priest didn't satisfy you? Rustling cattle made you crave killing? And killing derelicts at that. You, Mr. Tate Nolan, are a waste of skin. Your mere presence takes up valuable room for someone who matters."

Mr. Efronton jumped to his feet. "I object, Your Honor. I demand a change in judges. Change of venue. You're obviously not impartial."

Flurries of voices and people moving filled the room. The judge smacked the gavel three times. "Sit down, Counselor." He used the gavel to point. "Silence. This is a court of law. This is my court and I'll not have it disgraced with threats."

"Change of—"

"Mr. Efronton. *I* am the only district judge within a hundred miles." His eyes narrowed. "This young man gets me...or a rope. Which would you prefer?"

My lawyer eased to the edge of his chair, ready to pounce again. Like that would help. At least I knew where I stood with the judge. I wasn't surprised, exactly.

The judge eyed me and then Efronton. "I see you've hired yourself top counsel, Nolan. You must have good friends. So, since you have such ace-high representation, I'll let you testify, give your side of the story." He crooked a finger. "Approach the bench."

Shocked was a word. I'd never had the chance to speak in my own defense before and had no idea what to say. Both Mr. C. and my lawyer leaned over and whispered a couple words of advice. Hearing only disconnected noise, I nodded as the bailiff stepped toward me. What to say? The truth, Ma had always said.

After swearing I'd tell the truth, I sat next to the judge facing the courtroom, which turned out was packed. To my surprise, Mr. Efronton walked with me, standing nearby. I began with talking about my family, then borrowing the sheriff's horse, my time with his daughter, and then rambled, always with candor. Being prompted by my lawyer, I mentioned how my time on Mr. C's ranch had helped me grow into the man I wanted to be. How I came to Fredericksburg and even mentioned living with Mrs. Steinmaker. Her name caused many heads to bob. I talked about a future with Hilda, or what I hoped was a future and that I wanted to be part of this town.

I ended with the fact I always seemed to be in the wrong place at the wrong time. I shook my head and blew out a sigh. Done. No more words. I'd said what my heart told me to say and that would have to be enough. No doubt it wasn't, but at least I didn't lie, and I didn't run away. And I hadn't mentioned wanting to best Jesse James.

"Anything else, Mr. Efronton?" The judge raised one eyebrow as if bored.

"No sir." My lawyer addressed the people in the room. "My client is a good man. Yes, he lacks a bit of good judgment at times, but...don't we all? He's building a life for himself here and should be allowed to continue doing so."

Old Man Andersen grunted up to his feet and shuffled to my chair. I leaned back at his stale beer breath now ringing my head. He must be a delight for the ladies.

He asked questions I'd already answered. I supposed he was trying to catch me off guard, seeing where I was lying. I answered truthfully and carefully.

My lawyer objected a time or two but was gaveled back to his seat.

Halfway through Andersen's questioning, the courtroom's back door opened and in walked Sheriff Samuels of San Antonio fame. Great. Now I had Sheriff Wagner, Sheriff Driggs, and Samuels. All I needed was Marshal Becker and my day would be complete.

Attention returning to the prosecutor, I pushed down pure panic and forced myself to stay seated, to answer truthfully without shaking. What could have been a year crawled by until the judge said, "Thank you Mr. Andersen. Mr. Nolan, you may step down."

That was it? The trial was over? Now what? Neither of my two previous trials had ever gone this long. Heart in my throat, I took my seat, looked at Mr. C. and then Mr. Efronton. I shrugged.

The judge pulled in a long drink of air, shuffled more papers. Like a man on a mission or in desperate need of a drink, he stood which forced the spectators and me to jump to our feet. The judge looked at the six men, still stoic and looking oh so bored. "Jury, you're released to deliberate." He glared at me. "Court's adjourned until they return with a verdict."

Still standing, knees weak, I stared at the backs of the men who held my life in their hands. What would they say about me behind closed doors? Had they been paid off by the judge to bring in a guilty verdict? Or paid by Mr. Andersen who wanted to keep a perfect record. Maybe were they truly honest, decent men who would weigh the evidence and listen to my words? How could I become a mouse in that room?

"No need to stay in here and wait." Mr. C. nudged my shoulder. "Let's get some fresh air." He leaned closer to Sheriff Driggs. "If that's all right with you."

Driggs nodded. "Could use air myself." He gripped my arm like I was about to fly away, and we walked, the four of us, through the staring throng and onto the courthouse steps. We pushed past a group of men and one woman on the veranda and down the three steps to the boardwalk.

Glad my legs and knees kept my weight, I stood enjoying the sunshine and slight breeze. Was that a hint of a chill? This was only what? September? Too early for a cold snap. Must be my nerves.

Three, possibly four minutes passed before our little group was joined by Sheriff Samuels of San Antonio and Sheriff Wagner of Blanco Hill. Great. Surrounded by the law produced bumps running up and down my back.

Being the bully that he was, Wagner started in first by addressing the other two lawmen. "Once he's convicted, wanted you to know, I'll be collecting that reward money." He hitched a thumb in his vest pocket. "Should be riding back this evening with coin jinglin' in my pocket."

"Told you before," Driggs said. "This's *my* town, *my* jail. I arrested him which makes him *my* prisoner and that makes the reward *mine*." He stepped closer to Wagner who had at least five inches and thirty pounds on Driggs.

"Hold it, boys." Sheriff Samuels snarled at the men, me, then back to them." He was in *my* jail earlier this year, which makes him *my* prisoner first. Reward is mine."

I wanted to tell Samuels I'd never been *in* his jail, and he was lying, but figured this wasn't the time to mention details.

Mr. C. held my arm pulling me aside. He and Efronton stepped away allowing room for fisticuffs or gunplay, whichever was about to happen. I stood watching grown men chest bump with words and then shoulders and then actual chests. Badge clashed with badge until I was certain one of the men would pull a gun. A hand or two twitched that way and just as Wagner reached for his revolver, the courthouse door opened, and the bailiff appeared.

"Jury has reached a decision. Trial resumes immediately."

Could I manage to walk back to my seat? Frozen on the spot, my feet and legs refused to budge. I couldn't spend the rest of my life in prison. Nine months was too long and there was no way I could do even a day more.

A push on my back and then a light pat moved me forward. All right. I pushed my shoulders back, stood up straight. I wanted the people in my life to be proud of me. I wouldn't run, like I'd promised. As I took the steps, I couldn't help thinking what would Jesse James do? Would he be brave like me or fight with every last breath. I wasn't sure and by the time I decided he'd fight, I was at my chair, Sheriff Driggs on one side, Lawyer Efronton on the other.

The jury filed in followed by the bailiff and then the judge.

We sat after he did, and all eyes turned to the jurors. The six men sat there like statues waiting to be visited by pigeons. I grinned at the vision of them sitting there with—

"Rise, Mr. Nolan." I rose along with Mr. Efronton. The judge continued. "Jury, have you reached a verdict?"

Could my heart pound harder? It thundered in my chest and throbbed in my throat.

The man at the end stood. "We have, Your Honor."

"What say you?"

Hesitation on the foreman's part brought pure panic to my soul. Guilty. Of course it's a guilty verdict. What else could make him wait? Unless he enjoyed torturing me.

He glanced back at the other five men, took a breath and stated, "Not guilty, Your Honor. We, the jury, find Mr. Tate Nolan not guilty."

What? Had he just said I was innocent? Efronton bearhugged me and I bearhugged back. Those two words were the sweetest in the world.

"Mr. Nolan." The judge pounded the gavel until the courtroom fell silent. "Mr. Nolan. Against my better judgment, I'm duty-bound to accept the jury's verdict. I'd much rather watch you hang, but I am, after all, a man of the law." He stood and leaned far over the desk and pointed the gavel at me. "If I catch a whiff of wrongdoing by you, a hint of a scent of breaking the law, even a nub of a hint, I'll string you up personally. And enjoy every minute."

He glared at me with a combination frown and sneer, then turned and swept out of the room, that black robe flapping behind. I stood stunned. A roar in my ears. Stomach flip flopping. Many hands thumped my back and a few shook mine, but nothing made sense. Words, tons of words floated around my head.

Somehow, I managed to get down the steps to the boardwalk. While standing there with Mr. C, Mr. Efronton, and Sheriff Driggs, one of the jurors approached my lawyer. "Thought you'd be interested to know, Mr. Efronton. Your client missed the noose by two votes. It was four to two at first count for guilty. Then we talked about Nolan's claim he was in the wrong place at the wrong time. Seems we've all been there." He adjusted his hat.

"That changed two votes, mine included, over to not guilty."

I shook his hand. He walked away, stopping to chat with friends.

Breathing in the fine fresh air brought clarity to what had just happened. I was free. Free to walk the street. Free to ride off. Free to do whatever I wanted to do.

Free to rob a bank.

No, that idea needed some thinking first. I'd dodged the bullet this time and wasn't ready to try riding the owl hoot trail again. Not quite yet.

CHAPTER THIRTY-SIX

Late that same afternoon, flowers gripped in hand, I stepped up to Mrs. Steinmaker's door. Knocking, I then let myself in. "Mrs. Steinmaker? It's Seamus! I'm back."

Voices from the kitchen and the scent of baking ham brought me into a room I'd grown to love. I froze at the doorway. At the table sat Mrs. Steinmaker and a man I'd never seen. Dark circles under his eyes, a haunted look in them, told me this was Karl. A man I took for dead.

She jumped up when she spotted me, a gleam in her eyes I'd never seen before. "Oh Seamus! Look! Look who came home! My Karl. He's really, truly here."

I presented her with the flowers. I thought my news was big. Hers topped it all. Was this fella indeed Karl? I'd find out.

I hugged her, then shook hands with Karl. Mrs. Steinmaker flapped a hand. "Oh my, where's my manners? Seamus, would you like a cup of coffee? We're having our second one now."

"I would, ma'am, but let me pour. Sit down. I'm sure

you've been on your feet all day." I turned to Karl. "She cooks all day. And what a cook she is."

He nodded and picked at a piece of bread, butter spread edge to edge. "I remember her dewberry pies. Melts in your mouth."

"And the roasts." My mouth watered in remembrance.

"Oh yes. Ham was my favorite, but her chicken on Sundays was wonderful."

I sat at the end of the table and regarded this man. He was about Karl's age I figured, but didn't look anything like her. Probably after being gone and in the war, he'd changed. I had to find out and took the direct route. "Mrs. Steinmaker tells me you were in the war. What'd you do when it was over?"

He laughed, then quieted. "In Vicksburg, got captured. Spent years as a prisoner. Lost my memory there and have been trying to figure out who I was and where I lived ever since then. Spent a few years on the streets until I got kicked in the head."

"I'm sorry. We have a few veterans on the streets in Blanco Hill." I immediately thought of the derelicts I'd borrowed a cap from. Was one of them him?

Karl looked at his cup. "Time was, this cup of coffee would have meant everything to me." He glanced up at Mrs. Steinmaker. "Still does."

She sniffed and held a cloth handkerchief to her nose, then dabbed at her eyes.

"After getting hit, images kept coming to me. My ma, pa mending a fence. This house. My room." Karl paused. "I knew I had to get home, back to my family. Took a while, but here I am. But Pa's dead and you've got my room."

I rocked back like I'd been punched in the chest. I was

welcome here, but this wasn't my home. Not now. Not anymore. "Sorry about your da. But your room is still yours and your ma is still your ma. She's been waiting for you. Talks about you all the time."

Standing, I finished my coffee, put the cup on the sideboard. "Mrs. Steinmaker, now that your son's home, I'll be going. Can't thank you enough for everything. You've saved my life."

She hugged me, tears welling. We hugged again. I shook hands with Karl.

Standing outside, I decided to stop by Hilda's store to apologize and say goodbye. As I did, her nose turned a little redder, as did her eyes, but she had already promised her da she wouldn't marry me. I agreed, figuring it was for the best. I didn't want a father-in-law to hate me from the beginning of our marriage. This was best I told her and myself.

Yet, why did it hurt so much?

I joined Mr. C. and Mr. Efronton for an early supper when they had decided to wait until morning to ride home. We'd ride back together.

With Fredericksburg in my memory, I set my sights on the future. At supper, Mr. C. offered me my old job back and I accepted. Maybe when I got settled, I'd write a letter to Jesse James to see how he was doing.

For me, I was doing well.

A LOOK AT BOOK TWO:
EAGAN'S REVENGE

Eagan Nolan's goal is simple—remain hell-bent on seeking revenge after a humiliating assault.

When Eagan faces a harrowing encounter on Main Street, three menacing accomplices demand not just his hard-earned pay, but also payment in flesh. Although Eagan's friends intervene, the incident leaves him emotionally shattered, his pride and confidence in pieces.

Driven by the belief that a gun will protect him from further harm, Eagan resorts to lies and theft to obtain one. On his troubled journey, he crosses paths with Molly, a seemingly sweet companion who offers him affection—on the condition that he transform into a steely-eyed, vengeful force.

Caught between his first love and his conscience, Eagan prepares for an ultimate showdown and explores whether his quest for revenge is leading him down a path of redemption... or self-destruction.

AVAILABLE JULY 2024

ABOUT THE AUTHOR

Growing up in southern New Mexico, Melody Groves' mind raced with characters from the Old West—gunfighters were her favorite. Now, her novels reflect her fascination—and ties—from that era.

As a New Mexico Gunfighter re-enactor, Melody loves to entertain visitors at Albuquerque's Old Town, allowing them a glimpse into earlier times. Her books reflect her passion for rodeo and her appreciation of historic wooden bars. Yes, bars—the front and back wooden structures, which Melody feels are just as amazing as rodeo performers.